FOR JAMI  **'S NOVELS**

"J   vorites!"

James Houston Turner is the bestselling author of the Aleksandr Talanov thriller series, as well as numerous other books and articles. Talanov the fictional character was inspired by the actual KGB agent who once leaked word out of Moscow that James was on a KGB watch-list for his smuggling activities behind the old Iron Curtain. James Houston Turner's debut thriller, *Department Thirteen,* was voted "Best Thriller" by USA Book News, after which it won gold medals in the Independent Publisher ("IPPY") Book Awards and the Indie Book Awards. A cancer survivor of more than twenty-five years, he holds a bachelor's degree from Baker University and a master's degree from the University of Houston (Clear Lake). After twenty years in Australia, he and his wife, Wendy, author of *The Recipe Gal Cookbook,* now live in Austin, Texas.

For more information about Wendy Turner's gluten-free, sugar-free recipe book, visit *www.recipegalcookbook.com.* For more information on James, visit his global website at *www.jameshoustonturner.world.*

BY JAMES HOUSTON TURNER

FICTION
The Search for the Sword of St Peter
The Identity Factor
Department Thirteen
Greco's Game
November Echo
Dragon Head

NON-FICTION
The Earth of Your Soul
The Spud Book
The Recipe Gal Cookbook (photographs)

JAMES HOUSTON TURNER

GRECO'S GAME

AN ALEKSANDR TALANOV THRILLER

REGIS

Published by Regis Books
An imprint of Ruby Rock Films LLC

Regis Books first edition, 2017

Copyright © James Houston Turner, 2011, 2017

James Houston Turner has asserted his right to be identified
as the author of this work.

For more information about James Houston Turner, visit
www.jameshoustonturner.world

To follow James Houston Turner, visit his official Facebook page:
@*officialjameshoustonturner*

Cover design by Frauke Spanuth

ISBN
9780958666466 (eBook)
9780958666473 (paperback)

Manufactured in the United States of America

3 2901 00644 0433

ACKNOWLEDGMENTS

I love spinning yarns that inspire, entertain, provoke, and satisfy. Writing is solitary but exhilarating work, and no one understands the process better than my gorgeous, dark-haired Aussie wife, Wendy, who endures the highs and lows of being married to this idealistic writer with her unique brand of spunky Aussie humor. We have done this together, my love, and I cannot thank you enough.

I would also like to acknowledge my friend and mentor, the late Sherwood "Woody" Wirt, founding editor of *Decision* Magazine and author of more than forty books, and the late Hollis "Lee" Holthaus, then executive director of the famed Union Rescue Mission, in downtown Los Angeles, California. Thanks to the faith those two men placed in this budding young writer, I landed my first job as a journalist for the mission's magazine, *Lifeline*. Little did I know how that job would lead to the writing of this book, and the creation of a fictional character who was not yet a gleam in his father's eye, as the old saying goes. While working for the mission, I met several young women who were victims of human trafficking. I barely knew such a horrific practice existed, but their stories opened my eyes to the reality of this monstrous crime. *Greco's Game* is therefore a tribute to those quiet, heroic women I met at the mission's women's shelter, Bethel Haven. Having grown up in a family of strong, capable women, my books typically feature kick-ass females who pack as much punch as most men. With Larisa in *Greco's Game,* I did something different. I created a strong, capable lead woman who was understated and shy. Why? Because I witnessed that same kind of quiet, triumphant, fighting spirit in many of the women at Bethel Haven, as well as during my dozens of trips behind the old Iron Curtain as a smuggler.

A lot of deliberating went into the structure of this novel. My dilemma was this: do I take more of a documentary approach that focuses on the crime of human trafficking, or do I focus more on Talanov and his personal odyssey against the perpetrators, which, in this case, are his old colleagues from the KGB? Rightly or wrongly, I opted for the latter. This book is therefore a chapter in Talanov's ongoing story of struggle and triumph over loss, failure, guilt, and old enemies who simply will not leave him alone. That being said, I still wanted to portray the despicable practice of human trafficking in an accurate light. Helping me was a terrific journalist, Irina Sandul, plus Ulyana Panchishin, and Corinna Wengryn Caudill. Thank you for your help. For other elements in the book, I would like to thank the "Happy Hospitalist," for fielding medical and hospital questions; Al Nofi, "Felix," and others who prefer to remain in the shadows when it came to weaponry and practices of the CIA; to longtime friend, George Nassif, for poring over countless emails and documents relating to the Russian electoral hacking scandal; and Charles S. Faddis, for his generous assistance with other matters relating to the CIA and the JRIC. And a *very* special thanks to the rock star of graphic artists, Frauke Spanuth, who designed the *Greco's Game* book cover.

Nor would I be where I am today as a writer had it not been for the generous support of good mates Wally Mariani and Mandy Bluett, plus all of the wonderful people at Qantas Airways and G'day USA. Thank you for helping launch my career.

A *very* special shout goes out to the visionary team at TideRock Media, LLC, and Wonderfilm Media Corporation. *Thank you* Thomas B. Fore, Jeffrey Bowler, Bret Saxon, Daniel Grodnik, and one of the true legends of filmmaking, Kirk Shaw, for adapting Talanov to the screen. Thanks also to Jim Shoaf. You guys rock.

I would also like to acknowledge film director Phillip Noyce. As many of you know, I took time off from my novels to write some film scripts. Phil read several of them, made invaluable comments, and offered priceless encouragement to me as a writer. Thank you for being such a good mate.

In closing, I want to thank the actual KGB agent who inspired the creation of Aleksandr Talanov. You know who you are and what you did, and for that I give you thanks.

For the untold victims of human trafficking

Whose names I will never know

Whose plights I will never forget

CHAPTER 1

TALANOV slowly opened his eyes to the sound of canned laughter. *You stupid idiot,* he thought, fumbling for the remote. After switching off the TV, he swung his feet down onto the floor and sat hunched over for a long moment. Finally, he stood and looked around the bedroom for his clothes. In the wash of light coming in through the window, he could see them strewn across the floor. He remembered kicking them in various directions when he and "Tash" had giggled their way into the hotel room earlier that night.

Tash sure knew the routine. With legs like a sprinter and hair the color of honey, the twenty-something Ukrainian had moved up and down him like a pole dancer while slow-waltzing him into bed. Talanov knew it was a set-up long before his head began to spin from whatever it was someone had slipped him back in the nightclub. Even so, he didn't care. He had quit caring long ago.

He picked up his underwear from a tangle of covers at the foot of the bed. A remnant of what would never be a memorable night of lovemaking. He could still see Tash jumping from the bed in her hot pink g-string, contemptuous at his inability to "do it." It was always the same, whether with Tash or any of the other hookers he had picked up over the last few months in an effort to try and forget. But try as he did, he could not get Andrea out of his mind.

Memories of that night were still embedded in him like shrapnel. On stage for the award. Waves of applause. Andrea's sudden urge to lean over and kiss him. Suddenly a shot. An explosion of blood. The brilliant red spatter floating before him like a nightmarish special effect in a movie. And in that split second before his wife hit the stage, Talanov saw movement high on the catwalk. A fleeting shadow making an escape. Then came the shrieks. People scattering. Andrea's fingers desperately reaching out for him while she lay quivering in a spreading pool of red. In all his years with the KGB, Talanov had never felt panic. *But he felt it then.* Diving to her side, he placed his hands over the gaping holes in her neck. He screamed for help while Andrea's life continued to squirt through his fingers. He looked down and saw Andrea's eyes smiling up at him. She tried to speak.

"Save your strength, help's on the way," he instructed, his eyes betraying the confidence he tried to portray.

"Love ... you," Andrea whispered as her eyelids sagged closed.

"Stay with me!" Talanov shouted as the tears streaked down his cheeks. He screamed again for help.

Sitting in the ambulance minutes later, Talanov strained to breathe. But the coils around his chest were crushing, relentless, and cruel. The hope once visible in his eyes had melted into dark puddles of despair. Suddenly, a high-pitched squeal sounded and the paramedics sprang into action. Readings were shouted, drugs were administered, heart massage was commenced. Then came the paddles.

"Clear!" one of them shouted an instant before a jolt of electricity convulsed Andrea's ghostly white body. The high-pitched squeal did not waver. The paddles were charged again.

Talanov did not know how many attempts were made to save his wife before she was finally pronounced dead. He did not remember the hospital waiting room or the questions asked by police, or the young female officer who finally drove him home. Numbness was all that he felt as he lay curled up on the side of the bed where Andrea had fallen asleep on countless nights, wrapped in his arms.

And numbness was all that he felt now as he stood at the hotel room window, buttoning his shirt.

After staring absently at the lights of West Hollywood for several minutes, he looked toward the nightstand for his watch. It was nowhere to be seen. With a sarcastic snort, he walked over and picked up his slacks. A wrinkle of worry then creased his brow. *My wallet,* he thought. *It's gone.* He felt his pockets, then turned a full circle, hoping to see it on the floor. He then dropped down onto all fours and searched under the bed.

You little bitch.

Jumping up, Talanov yanked on his slacks, pulled on his shoes and stormed out of the room. Outside, he paused on the sidewalk and tried to remember which way he and Tash had come. He looked right and saw a darkened stretch of asphalt lined with apartment blocks and parked cars. Half a block to his left was an intersection with a traffic light. *I remember that light,* he thought. He ran to the corner and paused. Which way now? Both sides of the boulevard in both directions were lined with cafés and clubs. *Think,* he told himself. How far had they walked? A few minutes at most was his recollection. That meant the club was not far away. He remembered its green awning, long and narrow. The kind that stretched out over the sidewalk. With bushes on each side. And black walls, half a block wide, like a warehouse.

He looked right and saw it, a hundred yards or so on the other side of the street. He waited for a break in the traffic and crossed against the light. When the next wave of cars rushed past, he felt a blast of exhaust fumes.

Guarding the front door were two bouncers dressed in black slacks and t-shirts. Flirting with them were several girls in micro skirts. Everyone was laughing. The more muscular bouncer, Gunner, was taller and bald, while the other one, Daz, had a ponytail to the middle of his back. Talanov ignored them and headed straight for the door. Gunner stopped him.

"I need to see some ID," Gunner said.

"You're kidding. I'm over fifty."

"Fifty?" blurted one of the girls named Tracy. "I thought you were, like, thirty-something."

"Shut up," snarled Gunner, glaring at Tracy. To Talanov: "Do I look like I'm kidding?"

"Someone inside has my wallet."

"Not my problem."

Talanov took a calming breath. He was furious. Tash, or whatever her name was, had stolen his wallet and he wanted it back, assuming, of course, that Tash was inside, which was entirely doubtful. "Ten minutes, that's all I ask," he said. "I go in. I look around. I get my wallet and leave. If she's not there, I leave, anyway. You never see me again."

"And I'm telling you that's not going to happen."

Talanov took another calming breath. This one was not as effective. "I'm not looking for trouble," he began.

"Then get the hell out of here. Or trouble is going to find you."

According to Gunner, the choice was simple. Leave voluntarily or leave forcibly. And it didn't seem to matter to Gunner which choice Talanov made. For Talanov the choice was likewise simple. Was his wallet worth a fight? Logic told him to either forget the wallet or try and work things out peacefully. He opted for option number two. After all, Gunner was a big guy. He was also twenty, maybe twenty-five years younger. Besides, what were the odds that Tash was inside? His wallet had had nearly two thousand dollars in it. More than likely, Tash was partying someplace else.

Talanov looked at the other bouncer, who was staring at him with unfriendly eyes. The groupies were also watching. Everybody was waiting to see what the old guy was going to do. "Don't make this worse than it is," he said. "Ten minutes. Then I'm gone."

There was a long moment of silence, almost like a vacuum. Nobody seemed to breathe. Then Gunner's arms shot forward, the heels of his hands like battering rams aimed straight for Talanov's chest. It was a preemptive two-handed blow designed to knock the wind out of Talanov and send him flying into the bushes. A lesson about who was boss.

But Gunner had made the mistake of broadcasting his intentions with a number of subliminal signals. Flaring of the nostrils, tightening of the lips, setting of the jaw, the drawing in of a breath and holding it. So when Gunner's hands shot out, Talanov stepped to the side, grabbed Gunner's wrist and twisted it down and back. This forced Gunner to compensate by straightening his arm and bending left in an effort to pull away. That allowed Talanov to twist the outstretched arm behind Gunner. He then used Gunner's momentum to drive him facedown to the sidewalk in one smooth motion. The whole maneuver took less than four seconds. Kneeling on Gunner's back, Talanov lifted the arm in a direction that could easily pop it from the socket. Gunner cried out and Talanov eased off.

"I asked you not to make this worse than it is," Talanov said, glancing at Gunner then up at Daz. "What's it going to be?"

Daz glared angrily down at Talanov but knew better than to try anything with Gunner's arms bent backward like that. Talanov raised an eyebrow expectantly. "Ten minutes," growled Daz. "But if you cause anyone any trouble – and I mean, *anyone* – I guarantee you won't be leaving in one piece."

Releasing Gunner's arm, Talanov glanced at Tracy and stood. And with a hint of a smile, he disappeared inside.

"Did you see the way he took Gunner down?" Tracy whispered excitedly to her friends. "Man, he's like friggin *McDangerous!* C'mon, let's go and meet him."

"What is *wrong* with you, Decker?" a friend responded. "You don't even *know* that dude! Know anything about him."

"Yeah, but he's, like, totally hot."

The inside of the nightclub had a high ceiling, exposed truss beams and flexible ductwork, all painted black. On the dance floor, a churning mass of young people gyrated wildly to a deafening blast of music played by a DJ with dreadlocks and sunglasses. Mounted above the dance floor were numerous tracks of colored stage lights that kept time to the music.

There's got to be three or four hundred people out there, thought Talanov, squinting through the noise at the waves of arms bending back and forth. But he had to start somewhere and the dance floor was the logical place.

Finding Tash, however, was not his only problem. She also had a partner: the person who'd spiked his drink. He'd been in enough nightclubs to know one should never leave a drink unattended. And he had not. So who had spiked his drink? The waitress? One of the bartenders? Someone watching him from the service area? Whoever it was, it was imperative that he spotted Tash before she or her partner spotted him. Which meant he had to work fast.

Threading his way through the crowd, Talanov was grabbed by several laughing girls. Lost in the rhythm of the music, they whirled and swayed enticingly around him while motioning him to join in. Talanov pushed past them and made his way to the end of the bar, where he stationed himself unobtrusively in the slashes of spinning lights. There, he allowed his eyes to systematically comb the dance floor. There were lots of blondes, but none of them was Tash.

Suddenly, on the far side of the nightclub, Talanov saw Daz and Gunner enter the club. Daz spoke into a filament mike positioned near his mouth. Within seconds a large man in a suit approached. Standing a full head taller than either of them, the man looked like a Sumo wrestler, with a buzz cut and folds of flesh creasing the back of his neck. The two bouncers spoke to him briefly, then fanned out to begin sifting their way through the crowd.

So much for getting ten minutes.

To his left was a short flight of steps that led to a mezzanine full of café tables and booths. Talanov waited for a group of young people to climb the stairs and fell in behind them. At the top he stepped to one side and surveyed the room. People were everywhere. At tables, in booths, standing in the aisles. Most were laughing and drinking. Many were sending text messages or talking on their cell phones. Again, lots of blondes but none of them was Tash.

Talanov started back down the stairs, then abruptly reversed direction and excused his way to the top. *You're angry and in a hurry. This time, do it right.* Thus, calling on skills learned more than thirty years ago at the Balashikha training center near Moscow, former KGB colonel Aleksandr Talanov stood in a darkened corner and methodically double-checked each face in the room. In less than a minute he saw her, seated with a businessman in a darkened booth.

"We go to quieter place now, yes?" Tash asked the businessman in broken English. "Get comfortable. Have some fun." With a seductive smile, she kissed his ear and began stroking his thigh.

"I don't normally do this," the businessman replied nervously.

He was a florid-faced man in his fifties, with fleshy jowls and thinning hair.

"Me, too," Tash replied, scooting closer.

"Where are you from, anyway?" the businessman asked, staring into her gothically-shadowed eyes.

"Wherever you want," answered Tash. Her hand suddenly went higher and the businessman's eyes widened. "Hurry. Finish drink," she cooed.

The businessman was gulping the remainder of his mojito when Talanov slid into the booth. *"Zdravstvuy̆te, Tash,"* said Talanov in Ukrainian.

Tash's mouth fell open.

"Who are you?" the businessman asked, blinking several times.

"I came for my wallet," answered Talanov, his eyes on Tash. "You know, the one you stole?"

The businessman looked at Tash, who shook her head emphatically.

"I think you've got the wrong table," the businessman said.

"Oh, I've got the correct table, all right," answered Talanov. "Tash here slipped something into my drink a few hours ago. And by the look on her face, I can tell she wasn't expecting me to wake up anytime soon."

"He is lying, Tom!" cried Tash. "I don't know who this man is. Or what he is talking about."

"It's Todd," muttered the businessman, glancing at his empty glass.

"Let me out," demanded Tash.

"Not until you hand over my wallet," said Talanov.

"She said she doesn't know you," responded Todd.

"Then how did I know her name?"

Todd started to respond then looked at Tash with a wrinkle of doubt. "How *did* he know your name?"

Tash replied with a disdainful huff. "I *told* you, I am model! He see me somewhere."

Todd gave Tash a dubious scowl.

"Whatever," said Tash. "Let me out."

"As soon as I get my wallet," declared Talanov.

"How many times do I have to tell you? I don't have your stupid wallet."

"Let's just see about that," said Talanov, grabbing Tash's tiny pink leather purse.

"Give that back!" cried Tash, lunging for it.

Blocking her hand, Talanov opened the purse and turned it upside down. A tube of lipstick, mascara, two condoms, and a folded wad of cash landed on the table.

Talanov stared at what was not there.

"See, I don't have wallet," said Tash, snatching back her purse. "Now, get out of here. Leave me alone."

A petite Asian waitress named Jade came up the stairs with a tray of drinks. She had blue streaks in her hair and wore bright red lipstick. When she saw Talanov, she placed the drinks on a table, ran back down, and pushed her way through the crowd. She found Gunner and grabbed him by the arm.

"Not now," Gunner replied, shaking off her hand while continuing to scan faces in the crowd.

"Upstairs. The Russian guy that was here earlier with Tash. He's back and he's causing trouble."

Gunner stared at Jade for a moment then touched the microphone near his mouth. "On the mezzanine. We've got him."

Sliding out of the booth, Todd stood. "I'm calling the police," he said, fumbling clumsily with his cell phone.

"Go for it," said Talanov. "When they get here, tell them to run a drug test on your glass. Provided you're still conscious by then."

Tash tried scooting out of the booth. Talanov grabbed her by the wrist.

"Hey, wut're you doing?" said Todd, fumbling his words as much as his phone. "I think you'd bedder leave."

"You've got ten, maybe fifteen minutes before you pass out," said Talanov while Todd wobbled in front of him. "If I were you, I'd get some help."

Todd blinked several times but did not move.

"Go!" commanded Talanov.

Todd nodded and hurried off.

"Okay, where is it?" Talanov asked Tash, turning to face her. Tash folded her arms and looked defiantly away. Talanov grabbed her by the chin and forced her to look at him. "For the last time, *where's my wallet?"*

Talanov and Tash locked eyes.

"Out back. In dumpster," she said quietly.

Talanov let go and settled back in the booth.

A long moment of silence passed while Tash rubbed her chin. "I want to go now," she said.

"No driver's license. No credit cards. No keys."

"What are you talking about?"

"You're carrying no driver's license, no credit card, and no keys."

"So what? Why do you care?"

"That tells me you're part of something you probably don't want to be a part of," Talanov said. "That maybe someone's holding you against your will. Making you *do* things against your will."

"I don't know what you are talking about."

"I think you do."

Tash stared at Talanov for a long moment then looked away. Talanov watched her for a moment. Tash – or whatever her name was – was a pretty girl. A pretty girl with a look of fear in her eyes.

"Sorry for getting so rough," he said.

Tash gathered her lipstick and mascara and slid them into her purse. She placed her hand on the cash but paused when she saw Talanov watching her. "Here," she said, sliding the money toward him. "It is all there. Count, if you wish."

"It was never about the money," Talanov replied, ignoring the cash and sliding out of the booth.

"Then what is this about?"

"Her photo. It's all I've got left."

"You do this for *picture?"* Tash asked incredulously.

"I wouldn't expect you to understand."

The next few seconds were one of those rare moments when time seemed to linger. And in that moment, Tash saw

Talanov's anguish. She remembered the photo – a wedding shot – in a plastic window where a driver's license should have been. The picture was of Talanov and his bride, happy and smiling, holding flutes of champagne on a beach. Tash studied him more closely and saw desperation and a certain "lostness" in his eyes. *Her photo. It's all I've got left.* No divorced man thinks that way. *My God, she's dead, you're in mourning,* Tash realized. *No wonder you couldn't do it.*

By now, Talanov's thoughts had drifted back to happier times, what few there had been, mainly because he had been unable to love his wife the way she deserved. Transparency and love – qualities that defined a good marriage – were contrary to what had been hammered into him at Balashikha. Love would get you killed. *Or worse: those you loved.*

Then the world changed. But Talanov could not change with it. And just when he was beginning to learn how—

Talanov noticed Tash's eyes widen an instant before the room flipped upside down as he crashed hard on top of a table before tumbling head-over-heels to the floor. Around him, people shouted and ran.

For a long moment, Talanov lay stunned and motionless. *What the hell just happened?* He opened his eyes and saw Gunner standing over him like an angry bull. Gunner grabbed Talanov and pulled him effortlessly to his feet. When Gunner drew back his fist, Talanov closed his eyes. *Do what you want. I'm already dead.*

The blow hit Talanov like a freight train and sent white spots exploding through his brain. He floated limp for an instant, then landed on another table before rolling down onto the floor. In the distance he heard Tash screaming. Talanov groaned and rolled onto his back. His head was pounding and it hurt to breathe. He saw Gunner push an overturned table out of his way and bear down on him, teeth bared, hands like claws, his neck muscles taut and veined. Gunner took a quick half-step and swung his foot at Talanov's head. Talanov rolled away and Gunner missed.

"Leave him alone!" cried Tash. She grabbed Gunner and

tried to stop him but he brushed her aside and kicked again at Talanov's head. Like an extra-point kick in a football game. Full-force after a quick hop, aimed straight at Talanov's head. That meant one foot was in motion while the other foot supported all of his weight. Talanov swung his leg like a scythe and caught Gunner in the back of his ankle. Gunner's leg flew out from under him and Gunner hit the floor hard. When he did, the crowd of young onlookers cheered. Gunner immediately scrambled to his feet just as a winded Talanov struggled to his, one hand holding his ribs, one hand waving back and forth, an indication that he wanted to stop.

"I'm leaving! I got what I wanted!" gasped Talanov.

"You're leaving, but not in one piece," growled Gunner just as Daz pushed his way through the circle of spectators, many of whom were recording the action with cell phone cameras.

"There's no need for this!" said Talanov, looking back and forth between the two bouncers.

"Stop it, Gunner!" yelled Tash. "He got what he wanted. Leave him alone."

"Shut *up,* you worthless whore!" shouted Gunner. He clamped a meaty hand across Tash's face and shoved. Tash crashed into a table and back-flipped down onto the floor, where she lay crying, legs sprawled, her short skirt hiked up to her waist. Her blonde hair was tangled and her lipstick was smeared. Her cheeks were streaked with mascara.

Talanov saw the crowd laughing as Tash rolled slowly onto her side and looked helplessly over at him. She tried to get up but Gunner pushed her back down and kicked her. Tash tried crawling away but Gunner grabbed her by the hair.

Five minutes ago, Talanov would have been happy to let Tash get what was coming to her. She had drugged and rolled him. She had taken the only item that meant anything to him. She had left him passed out in a hotel room in order to fleece some other guy. And now, here she was, trying to defend him. A thieving whore. *Why couldn't she have left well-enough alone?*

Gunner lifted Tash to her feet by the hair and drew back a fist just as Talanov slammed one of the aluminum café chairs on the floor. Gunner paused when he heard the noise and saw Talanov fall into the chair. With his head lowered, Talanov sat motionless against the pulsating reflections of light keeping time with the music. Surprised by this apparent act of surrender, Gunner let go of Tash and looked over at Daz. An instant later, they both rushed forward.

Sensing their decision to attack milliseconds before any movement occurred, Talanov grabbed the leg of his chair and sprang left, slinging it straight at Daz, who stumbled backward while trying to wrestle it away from his face. Continuing his pivot, Talanov sank a roundhouse kick into Gunner's kidney. With a bellow, Gunner stumbled forward. Talanov stepped behind him, seized Gunner by the back of the neck and hammered his forehead onto a table to the crazed delight of the crowd. He then whirled to face Daz while Gunner slid limp to the floor.

Daz picked up a chair and threw it. Talanov grabbed one of the café tables and used it to deflect the chair. Daz hurled another chair, then another, but Talanov used the lightweight table like a shield and sent each of them tumbling to the floor. Daz turned to flee but was stopped by the wall of spectators. Cut off, he turned and charged. Talanov blocked several wild punches, stepped inside and smashed Daz in the jaw with an elbow. He then grabbed Daz by the shirt, twisted inward and flipped him over his shoulder. When Daz landed on his stomach, Talanov grabbed him by the ponytail and slammed his face on the floor.

"I told you not to make this worse than it is," Talanov said, leaning close.

With his nose dripping blood, Daz swallowed and coughed.

Talanov leaned closer. "So I'll ask you one more time. Are you ready to call this off?"

Daz coughed again.

"Are you?" Talanov demanded.

With his attention focused on Daz, Talanov did not see the big Sumo move in from behind. He did not hear the collective gasps as Sumo's hand came down like an axe. All he felt was an explosion of pain. An instant later, everything went black.

CHAPTER 2

TALANOV felt as if he were floating in deep water. Dark. Peaceful. Insulated from the distant pounding, which was a violent commotion of some kind, like a riot. He could feel the vibrations and hear the shouts, but he was floating in the opposite direction, suspended, adrift.

He was also aware of the pain. Not physical pain, but the agony of remorse and guilt. And he knew why. *His wife was dead because of him.*

God, how he longed to see her again. To feel the warmth of her smile and the embrace of her love. He could see her sitting in a corner of Don Adan's coffee shop in Sydney on a typical Sunday morning. "The Don," as Andrea loved calling Gerardo, the owner, would bring her a mug of his strong *pacamara* coffee, grown on his family's plantation in Honduras. He would then sit across from her to argue recipes and cooking techniques while Talanov went for his morning run. Up before dawn, he would work up a sweat jogging the side streets to Neutral Bay, then following the jagged contour of the coast out to Middle Head before returning to Don Adan's, where he would join Andrea for one of The Don's special breakfasts of eggs, black bean *frijoles,* avocado, fresh salsa, and sourdough bread.

Andrea was always trying to pry the *frijoles* recipe out of The Don, who steadfastly refused to give up his mother's secret formula. Andrea employed every trick in her arsenal. Charm, tears, and briberies with various cakes, jams, and pies, and once even a fit of anger, when with one swipe of her hand she sent three breakfast plates crashing to the floor.

"You are not getting this recipe," The Don laughed while one of his waiters swept up the mess.

Talanov continued floating. Why was he thinking of this? Why was he remembering Andrea arguing recipes? How is it that he could see Don Adan's so clearly, with its turquoise paint and local artwork hanging on the walls? He could even see the old guitar on its stand in the corner. He could see people of all cultures and nationalities standing at the door waiting for a table. He could hear the clinking of silverware, the laughter, and the overlapping conversations. He could see Andrea wiping her breakfast plate with the last of her sour-dough bread, as she always did, to The Don's delight. Andrea loved to eat and did so with gusto, which annoyed her gym-junkie girlfriends, who were perpetually on starvation diets and exotic juice drinks in an effort to look like her. He could hear them hissing on their treadmills. *How can anyone that elegant eat so much?*

Elegant. The word was used frequently to describe Andrea. In truth she was that and more. And anything but.

They met because of the party she was catering for him. During his initial phone call to *Elegant Cuisine,* she had simply been a voice. Precise, authoritative, and courteous. And she remained just a voice over the next few weeks, with all matters pertinent to the event handled by e-mail and phone. In fact, it was not until the morning of the event itself that he actually met the owner of that voice. He was standing in the kitchen drinking coffee when she strode in with two boxes of Champagne flutes. She was wearing tight blue jeans and a caterer's jacket, and her auburn hair was tied back in a ponytail.

At first Talanov thought she was merely one of the food-prep staff. That misconception was soon corrected, and not because of anything she had said. It was the way she calmly orchestrated a kitchen full of cartons, portable ovens, coolers and platters into an elegant presentation of fresh lilies, starched linen and impeccably-garnished hors d'oeuvres.

Throughout the day, Talanov could not keep his eyes off her. For not only was Andrea the most beautiful woman he had ever seen, she was a boss who was not afraid of hard work. Once she had taste-tested everything, from the *pelmini* and *syrniki,* to the smoked salmon and caviar canapés, to the spicy beetroot dip, she turned the kitchen over to her assistants.

"You're in good hands now," she said before leaving.

Talanov remembered the deflation he felt when she drove off, as if the whole party was now pointless. He also remembered the elation he felt when she reappeared two hours later wearing a snug, chocolate-colored cocktail dress that showcased sublime collarbones, a slender waist, and absolutely magnificent legs. *I'm going to marry this woman,* he told himself as he watched her stroll the floor chatting with guests, as if the party were hers. Which it was, in a very real way, because Talanov virtually ignored everyone else.

"Flawless and elegant," was how the *Sydney Morning Herald* described Andrea-the-caterer. And yet Andrea-the-wife had a different profile at home. The floor on her side of the bed was littered with piles of magazines, novels, cookbooks, and empty coffee cups. Her side of the closet was much the same. There were piles of shoes everywhere. Clothing and bras were strewn about, with drawers and shelves crammed with underwear, belts, and sweaters. His side of the closet was the exact opposite, with racks of neatly-paired shoes. Shirts, slacks, and suits were arranged and hung by categories and colors. Each pair of underwear had been folded and stacked. Felix and Oscar. The Odd Couple.

It was much the same in their kitchen, especially during "Guinea Pig Trials," as she liked calling new recipe experimentations, where she would cook and Talanov, the "guinea pig," would taste while washing dishes in a futile attempt to keep pace with her frenetic mixing, simmering, baking, and boiling. It was not that they didn't have a dishwasher. They did. It was one of those quiet, Scandinavian kinds. Nor was it because Talanov was proficient at washing dishes. He wasn't. Simply put, dishwashers took way too long. They were also machines, and as such, were incapable of being made to work faster.

"I should have invested in soap stocks," he remembered grumbling while washing a handful of utensils.

"I need that whisk," she replied.

"What whisk?"

"The one you've got in your hand."

"Why'd you drop it in the water if you still needed it?"

"It was dirty."

"With what?"

"Marinara sauce."

"You're cooking marinara sauce."

"I added some herbs."

"What difference does that make?"

"You are so cute!"

How can one argue with that? It wasn't logical, which, of course, drove him crazy, because he was used to functioning on logic. And precision.

"Alex, I need that whisk."

"I'm washing as fast as I can."

"The sauce is burning!"

"Then quit making me wash it each time."

"You are *so* cute! By the way, could you wipe the counter for me?" She nodded toward some spills.

"You're a slob."

"I'm an artist. Being sloppy is a sign of creative genius."

"Do you seriously expect me to believe that?"

Andrea responded by grabbing a clean spoon, scooping out some of the sauce and lifting it to Talanov's lips. He scowled, then tasted the slow-cooked harmony of Roma tomatoes, spices, olive oil, red wine, and veal.

"Okay, you win," he said.

Why am I remembering these things?

Talanov knew the answer before he had posed it. It was how life had been. It was everything he loved, and everything he had lost.

And he would hate God forever because of it.

CHAPTER 3

WITH Sumo standing guard inside the back door to keep spectators from witnessing what was happening outside the back door, Gunner and Daz continued kicking Talanov where they had dropped him. Whatever his condition – unconscious or dead – they didn't care.

Suddenly, a police car squealed around the corner and sped down the alley. Hearing the siren, Sumo melted away into the crowd at the same time Gunner and Daz fled down the alley into a walkway between two buildings. The patrol car screeched to a halt and two officers jumped out. Carlos, the driver, chased after the bouncers while his partner, Diego, hurried over to the body. Diego checked Talanov's neck for a pulse. *Not the way you thought this day would end, huh, pal,* he thought as spectators began streaming out the rear door of the club. Seconds later, the wail of another siren filled the air. Seeing the ambulance, Diego waved the crowd back.

"Let the ambulance through!" he shouted.

The ambulance parked at an angle near the dumpster, which was filled with flattened boxes and trash. Two paramedics jumped out, ran to the back of the ambulance and retrieved a medical kit and gurney. They met Diego at the body.

"What have we got?" asked the driver.

"Middle-aged male. Wrong end of a fight," answered Diego. "No pulse that I could find."

"He's still alive, but just," the other paramedic announced in the flashing strobes of red and blue.

"Insert an airway and bag him," said the driver. "I'll work on his vitals."

While the paramedics attended to Talanov, Carlos trotted back to the squad car, winded from the chase. "They got away," he said to Diego, as the crowd of young onlookers pressed closer. "I'm guessing they were the club's bouncers, judging from what the caller said. But I never got a good look."

"Is he dead? What happened?" several onlookers asked.

"This is, like, *so* amazing!" others remarked. "Yeah, like totally *cool!*"

Something is wrong, thought Talanov as the distant commotion grew louder. He was in a strong undercurrent that was pulling him toward the noise. He fought to break free, to return to the peace and quiet he had felt moments before. But he couldn't move. What was happening? *Leave me alone!*

Talanov gasped and opened his eyes. Dark shapes were bent over him but everything was a blur, as if he were looking through wax paper. Garish lights jabbed him from all directions. Knives of red and blue. *Where am I? Where's Andrea?*

"He's back! Let's load and go," shouted the ambulance driver. She and her partner hoisted Talanov onto the gurney and fastened him with straps. When they lifted the handles and stood, the legs of the gurney extended downward and locked in place. The paramedics then rolled Talanov over the broken asphalt to the rear of the ambulance, where they loaded him inside and secured him in place. One paramedic climbed in beside him.

"Think he'll make it?" asked Diego.

"Hard to tell," the driver replied. "We'll take him to County."

Diego nodded and the driver slammed the door, ran to the cab and jumped behind the wheel. Shifting into gear, she reversed out of the alley, hit the siren and sped off down the street.

Standing in the crowd of onlookers was a forty-six year-old man named Roman Borzakov. He had wavy black hair, an angular jaw, and a slight paunch. He was fashionably stubbly and wore a black Armani suit and a gray mandarin shirt, which was unbuttoned almost to his navel. On his chest was the tattoo of a cross. Around his neck were several gold chains. He took out his cell phone and dialed.

"Da?" answered a voice.

"Eto Borzakov," he said.

"Kak Talanov?"

"The police arrived," Borzakov explained in Russian. "He's alive."

"Will he live?"

"I think so."

"I presume you got what we needed?"

"In my pocket."

"Good. You know what to do."

Borzakov ended the call and joined the last of the spectators trailing back inside.

With a bottled drink in one hand, a black-haired girl approached Diego. She had eyebrow piercings, bright red lips, a tight black and green dress, fishnet stockings, clunky boots, and white breasts that bulged from a lacy bra.

Diego looked the girl over. *What is it with kids these days?*

"Hey, don't judge!" the girl barked, reading his expression.

"May I help you?" Diego asked.

The girl kept scowling at Diego, who shrugged and turned.

"I kinda saw what happened," the girl called out.

Diego looked back at the girl.

"That dude the Ems took away was Russian," the girl continued. "I was sitting in the next booth having one of these *amaz*ing Vodka Epidurals when he said something that sounded like Russian to this hooker. The hooker was pissed off because she was about to score with some other dude. A real creampuff. Balding. In a suit."

Diego began to take notes.

"The hooker must have slipped something into the creampuff's drink," the girl said, "because the Russian told him he'd better get some help, that he didn't have long before he passed out. I don't know where he went."

"Were any names mentioned?" asked Diego.

"The Russian called the hooker Tash. I think the creampuff's name was Tom. No, wait, it was Todd."

"Tash, did you say?" asked Diego.

"And Todd."

"Okay. Go on."

"Anyway, the Russian accused the hooker of stealing his wallet. Like I told you, he said something in Russian."

"How do you know it was Russian? Do you speak the language?"

"No, but I've heard accents like that on TV. I know somebody from Lithonia and she talks like that."

"Lithuania?"

"I guess. It's all kinda the same, I think. And the Russian only said a word or two. Kind of like hello or something."

"They spoke English after that?"

"Yeah, and he spoke it really good. No accent at all. She was a different story. Like she hadn't been here all that long."

"What did she look like?"

"Blonde. Nice tits. Twenty-something."

"Go on."

"Anyway, the Russian wanted to know where his wallet was. She said she didn't have it. So he dumps her purse out on the table and grabs her by the chin. Then she says something I couldn't understand. Then she offers to give his money back – a big wad of cash – but he says he doesn't want it. So he gets up and says something about a photo. Then Daz and Gunner jump him and begin beating the crap out of him. And the crazy sicko just let 'em, like he didn't care."

"Do you know who called this in?"

"Called what in?"

"The fight. Someone called the police. Was it someone you know?"

"It wasn't me, if that's what you mean."

"Whoever called probably saved the Russian's life. Are you sure you don't know who it was? They're not in any trouble. I'd just like to know what he or she saw."

"Like I said, it wasn't me."

"Did you see anyone using a phone?"

"Dude, *every*one was using a phone. It's probably on YouTube by now."

"You said you saw what started the fight?"

"The Russian must have done something to piss off Daz and Gunner, 'cause they came upstairs and jumped him. Then the hooker tries stopping Gunner and he shoves her to the floor and starts to bash in her face. So the Russian suckers Daz and Gunner into coming after him instead."

"Wait a minute. Are you saying the Russian and the hooker were helping each other? Like maybe he was her pimp and she was one of his girls?"

"I dunno. Maybe. When Gunner started to bash the hooker, the Russian sat on a chair in the middle of the floor and it suckered Daz and Gunner into attacking him. It was, like, awesome the way he took 'em out using some kind of karate shit. Both of them! But then he gets a neck chop from Kato, and it's, like, game over."

"Who's Kato?"

"One of the bouncers. None of us know what his real name is, so we call him Kato. You know, from the Pink Panther. He's, like, part Chinese and part something else. A big dude. Really big. Like one of them Chinese wrestlers. Anyway, Kato gets Gunner and Daz back on their feet and they drag the Russian out back. I didn't see what happened 'cause Kato wouldn't let us go outside. He just stood there blocking the door, like a massive tree across the road. Except he was standing upright. He wasn't lying down or anything. Then we hear sirens, Kato takes off, and we all run outside to see what was happening."

"What's your name?"

"Amy Stryzak."

"How do you spell that?"

Amy told him and Diego wrote it down, along with her address and phone number.

"Do you think there'll be, like, a reward or anything?" Amy asked.

"I doubt it."

"What about job openings? I watch lots of cop shows and they have, like, these awesomely amazing computer chicks that help solve cases."

"I wouldn't know."

"Do you think you could let me know?"

"Not my department," said Diego, turning away.

Amy shrugged, finished her drink and tossed her bottle in the dumpster before going back inside. When she opened the door, a blast of music filled the alley.

Diego slid behind the wheel of the squad car to see Carlos pouring coffee from a thermos.

"Want some?" Carlos asked.

Diego shook his head.

"What'd you get?"

"Descriptions on a couple of possible Russian nationals. Our John Doe and a hooker named Tash. Seems John Doe accused the hooker of drugging him and stealing his wallet."

"Never leave your drink unattended," said Carlos, slurping his coffee. "Man, this stuff is good. Mandy makes it in one of those French plungers with non-fat powdered milk that she mixes in a shaker. Makes it froth up just like one of them fancy machines."

"Seems John Doe also knew the hooker," Diego continued, "like, maybe, he was her pimp. There was also a third victim named Todd."

"Sounds like Tash was involved in something more than spreading her legs."

"My witness said Tash spoke broken English. Like she hadn't been here very long." Diego drummed his fingers on the steering wheel for a moment. "Where would you go if you had fifteen minutes before you passed out from a spiked drink?"

"The nearest ER," said Carlos.

Diego started the car. "Call dispatch. Tell them to put out an ATL for a middle-aged male named Todd."

CHAPTER 4

THE USC Medical Center, otherwise known as County General, is one of the busiest hospitals in the world. Containing eight hundred beds, the original Art Deco facility was featured in several television shows and films, including *General Hospital.* Marilyn Monroe was born in its charity ward in 1926. The newer replacement facility, a stark, low, white building with sharp corners, housed only six hundred beds, which in a glutted metropolis like Los Angeles made it vulnerable to overcrowding.

The driver pulled into the ambulance bay beside two other ambulances, where an emergency crew was waiting. The driver jumped out and hurried to the rear of the vehicle, where she opened the door and pulled out the gurney. As before, the legs extended downward and clicked into a locked crisscross position. The other paramedic accompanied the emergency crew as they wheeled Talanov into the hospital.

"What have we got?" asked the attending physician Dr. David Ross, over the sound of patients' cries and rattling gurneys.

"Middle-aged John Doe," answered the driver. "No wallet, no ID, conscious but delirious from repeated blunt force traumas."

"Plus some facial lacerations, a few abrasions, one eye swollen shut," added the other paramedic.

Ross glanced down and saw Talanov's good eye was partially open. On his neck was a padded white collar. Over his mouth was an oxygen mask.

"Where is she? I don't see her," said Talanov weakly, moving his head from side to side. His voice was muffled beneath the mask.

"Who's he asking for?" said Ross.

"No idea," answered the second paramedic. "He's been talking like that the whole way over. Drifting in and out. He took quite a beating and was unresponsive when we found him in an alley."

"Where is she?" Talanov asked again. He tried sitting up but Ross kept him down.

"Lie still. We're almost there," instructed Ross.

The fact that John Doe was moving was a good thing. It meant that his spinal cord was intact and his extremities were responding. The fact that he was speaking and moving his head back and forth was also a good thing. It meant that his airway was clear and his neck injuries were minimal, although an x-ray would be needed to confirm the extent of any possible damage. His delirium, however, was a concern. If the victim had been deprived of oxygen for any length of time, brain function might be impaired.

"Why didn't you intubate?" asked Ross.

"I was about to," answered the driver, "because the attending officer couldn't find a pulse, but when I checked, he was breathing steadily on his own. It was shallow and almost undetectable, but steady nevertheless."

"He looks to be in pretty good physical condition," observed Ross.

The driver agreed. "Given what he's been through, his fitness no doubt saved his life."

They turned a corner and narrowly missed hitting a gurney coming the other way. On it was a gunshot victim whose chest was a mass of blood.

"What's his BP?" asked Ross just as they were passing a cluster of beds near the nurses' station. Doctors and nurses hovered over more victims of stabbings and shootings. Orders were being shouted. Portable monitors beeped and squealed.

"One-ten over seventy-five," answered the driver. "No fluctuations. No signs of internal bleeding."

Ross glanced back to make sure his nurse was recording the information on a chart.

"I've never seen the place like this," the driver remarked. She started to comment on it being a full moon but had made that mistake before and been corrected by none other than David Ross himself, who told her full moons had no bearing on violent behavior.

"Saturday night, with temperatures climbing," she said instead. "Brings out the worst in the best of us."

"Where is she?" asked Talanov again. His voice was distant and faint.

"Don't worry, we'll take good care of you," said Ross, patting Talanov on the shoulder.

"By the way," said the driver, "the attending officer called and said he'll come by later to question John Doe about possible involvement in human trafficking and drugs. He wants you to hold him until he gets here."

"Not a problem. From the looks of his condition, he won't be going anywhere, anyway."

Talanov was wheeled into an examination room and lifted onto a hospital bed, spine board and all. A cart with stainless steel instruments was wheeled over and Talanov's clothes were cut off. Overhead was a large, round, high-intensity surgical lamp. It bathed the area in light.

"Save his clothes for the police," instructed Ross. "Don't forget to record the chain of evidence."

"Yes, doctor," answered one of the nurses. She placed Talanov's clothing in a large plastic evidence bag, sealed it closed, then recorded the attending physician's name, her name, the time, date, and patient's assigned name of John Doe 061003 on the manifest. She then handed everything to an orderly, who signed the manifest and left with the bag.

Beneath the glare of the surgical lamp, Ross looked carefully at the topography of bruises discoloring Talanov's face and midsection. One eye was swollen closed. His forehead was gashed and seeping. Ross ran his fingers gently across several areas of abdominal swelling. Talanov responded with flinches and groans. Ross pricked the tips of Talanov's toes with a pointed instrument and saw them twitch. "Very good," he said. "Can you tell me your name?"

"Where is she? I don't see her," Talanov said weakly.

"Who are you? What's your name?" repeated Ross.

With a plaintive moan, Talanov made another feeble attempt to sit up.

"Lie still," said Ross, holding him down. He nodded and a warm blanket was placed over Talanov. With a brief shiver, Talanov sighed and relaxed.

Ross made several comments to his nurse, which she recorded on the chart. He then continued his physical examination and commentary, with each of his observations and assessments recorded on the chart, including remarks about the patient's remarkable physical fitness and the presence of several old scars on his shoulder and stomach. Ross then ordered a battery of blood tests, an abdominal ultrasound, and x-rays of John Doe's neck.

"Let's close that wound near his eye," Ross said, and Ross's team gathered around to assist. When Ross had finished stitching the gash, the tests Ross had ordered took another forty minutes, after which Talanov was dressed in a hospital gown and his bed placed in the corridor, head to toe, in a line with three other beds.

The corridor was wide and long. At the far end was a junction that intersected another corridor. There were also some bathrooms and an exit. The front end of the corridor faced the admissions counter, where a hum of activity was taking place. The waiting room was full. Phones were ringing. Doctors and orderlies flew by in both directions. No one paid the slightest attention to the sleeping patient lying motionless on a portable hospital bed.

Talanov, however, was not asleep. Nor had he been unconscious or delirious on the ride over. Instinct told him to maintain that appearance, which enabled him to not only learn that he had no serious injuries, but to overhear the paramedics' conversation about the police wanting to question him.

In theory, he should be presumed innocent until proven guilty. In reality, that was not the case, especially with so-called "persons of interest," which is what he would become the moment they learned he was Aleksandr Talanov, a former colonel in the KGB, who was in the United States on a pending Green Card application. And once they did find out who he was, his application would be revoked and he would be deported, especially after he had been taken into custody for questioning about his suspected involvement in a human trafficking and drugs ring. No matter what explanations he gave about his innocence, he would be guilty by assumption and linked – at least in their minds – with the Russian mafia, which was full of his old KGB colleagues.

Without moving his head, Talanov opened his good eye and saw two security guards at the mouth of the corridor. One of the guards was chatting with a gorgeous young intern with ebony skin and a radiant smile. She sounded Jamaican. The other guard, a big guy, was keeping a casual eye on the waiting room crowd. Talanov discreetly flexed his muscles. Everything seemed functional.

A commotion drew the guards' attention. Someone was fed up with waiting and decided to protest. The guards stepped over to calm things down. When they did, Talanov slid off the bed and stood. He steadied himself by holding onto the bedrail for a moment. His whole body ached. Joints, ribs, stomach, back, head. Everything. But he forced himself to start walking toward the exit sign at the end of the corridor.

It was his own fault that he was in this predicament. If only he'd not gotten involved with Tash. If only he'd done what he set out to do, which was retrieve his wallet and leave. But no, he had to stick up for her and place his entire future in jeopardy. What the hell was he thinking?

Andrea would have stuck up for her, and in his former days, before her murder, he would have, too. In those days, he cared. These days, he did not. So why had he made such a stupid decision? Why had he gotten involved? It wasn't simply because she was a woman. Well, maybe partly. She was, after all, being picked on by a bully named Gunner. So maybe that was part of it, although not all of it, because he had once shot a woman in Spain who was trying to kill him, and would have if he'd hesitated. This was different. This girl, Tash, was just trying to survive.

Oddly enough, he didn't blame her for stealing his wallet. When she first slid onto the barstool beside him and made her intentions known, her accent told him she was from the Ukraine, the southern part most likely, near the Black Sea. Her actions and appearance, however, told him something else. Here was a beautiful Ukrainian girl in her mid-twenties, who spoke broken English, working as a prostitute in Los Angeles. That meant only one thing: she had been recently lured here by some kind of scam and then forced into prostitution to pay off her so-called debt. And the people running those kinds of operations here in Los Angeles were the Russian mob. Which was precisely what the police wanted to question him about.

Talanov passed an open hospital room and a woman gasped when she saw him. Under ordinary circumstances, his presence would not have attracted attention. But these were not ordinary circumstances. His hair was matted and dirty. One eye was swollen shut. His face was scabbed and bruised. Iodine stains surrounded his sutures. Everything about him attracted attention as he limped by in his hospital gown.

Washing up in the bathroom was out of the question. His absence would soon be noticed and the security guards would come looking. He had to get out of the building and he had to do it a lot faster than at this slow pace.

Outside the emergency entrance where Talanov had been wheeled in, Diego parked the squad car in a reserved space. He and Carlos got out, slipped their batons into metal loops on their belts and headed for the door.

"Todd Martin didn't give us a lot," remarked Diego.

"Yeah, but did you see his face when we showed up to question him?" asked Carlos with a grin. "How the *hell* did you find me? That's what he was thinking, and I *love it* when that happens. Total shock. He was lucky John Doe clued him in about the spiked drink. You gotta give Todd Martin credit for flagging down a taxi and getting to a hospital so fast. I wonder if he threw up in the backseat of that taxi?"

"I was hoping Todd Martin could have given us a name," said Diego. "I was hoping he might have overheard something that would help us identify John Doe."

"Who checked John Doe into the hospital?"

"David Ross."

"Did Ross get any information?"

"He tried asking his name but Ross said John Doe was delirious, although he did say he was in pretty good shape considering the beating he'd taken."

"What if he's still unconscious?"

"We wake him up. I want answers about what the Russian mob is doing on our side of town."

"Just because he's Russian, which we don't know for sure, doesn't mean he's involved with the mob."

Diego knew Carlos was right. John Doe may not be Russian. And even if he were, it didn't mean he was involved with the mob. John Doe could simply have been in the wrong place at the wrong time, just as Todd Martin had been. The fact that he, too, had been drugged seemed to support that conclusion.

But from the sound of it, John Doe *was* a Russian, as was the hooker, assuming she was not from some neighboring country whose language sounded like Russian. She also spoke broken English, which probably meant she had arrived here recently, no doubt as part of some scam. And since human trafficking for purposes of forced prostitution was on the rise, this gave the whole case an organized crime smell. And since John Doe and the hooker had tried helping each other, that meant John Doe was probably her pimp, which meant they were both involved in the operation together.

"He's involved, all right," said Diego. "To what degree, I can't tell. But we're sure as hell going to find out."

Inside the hospital, at the far end of the corridor, Talanov hobbled toward the exit sign as fast as his aching legs would take him, which wasn't fast by any definition. He had already passed several nurses and orderlies and sensed them turning around to look. He smiled at the thought of his bare ass staring back at them through the gap in his gown. And he made no effort to hide it.

His plan was simple. Once he was out of the building, he would make his way to the street and circle up the hill and find a service station, where he could clean up and call for a taxi.

The problem would be inventing a believable story about why he was walking around barefooted at night in a hospital gown. That last thing he wanted was someone phoning the cops. Four more steps. He was nearly there.

A hand suddenly grabbed him from behind. "Where do you think *you're* going?" The hand spun him around and Talanov found himself staring up into the glaring eyes of a security guard. And not just any guard, either. It was the big one, who stood maybe six-foot-four. He had short hair, which probably meant he was ex-military. But he also had a big gut, which probably meant he would be slow. Nevertheless, he had plenty of muscle and plenty of size, which meant there was no chance of overpowering the guy.

"Man, I *gotta* take a leak!" said Talanov, holding his groin and crossing his knees, as if he were about to burst. "I've been on that stretcher for *hours.*"

"And back to that stretcher you're going," the guard replied." We're holding you for the cops." He took out a disposable handcuff, which was a self-locking double-loop of nylon.

"C'mon, man. I've got to take a leak or I'm gonna do it right here on the floor. The bathroom's right over there." He pointed toward a "male" symbol on a door.

The guard hesitated.

Talanov grimaced and bent over even more. "Please, man, I gotta go."

"All right. But I'm coming with you."

"Fine. Hold my hand if you want. But no funny business while I'm doing my thing."

The guard gave Talanov a dubious scowl and followed him toward the bathroom. Before pushing opening the door, Talanov noticed an exit sign above a door that led outside.

The men's room was clean and smelled of sanitizer. Talanov stepped into the stall and closed the door while the guard waited by the sink, arms folded and relaxed. After urinating in the toilet bowl, Talanov flushed the toilet, opened the stall door and shuffled unsteadily to the sink. The guard moved aside to let him wash his hands. After a squirt of liquid soap,

Talanov paused with his hands in the running water and stared at his reflection in the mirror. He brought a wet hand up and gingerly touched his swollen eye.

"Someone did a number on you," the guard remarked.

"I don't remember," said Talanov, dripping water on the floor with one hand while staring absently at his face. He refocused and cranked off the faucet. When he turned from the sink, he slipped.

Talanov tried catching himself, but his bare feet had already flown out from under him and he fell against the wall, where he bounced forward and clubbed his head on the edge of the counter before crashing to the floor. Blood began streaming down his face.

At the other end of the corridor, Diego and Carlos approached the admissions counter, where phones were ringing and computers were being worked frantically in an effort to keep up with demand. The counter was piled high with charts. Doctors barked orders to nurses and orderlies, who dodged one another and hurried off. Two receptionists were arguing in Spanish with several people at the counter. Behind them, the waiting room was full of coughing children, harried mothers, morose teenagers, and moaning adults. Other children were chasing one another among the chairs, their wearied parents having long ago given up trying to control them. Several people were sitting on the floor, backs against the wall, waiting for their names to be called. Bypassing the congestion, Diego and Carlos circled the counter and flagged down a passing doctor.

"We're here to see David Ross," said Diego.

The doctor looked around, saw Ross and pointed him out. The officers threaded their way over to where Ross was conferring with a nurse beside a gurney. On the gurney was a patient under a sheet. Ross issued instructions and the nurse wheeled the gurney away.

Diego said, "Dr. Ross, we're here for John Doe."

"Which one?" asked Ross. "We have four."

"Middle-aged Caucasian male. Dark hair. Beaten up pretty badly."

"In a nightclub brawl, that's right, I remember. He's the one you wanted us to hold on suspicion of drugs and human trafficking."

"Where is he?"

"Follow me."

In the bathroom down the hall, the guard rushed over to Talanov, who was trying to sit up. "I should never have let you to come in here," said the guard.

"I had to pee."

"I'll get help. Your forehead is bleeding."

"I'm okay. Give me a hand." Talanov tried standing but slipped again.

"Take it easy," said the guard. He stepped behind Talanov, looped an arm under each of his armpits and lifted him to his feet.

Talanov grabbed the front edge of the counter and steadied himself in front of the mirror. The blood was running down his face.

"Grab me some toilet paper," said Talanov, turning on the water.

"You need a doctor."

"I need to get some cold water on this wound. It'll stop the bleeding. Hurry."

"Are you okay there on your own? You got your balance?"

"I'm good. I'll be all right."

The guard stepped over to the stall, pushed open the door and leaned in to unroll a wad of paper. Talanov quietly followed.

In truth, Talanov liked the guard. He wore a wedding ring and seemed like a decent guy. Had he made it out the exit undetected, he would not be in this predicament. But that had not happened. Without question, he could not allow himself to be questioned by the police. Nor could he allow himself to be identified, which he would be once the police took him into custody. That meant the guard had to be taken out. He didn't like the idea, but it had to be done.

In a situation like this, timing was everything, especially in his weakened condition. To try and overpower the big security guard was not an option. Trying to outrun him was equally impossible. An old man in a walking frame would be faster. His only choice was to catch the guard in an awkward position. Even better would be some kind of a confined space, like a toilet stall, with his defenses down and his focus elsewhere.

Bluffing his way into the bathroom had enabled him to get out of sight while keeping the security guard from cuffing his hands and hauling him back down the corridor to his hospital bed. Besides, he actually *did* have to pee. Once inside the bathroom, he knew he had to think fast. He had maybe two or three minutes at most, which was the time it took to urinate and wash his hands. But instead of choosing the urinal, he chose the toilet stall. For someone in a hospital gown, it was a natural choice. His hope: that the security guard would use the urinal himself, which would leave him in a vulnerable position, with his attention focused in one direction and both hands dutifully occupied. But that hadn't happened. Nothing, it seemed, was going to plan.

Then Talanov stepped over to the mirror and saw his swollen eye and stitches. He just stood there, water running, hands dripping on the floor, staring at a face he hardly recognized. And that's when the idea hit him.

Head wounds were known to bleed more profusely than other wounds, so the stitches on his forehead presented an opportunity for him to create a crisis. Splitting open the wound would hurt, but these days he was accustomed to pain. So he remained in front of the sink long enough to drip a large puddle of water on the floor. The floor was linoleum and therefore would be slippery. Then came the tricky part of hitting his head hard enough to open the wound, but without seriously injuring himself.

Immediately after the "accident," the guard, as predicted, rushed to his aid. Talanov then convinced the guard he was not hurt. He then asked the guard to help him stand, a move calculated to keep him inside the bathroom rather than calling for help. All that was required next was getting the guard to lean into the toilet stall and turn his back. And when he did, Talanov shoved.

"Sorry," Talanov said when the guard's head smashed into the wall and with a moan he slid to the floor. Talanov could not tell whether the guard was unconscious or merely dazed, but for the moment, he was not moving. He grabbed the guard's feet and pulled. His aim was to switch clothing, which would make him a lot less visible on the street. But the guard weighed over two hundred pounds and was wedged tightly between the toilet and the wall. Talanov strained but could not work him free. In his present condition, he did not have the strength.

What to do? A man walking along the sidewalk at night in a hospital gown would attract attention. An escapee, people would think, which, of course, would be true. Yet what other choice did he have? Some hospital scrubs might work. But that would mean luring an orderly into the bathroom and knocking him out.

The guard suddenly groaned. He was regaining consciousness.

Dammit, thought Talanov. *Nothing was going to plan.* And after grabbing the guard's walkie-talkie, he hobbled out of the door.

CHAPTER 5

ROSS walked over to Talanov's empty bed and looked around. John Doe was missing and so was one of the security guards. "Your buddy and this patient, where are they?" he asked over the din of coughs and moans. The other guard glanced at the empty bed where Ross was standing and shrugged. Ross marched over and got right up in his face. The Jamaican nurse picked up a chart and melted quickly away.

"Do you know what time it is?" asked Ross.

"3:00am," the guard replied, backing away slightly.

"If you want to make it to 3:05 as an employee of this hospital, then you'd better find the occupant of that bed."

The guard swallowed hard and nodded.

Outside, Talanov felt the warm night air brush across his face as he hurried along a railed walkway at the base of the hospital. A wall of lighted windows rose above him. The exit had spilled him onto a wide plaza between the hospital and another medical building. During the day, the open plaza was filled with patients and hospital staff wanting fresh air. It was a favorite place to eat lunch, catch some sun, or take a break. Now it was deserted and dark. Even so, Talanov elected to stay in the shadow of the hospital. He tried running, but could not because everything ached. So he walked as fast as he could.

He realized he was a bundle of contradiction. Since Andrea's murder, he had been on a destructive, downward spiral. Without her, what was the point? His whole life had been a lie, and the one true part of it was now dead. Because of him. Bright and open and honest, she had been his polar opposite in so many ways, coming as he did from a life of secrecy and mistrust. Shades of gray compared to a rainbow.

And yet if that were completely true, why go to all of this trouble? If life were so pointless, why not surrender and let the police do what they wanted? So what if they deported him? So what if he were accused of being involved in some ludicrous narcotics ring operated by the Russian mob, or one of their despicable human trafficking operations? So what? He stopped in the darkened hum of some air conditioning fans. Why run? What was the point?

A guard's voice crackled over the walkie-talkie he was carrying. A Caucasian male patient had assaulted a security guard and escaped. A description then followed of a middle-aged barefooted man in a hospital gown.

Continuing on, Talanov knew why he was running, or at least part of the answer. He wanted vengeance for what had happened. His past had followed him to Australia in the form of a group of assassins from an old KGB assassination unit called Department Thirteen. And for what? *Money*. It wasn't for anything he had done, but for a secret bank account in Switzerland that had been manipulated from seven million to nearly one-and-one-half billion dollars. And after losing nearly everything because of that wretched money, which then disappeared to God-knows-where, Andrea had reluctantly followed him here, to Los Angeles, in search of anonymity and peace. But that had not happened. Instead, someone killed his wife in a botched attempt to kill him.

For a long while, he was the prime suspect. His KGB past had unleashed a feeding frenzy, like raw meat to sharks. And everybody wanted to be the first to bring him down. Assumptions and theories ran rampant. Perhaps his wife had stumbled upon some deeply buried secret, and he had killed her to keep it quiet. Perhaps she found out he was working with the Russian mafia. Perhaps he was a terrorist. He tried explaining his role with the KGB, but his refusal to reveal details of classified operations only fueled their determination to prove his guilt. He could not tell them he was November Echo, which was his codename while operating as a deep cover informant for the CIA, because some agents and operations might still be active. Detectives tried every trick in the book to make him talk and catch him in a lie. There was endless grilling, with repeated variations of good cop versus bad cop. They searched his house, investigated his financial records, insurance policies, and business dealings. Everything was torn apart and scrutinized. Nothing was spared. The case against him eventually collapsed but the police resented him for it. In their minds, he had merely outwitted them.

Innocent until proven guilty. What a laugh.

For Talanov, the real killer was still out there, and one day he would find him. However, getting hold of the evidence file on his wife's murder turned out to be impossible. He had tried but the police were not about to hand over evidence to their prime suspect. So his determination to find the killer waned, and in the end, became futile and pointless. *So why keep running? Why put yourself through all this pain?* He heard shouts and quickened his pace. If only he could run.

At the top of an embankment he could see the headlights of cars moving along a street. If he could reach that street, maybe someone would give him a ride. The embankment, however, was steep and covered with shrubbery, and there was a chain link fence at the top, so even if he could manage to climb the steep incline, he would never get over that fence. The only way to get there was up a flight of concrete steps off to his right.

Leaving the protective shadow of the hospital, Talanov limped along a sidewalk. He descended a small flight of steps and paused beside a railing to catch his breath. He looked down over the railing and saw that he was at the top of a high retaining wall. Below was a freight yard with some trucks backed up to a loading dock. On the platform were piles of pallets and crates. The dock offered numerous places to hide, but a two-story drop would break his legs. Hurrying onward, Talanov followed the walk, which angled right a short distance before reaching the concrete steps he had to climb. Grabbing hold of the railing, he hobbled to the top, where he paused again to catch his breath. He had made it to the street.

Talanov looked right. Down the hill half a block was a stop light. The intersection was well lit and he could see the illuminated red dot hanging above the intersection. Cars were passing beneath the light in both directions. A steady flow. That meant the chances of getting a ride were good. It also meant the chances of being seen by the police were good. So he turned left, and with his hospital gown flapping behind him, started up the hill.

Hearing voices behind him, Talanov glanced down the embankment and saw two men pause at the top of the retaining wall where he had paused. They were looking down into the freight yard, no doubt wondering if their escapee was hiding down there. They were deliberating what to do when a car turned a corner at the top of the hill. Talanov ducked but not in time.

"Up there, I see him!" one of the guards shouted.

The walkie-talkie in Talanov's hand crackled. "We see him! He's heading up Chicago Street hill."

"Copy that. On my way," a voice replied.

Hearing footsteps bounding up the concrete steps, Talanov struggled to run barefooted up the hill. His body ached. His chest was pounding. His legs were beginning to seize. Spasms of pain shot through them. He began to wobble. *"Not now,"* he growled through clenched teeth, willing himself onward. But he couldn't go on and finally staggered to a stop, bent over, gasping for air. He was spent and exhausted. It was over.

The headlights coming toward him were blinding. Footsteps closed in from behind.

The walkie-talkie crackled again. "Subject is in view. We've got him!"

Talanov looked up just as a black Lexus screeched to a stop inches away from him.

The door flew open.

"Get in!" a woman's voice shouted.

CHAPTER 6

TALANOV stared at the gaping opening staring back at him. It was like an escape tunnel, or a steel trap, he wasn't sure which. The interior light was not on, so he couldn't see who was driving.

"Get in!" Tash shouted again.

Talanov dove into the empty back seat. "Go the other way," he gasped, tumbling to the side when the Lexus did a squealing turn and roared back up the hill. The torque of the acceleration caused the door to slam shut.

The security guards sprinted after the Lexus but it was no contest and they soon stopped in the middle of the street, where they watched the tail lights of the Lexus reach the top of the hill and disappear to the right.

"Where are you?" one of the security guards yelled into his walkie-talkie. "The subject got into a car!"

"Turning onto Chicago Street now," Diego replied.

The guards looked back down the hill and saw the black-and-white squad car peel around the corner and speed toward them, its red and blue lights flashing. The guards moved to the curb and pointed up the hill as the squad car roared past.

The Lexus raced down Charlotte Street. It was a gentle downhill grade through an aging residential neighborhood being invaded by new zoning laws. They roared around several slower cars, through an intersection, and past a three-story parking garage.

Talanov sat up and looked out the rear windshield at the flashing lights of the police car at the top of the hill where they had turned. He was still not sure what had just happened. Turning around, he looked at the two girls in the front seat. In the wash of light from passing streetlamps, he recognized the face of the driver.

"It's you, from the nightclub," he said, rocking from side the side when Tash passed cars. "Tash, I think it was."

Tash did not reply.

Talanov studied her face and saw that she was even more beautiful than he remembered. Back in the nightclub, her hair had been teased and gelled or whatever women did to make it look skanky. In the nightclub, she had had a hardened look, with heavy eye shadow and maroon lipstick to go with the rest of her provocative image. She had worn a tight microskirt and even tighter halter top with a bit of lace to give her that innocent baby-doll look. Her breasts then had been packed in so tightly they all but screamed to get out. Which she was willing to accommodate, for a price.

But now, her honey-blonde hair had been pulled up into one of those loose, messy, alluring ponytails with playful wisps hanging in random directions. She was still in the halter top and microskirt, but she was wearing an unbuttoned oversized shirt. She had scrubbed off all of her makeup so that even in the dim, occasional light of a passing car, Talanov could see she possessed a natural, wholesome beauty. What a contrast to the woman he had met earlier.

"Thanks for showing up when you did," said Talanov. Neither Tash nor her friend replied. "My name is Alex, by the way." Tash glanced at him in the rearview mirror but said nothing. "Mind telling me yours?" He looked at Tash, then at the petite Asian girl sitting in the passenger seat beside her.

"Why do you want to know?" asked Tash.

"Because you just saved my ass. You tried saving it before, back in the nightclub, and nearly got hammered. So here I am, sitting in the back seat of your car in a hospital gown. Why, I don't know, but here I am. So ... *thank you,* whoever you are. I know your name isn't Tash. But if you don't want to tell me what it is, that's okay. I'm not trying to hustle you or anything. Not that I could, in my condition."

When Tash sped around another car, Talanov grimaced and fell back in the seat. Tash eyed him in the rearview mirror again and saw him holding his ribs.

"You are hurt," she said. "What did doctor say?"

"Don't worry about it," Talanov replied.

Tash kept glancing at him in the rearview mirror. "Larisa," she finally said as they raced past some office buildings. "My friend here, she is Jade."

Jade looked sharply at Larisa. "I told you not to tell!" she whispered harshly.

"It's all right, I'm not a cop," said Talanov. "And I don't blame you for stealing my wallet, if that's what you're worried about. Especially after what you just did." He began looking around at the interior of the car. Something about it looked familiar.

"Go through the intersection," said Jade. "The freeway is straight ahead."

Talanov forced himself to sit forward when they slowed for the stoplight at North Soto. He glanced at Jade's delicate, almost porcelain-like features in the dim wash of light from the instrument panel. She had large, dangling earrings and blue streaks in her hair. "I remember you," he said. "From the nightclub. You served us drinks."

Jade did not reply as they came to a stop behind several other cars. On their right were a couple of SUVs. On their left was a Chevron station with a flat canopy over the pumps. Everything was brightly lit.

"Whose car is this?" asked Talanov.

Larisa did not answer. She was looking anxiously in the rearview mirror at the approaching police car. It was still a long way back but was closing in fast. Even worse, two other cars had pulled up behind her, boxing her in.

Talanov leaned forward and looked at the ignition key. "This is *my* car!" he said, recognizing a small medallion hanging from the key ring.

"Come on. Come *on!*" Larisa mumbled, gunning the accelerator and jerking the car forward in small increments, as if it would speed up the light.

"Where did you get my *car?*" demanded Talanov, squirming in the backseat, trying to get comfortable. But whatever position he tried, his body still hurt. Especially his abdomen, where he had been kicked.

In her side mirror, Jade was looking worriedly at the approaching police car while Larisa gunned the Lexus and honked.

"Stop it!" said Talanov, glancing behind them at the flashing lights. "The cops are looking for someone driving like a maniac."

"They will catch us if I don't," said Larisa.

"They'll catch you *for sure* if you do," Talanov replied.

"What am I to do?" she asked just as the light changed and traffic began moving forward.

"Through the light, then turn left, then a quick right into that side street," said Talanov, pointing. "Normal speed or they'll know it's us."

Larisa did as Talanov instructed. The street was dark and quiet and lined with trees. No streetlamps. Plenty of shadows.

"Into that driveway," he said. "Park and turn off the engine."

Larisa turned into a handicapped slot beside a two-story apartment building of white stucco. Near the curb was a stuffed couch surrounded by black garbage bags full of trash.

"Everybody down," said Talanov once Larisa turned off the ignition.

They all slid down in their seats.

"Where did you get my car?" he asked, sitting up after a brief burst of flashing red and blue.

"Your keys were in alley after ambulance leave," said Larisa. "I pick up. Later, in parking lot, I push button. See parking lights flash."

"And your friend there beside you, Jade. She's the one who spiked my drink." A statement more than a question, and neither girl replied. "I'll take that as a yes," said Talanov.

A hand banged on the hood and everyone jumped.

"Estas en un de estacionamiento para discapacitados!" shouted a man in a cowboy hat.

"Go," said Talanov. "We're in handicapped parking."

Larisa started the car, backed out, and drove to the corner. After a couple of turns, they were in a river of traffic heading northwest on the Hollywood freeway.

"Where do I take you?" she asked.

"Why'd you come back?" Talanov replied.

Larisa retrieved Talanov's wallet from between her legs and held it back to him. "For you," she said.

Talanov accepted the wallet and slowly opened it. His driver's license and Amex card were gone, but his wedding photo was still in the plastic window. He stared at it in the intermittent flashes of light on the freeway. A sad smile formed on his lips. "How did you know where to find me?" he asked.

"I hear ambulance say they bring you to County Hospital. We drive around to find place to park. See you running up hill."

Talanov ran his finger over the photo.

"You miss her, yes?" asked Larisa.

Talanov closed the wallet and looked out the window at the passing lights. They were heading northwest on US 101, toward Ventura. In the distance was the lighted thirteen-story Capitol Records Tower, which resembled a stack of 45 records piled on a turntable.

"I am sorry, I should not have asked," Larisa said.

"Forget it," Talanov replied.

Larisa looked over at Jade and nodded. Jade responded with a scowl of disbelief. Larisa nodded more emphatically. With a grumble, Jade handed Talanov the wad of money Larisa had taken earlier that night.

"Here," Jade said. "This is yours."

"Keep it," Talanov replied.

Larisa and Jade exchanged glances.

"It's okay. You can keep it," Talanov said again.

"Why do you do this?" asked Larisa. "The money is yours."

"He said we could keep it," said Jade.

"Why you not want to take it?" asked Larisa.

"It was never about the money," said Talanov. "I told you that."

"I do not understand."

"Let him do what he wants," said Jade. "We kind of like need it, you know?"

"Next exit. Get off," said Talanov. "At the corner, turn right, then—" He suddenly started coughing. Seconds later, he was struggling to breathe.

Larisa took the exit ramp, made a quick right turn at the light and pulled over quickly. There wasn't much around. No commercial outlets. No gas stations. No fast food outlets. Just some unimaginative apartment blocks and houses. She jumped out, opened the rear door and bent in to help Talanov. A pickup truck sped by and honked at her long legs and high heels.

Talanov was holding his ribs and grimacing in pain. His hospital gown had fallen away and Larisa discreetly wrapped it up over him.

"You need to lie down," she said. "How far to house?"

"Help me up," he replied hoarsely. "I need to show you the way."

Larisa felt his forehead with the back of her hand. "You have fever. We must hurry."

Placing one foot in the car, Larisa carefully reached an arm around Talanov. Even in the dark and with one eye swollen shut, he could not help but stare directly into her cleavage. It was right there, in his face, two perfect breasts packed snugly into a halter top that was way too small. She smelled good, too. Really good. Talanov could feel the heat of her breath on his neck as she helped him sit up. He felt strands of her hair brush delicately across his cheek.

Her behavior had been different back in the hotel room. "Tash" had been aggressive and seductive, as if she had been on a mission and time was limited, which, when he thought about it, was true. She was a hooker, and the more tricks she turned, the more she got paid. Money was her lifeline, being, as she no doubt was, a sex slave for some Russian pimp. And if she did not pay her weekly debt, which probably ran into the thousands, she would get punished. And not in ways that would tarnish her beauty. Russian pimps were shrewd businessmen. Not the kind to damage their chattel so long as a girl maintained her usefulness, which in most cases was both her beauty and her willingness to do whatever a client wished, no matter how twisted or perverse. That was Tash.

But this was Larisa, and the Larisa who was helping him right now was a full one-and-hundred-eighty degrees different.

She wasn't Tash, the aggressive hooker. She was Larisa, a gentle, caring, almost innocent yet surprisingly capable young woman.

Reality check. She's a hooker who drugged and robbed you.

A hooker who saved your ass.

Larisa didn't seem the sentimental kind. Which made him wonder if his wedding photo had really inspired her to climb into that dumpster and retrieve his wallet, then drive to the hospital to try and find him? Was she being nice for some other reason? Was this merely an act? Was she hoping to make an even bigger score by taking him home?

Talanov groaned when he sat up. The upright position caused the weight of his torso to compress every vertebra in his back. And each of them was screaming in protest. It also made breathing an excruciating exercise.

"You are certain you wish to sit up?" Larisa asked. Talanov grimaced and nodded. Larisa clicked the seatbelt around him and closed the door. She then jumped back into the front seat and soon had them speeding along Cahuenga. The patched concrete beneath the tires made rhythmic noises, like a train.

Following Talanov's directions, they began zigzagging up into the canyons and bluffs of the Hollywood Hills. Even in the darkness, the influence of old Mexico was apparent. There were terraces with charming narrow stairways, white plaster walls, and wild cascades of brilliant bougainvillea. Houses had been set into the steep slopes at various odd angles to capture ambient sunlight and spectacular views of the city. The street dipped and curved before winding higher. Above them, the lights from surrounding homes merged with a tapestry of stars overhead.

A few more winding curves brought them to a rambling Spanish-style house built in three sections, like half of a hexagon, but with a carport extending from one end. The concave side faced the city and had been cut into the contour of the hill. Although the house was positioned beside a winding street, much of it was obscured by thick shrubs and trees. The apex roof had been freshly covered with barrel-shaped terra cotta tiles.

Larisa parked under the carport and switched off the engine. There were no street lights up here and the carport was made even darker by a dense tangle of jasmine spilling over a high wall that served as a backstop for the carport. Moving slowly, Talanov unbuckled his seatbelt and opened his door. Larisa was there waiting to help him out.

"I'll take it from here," he said. "You two can go on. Take the car and phone me in a few days to let me know where it is. I'll come get it."

"Don't be stupid. I am nurse. I will help you into house. Get you into bed."

"I can manage."

"Do you think I want to rob you? Is that what you think?"

"You tried it once."

"And I came back to return what I took. So stop being an idiot." Taking Talanov by the arm, she led him to the side door, found the correct key, inserted it into the lock and twisted. The door swung open.

They entered a darkened kitchen, which was filled with shadows and reflections. On the right was a long counter with a sink. It was positioned against a wall of windows overlooking the city. In the middle of the kitchen was an island. It contained a four-burner stove. Racks of pots and pans hung overhead. On the left was another counter, a walk-in pantry, the oven, some cupboards, and a humming refrigerator.

With Jade trailing silently behind, Larisa walked Talanov through the kitchen. Ahead of them was a wide archway that led into a darkened dining room. "Where do I turn on lights?" she asked.

"Around the corner, on the left."

Larisa felt along the wall and found the switch. When she flipped it, she screamed and froze.

Facing them was a wild-haired man quivering with rage. His teeth were bared and he was holding a revolver.

"Say your prayers and get ready to die!" he snarled.

CHAPTER 7

DEATH is something a person never quite gets ready for, even if that person thinks life is not worth living. And Talanov didn't.

During the harrowing ride up into the hills, he realized he was actually relishing the pain he was feeling. It was cleansing, like penance. And when death finally *did* come calling, he would ask what had taken so long. He did not anticipate a grand, heroic death, like the firemen who were killed in the Twin Towers. They died as heroes and would be remembered forever that way. He himself deserved something else, something ignoble, something that punished him for the pain inflicted on his wife. Maybe those weirdo monks who flogged themselves were not so weird after all. He had always regarded them as a bunch of lunatics, but now he understood. They were the ones with clarity. They were the ones with an understanding of the human condition. Like them, he deserved to suffer.

It had taken all he could muster to get out of the car minutes earlier. His knees hurt. His back hurt. His head and neck hurt. His hips and shoulders ached. His stomach was uneven and tight from pools of blood that had coagulated beneath the skin and formed hard lumps. *Praise God,* he wanted to shout. Except right now, he hated God for taking Andrea. Hated God for letting those paramedics revive him. Hated God because he didn't know who else to blame, and he wanted to blame somebody – anybody – other than himself.

The small step up into the kitchen from the carport was only four inches high. But lifting his legs those inches sent spasms through his hips and back. His whole body was one intercon-nected network of pain.

Bring it on, you son of a bitch.

There was nothing that didn't hurt as he limped across the kitchen floor of glazed terra cotta tiles. Each breath was labored. Each step was slow and excruciating.

You pussy. Is that all you've got?

Larisa's fingernails digging into his flesh made him refocus. He looked into the eyes of the man glaring at him then down at the pistol he was holding. It was a Ruger SP-101, which was a snub-nosed, double-action revolver. He then looked back at gunman, who like Talanov was in his early fifties. But that was all they had in common. Where Talanov was athletic and tall, the man holding the Ruger was short and stocky, with a watermelon belly and narrow hips. Although disheveled from his ordeal, Talanov's hair was still dark and fashionably cut. The gunman's hair was shaggy and gray and dry from cheap shampoo.

"You don't look surprised to see me," the gunman said. "Do your girlfriends there know what you did?"

"Leave them out of this," responded Talanov. Without losing eye contact with the gunman, he peeled Larisa's fingers off his arm and eased her aside. "Go on. Get out of here," he said.

Larisa started to move.

"Stay the bloody hell where you are!" shouted the gunman. He pointed the Ruger at Larisa and she froze. He then saw Jade standing in the shadows of the kitchen. "You! Get in 'ere!" he yelled. He walked over and yanked her into the dining room. Jade ran over and cowered beside Larisa, looking down, not making eye contact.

"Come on, Harry," said Talanov. "You came here for me. Not them."

"So the heartless bastard cares about somebody other than himself," said Harry with a sarcastic snort. "Well, well, well."

"Let them go. It will be you and I, then, and you can do what you want."

"It's a bloody sight late for that!"

Talanov replied with a thoughtful sigh. Harry was shaking now, which was not a good sign. It meant he was starting to panic and that his anger was surging out of control. It also meant Harry was coming to grips with having to kill three people now and not just one. Which meant his window of opportunity for reasoning with Harry was quickly slipping away.

"Which one is your girlfriend?" hissed Harry. He licked his lips and blinked several times before wiping perspiration from his eyes. He was holding the Ruger with two hands now, but even so, he was starting to shake.

"Let them go, Harry," said Talanov again, steadying himself on a chair to keep from wobbling.

"Which one?" shouted Harry. "The blonde?" He looked Larisa up and down with a sneer. "It's the blonde. I can tell." He pointed the gun at Larisa.

"It won't bring Andrea back," said Talanov.

Harry backhanded Talanov with the Ruger and knocked him to the floor. Quivering with rage, he stood over Talanov and aimed the gun at his head. "My daughter is *dead!"* Harry screamed. "And for what? So you could run from your past? You dragged her here, half-way around the world, made her *leave* her family, her friends, and her business. And *still* they found you. But was it you they killed? *No!* It was her! *She* was the one who paid. She was *miserable* because of you!"

"It wasn't all bad," said Talanov, slowly sitting up.

"Yes, it was! She knew you didn't love her. She made up all kinds of excuses, of course. Said you had this damaged past with the KGB that made it hard for you to open up. We tried to get her to come home, to leave your sorry arse, but she wouldn't do it. She said you were trying to change. Well, you didn't try very hard! And who paid the price for your miserable excuse of a life? *She did!* Well, I'm going to take someone from you, just like you took someone from me." He pointed the gun at Larisa again.

Larisa flinched and closed her eyes.

"She's a prostitute, Harry, a whore," said Talanov, climbing to his feet. Blood was oozing from the gash on his head. "Someone I picked up in a nightclub."

"You're lying!"

"Look at her. Look at both of them. At the way they're dressed. She's a *nobody!* A stupid country girl from Ukraine whose only asset is between her legs. That's why I brought her here, Harry. I'm using her. Because that's who I am and what I do. I use people. Does it bring Andrea back? No. Does it make me forget who I am? Never. It makes me hate myself even more. Can I run from my self-loathing? I wish I could." He stepped forward and Harry aimed the Ruger directly at his face. Talanov stared straight over the barrel into Harry's eyes. "Killing those whores will accomplish nothing. It's me you want. Let them go."

With his one good eye focused on Harry, Talanov did not see the tears trickling down Larisa's cheeks.

The two men stared hard at one another for a long moment.

"Like I said, I want you to know how it feels," Harry growled with a sneer. Taking a step back, he swung the gun toward Larisa.

Talanov had seen the resolve in Harry's eyes and knew he would not let the girls go. He had tried talking sense into Harry. Had tried making it easy for him to get what he wanted without any unnecessary casualties. But Harry wouldn't listen. The time for talking was over.

By now, Talanov was in a state of anticipation and his adrenal glands were pumping epinephrine throughout his body. His senses were on high alert and his pain threshold had been hormonally elevated to a point that he felt no pain. Hence, when he saw the gun move toward Larisa, his black belt instincts took over.

Talanov's immediate reflex was a circular sweep upward with his left hand. It knocked the gun away from the girls. A right-handed block to the side would have risked one of the girls getting shot. An upward block eliminated that possibility. Grabbing the gun, Talanov continued the circular sweep in a high overhead arc. The motion lifted Harry's arm with it, leaving his midsection exposed.

With a quick twist, Talanov hammered a knee up into Harry's solar plexus, like a punch, and Harry doubled over and fell to the floor, leaving the gun in Talanov's hand.

"Why'd you have to go and try that, Harry?" asked Talanov, standing over him in his hospital gown. "I gave you every opportunity to handle things right and you had to screw it up."

Harry lay on the floor, moaning and writhing.

"I know you hate me," said Talanov. "But it's not even close to the hatred I feel for myself. I understand how you feel, I really do, and I understand why you blame me for everything that's happened. But you need to be clear about something. I would not have married Andrea if I'd thought she was in danger. I may not have known how to love your daughter, but she was a good person. The only good person I ever knew. Sure as hell better than me."

Jade sank into a chair at the dining table while Talanov watched Harry gasping for air on the floor. Larisa knelt beside him. "Relax. Breath will come," she said.

"I know I dragged her away from Australia," Talanov continued. "And I know she wanted children." He paused and looked up, fighting back emotion. "If I could have tracked down the killers who took her life, I would have. And I would have made them pay. But the police weren't about to open their files to their number one suspect. So I was shut out, with nothing to go on and nowhere to look."

Harry finally regained his breath and sat up.

"I know it's of no comfort to you that I've wrecked my life," said Talanov, clutching his stomach. The adrenaline was wearing off and the spasms were returning. "I know it won't bring her back." He staggered over to one of the dining room chairs and sat.

"You pathetic, worthless bastard," rasped Harry. "I hope you *die.*"

"So do I," said Talanov, laboring to breathe. He looked at Larisa, who was now on her feet. "Use my car. Take Harry to the airport. Drive it home. Put key on a tire."

"I will stay. You need help."

"Go," said Talanov. "I'll pick up my car another time." He then looked at Harry and said, "Go with them, Harry. Go home. Because if you try something like this again, I'll kill you. Don't make me do that, okay?"

Harry pushed Larisa away and climbed to his feet.

"Now, get out of here," Talanov said, waving Harry away with the Ruger.

With a growl of hatred, Harry stormed through the darkened kitchen and out into the carport. After a couple of nervous glances, Jade followed hesitantly behind him.

Larisa looked tearfully at Talanov. "Did you mean those things?" she asked.

Talanov tossed the Ruger onto the table. "Go," he said with a grimace, wrapping his arms around his midsection.

"You need help!" Larisa replied, reaching for him.

Talanov knocked her hand away. "I told you to get *out of here!*"

Moments later, the kitchen door slammed.

Talanov stood and grabbed the edge of the table, and after several breaths, looked in the direction of the bedroom. He could do it. He had to. There was no other choice. Down four tiled steps, across the Persian rug, up two steps and through an arched doorway. Then along a short hall into the bedroom. He could do it.

He took one step but one step was as far as he got. His knees buckled. He grabbed for a chair. He missed and hit the floor.

And for the second time that night, everything went black.

CHAPTER 8

JADE'S stiletto heels echoed off the sidewalk in the early morning quiet when she approached the block of apartments. Six stories of tiny balconies. Security bars on the windows. Walls of faded pink stucco. Fan palms in patches of dirt.

"I sure hope you know what you're doing," Jade muttered to herself. She stepped up to the heavy steel security gate and pushed a call button near a small glass panel. The panel shielded a closed circuit camera. Folding her arms around the strap of her handbag, she waited nervously beneath an overhead floodlight. Another hour and it would be dawn.

Jade could feel Borzakov looking at her through the closed circuit camera. Other cameras were mounted high on the walls of the apartments, with two more on the fascia, near the roof.

The electronic lock finally buzzed and Jade pushed the gate open. When she was through, the gate slammed closed behind her. The sidewalk ahead led to a front door. When Jade reached the door, she pushed another button near another small glass panel concealing another camera. Overhead was a smoked glass dome concealing yet another camera. After several seconds, the electronic lock buzzed and Jade opened the door. A carpeted hallway stretched out before her.

An enameled red door opened on the right and out stepped Borzakov in a thick eddy of cigarette smoke. He was still in his Armani suit and gray mandarin shirt. "Where have you been?" he demanded. The smell of Scotch was strong on his breath.

"Trying to score," answered Jade with a submissive bow. She kept her eyes averted, toward the floor.

Borzakov looked Jade over. She was thin, almost boney, and with tiny breasts. But she had sex appeal and knew how to move. "Where?" he asked.

"Up and down the boulevard," she replied. With her hands folded in front of her, Jade shifted nervously in place before suddenly opening her handbag. "Here, for you," she said, taking out Talanov's money. She handed it to Borzakov, still avoiding his eyes.

Borzakov counted the wad of nineteen one-hundred-dollar bills. "Not bad," he said, pocketing the cash. "Not bad at all."

Jade said nothing and stood there, looking down.

Borzakov liked the fact that Jade could never look him in the eye. His Chinese prostitutes were nearly all that way. They were scared of him, to be sure, but they also knew how to show respect, and that really appealed to him. Not many people had manners like that today.

And yet maybe Jade *wasn't* afraid of him. Maybe she avoided looking him in the eyes out of habit. Maybe she did it to make him *think* she was afraid. He grabbed Jade by the hair and made her look him in the eye. Her hair was dry, like straw, probably from all of the teasing and blue color. Borzakov cocked his head and peered down into her frightened eyes. Her bright red lips were quivering. If she had not been afraid of him before, she was afraid of him now. Yes, sometimes these bitches needed a reminder.

Without letting go, Borzakov opened the red door and muscled her into the office, which was the living room of a converted two-bedroom apartment. Three men looked up from a card game they had been playing. Dressed in black t-shirts and slacks, two of the men – Nick and Vic, who were Borzakov's six-foot-four muscle men – wore shoulder holsters packing forty-four caliber Colt Anaconda revolvers. Eight-inch barrels. Polished stainless steel bodies. Heavy, imposing weapons with plenty of punch. The other man looked like an accountant because he was an accountant. He was balding, with glasses, and had a paunch. His suit jacket was hanging over the back of his chair and his tie was loosened. Bottles of Scotch and the anise-flavored "Green Fairy," absinthe, cluttered the table. Ashtrays were piled high with butts. A smoky haze hung in the air. On the floor were some discarded pizza boxes.

"Eta suka nuzhno prepodavat' urok," announced Borzakov.

"Good. I like entertainment," Nick replied. He disappeared

down a short corridor to one of the bedrooms while Vic dragged an empty chair into the center of the room. The room was furnished with several couches, a coffee table, and a large flat-screen TV. The TV was flanked by four tall speakers. Near the red door was a desk on which were several monitors featuring live feeds from the various exterior cameras.

Borzakov made Jade sit in the chair just as Nick reappeared and tossed Vic a roll of gray duct tape. Vic pulled Jade's hands behind her and taped them securely while Borzakov emptied the contents of Jade's handbag on the floor. With his foot, he sorted through a meager selection of cheap cosmetics, condoms, and crumpled-up one dollar bills. Finding nothing, he tossed the bag aside.

"I do what you say. Not make trouble," Jade said. She was looking up at Borzakov now, eyes pleading, tears welling, lips quivering.

Borzakov showed Nick and Vic the wad of cash Jade had given him. They counted the money and looked at Borzakov with disbelief.

"All of this? One night?" asked Nick.

"No way," said Vic. "Not her. She's never produced more than a grand. She has to be working on the side. Stashing money away. Maybe to try and run."

Borzakov looked back at Jade and stooped over to stare at her directly in the eyes. He cocked his head again and said, "You see, they not believe. So I not believe."

"I have good night. Give you *everything*. Not try to run!"

"Maybe. Maybe not," said Borzakov. He nodded and Vic slapped a piece of duct tape over Jade's mouth, leaving only her nostrils for breathing. Vic then handed Borzakov a dry cleaning bag. It was the kind that protects suits and shirts when they came back from the cleaners. On the front of the bag was a warning about the dangers of suffocation. It was followed by another reminder that the bag should be kept away from children.

Yanking the plastic bag over Jade's head, Borzakov pulled it tightly around her neck. He watched her eyes bulge as she began jerking back and forth, the bag inflating and deflating rapidly as she fought to breathe. Nick and Vic giggled and pointed at Jade thrashing back and forth. Duct tape was handy for *so* many things. They listened to a few muffled nasal screams before Jade had nothing left in her lungs with which to scream.

Borzakov wondered what was going through the bitch's mind. Was her whole life flashing before her? It couldn't have been much of a life, being sold as she had been by parents wanting a son instead of a daughter. Some peasants preferred oxen or chickens over a daughter. At least chickens could produce eggs.

When Jade's eyes began to flutter closed, Borzakov removed the bag and ripped the tape off her mouth. Jade's eyes flew open and she began gulping air, her chest heaving, her cheeks and forehead damp, almost wet.

Once Jade caught her breath, Borzakov grabbed her by the hair again and got right in her face. "Where you get money?" he shouted. "Are you working on side? Selling drugs and keeping for self?"

"No drugs. Do only what you say," gasped Jade.

Borzakov plunged the bag over Jade's head again and tightened it around her neck. He repeated the procedure until Jade slumped forward. The bag then came off and Borzakov slapped her in the face to get her breathing again. Standing together were Nick and Vic, who were howling with laughter.

"You work on side!" shouted Borzakov. "Save money to escape!"

With her head slumped to her chest, Jade panted hoarsely in a desperate attempt to regain her breath. Her face was wet. Her throat was dry. It hurt to swallow and she couldn't speak. But she had to speak. She couldn't take more of Borzakov's torture. She had to tell him the truth. She had to tell him that Larisa had given her the money. But that would mean telling him *why* Larisa had given her the money. And that meant Larisa would suffer worse than what she was suffering. But what other choice did she have? She couldn't take any more.

She had tried talking Larisa out of going to the hospital, but

Larisa had been insistent. She *had* to return Talanov's wedding photo. "Why?" Jade has asked.

"Because I have to," Larisa replied.

"Why?"

"Because I have to."

"Give me a *reason.*"

"Because I *have* to!"

Back and forth they had argued, but there was no changing Larisa's mind. Larisa was like that. She was a gullible, innocent flower on one hand, and a stubborn, tough bitch on the other. Naturally, she had wanted someone to ride along with her, in case Talanov turned out to be some kind of weirdo. Jade reminded her that taking the rest of the night off would mean lost earnings. So Larisa had promised her the money she had taken from Talanov. Then she changed her mind and offered to give it back. Then Talanov – to her utter amazement – replied that he didn't want it. So Larisa was able to make good on her promise, which she said would make Borzakov happy.

But Larisa had been wrong.

Borzakov was not one to be crossed, and neither were Nick and Vic. She had seen the two muscle men strangle a young girl from Cambodia just to make a point in front of the other girls. "You lie, you die," they had said.

The girl, of course, had done nothing. They had simply chosen her out of the group and choked her to death to show everyone what would happen *if* they lied. That was in addition to the photo board they kept of the girls' family members. Borzakov knew where they lived. He knew their addresses, knew what their parents did, knew the names of their siblings. Try and escape and someone back home would die. Fail to pay your debt on time and someone back home would die.

Not that they had much chance to escape, at least not during daylight hours, when they were locked in their rooms, eight to ten girls per room behind solid metal doors with double deadbolts and security bars over the windows. No fresh air, no sunlight, no freedom, with torture a random occurrence to remind the girls who was in charge. And Borzakov was an expert. He knew how to punish without "damaging the goods," as he called it. Injured prostitutes meant less money from clients, who weren't about to select someone with a black eye or a broken arm. No, Borzakov protected his investments, which in a perverted way kept him and the others from seriously injuring anyone. Unless, of course, you crossed him. Then you were dead.

You lie, you die.

After several more breaths, Jade was finally able to swallow. She would tell him the truth. She looked up and started to speak.

"You look like shit," said Borzakov, wiping a finger through the trails of mascara running down her cheeks. "We are finished. Go take a shower."

CHAPTER 9

TALANOV groaned and looked toward the double French doors that led out onto the deck. They were open and a warm breeze was wafting in. The sun was shining and in the distance he could see the skyline of Los Angeles.

He sat up slowly in bed and touched the side of his scalp. There was a lump the size of an egg. He remembered losing his balance and falling but that was the last thing he remembered. He looked around, confused. How did he get in bed? The accident had occurred in the dining room. That meant he would have had to crawl down four tile steps, across the living room, up two steps and down the hallway to the bedroom, then climb up into bed. Had he done that? If so, why couldn't he remember?

A quick look at the glowing red numbers of the bedside clock told him it was nearly five in the afternoon. He had been asleep for almost twelve hours. He threw back the covers and stood. When he did, he caught a glimpse of himself in the mirror.

Something is definitely wrong.

For one thing, he was dressed in the ugliest pajamas he had ever seen. They were covered with koalas, kangaroos, wombats, and eucalyptus leaves. A happy little Australian jungle scene, which had been a gift from Andrea back in Sydney as revenge for his having given her a pair of sequined nipple tassels for Christmas the year before. They had even dared one another to wear their respective gifts to a friend's Christmas party. Never one to turn down a dare, Andrea wore the tassels in an otherwise spectacularly topless outfit that showcased her spectacularly perfect breasts. He, meanwhile, had to uphold his end of the bargain by wearing these pajamas. Talk about a conversation stopper when they walked in together. The memory brought a smile to his face.

But what surprised him most was his eye. Swollen shut the

night before, it was now almost back to normal. The surrounding skin was still faintly black and blue, but the swelling was nearly gone. What had happened between then and now? He touched the bruises and looked around. Was that pineapple he smelled?

You're losing it, he thought as he switched on his cell phone and checked for messages. There were several missed calls from numbers he didn't recognize. Tossing his phone on the bed, Talanov padded into the bathroom and cranked on the shower. He pulled off his pajamas, stepped under the torrent of steaming hot water and just stood there, head tipped forward, absorbing the heat. Thirty minutes later, he stepped out to find a folded towel on the sink. He stared at the towel but for the life of him could not remember putting it there. "You really *are* losing it," he muttered, flapping it free of its folds.

While drying himself, he tried to recall what had happened over the last twenty-four hours. He remembered the fight at the nightclub. Remembered waking up in an alley and being taken to the hospital in an ambulance. Remembered his escape and Larisa picking him up in his Lexus while he was staggering up the hill. Remembered ditching the police, and the scene with Harry, here at the house. So his memory appeared to be working. So did his arms and legs. And the aching was nearly gone. He walked naked through the bedroom and into his walk-in closet, where he expected to sift through a huge pile of dirty clothing for something to wear. To his astonishment, his clothes had been washed and ironed and were now hanging neatly on hangers.

What the hell?

He grabbed some clean jeans off a hanger and pulled them on. He then pulled a t-shirt off another hanger just as his cell phone rang. He walked over to the bed and picked it up. "Yes?" he answered, pulling on the shirt.

"Mr. Talanov, this is American Express. We've been trying to reach you regarding an unusual purchase made earlier today with your card."

"Today? My card was stolen two days ago."

"Have you reported the theft?"

"I just got out of the hospital. What kind of purchase?"

"A Mark-12 sniper rifle, two scopes, a suppressor, and two boxes of ammunition, for a total of five-thousand-four-hundred-and-thirty-five dollars."

"What?"

"The purchase was made in Los Angeles."

"I didn't make that purchase!"

"We'll need you to submit that in writing."

"Gladly. Where was the purchase made?"

The agent told him the name of the store.

"So this was an over-the-counter purchase?" asked Talanov.

"Yes, and it was made with your ID."

"My driver's license was stolen, too."

"You'll need to report that as well."

"Cancel my card immediately."

The agent agreed and Talanov ended the call.

A sniper rifle purchased with his credit card *and* ID? This did not look good. Talanov tossed his phone on the bed again and hurried down the corridor into the living room, where he stopped abruptly. In the kitchen was Larisa, standing at the stove, still dressed in the same clothes and stilettos she had been wearing the night before. He stepped up into the dining room and saw the Ruger was missing from the table.

"You do not have much to eat," Larisa said as he entered the kitchen. "But I make – how do you say – *deruny?*"

"Potato pancakes."

"Yes. You may have with applesauce, if you like. I find jar in pantry."

"What are you doing here?" he asked, stealing a pancake from the skillet and tossing it back and forth in his hands to cool it off. It had been made with grated potatoes, flour, an egg, powdered garlic and spices. It had a coarse texture, like hash-browns, and was golden brown.

"I tell Jade take Harry to airport. When I come back inside, I find you on floor."

"So you were the one who undressed me?"

"Do not worry. I have seen you before without clothes."

Talanov chuckled. "I guess you have."

Larisa scooped out the pancakes, stacked them on a plate and poured more of the thick batter into the skillet.

"Thanks for doing my laundry," said Talanov. "It hadn't been done in a while."

"A very long while, I think."

Talanov laughed and headed for the espresso machine. It was a stainless steel unit sitting on the rear counter. It had all the features of a fancy commercial unit. "One for you?" he asked, looking over at her.

Larisa smiled and nodded, so Talanov took two mugs from the shelf and made them each a fresh cappuccino. When finished, he handed one to Larisa.

"The pistol," he said. "Where'd it go?"

"I take it."

"What for?"

Larisa looked at the clock. "I must go. It getting late."

"You didn't answer my question."

"I will sell it. Need money," she said, flipping the pancakes.

"I thought I gave you some money."

"I give it to Jade."

"You gave two thousand dollars to Jade?"

"She come with me last night to find you at hospital. Not work. She will be in much trouble if she does not pay."

"Pay who, your pimp?"

Larisa did not reply.

"What about you?" he asked.

"I will sell gun. How much is it worth?"

"Two, three hundred, max."

Larisa bit her lip anxiously while scooping the final batch of pancakes out of the skillet. She looked worriedly at the clock again. Talanov watched her switch off the burner and place the spatula in the sink. On the counter was the bottom half of an old pineapple. Beside it was a bunch of cut parsley. He looked at the fruit bowl and saw the pineapple he'd bought weeks ago was gone.

"What did you do for my eye?" he asked.

"I must go," Larisa said, opening her purse and pulling out a crumpled wad of cash. She unfolded the money and counted two hundred and eleven dollars. "How much for taxi?" she asked.

Talanov placed his mug in the sink. "How much for another night?"

"What are you talking about?"

"You and me. Another night. How much?"

Larisa did not reply. All she could do is stare back at Talanov, who smiled at her perplexity.

"Will fifteen hundred cover it?" he asked.

Larisa's mouth fell open.

"All right, two thousand," he said. "I'll get the money."

He turned to go.

"Why you do this?" she asked.

"Why did you do what *you* did?" he asked her in return. "You didn't have to bring me my wallet. You didn't have to carry me all the way down the corridor to bed then stay here all day cleaning the house, doing the washing and cooking *deruny*. Which, by the way, were very good. Two thousand. On one condition."

"What kind of condition?" she asked warily.

"That you tell me the truth about what's going on. And I mean all of it."

CHAPTER 10

TALANOV went to his floor safe, got the money and immediately paid her so that she would know he was on the level. Two thousand dollars cash, in crisp one hundred dollar bills, plus an extra five hundred for the Ruger.

"You say gun worth only three hundred," she said, handing over the weapon.

"If I were buying it retail, I'd have to pay five. A gun dealer, which is where you'd have to go and sell it on such short notice, would only give you half of that, if not less. He would then turn around and sell it to me for five. So I might as well pay you what he would have charged me. Saves us both some time and trouble."

"What will you do with gun?" she asked.

"Keep it. I collect them."

Larisa responded with a skeptical frown.

"Seriously, I do. I'm not a gun freak, but I believe in them when necessary, so I guess I'm a real American in that regard. Russia has some of the strictest gun laws on earth, and the homicide rate there is four times what it is here. That is why I carry one most of the time, which I'm licensed to do."

"I do not like them," said Larisa.

"Then it's a good thing I'm buying it off you. Both of us get what we want."

"I think you are being too nice."

"Not at all. I know you're in a jam because of what you did for me. And I'm grateful, really, I am."

Larisa placed the money in her purse and did not reply. Talanov watched her for a moment, thinking she would at least smile or say something and look happy. But she didn't. She only looked guilty or insecure. He couldn't tell which.

Sticking the gun in his pocket, he said, "Those pancakes were good but I'm still hungry. How about you? Have you eaten?"

"You do not have much in kitchen."

"It's been a while since this kitchen has seen much action."

Larisa offered to make him something else but Talanov waved it away.

"It's dinner time," he said. "Let's go out. Someplace nice."

"How? Jade take your car."

"I have a spare."

"What do you mean, you have a spare? Who has a spare car sitting around?"

"Actually, the Lexus belonged to my wife. The spare car is mine."

"I am not dressed to go out."

"Second bedroom. My wife's clothes are in the closet. Look through them. Find something you like."

Larisa looked suddenly uncomfortable.

"They're just clothes. I mean, she wasn't nearly as generous up here," he said, gesturing awkwardly in front of his chest with both hands. "But otherwise, you're about the same size."

"But they are your wife's clothes," she said.

"I'm only going to throw them away. Or give them away. So letting you wear them isn't like I'm trying to bring her back. Like I said, they're just clothes. It's up to you."

Larisa reluctantly agreed to have a look, so after changing his shirt and putting on a linen sports jacket and pair of deck shoes, Talanov stuck the Ruger in a low profile shoulder holster and waited outside on the deck. Above the kitchen windows was an arbor of bougainvillea that ran along the western side of the house. It protected the kitchen from the harsh afternoon sun. With his elbows resting on the stainless steel railing, Talanov gazed down the steep embankment at the houses below. The canyon walls that fell away from the deck were steep and rocky. At the bottom was a thicket of scrub.

Admittedly, events over the last twenty-four hours had made him feel alive again. It had been a year since Andrea's death and those months had been the darkest he had ever experienced. And he'd felt it all: shock, denial, resignation, guilt, anger, self-loathing, depression, and loneliness, and all while spiraling downward on a path of self-destruction. So maybe the last twenty-four hours was an indication that he was finally coming out of his grief. That he was starting to care again. The acute physical pain of getting beaten up had certainly forced his hand, penetrating as it had the comfort of his loathing and self-pity. His encounter in the nightclub had propelled him into action and he had responded.

The door behind him opened and Larisa stepped onto the deck. She had chosen a fitted black mini dress with a high neck and open back. Her hair was pulled to one side and clipped behind her ear, and her loose blonde curls contrasting stunningly with the black of the dress.

"Wow," he said. "You look great."

"You are sure you do not mind? Perhaps it is painful for you?"

"To tell you the truth, I don't remember having ever seen my wife in that dress."

After locking the house, Talanov led the way across the empty carport to a locked metal shed. He deactivated the alarm and touched a button that opened a wide roller door. Inside was a black Porsche Boxster convertible. He opened the passenger door and helped Larisa down into the seat. Once she was in, he jumped behind the wheel, fired up the engine, and backed out onto the street.

"You call this a spare car?" she asked, inspecting the luxurious interior. "A spare car to me is an old Lada that rattles and sputters like the fat Russians who make them."

With a grin, Talanov touched a button on the remote that closed the roller door. Once it was down, he shifted into first, released the clutch and took the Boxster down the winding canyon road like he owned it.

CHAPTER 11

TALANOV squealed around several turns in the road. The Boxter's headlights stabbed the night and the warm air whipped Larisa's blonde hair as she sat with her knees drawn together. "Okay, talk," he said. "What did you do for my eye? I can see. The swelling is gone."

"In Kherson, where I am from, near Black Sea, I was nurse. But I also learn – how you say – *natural'noï medytsyny.*"

"Natural medicine."

"Yes. I learn from my grandfather. We lived on farm, near forest. Very poor. We did not have *farmatsevtychna.*"

"Pharmaceuticals."

"Pharm-a-ceuticals," she said, repeating the word to learn it.

"So what's with the pineapple?" he asked. "Made me smell like a bowl of fruit salad."

Larisa laughed. *"Protyzapal'na,"* she said.

"Anti-inflammatory."

"Yes. It must be fresh. No canned."

"And the parsley?"

"Anestezii"

"An anesthetic."

"I mix with ice, put in washcloth and hold on eye while you sleep. Gentle, so not to wake you. Then a warm cloth. Then cold. Back and forth. It make swelling go away."

"Well, it did the trick. I'm impressed."

Larisa smiled as they took another turn. The Boxster's custom exhaust system whined powerfully as Talanov hit the gas again at a straightaway and the car shot forward.

"How did your wife die? May I ask?"

"Gunshot to the neck," he replied.

"My God. I am sorry. I should not have asked."

"It's okay. Really, it is."

"I cannot believe something like that would happen. Why would someone do this to your wife?"

"A mistake. It was meant for me."

Larisa stared in horror at Talanov as they wound through the lower residential streets of the hills before turning right onto Beechwood Drive and heading south along the bottom of the canyon. Houses blanketed the earth in all directions and up the sides of hills. Concrete and stucco and landscaped lawns.

Talanov looked over and saw that Larisa was genuinely disturbed. He took her hand and squeezed it to let her know that everything was okay.

"I cannot believe someone would do that," she said.

"Ever had paella?" he asked, changing the subject while downshifting for a stop sign.

Larisa shook her head and Talanov told her about the sexy little restaurant where they were going. It was noisy and intimate, with linen tablecloths and a Bohemian mix of clientele. The place served individual skillets of Spanish rice chocked full of clams, mussels, chorizo, chicken, spices, and that all-important golden crust along the bottom. They would then go to a café that served sticky date pudding with dark brown butterscotch sauce. With French vanilla ice cream, of course.

The description did the trick, and before long, Larisa was chatting happily about her favorite foods from back home. Potato dumplings, stuffed cabbage, vereniki, borscht, and homemade breads of all varieties, both sweet and savory. Talanov responded by describing the most delicious borscht he had ever had.

"It was made with herring," he said. "So thick you could stand up a spoon."

Larisa replied that beet soup made with fish was not borscht. Ham or sausage was acceptable, but definitely not fish. Talanov countered by saying that there were many varieties of borscht, with some served hot and some served cold. The only requirements were potatoes and beets. Larisa informed Talanov that borscht was a Ukrainian creation, which the Russians stole, so any Russian opinion on the matter had to be seriously questioned. They both laughed just as Talanov's cell phone rang. He glanced at the screen, saw it was a number he didn't recognize, and switched it off.

At the next intersection, they turned right, and when they came to North Gower, turned left again. The houses here had been built with imagination and flair. There were stately homes with dormers and turrets nestled beside quaint cottages tucked among the fan palms and birds-of-paradise. It was a mix of English style and Spanish romance. But style soon gave way to stuccoed two-story apartments and endless rows of garage doors and carports.

After speeding beneath the 101 overpass, Talanov turned right onto Hollywood Boulevard, and within twenty minutes was handing his keys to a valet outside the restaurant. Inside, Talanov spoke quietly to the manager and they were seated immediately.

The restaurant was abuzz with conversation and laughter. Every table was occupied. Waiters crisscrossed the floor serving drinks and sizzling hot skillets of paella. Clanging pans and harried shouts echoed from the kitchen. A waiter slid menus in front of them and Talanov ordered a bottle of wine. The waiter nodded and hurried off.

"The dress. You are sure you do not mind?" Larisa asked again.

"Not at all. In fact, I want you to have it."

"It is too expensive, I think."

"If you don't take it, I'll just have to throw it away. Please. I'd like you to have it. With anything else that fits. Except the car, of course."

They both laughed.

"You must have loved her very much," Larisa said quietly.

Talanov did not reply.

"Her father was very angry. I cannot believe he would say such terrible things."

"Actually, Harry was right," Talanov replied. "I didn't know how to love her."

Larisa looked at him curiously.

"The KGB taught us to use and exploit people. Love was a vulnerability that an enemy could use. So I became hard and cold. Then the Wall came down and everything changed. Unfortunately, I didn't change with it."

The waiter arrived, poured their wine, and took their orders. After clinking glasses with Larisa for a quick toast, Talanov continued.

"Even worse, I didn't try. Until, that is, a team of killers from my past caught up with me. It was only when Andrea was kidnapped that I finally woke up."

"So you did love your wife after all?"

"I'd like to think so, but sometimes I wonder."

"The police. Did they catch the killer?"

Talanov shook his head.

"Why would somebody want to kill you?" she asked.

"People in my line of work make enemies," he said simply.

When Larisa asked what his line of work had been, Talanov told her how he had been a surveillance specialist with the KGB. When Larisa asked what that meant, he skipped over the fact that he had once been a spy for the CIA. Instead he said, "I protected people."

"Like a guard dog?" she asked.

"I prefer bodyguard, but guard dog sums it up."

"And you bited someone?" she asked.

Talanov chuckled at the mispronunciation. "Someone tried biting me," he said. "And one day, I'll bite 'em back. If I can ever find out who they are, that is."

"Why did they do this?" she asked.

"A bank account in Switzerland that had secretly been put in my name. Some bad guys found out about it and tried killing me so they could steal it. Before they could, though, the money vanished."

"How can money vanish?"

"No idea."

"Why they kill your wife, then, if money is gone?"

"I wish I knew."

Larisa thought for a moment. "Her father, he was wrong," she said. "I know he blame you. But what happened was not your fault."

"I took her away from them. I dragged her halfway around the planet. We had a comfortable lifestyle but she was unhappy."

"Why?"

"Because I wasn't giving her what she really wanted. Emotional starvation was why she began supporting an orphanage called The Shelter that rescues children from being sold into slavery. Some kids were as young as four. The older ones became child soldiers. She even made several trips abroad to help teach basic cooking skills. She also began teaching English. Those children adored her. We were on stage here in Los Angeles receiving an award when she was shot."

"Your wife sounds amazing," said Larisa, holding the stem of her wineglass with both hands while staring despondently down into the ruby liquid.

Talanov noticed the sudden change in her body language. Larisa was pulling back into her shell, feeling inadequate and awkward. A hooker comparing herself to a successful business-woman and philanthropist.

"Everyone has gifts and abilities," Talanov replied.

Larisa smiled but did not look him in the eye.

"Take you, for instance," he said. "You're a nurse, aged – what – twenty-one?"

"Twenty-six."

"Who's been to nursing school, right?"

Larisa nodded.

"Did you graduate with a degree?"

Larisa nodded again.

"That's quite an accomplishment," he said. "Plus, how many people know how to take parsley and pineapple and smear it all over a person's face?"

Larisa chuckled.

"Yes, my wife was an amazing woman," said Talanov, "but you are, too." He leaned forward for emphasis and lowered his voice. "So what the hell are you doing working as a prostitute?"

Larisa looked away and said nothing.

"Let me guess. Some kind of a scam?"

Larisa lowered her eyes and nodded.

Talanov took her by the hand. "You're from Kherson, the mail-order-bride capital of the world, where the sex-scam industry is huge. Surely you had to know about those kinds of things?"

Larisa fidgeted nervously with her wineglass.

"Look, I'm not trying to embarrass you," he said. "I'm simply trying to help."

"There is nothing you can do to help. There is nothing anyone can do."

"How much do you owe them?" he asked.

"Sixty thousand dollars."

CHAPTER 12

LARISA told Talanov about life in Kherson, which was a grim port city on the mouth of the Dnieper River as it entered the Black Sea. Her father was an engineer, her mother a housewife, and she was the eldest of three children. She had a sister who was seventeen and a brother who was fifteen. Living within sight of the river, their home was a tiny three-room flat on the eighth floor of a high-rise apartment block overlooking the railroad tracks.

"We were happy, even with all of those steps," Larisa said, recalling how the elevator seldom worked and the vandalized stairwells smelled of urine. She went on to explain how her father had spent most of their savings to send her to nursing school, after which he got laid off because of the economic downturn.

"What kind of work did he do?" asked Talanov.

"He worked for manufacturer of farm equipment. With hundreds laid off across country, my father was unable to find another job. So my mother began selling shoes in department store. We barely survived, and my brother and sister had no hope of education, because everything had been spent on me."

"So you felt guilty and desperate," said Talanov as their food was served.

Larisa nodded, then related how Olga, a friend from school, suggested she apply for an overseas modeling job through a local agency. "She say agency was looking for beautiful women to model latest fashions like we see in Elle and Cosmo. She say maybe I get part in movie, since I can dance and a little bit sing."

"And because nursing pays peanuts in Ukraine, you saw this as your chance to get ahead and pay back your parents."

"Olga live in neighboring block of flats. She left town for a while, and when I saw her again, she was very glamorous. She took me to see a man from agency and he showed me signed photo from Ukrainian fashion designer, Oksana Mukha. Well, supposedly it was signed. But who can know if it was genuine, right?"

Talanov smiled sadly and nodded.

"At first I was wary," Larisa continued, "but Olga convinced me agency was – how do you say – *zakonnymy.*"

"Legitimate."

"Yes. She said they represented many beautiful women in Los Angeles. Olga took me to studio for pictures. She said I could make lots of money and pay back my family. Maybe even move them to US and find job for my father, who is very smart."

"So you agreed. Then, once you got here, you found out it was a scam because they took your passport, locked you away, and said the only way for you to pay back the money you owed was to work as a prostitute. Refuse and they break your legs. Or worse."

"How do you know this?" she asked.

"Because a lot of my KGB colleagues went to work for the mob once the Soviet empire collapsed. So I know a lot about what they're into. Also, when you first hit on me in the nightclub, I recognized your accent. My guess was Odessa or Kherson, or maybe the Crimea. Plus, you carried no keys, no credit card, and no ID, which suggested one of two things. Either you were extremely careful, or everything had been taken away. If you'd been a high-priced American call girl, I'd have assumed you were merely being careful. But you were from Ukraine, and your English was average, not great. That meant you hadn't been here very long. You were also taking a very dangerous risk drugging and rolling a client. That meant you were desperate. And a desperate Ukrainian prostitute means only one thing: an innocent girl in *way* too deep."

Larisa lowered her eyes.

"Look, there's no way they spent sixty thousand dollars getting you here," Talanov said, taking Larisa by the hand. "They're simply trying to extort the money out of you by using scare tactics. Pay them a few thousand to cover their costs, then go to the police and tell them what happened. They'll deport you back home, which means a free ticket. The mob won't do anything because they recouped their expenses and have bigger fish to fry."

"You are either naive or foolish if you think they would do nothing."

"What would they do? Spend thousands of dollars going to Kherson to try and squeeze blood from a rock? You and your family are poor. They would gain nothing except trouble from the local police. The risk and cost would be too much. Like I said, they have bigger fish."

"They would do something to teach me a lesson. To keep me from telling the truth."

"Look, I'm not saying you wouldn't have to go visit relatives for a while. To lay low and let things blow over."

"You seem to have it figured out."

"That part, yes, I think. What I *haven't* figured out is why you brought me my wallet. Because if my wallet was indeed in that dumpster, then you would have had to climb in that dumpster and sort through all that trash. In stilettos and a micro skirt. Then give up a whole night's work – and that's for both and Jade – in order to drive across town to the hospital to try and find me. The mob is brutal. We both know that. Which means you took a huge risk helping someone you just robbed. I want to know why. What is it you're not telling me?"

Larisa withdrew her hand and leaned back.

"I'm not your enemy," Talanov said, leaning forward casually. "I paid you for tonight because I know you're in a jam. Because I appreciate all you've done. But I need you to tell me the truth. That was our deal. Remember? So let's have it. Why did you bring me my wallet? Why did you stay behind and take care of me?"

A long moment of silence passed while Larisa toyed with her wineglass. "Why did you help me?" she asked in return, raising her eyes to meet his.

"Quit answering my question with a question," he said.

"You had your turn. Now it is mine. Why did you help me?

Gunner was ready to hit me but you stopped him. You make him come after you. Make him attack you. Why did you do that? You are the only man who has ever helped me."

It was Talanov's turn to thoughtfully toy with his wineglass. "When I was lying on the floor," he said, "I heard you trying to stop Gunner from pulverizing me. Who names their kid Gunner, anyway?"

"He would have killed you, I think. And you looked so unhappy, so empty. That is why I get wallet from dumpster and bring to you. Because I see in your eyes how much she mean to you. That you miss her very much. Every woman wants to be loved in such a way."

"Every man, too," said Talanov.

"So why did you stop him from hitting me?" she asked. "You said in your house that I am nothing. That I am worthless. A stupid whore."

"I didn't mean that," Talanov replied. "I was afraid that Harry might shoot. So I said it to deflect his attention away from you and onto me."

"But this is what you think this about me, yes?"

Talanov bit his lip. A part of him – the old KGB part – regarded her as a naive if not foolish young woman who had fallen for an obvious scam and was therefore getting what she deserved. He was trained to make factual observations and that was a cold, hard fact. And yet another part of him did not regard her that way.

On the surface, the reasons seemed obvious. She was a spectacular blonde with knockout looks and a smile that could melt you on the spot. But Larisa was a more than that. She had a depth of character and a quiet strength that he found hard to define. Which was a miracle in itself, given everything she'd been through. Instead of being cynical and hard, she was inexplicably soft and caring. Which were qualities that definitely attracted him.

Which of course begged the question: *was he being sucked in by some deeper scam?* By a gravitational pull Larisa understood all too well and was not afraid to use against him? Or did she genuinely care? Who was sitting across from him? Was it Tash or Larisa? The hardcore hooker or the caring nurse?

Talanov focused on the growing dejection in Larisa's eyes. She had taken his silence to mean an implicit agreement that he did, in fact, consider her to be nothing more than a worthless whore. A scammer would not care. Larisa *did* care, and her dejection was evidence of that. It was an involuntary response that let Talanov know exactly who was sitting across from him.

"No one is worthless," he said gently, "and certainly not you. What you did back there was heroic. In fact, everything you've done is heroic." He smiled and took her by the hand again. "Thank you for what you did. For tonight. For helping me start to move on. It's the first time in a long time I've had a good time."

When they left the restaurant it was dark. Too full for sticky date pudding, they drove to the coast and headed south, riding mostly in silence, contented, the night air blowing their hair. To their left, sandstone hills were dotted with lights. To their right, a seawall of large rocks fell away to a wide swath of lapping ribbons of foam. Talanov glanced over and saw Larisa staring at a dot of light far out to sea. A ship was floating out there in the midst of all that darkness. A tiny dot of light. A sign of hope.

His mind skipped back to a snowy night in Siberia. Winter in that part of the world can kill a person in a matter of minutes. On a clear night, the surrounding terrain was vast and beautiful. But when the cloud cover settled in, hanging low as it did for weeks on end, it was depressing and claustrophobic. No wonder alcoholism was so rampant.

He had been in Siberia investigating a spurious report that his father was actually alive in a detention center near the remote city of Yakutsk, which was about as far from anyplace as you could get. The report was a lie, of course, because his father had been killed when he was an infant. Why then had an anonymous note been slipped under his door saying his father was alive? Who would pull such a prank, and why? Regardless, he knew he must investigate.

He remembered being the only passenger aboard the drafty commuter jet when it took off from Moscow in the early morning darkness. Ahead of him was a three-thousand-mile journey to the northeast. The plane had a single flight attendant, a fifty year-old woman with the figure of a fire hydrant and an attitude to match, who for most of the trip sat in one of the front seats, smoking and drinking and occasionally getting up to go to the toilet. Near the end of the day, the drafty plane finally dropped down through the cloud cover and landed.

The landscape of Yakutsk was dismal. Gray sky. Gray snow. Gray concrete. Gray everything. From the airport, Talanov went to the local Communist Party headquarters, where an old red Lada had been reserved for him. It was parked near the towering gray statue of Vladimir Lenin. His car was the only splash of color in the midst of all that gray.

After coffee with the local head of the KGB, who was a large man with glassy eyes and a flushed complexion, he headed east in the fading light of the afternoon in the sputtering old car. He had to drive across the ice of the frozen Lena River because there was no bridge. From there he angled north into the forbidding Siberian wilderness. The cracked pavement of the highway soon turned into a potted road of frozen ruts. Sixty miles farther, his car broke down.

Normally, to have a car break down at night in that part of the world meant certain death. The wilderness was remote and unpopulated. Packs of wolves roamed the countryside and forests. Temperatures at night dropped to minus sixty. Even now, he still suspected the whole trip had been an assassination plot.

But even more memorable as he trudged along that frozen road was a lighted window in the midst of all that darkness. A farmhouse in the distance. A tiny dot of light. A sign of hope. "And a light shines in the darkness," he said, staring reflectively at the dot far out to sea.

"Where did you hear that?" asked Larisa.

"From an old couple in their eighties," said Talanov, recounting the story of how he had seen the light in their farmhouse window. How he had knocked on their door, half frozen. How they had warmed and fed him, and prayed for his safety. "Beautiful people. Godly people. Served me the best fermented horse milk I've ever had."

"So you believe in God?" she asked.

"I was educated in a system that did everything possible to stamp God out. Atheism was hammered into us. Evolution became our religion. But the closer I looked, none of what they were teaching made sense. Look at the world. At the complexity of life. At the order of things. All this by random chance? For me, it was much more logical to believe in a creator. So, yes, I believe in God, which is why I wanted to blame him for the death of my wife. I wanted to blame anyone but myself, and God was an easy target."

Within an hour, they were winding their way up into the Hollywood Hills again. Larisa was curled up in the seat facing Talanov, staring at him with a mellow smile, one hand holding her hair to keep it from blowing in the wind, although a few loose strands flicked playfully about her face.

Talanov noticed her staring up at him. "I thought you were asleep."

"I am too happy to be asleep. I have not been happy for very long time and I do not want to sleep through it."

"I'm having a good time, too," he said, "much to my surprise. I was so messed up the night we met. I felt guilty and lost and full of anger."

"What made you change?" asked Larisa.

"You wouldn't believe me if I told you."

"Perhaps I will surprise you."

"Okay, it was Gunner."

"Gunner?"

"Told you," said Talanov with a chuckle. "When Gunner first started pounding on me, I didn't care. *Do what you want, I'm already dead.* That's how I felt. But you tried defending me, so Gunner started pounding on you, and something inside me snapped. But it didn't end there, which it might have if you and Jade hadn't come to the hospital. But you did, and here we are. But that's not the end of it, either. It wasn't until I heard myself telling Harry that nothing he could do would bring back his daughter, which, by extension, meant nothing I could do would bring her back, either. No amount of loathing or self-destruction. So in a real way, it wasn't Gunner but you who caused me to change. I don't know where this is going, Larisa, or even what it is. I am, after all, twice your age. But this feels really ... good. "

"I think it feels good, too," Larisa said with a smile.

"Still, doesn't it bother you a little?"

"What?"

"Our age difference."

"My grandmother was fifteen when she met my grandfather, who was forty-four. He tried shooing her away, like a fly, but my grandmother would not be shooed. Ukrainian women can be very stubborn."

"Really? I never would have guessed."

Larisa laughed. "My grandmother was very independent, and very strong, and she was the most beautiful woman I have ever seen. I have a picture of her on her wedding day, when she was sixteen. Like me, she had long blonde hair. She was very – how do you say – *khtyvyy̆?*"

"Voluptuous."

"Yes. And she had many suitors. Young men from all over the region tried winning her heart. But she had eyes only for my grandfather, who was very dashing and strong. A man among boys, she called him. He is today one-hundred-and-six and she is seventy-seven, and still they go dancing. So I am perhaps not bothered as much about your age as you are about mine."

"Yeah, well, maybe you should be bothered."

Larisa laughed. "I am making you nervous?"

"Yes!" he said, steering the Boxster around a corner. "You are – how do you say – very *khtyvyy̆.*"

Within a minute, Talanov had steered the Boxter around another turn and into the carport, where the low rumble of its engine echoed in the empty space. After switching off the ignition, he climbed out and walked around to open Larisa's door. Accepting his hand, she climbed out. Talanov slammed the door but neither of them moved. They just stood there in the darkness, their faces inches apart, looking at one another.

Talanov circled his hands around Larisa's waist and brought her to him. Pelvis to pelvis, pressed tightly. With a finger, he looped a strand of Larisa's hair behind her ear, then ran his fingers through her hair and around the back of her head. Larisa closed her eyes and felt him gently twirling, investigating, caressing.

She pressed herself closer to him. "You are making big mess of my hair, I think," she said, opening her eyes. It was dark and she could only see his darkened silhouette. She could feel the warmth of his breath.

"It's so inviting ... so messuppable," Talanov replied, "if that's even a word. I can stop, if you'd like."

"Or you can ... not," Larisa replied with a smile.

Talanov leaned in to kiss her but Larisa leaned back and touched a finger to his lips.

"What's wrong?" he asked.

"There is something I need to tell you."

"Okay."

Larisa took a steadying breath, and in the ensuing seconds of silence, Talanov heard a tiny scuff that was barely audible against the sound of rustling palm fronds. With a smooth pirouette, he scooped Larisa behind him while sliding the Ruger from its holster.

"Face down on the pavement! *Now,*" shouted Talanov, aiming the Ruger at a dark figure coming toward them.

"*Net! Ne strelyaĭte!*" a man called back, holding his hands in the air.

"I said, face down on the pavement!" commanded Talanov.

The man lowered himself onto the concrete.

Talanov circled the man and scanned the surrounding darkness.

"I'm a friend. I come alone," the man said.

"I have no friends," answered Talanov.

"You have more friends than you realize," the man replied.

"And you are?"

"My name is Ilya Filishkin," the man replied. "I am from the FSB."

"What does the Russian Federal Security Service want with me?"

"We need to talk."

"Your ID. Where is it?" demanded Talanov.

"Hip pocket."

Talanov retrieved Ilya's wallet. "Get up," he said, placing the Ruger to Ilya's head and pulling him to his feet.

"*Svynya,*" muttered Larisa, calling Ilya a pig.

"My keys. They're in my pocket," Talanov said to Larisa.

Larisa took the keys from Talanov's pocket, unlocked the door, and turned on the lights. Talanov guided Ilya into the kitchen and made Ilya lie face-down on the floor.

"Is this really necessary?" asked Ilya while Larisa closed and locked the door.

"I could have shot you instead," remarked Talanov, looking at Ilya's ID. "I remember you," he said.

"We were in the First Chief Directorate during Gorbachev," Ilya replied. "May I get up now?"

"Actually, you were in Department Thirteen and training for a covert posting in ... where was it, again?"

"Brussels."

"That's right. As a ... "

"Sniper. Targeted dispatch. For those on our list."

"Hell of a chess player, too. You loved that famous player. Who was it again?"

"Petrov."

"Ah, yes, Petrov's Immortal," said Talanov. "Queen sacrifice. Legendary game. Checkmate in twenty moves."

"Are you satisfied now?"

"For now," said Talanov. He tossed Ilya's ID on the counter and motioned for him to get up.

"I tried phoning you a number of times," said Ilya, springing to his feet. In his mid-fifties, he stood five-foot-five and was slender, with thinning hair that had been dyed light brown to cover the gray. He was dressed in a rumpled blue suit and white shirt, with the collar unbuttoned.

"About?" asked Talanov, keeping Ilya covered.

"Is that really necessary?" Ilya asked, nodding at Talanov's gun.

"It is until I know why you're here."

"I showed you my ID."

"Which tells me who you are, not why you're here."

Ilya glanced sharply at Larisa. "Who is she? The Ukrainian?" he asked.

"Answer my question."

"I prefer we talk alone."

"And I prefer to be left alone. But here you are, interrupting a very promising evening, which puts me in a very bad mood. So either you tell me what I want to know or the rest of your evening isn't going to go very well."

"I am here on official business, Colonel. I am not used to being treated this way."

Three seconds later, Ilya again found himself lying flat on the floor, this time with Talanov's knee on his chest and the Ruger aimed directly at his forehead.

"Last time," said Talanov. "Why are you here?"

"I know who killed your wife."

CHAPTER 13

WHILE Larisa prepared coffee, Ilya spread the pages of an LAPD report across the dining room table. The report contained photos of Andrea, Talanov, and the crime scene where Andrea had been killed. There were copies of other reports from paramedics, doctors, eyewitnesses, and the coroner, plus photos of Talanov's house, copies of his bank records, insurance policies, and a copy of Talanov's old KGB file.

"Where the hell did the Los Angeles Police Department get hold of my KGB file?" asked Talanov, flicking through the pages. Some had been completely redacted, with other lines partially blacked out.

"We emailed it to them," said Ilya.

"You did *what?*"

"After the death of your wife, the police began their investigation by scrutinizing those people closest to the victim – sorry, your wife – and quite naturally your records became a matter of great interest once they found out who you were. So when they reached out to us, we complied. You know how it is these days, with interdepartmental cooperation and all."

Talanov snorted sarcastically and tossed aside the report.

"Understandably," added Ilya, "the file we sent contains only generic information as to your background and training. There is nothing classified or sensitive."

"In other words," said Talanov, "you were protecting your asses while volunteering mine."

Ilya did not reply.

After preparing and serving the coffee, Larisa took her mug into the living room, kicked off her shoes and curled up on one of the sectional couches, where she watched Talanov sort through other reports scattered across the table.

"The bruises on your face. What happened?" asked Ilya.

"I was beaten up by a couple of bouncers in the nightclub where I met Larisa."

"Why would they do this to you?"

"Things got out of hand when I tried going back for my wallet."

"I do not understand. If you lost your wallet and went inside to get it, why would they care?"

"Actually, my wallet was stolen, by Larisa, who drugged me first before taking me to a hotel room, which is where she stole it once I was passed out. When I woke up and saw that it was gone, I went back to the same club where I met her to get it. That's when the trouble started."

After a sharp glance at Larisa, Ilya stepped closer to Talanov and lowered his voice. "So this *prostitute* stole your wallet, and you are still with her? Why would you do something like this?"

"What's your point?"

"She drugged you. She stole your wallet! And yet when I arrive, I see you have brought her to your house. What is going on?"

"No offense, but that's none of your business."

"She's Ukrainian! They are liars and thieves. All of them! And yet, here you are with her, in your *house*. You are much more trusting than I would be, my friend."

"I'm not your friend," said Talanov.

Ilya held up his hands in surrender, then took a thin box of Sobranie Black Russian cigarettes out of his jacket pocket and offered one to Talanov.

"Smokers outside," was Talanov's reply.

Ilya shrugged agreeably and left through the kitchen, a cigarette dangling from his mouth. Once he was gone, Larisa got up from the couch and padded barefoot back to the table.

"He is a pig. I do not like him," Larisa said.

"I never would have guessed," Talanov replied.

"He works for FSB, who do nothing to stop mafia. I am here because of mafia. A prisoner because of mafia."

"He knows who killed my wife."

Without responding, Larisa took her mug to the kitchen and rinsed it. "Where would you like me to sleep?" she asked.

"My bed, but don't wait up," Talanov replied. "I'll probably be working all night."

"May I fix you another coffee?"

"Thanks. A cappuccino," Talanov replied just as the door to the carport opened and Ilya stepped back inside. Larisa did not look at him when he passed by.

"You have a beautiful home," Ilya said, entering the dining room. On the wall was a framed painting of the Australian outback. It was a scene of dry mountains in rich reds and ochres set against an aquamarine sky and wispy white clouds. "Is it like this in Australia where you lived?"

"You were saying you know who killed her," said Talanov. "How can you say that when the police themselves never figured it out?"

"Because the police could not decipher the evidence."

"And you could?"

Ilya withdrew another manila folder from his briefcase and handed it to Talanov. Inside was another police report, this one in Russian and on cheap Russian paper. Several pages featured the gray shield of the FSB, with its golden, double-headed eagle. Others sheets had the mastheads and logos from the Ministry of Internal Affairs, the Special Purpose Units of the Moscow City Police Department, as well as the Moscow Oblast Police Department.

"Give me the short version," said Talanov as Larisa brought him a frothy cappuccino.

"I go to bed now," she said, touching him on the arm.

"See you in the morning," Talanov replied.

Larisa descended the steps and crossed to the arched doorway leading into the hall, where she paused and glanced back. With his cappuccino mug still in hand, Talanov was busy looking over photos while Ilya related how the LAPD had found a fingerprint on a forty-five caliber shell casing found on the floor of the convention center. With a dejected sigh, Larisa continued down the hallway into the bedroom.

At the table, Talanov told Ilya how the shot had been fired from a catwalk nearly seven stories above the audience, meaning the casing had obviously been ejected from the rifle and then fallen down onto the floor. "So that fingerprint could belong to anyone," said Talanov.

"Perhaps," replied Ilya. "But this print was not in the system."

"Lots of people aren't in the system."

"True," said Ilya, "but an identical fingerprint was found in Moscow, seven weeks ago, on another forty-five caliber shell casing, which is how I became involved in this case. The bullet from that casing killed my boss and your former colleague, Ivan Moroshkin."

Talanov was stunned. "Ivan is *dead?*"

Ilya nodded.

"Why would anybody want to kill Ivan?" asked Talanov.

"I am guessing for the same reason they tried killing you."

"Which is?"

"That, we have not figured out. Whatever the reason, you survived and Ivan did not. So your life may still be in danger."

"Have you identified the killer?"

"Yes, we have. Do not ask me how we obtained this information, but the fingerprint belongs to an assassin named Connor Jax."

"Never heard of him," said Talanov. "Who is he?"

"A contract killer for the CIA."

Talanov nearly choked on his cappuccino.

"That is correct, Colonel," said Ilya. "You've been targeted by the Americans."

CHAPTER 14

TALANOV could not believe what he was hearing. *The CIA wanted him dead?* That he could not believe. And yet, after reading the police reports, including several pages from a leaked CIA document, it seemed undeniable that the fingerprints on both casings belonged to a contract killer named Connor Jax, whose fingerprints and employment record had somehow been retrieved from the Sensitive Compartmented Information Facility at Langley, which stores and protects information well above the "Top Secret" classification.

"Where did you get this information?" asked Talanov.

"I told you not to ask."

"Well, I'm asking. Where did you get it? Whoever gave it to you could be tried for treason."

"I honestly cannot tell you. I got it from a colleague in Moscow who got it from someone who knows someone. In our line of work, no one admits to anything, and those of us at the tail end of the food chain are powerless to investigate. I am sorry."

"I need to confirm this report."

"Our people think it is genuine, but of course we have no proof. What you are looking at is a copy of a copy of a copy. The CIA would no doubt claim the document to be a forgery. As we both know, the CIA is above scrutiny. Which is why my government sent me over here to speak with you and the LAPD personally. To find out why the CIA would want to kill you, which in turn may help us determine why they killed Ivan Moroshkin. If my government is to put pressure on the American government to stop Connor Jax, then we need to present them with a lot more evidence than we currently have."

By now, Talanov was pacing the floor.

"Can you think of any reason why the CIA would want to kill you?" asked Ilya. "Someone you know? Some*thing* you know?"

"Let me see that report again."

Ilya handed it to him and Talanov bounded down the steps into the living room.

"Where are you going?" asked Ilya.

"Wait there," Talanov replied. He tiptoed down the hallway into his bedroom. The room was dark but he could see the bed was empty. After retrieving his phone from the dresser, he walked over to the French doors and found Larisa outside on the deck, still dressed in the same black dress she had worn to dinner. "I thought you'd be asleep," he said, joining her at the railing.

"This view is very beautiful," she said.

Talanov stood beside her for a moment and watched the blinking lights of an airplane taking off in the distance.

"You are finished with pig?" she asked.

"He's not that bad," said Talanov with a chuckle. "And I'm afraid we're just getting started. Ilya thinks he knows who killed Andrea. I tried looking into it once before but the police shut me out."

"I am happy for you," Larisa said.

"If Ilya's right, I can finally track down the coward who did this. He's got the name of the killer, but something doesn't add up. So I need to check things out, which is why I came for my phone."

Larisa smiled and nodded.

"Can I get you anything?" he asked. "A glass of wine?"

"Nothing. I am fine."

With a smile, Talanov touched Larisa on the arm and left her standing on the deck. When he entered the living room, he saw Ilya was gone, no doubt to smoke another cigarette out in the carport. Pausing by the fireplace, he dialed a memorized number.

"Yes?" answered a man's voice after two rings. The voice was clear and precise, and by the pitch, Talanov guessed the man to be in his twenties.

"November Echo for La Tâche," replied Talanov. "I need an immediate callback to this number."

"One moment," the voice replied.

The wait was not long.

"Who is this again?" asked the voice.

"November Echo."

"I have no record of that name."

"Check again."

"I did. We have no record."

"Then check *again.*"

"One moment."

Again, the wait was not long.

"I'm sorry, but we have no record of that name," the voice stated.

"Then put me through to someone who can help me," Talanov replied.

"I can't do that without knowing who this is."

"I just told you who this is. November Echo."

"One moment, please."

Talanov shook his head. He understood protocol. That's why he had requested an immediate callback, which would have been over one of the CIA's encrypted telephone lines. He also had given his codename, November Echo, and Wilcox's codename, La Tâche. That should have been enough.

The voice came back onto the line. "Where, exactly, did you get this number?"

"From La Tâche."

"And who are you?"

"November Echo."

"We have no record of that name."

"Then call La Tâche and ask him."

"I'm afraid I cannot process this call without proper identification."

"Which I just gave you!"

"We have no record of that name."

Talanov was losing patience. "Then does the name Wilcox ring a bell? I can give you his first name, if you'd like, but he told me to ask for La Tâche, if ever I needed to call home, his codename being a reference to what is arguably the finest French wine in the world. You can be forgiven for not knowing how much the old snob loves wine, but not for ignoring protocol, which I have followed to the letter. Now, put me through, dammit! You've already forced me to use his actual name over an *un*encrypted telephone line. If that's not breaching protocol, I don't know what is."

"One moment."

Again, the wait was not long.

"Sir, my name is Frank," another voice said, this one deeper and older. "La Tâche is unavailable. What's this about?"

"It's about me needing to talk with La Tâche."

"As I said, he's unavailable."

"Then call me back on a secure line so that I can tell you what this is about."

"I cannot process such a request without knowing who you are or the specific nature of this call."

"Man, you guys are too much. All right *Frank,* this call's about a leaked report from your office identifying Connor Jax as one of your assassins. I got it from the Russian FSB. The report contains evidence that Jax assassinated a captain in the FSB, as well as my wife in a failed attempt to kill me. So I'm calling to find out what the hell's going on and why I've been targeted. Is that specific enough? So be sure and tell La Tâche that if I don't get some answers *right now,* I'm taking this to the media." And with that, he ended the call.

CHAPTER 15

TALANOV knew he had pushed the boundaries with Frank but he didn't care. He needed answers and he needed them now.

Back in the eighties, Bill Wilcox – La Tâche – had been the Chief of Station at the American Embassy in London the day he telephoned to offer his services against a totalitarian disease called communism. Operating as the embassy's "Third Viticultural Attaché," which meant he could roam the countryside tasting wine whenever he pleased, Wilcox was at the time an affable man of thirty-nine who loved pontificating about wine as much as he did about intelligence operations. At five-feet-ten, Wilcox was bald, had a pot belly, creased forehead, and a short salt-and-pepper beard, or Friesian roan, as he liked to call it. He always wore his trousers cinched beneath the overhang of his belly, which allowed him to declare his waist to be thirty-four inches when in fact it was forty-two.

Contrary to Agency protocol, the two had become friends to the point of meeting at the vineyard of Domaine de la Romanée-Conti, makers of several wines that included the *very* expensive La Tâche. Producing wine since 1232, the vineyard was located on the well-drained limestone slopes around the picturesque village of Vosne-Romanée, in the Burgundy region of eastern France. It was a late summer afternoon in 1986 when Talanov arrived at the winery dressed in a black Fedora, sunglasses, and a three-quarter-length jacket, which was all very sleek and stylish compared to Wilcox in his yellow Hawaiian shirt, walking shorts, brown socks, and sneakers. Seated at a small table beneath a tree near an ancient limestone building, Wilcox waved Talanov over while continuing to swirl a wineglass full of ruby Pinot Noir. Talanov approached the table guardedly.

"Met my second wife over a glass of Pinot Noir," mused Wilcox, using his foot to push the chair back for Talanov.

"Third wife, too, come to think of it." He beamed when the curvaceous black-haired waitress brought him another basket of French bread and olive oil. When she bent down to serve him, he repositioned himself slightly to get a better view of her cleavage. The waitress caught him peeking and gave him a token smack, but made no effort to move while fussing about with serviettes and glasses. Before leaving, she threw him a final scolding glance with just the slightest hint of a smile.

"How beautiful you are, my darling," Wilcox remarked poetically once she was gone. "Your love is better than wine. Curvaceous hips, incredible breasts." He shivered with delight before looking up to see Talanov staring down at him warily. "Song of Solomon," Wilcox explained.

"You read the Bible?" asked Talanov with surprise.

"Indeed I do," Wilcox replied. "Especially the juicy bits."

"Seriously? Curvaceous hips? Incredible breasts?"

"My friend, you've got no idea what you've been missing all this time." His eyes followed the waitress across the courtyard. When she disappeared into another building, he sighed longingly. "If I were ten years younger and twenty pounds lighter ..."

Make that twenty and forty, thought Talanov, his hands on the back of the chair while continuing to scan the grounds, alert for anyone paying them undue attention.

"Will you *please* sit down and relax?" said Wilcox. "And take off that coat and hat. It causes you stand out like a Brit, which could damn well get us kicked out of here."

"As if that Hawaiian shirt of yours make us blend in," said Talanov, removing his coat.

"A sense of humor. I love it! Yes, my friend, you and I will get on famously," laughed Wilcox just as a man in a blue apron came out of a nearby door. His hands were stained a deep plum color and he was wiping his hands on a rag.

"Qu'en pensez-vous?" he asked, an expectant smile on his face.

Wilcox closed his eyes and sniffed the glass, inhaling the wine's bouquet. He then lifted the glass to his lips, took a sip and sloshed the liquid briefly in his mouth like mouthwash before swallowing and exhaling with a slow, satisfied smile.

"Superbe, Aubert. Tout simplement génial," he replied. "Aromatic, soft, almost feminine on the palate, with wonderfully subtle hues of cherry, raspberry, and black currant. But that's the flirtatious – indeed, *capricious* – side to this deceptively rich, full-bodied varietal with outstanding complexity, smooth tannin, and a *hint* of Asian spice. I don't know how you do it, Aubert, but this is exquisite, insuperable, magnificent. I'll take a case."

"Merveilleux!" exclaimed Aubert, disappearing inside and shouting the order in French.

"Bring a glass for my friend!" Wilcox called out.

Standing in his living room in the Hollywood Hills, Talanov recalled how he and Wilcox sat together under that tree drinking a thousand-dollar bottle of wine paid for by the CIA.

"The best for the best," Wilcox had said, lifting his glass in a toast. *"Un pour tous, et tous pour un."*

"One for all, and all for one?" said Talanov, translating.

"From The Three Musketeers."

Talanov shrugged and shook his head.

"Porthos, Athos, and Aramis were the Three Musketeers," explained Wilcox. "D'Artignan, of course, was not officially a Musketeer, even though his name is synonymous with them."

Talanov responded with a blank look.

"The classic novel by Alexandre Dumas," exclaimed Wilcox. "'You fight like a man. Let's see if you can drink like one.'"

Wilcox waited for some sign of recognition from Talanov, but there was none.

"Or this one," Wilcox said: 'You, boy, are arrogant, hot tempered and entirely too bold. I like that. Reminds me of me.'"

Wilcox again waited for some sign of recognition from Talanov, but there was none.

"Then *surely* you've heard this one," declared Wilcox: "'Go home, find a wench, raise fat babies, live a good long life.'"

Talanov shrugged and Wilcox shrugged with surrender. "Well, then, here's to you and me," he said, finishing his toast. "To November Echo and La Tâche, the Two Musketeers, and to a long and happy partnership."

With a smile, Talanov remembered how they had hit it off. He just hoped the old fox still regarded him with the same trust and conviction.

"Is everything all right?" Ilya asked from the doorway into the kitchen.

"I tried getting through to an old contact at the CIA," replied Talanov. "To have him check on Connor Jax."

"What did you find out?"

"I couldn't get past the switchboard."

"I am not surprised," Ilya replied. "If indeed you have been marked for assassination, they may not want to talk with you."

"It was a long shot, I know, but if anyone could have told me what was going on, it was my friend."

"Try him tomorrow, during normal business hours."

"What continues to bother me is why I've been marked, and if I have, why haven't they finished the job? I'm not that hard to find."

"Perhaps you are harder to find than you think," said Ilya, coming into the dining room, where Talanov joined him. "Your wife, she was Australian?"

"She catered a party I gave in Sydney shortly before the renovation of my house. It was lust at first sight, at least for me. She, on the other hand, took a little convincing."

Ilya laughed.

"We were married six weeks later," Talanov said, pulling out a chair and sitting.

"She must have been an extraordinary woman."

"She was. Fantastic cook, gutsy, smart as a whip."

"Then what are you doing with this *prostitute?*" asked Ilya with a scowl. He pulled out a chair and sat across the table from Talanov.

"One of many diversions."

"And you do this – why – to forget?"

Talanov did not reply.

"Do not waste time with whores," said Ilya, "especially cheap ones like this Ukrainian. She is nothing but a liar and a thief. You do not honor the memory of your wife with such behavior, although your erratic hours with her may well have kept the CIA from 'finishing the job,' as you say. Perhaps I speak out of place, and if so forgive me, but I am here because I want to find the killer of your wife, same as you. I want to bring this Connor Jax to justice for what he has done. But get rid of that whore. She is trash."

Outside on the deck, at the railing near the open slider, Larisa stood alone in the darkness, waiting for Talanov to defend her. But silence was all that she heard. Fighting back tears, she ran into the bedroom, pulled off Andrea's dress and put on her hooker clothes. Grabbing her purse and stilettos, she slipped quietly out onto the deck, climbed over the railing, jumped down into the shrubs and hiked up the embankment to the road, where she began the long, lonely walk down the hill.

CHAPTER 16

THE Hollywood Hills are part of a network of east-west transverse mountain ranges that intersect the north-south coastal ranges of Southern California. Characterized by steep gorges and eroded canyons full of sage and chaparral, the hills have become a residential enclave of affluence and seclusion. Winding roads follow the contours of the rugged terrain. Houses dot the hillsides and sit at odd angles to maximize stunning views. Some sit precariously on cliff faces, with decks built out over ravines.

Having left an estate high up in the hills, the silver Chrysler squealed around the corner and sped along the winding street toward the next turn. Heavy *Gangsta Rap* music vibrated out of massive speakers mounted in the rear deck of the car. Sitting low in the seat and dressed in a black wife-beater, the muscular twenty-two year-old driver wore a black stocking "wave cap" of elastic fabric. A gangsta rapper from the wrong side of town, the driver's name was Dennis but he went by Slam-D. Around his neck were several gold chains. In the passenger seat was Dog, whose real name was Travis. He was the drummer in Slam-D's band. Dog had a bull neck, enormous biceps, and a large scar on one cheek. Dog's blond hair had been completely shaved and he had prison tattoos covering much of his body, including the sides of his veined bald head. In Dog's hand was a twenty-five caliber semi-automatic pistol, otherwise known as a Saturday Night Special.

"No shit?" Slam-D remarked.

"Burned that wangsta right then 'n' there," Dog said, mimicking a shot with his pistol, which he then stuck in the belt of his jeans.

"Off da hook, man!"

They bumped fists and began rocking to the beat of the music. Slam-D kept time by tapping his fingers on the steering wheel, while Dog slapped his knees, like drums.

They rounded a corner and the Chrysler's headlights beamed for an instant on a lone female in a micro skirt walking barefooted on the left-hand side of the road, stiletto high-heels in hand, a tiny purse on a chain swishing at her side.

"Whoa, man!" Slam-D exclaimed as they roared past her. He stared disbelievingly in his rearview mirror while Dog twisted his bull-neck to look. "Man, what's a dime like that doin' out here?"

Larisa watched the taillights of the Chrysler disappear around a bend. She had thought about trying to flag down the driver but didn't feel up for an hour of questions and small talk. At the moment her mind was on Talanov and how she couldn't believe he had just sat there and not said anything to that pig from the FSB. She looked back across the ravine to her left and saw the lights. The house was above her now, around a wide curving bend in the road, sitting up there in the darkness. She had felt safe with Alex, rescued if but for a moment from a dreaded life she knew she could not escape. That's because Borzakov would be waiting for her back in West Hollywood. Waiting for an explanation, waiting for payment, waiting to remind her of what would happen if she even *thought* about trying to escape. He would no doubt drag her over to a wall board and show her the photos of her family – her mother, father, brother, and sister – probably with that grinning monster, Gorsky, who along with Olga had suckered her into this horrible scam. Gorsky would be in all of the photos, almost like a friend of the family, no doubt reassuring them about how well she was doing in Los Angeles.

In truth, it was a cold reminder that if she failed to pay on time, or if she tried to escape, or if she did *anything* to anger Borzakov, the order would be given and Gorsky would torture and kill someone in her family. He knew where they lived, where her brother and sister went to school, and where all of their friends and relatives lived. Nowhere was safe and no *one* was safe. Borzakov would then do something as a reminder of his power. A plastic bag over her head to the point of suffocation. Or stun gun practice for his two muscle men, Nick and Vic.

She could still remember their last victim, another Ukrainian girl, from Lviv, lying on the floor, convulsing violently and urinating in her clothes while Nick and Vic laughed liked hyenas. No evidence of abuse. No damage to "the goods." A sobering reminder about who was in charge.

Walking along in the darkness, Larisa kept to the edge of the pavement. To her immediate left was a thin gravel shoulder that turned grassy before dropping steeply away into a canyon. Across the canyon were other homes, some with lighted windows. Far below, the headlights of a car followed a winding street.

She rounded the bend and paused when she saw the red glow of taillights. The Chrysler had pulled over and stopped. Its engine was still running and loud music vibrated into the night.

What to do? She could stand here in the darkness and hope they drove on. She could continue walking slowly along the edge of the street. She could turn back. Turning back was not an option because she was not about to knock on Alex's door with that pig still in the house.

Larisa was deliberating what to do when the Chrysler reversed up the street and stopped beside her.

"Whas goin' down?" asked Slam-D, gunning the engine.

Larisa brought one arm up across her breasts, knowing she was wearing no bra, which was fine for a hooker in a nightclub, not so fine for a woman walking alone at night. She continued walking forward and did not reply.

"Hey! I'm talkin' to you!" Slam-D called out.

Larisa kept walking and did not reply.

"She's dissin us, bro," said Dog. "That bitch is actually *dissin* us!" With an angry sneer, he yanked the Special out of his belt, jumped out of the car and ran over to Larisa. He grabbed her by the arm and shoved the pistol in her face. "Well, we are gonna school *you,* bitch."

"I do not know what you are talking about!" cried Larisa.

"I'm talkin' about you *dissin* us! That's what."

"What is dissin? I do not know what that *means.*"

"Yeah, well you's about to find out!" Dog said, jamming gun

in Larisa's side and muscling her over to the car. He pulled open the rear door, and in the dim glow of the interior light, saw the soft mounds of flesh that were Larisa's breasts. They were pressing tightly against the thin cloth of the halter top. With a grin, Dog grabbed the halter top and ripped it off. He then pushed Larisa into the back seat, laid his Special on top of the car and pulled down his pants. Larisa replied by kicking Dog in the groin. With a gargling gasp, Dog doubled over and collapsed backward to the ground, where he began moaning and writhing.

With a hand across her naked breasts, Larisa scrambled out of the car and ran toward the edge of the street. She knew it fell away into a ravine, but she would rather take her chances in a ravine than with these men. Slam-D sprang from the car and caught Larisa at the grassy shoulder before it plunged away into darkness. He grabbed her by the hair and dragged her screaming back to the car, where Dog was now on his knees.

"I'm gonna bust a cap in yo' ass!" shouted Dog.

Dog grabbed for Larisa, who jerked back, ducked under Slam-D's arm and dug her nails into his face. Slam-D grabbed at the blinding pain. Larisa broke free and ran for the ravine. Slam-D caught her by the hair again and dragged her back to the car, where Dog grabbed her by the arm and pressed the gun to her forehead.

"Not yet," said Slam-D, shoving Larisa into the back seat of the car again. Larisa tried kicking him but Slam-D grabbed her legs, held them apart, and climbed in on top of her. He pinned her arms above her head, and with *Gangsta Rap* music engulfing them, fumbled with his zipper.

Lying on her back, with Slam-D grunting and maneuvering on top of her, Larisa saw Dog's face slam against the rear windshield of the Chrysler. It stayed there a moment, distorted and crooked, before sliding out of sight. A hand then grabbed Slam-D by the belt and yanked him backward out of the car. Before Slam-D could even swear, Talanov had grabbed him by the throat and kneed him in the groin. Slam-D crumpled in agony to the pavement. Talanov took off his shirt and handed it to Larisa, who covered herself and sat up. Tears streamed down her face.

"Are you all right?" asked Talanov.

Larisa nodded and got out of the car.

Talanov looked down at Slam-D writhing on the pavement. "Get up!" he commanded, motioning with the Special.

Slam-D lifted his hands and stood.

"Put your buddy in the trunk," said Talanov.

Slam-D hobbled to the driver's door and pushed a button. The trunk popped open. Talanov followed Slam-D to the rear of the car and inside the trunk saw nearly a hundred CDs scattered across the carpet. Talanov took one out and looked at it while Slam-D lifted the two-hundred-plus pound Dog into the trunk with a grunt.

"This you?" asked Talanov, showing the CD to Slam-D, who was featured on the cover with Dog and the rest of his band. With their instruments as a backdrop, the group was making angry gestures into the camera.

"Whassit to you?" Slam-D replied sarcastically.

With a snort, Talanov tossed the CD on top of Dog and closed the lid.

"You got *no idea* who you messin' with old man," Slam-D said. He threw Talanov an icy glare and jerked his head defiantly. Two seconds later, he was flying over Talanov's shoulder and down onto the top of the trunk, where he hit hard with a thump and lay gasping for air.

"Your trouble," said Talanov, "is that you've got it all backwards." He slipped Slam-D's wallet from his pocket. "You see, I *do* know who I'm messing with." He opened the wallet and looked at Slam-D's driver's license in the red glow of the tail light. "But you've got no idea who *you're* messing with, Dennis." Talanov slipped the wallet back in Slam-D's pocket, yanked him off the car and jammed the pistol in his groin. "So if you don't want me paying you a visit one night to explain things further, here's what you're going to do. You and your band are going to donate a hundred thousand dollars to an orphanage called The Shelter. One hundred thousand dollars. Have you got that?"

Slam-D nodded.

"Within forty-eight hours," added Talanov. "And I *will* be checking to make sure they receive it. Tell them it's out of the goodness of your heart, take all the credit, I don't care. But they'd better receive that money. Do I make myself clear?"

Slam-D nodded again.

"I'm not sure you fully understand what will happen if you don't," said Talanov, hammering the Special into Slam-D's groin. Slam-D let out a whimpering gargle and started to collapse. Talanov grabbed Slam-D by the throat and propped him up until Slam-D caught his breath. "One hundred thousand dollars within forty-eight hours, or the little guy down there is going to suffer a serious accident. Now, get out of here before I change my mind and raise the pitch of your voice right here and now."

CHAPTER 17

WITH her arms wrapped tightly across her chest, Larisa walked barefooted beside Talanov up the hill. She had no idea what had happened to her stilettos and right now she didn't care.

"What the hell were you *thinking?*" asked Talanov, sticking the Special in his belt.

Larisa did not answer.

Talanov stepped in front of her but Larisa walked around him. Talanov jumped in front of her again and stopped her by placing his hands on her shoulders. "Will you tell me what's going on? Why did you leave like that?"

"Because you let pig say those terrible things. Yes, I may be stupid for thinking I could get modeling job in LA. But you do not know what it is like to be desperate. Have family threatened if I do not do what they say. But I am *not* cheap trash. I may be whore, but I do this because I have no choice. I do *everything* because I have no choice." She pulled angrily away and began walking alone up the hill.

"Will you please stop for a minute and listen to me?" Talanov said, hurrying to catch up with her.

"How could you let him say those terrible things?" Larisa cried. "How could you just *sit* there and say *nothing?*"

"What are you talking about?"

"I heard you! I heard you sit there and say nothing when he called me those terrible names."

"Then I take it you stormed away before hearing my response?"

"Your response was to say *nothing!*"

"Oh, I said something, all right. You just didn't stick around long enough to hear it."

Larisa stared at Talanov while continuing to walk slowly beside him. To their right were the lights of Talanov's house shining in the darkness. A light breeze swirled about them. "What did you say?" she asked.

"That if he *ever* said anything like that about you again, I would personally throw him off the deck of my house, where he would experience about four seconds of freefall before rudely encountering the bottom of the canyon fifty feet below."

A long moment of silence passed.

"You say that to him? Really?" she asked, wiping her nose with the sleeve of Talanov's shirt. The shirt was too big and hung loosely on her body. His long sleeves covered both of her hands.

"I also told him he needed to apologize, which he wasn't real happy about. But I'm not in the business of making him happy. I'm in the business of making *you* happy. You're the one who matters. If you want, I can break his legs."

"Break his legs? You would do this?"

"Absolutely. If I do, though, he'll probably need a pretty nurse to push him around in a wheelchair and give him sponge baths."

Larisa laughed and Talanov did, too.

"What if he will not apologize?" she asked.

"*Then* I break his legs."

When they entered the kitchen ten minutes later, Ilya was making an espresso. "You found her, I see," he said.

Talanov paused bare-chested in front of Ilya and looked him in the eyes. Ilya saw Talanov staring at him and shifted nervously in place.

"Well?" asked Talanov.

"*Izvinite,*" Ilya grudgingly mumbled.

"In Ukrainian," Talanov replied.

Ilya glared briefly at Talanov, then said, "*Vybachte.*"

With a satisfied smile, Larisa marched past Ilya into the dining room. "I will take shower now," she announced. "You may join me, if you wish." She looked over her shoulder at Talanov. "I mean you, not you," she said, glancing dismissively at Ilya before skipping happily down the steps and through the living room.

"I guess she told you," said Talanov.

With a scowl, Ilya took a sip of his espresso while Talanov

followed Larisa to the bedroom, where he put on another shirt before returning to the dining room table.

The next six hours were spent poring over the police reports again, with Talanov studying facts and memorizing details. Talanov tried placing another call to Wilcox, but still could not get past the switchboard. When the first signs of dawn began illuminating the eastern sky, Larisa walked barefoot into the living room still wearing Talanov's shirt.

"Take shower. I fix breakfast," she said, seeing Ilya sprawled out on one of the couches asleep, mouth open, snoring lightly.

"Are you wearing anything under that shirt?" asked Talanov.

Larisa smiled and shrugged. Talanov leaned in to kiss her but Larisa stopped him with her hand, like she had last time.

"Not again," he said.

"There is something I must tell you," she said.

"In a minute," Talanov replied, wrapping his arms around her. He felt Larisa press her bare thighs against him. He leaned back and saw her staring up at him as his desire for her grew. He leaned down and started to kiss her again.

Larisa suddenly pulled back. "Alex, please. There is something I must tell you," she said, this time with resolve. She took a steadying breath.

"This sounds serious," he said.

A fist began pounding on the door to the carport. "Police! Open up!" shouted a voice.

Ilya jerked awake just as Talanov broke away from Larisa.

"Open up!" the voice shouted again.

"Take it easy, I'm coming," answered Talanov while the pounding continued.

He opened the door and a river of detectives and police officers burst into his kitchen. Some were in suits. Some were in black LAPD uniforms. Some had ICE – Immigration and Customs Enforcement – emblazoned on their jackets. Four officers with drawn guns surrounded Talanov.

"Well, well, well, what have we here?" said Diego, striding through the door. "Didn't think we'd find you, did you, Mr. *Aleksandr Talanov,* former colonel in the KGB?" Diego was followed by an obese detective named Jones, who was eating the last of a jelly-filled donut.

"This him?" asked Jones, wiping crumbs from his mouth with a hand. "You're sure?"

"It's him, all right," Diego replied, taking out his handcuffs while other officers surrounded Larisa and Ilya. The remaining officers swept through the house and searched every room.

"What the hell is this about?" demanded Talanov.

Diego spun Talanov around and snapped handcuffs on his wrists. "Where shall I begin?" he asked rhetorically, spinning Talanov back around to face him again. "How about at the nightclub? How about your involvement with a drug and prostitution ring being run by the Russian mafia?"

"That's absurd!"

"Is it? I wonder if Todd Martin will pick you out of a lineup. You remember Todd. He got drugged by a Russian prostitute we think works for the mob. Todd told us you knew this prostitute by name, which in turn links *you* with the mob. And who *is* this mysterious Russian prostitute?" He glanced at Larisa then back at Talanov. "We'll put your girlfriend there in a lineup, too, and see what Todd Martin says."

"I can explain," said Talanov.

"I bet you can," said Jones, stepping in. To Larisa: "Put on some clothes." He signaled a female officer, who took Larisa by the arm and led her into the bedroom.

"But wait, that's not all," continued Diego. "How about that sniper rifle you bought with your American Express card? Along with a silencer and ammunition."

"I didn't make those purchases!"

"A shop owner says you did."

"He's lying."

"Let's see, a respectable, licensed gun shop owner versus a suspected drug dealer working with the mob." Diego rubbed his chin, as if perplexed. "Gee, I wonder who the courts are going to believe?"

"I tell you, *he's lying!*" insisted Talanov. "I did *not* make those purchases. My card was stolen. So was my driver's license.

Larisa can verify where I was the day those purchases were made. I was here, asleep, all day. I'd been in a hospital!"

"Who's Larisa?"

"The young woman who was just here."

"See if Larisa has some ID," Jones told Diego, who nodded and left the kitchen just as two other detectives appeared with Ilya.

"This guy says he's with Russian State Security," one of them said. "His ID looks legit, but it's in Russian."

The other detective held up the stack of reports. "From the looks of it, they've been working on something big. They've got copies of the LAPD files on the murder investigation of Talanov's wife, plus a bunch of other reports – all in Russian – and what looks to be a leaked report from the CIA."

Two men entered the kitchen from the carport. They were armed with holstered nine-millimeter pistols. One man almost six-feet-seven inches tall. His name was Tyrone. With him was a man who stood a mere six-feet-two inches tall compared with Tyrone. His name was Calvin.

"Let me see those," Calvin said, gesturing toward the stack of reports in the detective's hand.

"And you are?" asked Jones.

"Homeland Security," answered Calvin, showing Jones an ID. "Those reports. Let me see them."

Jones gave the nod, and after a nervous glance up at Tyrone frowning down at him, the detective handed Calvin the reports just as Diego and the female officer came back into the kitchen with Larisa, who was dressed in a pair of Andrea's jeans and a t-shirt. She was also wearing Andrea's Ugg boots, as none of her shoes would fit.

"No driver's license, no Social Security card, and no credit cards," said Diego. "She's got nothing but a big wad of cash, some condoms, and a few cosmetics."

"When I questioned her, she admitted to being a prostitute from Ukraine," said the female officer.

"You said I could trust you," said Larisa. "You said you wanted to help me."

"Oops, there goes your alibi," said Diego, grinning at Talanov and clicking his tongue. "I doubt the court will believe the testimony of a whore who works for the mob."

"Take them into custody," said Jones.

Diego grabbed Talanov by the arm. "Aleksandr Talanov, you have the right to remain silent. Anything you say can and will be used against you in a—"

"Hold up," said Calvin.

"What's wrong?" asked Jones.

Calvin handed the reports to Tyrone. "As of now, we're taking over."

"On what grounds?" demanded Jones.

"On the grounds that I've got a Russian intelligence officer with a leaked report from the CIA. That makes this a national security issue. Plus, I'm not even sure a Russian intelligence officer should be here. How did he get into the country? Is he legit? We'll need to look into that, too."

"This is outrageous!" cried Ilya. "I am here on official business."

"Get him out of here," said Calvin. "Put him in the back seat of our car."

Following Tyrone, two LAPD officers escorted Ilya out through the carport to the car.

"I've also got a foreign national working illegally as a prostitute," said Calvin.

"Prostitution's our turf," said Jones.

"She's Russian. She stays with us."

"Ukrainian," stated Larisa.

"Whatever," said Calvin. "As for you, Mr. Talanov, you're a former KGB colonel whom we suspect is involved with the mafia."

"This is *nonsense!*" exclaimed Talanov.

"You're also suspected of murdering your wife."

"I was *cleared* of that ludicrous charge!"

"We also have evidence that you purchased a sniper rifle."

"Which is a *lie!*"

"How a Russian like you ever got Australian citizenship after the Wall came down, I'll never know. But we're shipping you back to Australia, where they can do with you what they want. In fact, we're deporting all of you. And let me assure you of one thing right here and now: none of you will *ever* be allowed into this country again. Ever! Get them out of here."

CHAPTER 18

TALANOV, Larisa, and Ilya were seated together in the back seat of Calvin's sedan. Steel mesh separated them from Calvin, who was driving, and Tyrone, who was in the seat next to Calvin. A shotgun was mounted in a bracket near Tyrone's left knee. In the back seat, Ilya was by one of the windows, with Talanov in the middle and Larisa by the other window, her elbow on the armrest, head in hand, eyes covered.

"It'll be okay," Talanov said quietly. "You're getting a free ticket home. The opportunity to regain your life."

Larisa did not reply.

"Can you at least take off these cuffs?" Talanov called out.

"You'll be released once we're inside a secure zone at TBIT," said Calvin.

"What is TBIT?" asked Ilya.

"The airport," answered Talanov. "Tom Bradley International Terminal."

"What will happen once we are there?" asked Ilya.

"You'll be processed and put on a plane," Calvin replied.

"So I am to be deported without being allowed to call my consulate?"

Calvin did not reply.

"I demand your badge number and name," said Ilya. "This kind of treatment is unacceptable. I will be lodging an official protest."

Calvin smiled but did not respond. Tyrone did more than smile. He laughed.

"You think this is funny?" asked Ilya.

"Yeah," said Tyrone. "It's funny as hell. A couple of Commie spies lodging an official protest about being deported."

"Commie spies?" asked Talanov. "Seriously?"

"Commie ... Communist," said Tyrone.

"I know what it means," said Talanov. "I'm just wondering if you've been on a twenty-year drinking binge or something."

"Are you trying to be funny?"

"Are you trying to be stupid?"

"Laugh it up all you want," said Tyrone. "You and Ivan are gettin' shipped home."

"My name is *Ilya* Filishkin, and I am an officer Federal Security Service of the Russian Federation."

"Whatever."

"This is outrageous!" said Ilya.

"Yeah, you said that before," said Tyrone. "Made no difference then. Makes no difference now."

"The Federal Security Service is the equivalent of your FBI. I am here on official business."

"Of course you are," said Tyrone, slapping Calvin on the arm. "Can you believe this shit?"

"I came here to help this man solve the murder of his wife, which is something *you* should have done."

"Save your breath," said Talanov while Tyrone laughed.

"We cannot let them get away with this."

"I'm afraid it's no use. Those two *bruh-thuhs* are bigots, and there's no reasoning with a bigot."

With a quick glare back at Talanov, Tyrone stopped laughing.

"You see, Ilya," Talanov continued, "a bigot is an irrational, often spineless individual who exhibits intolerance or blind hatred toward groups of people based on race, nationality, religion, sexual orientation, gender, disabilities, or any number of physical traits. In short, they don't know how to think. Take us, for example. To the *bruh-thuhs* there in the front seat, a Russian *has* to be the enemy. A spy. Just like all black people can dance. And that's after mammy serves up a big platter o' watermelon, greens, chitlins, hushpuppies, and catfish. Right, *bruh-thuh?*"

"Watch your mouth!" snarled Tyrone.

"Or what, you'll shoot? You like pickin' on honkies, don'cha? Makes ya feel *big* and tough."

"I said, shut *up!*"

"Cool it, Tyrone," said Calvin. "He's just yanking your chain."

"That's right, massa Calvin," said Talanov. "You da boss-man."

Tyrone slammed his fist against the mesh, scaring Larisa. "Shut your mouth before one of us shuts it for you."

"If anyone should have been open to giving me a chance to prove my innocence about this sniper rifle nonsense, it should have been you. But you're no different than the red-neck bigots who persecute blacks. Yeah, I've been yanking your chain. But you genuinely don't care. You really *are* a bigot. You're disgrace to the uniform you wear."

"If I were you, I'd shut it right now," said Calvin.

"Scared of what I might have to say?"

"I said, shut up!"

"No, wait," said Tyrone. "I'd like to hear what our Commie friend has to say."

"What for?" asked Talanov. "You've already made up your mind."

"Because the LAPD interviewed the shop owner and showed him a set of pictures. Guess what? The owner picked you."

"He's lying."

"Gee, that's unique," said Tyrone. "Never heard that one before."

"Then let's go ask him, face to face, with me there looking him in the eyes."

"I'm not wasting time with this," said Calvin. "We're on our way to the airport and you're on your way home."

"You really *are* afraid of discovering the truth, aren't you?" asked Talanov.

"We ain't afraid of nothing," said Tyrone.

"Of course you are," answered Talanov. "You're just afraid of admitting it. That's because bigots like you are scared of finding out the truth. Afraid of finding out I didn't buy that gun. Afraid of watching your whole case collapse in front of your eyes." He laughed contemptuously and shook his head.

"Your little tactic ain't gonna work," said Calvin. "You're being deported. So shut the hell up."

"That's the spirit, *bruh-thuh.*"

Tyrone jabbed a finger at Talanov. "All right, mister, you're on!"

"We don't have *time,*" declared Calvin.

"It's on our way," Tyrone replied. "Five minutes. No big deal."

"The investigation's over. They're being sent home!"

"He called me a *bigot*. And I ain't puttin' up with that shit. Especially not from him. So we *are* doin' this, and I *will* be shoving his smug-ass words right back down his throat. I'll call Arnie and have him meet us out front. But if our Commie spy tries anything – and I mean *anything* – I guarantee I'll be shipping his ass back to Siberia in a little red box."

A beat-up white panel van was waiting in front of Arnie's Ammo Emporium when the unmarked sedan pulled into the parking lot. The store was in a rundown strip mall on a bend in the street. It was a single story building with a flat roof and security bars over the windows. In front of the building, a barricade of thick steel pipes protruded out of the ground to prevent ram-raids. A small hedge separated the parking lot from a meandering sidewalk near the street.

The sedan entered the lot and parked in front of the store. The door of the van creaked opened and a large man in jeans and a sleeveless flannel shirt got out. On his hip was a holstered nine-millimeter black pistol. "Arnie," as the owner was known to his friends and customers, had a long, thick beard and a head of thick wiry hair that had been tied back in a ponytail. Calvin got out and met Arnie at the front door.

"We appreciate you doing this," said Calvin.

"Anything to help the *po*-lice," said Arnie, his hand on his pistol.

Calvin noticed Arnie's precaution and smiled. "Want to step over to the car and have a look at their faces?"

"Being 'em inside," said Arnie. "Controlled environment. Not that I don't trust you boys."

"Yeah, sure," replied Calvin with a growl.

While Calvin returned to the sedan to get Talanov, Arnie unlocked a thick deadbolt at the bottom of the door, then another at the top, then a final lock midway, near the push bar. He then stepped inside and deactivated the alarms.

Calvin unlocked one of Larisa's handcuffs and fastened it to the mesh. "You're staying here," he said.

Staring despondently down at the floor mat, Larisa did not reply. Calvin eyed her for a moment then slammed the door just as Tyrone opened the other door. Ilya got out and Calvin took him by the arm and led him inside with his hands still cuffed. When Talanov slid out, Tyrone took him by the elbow.

"Can you at least take off these cuffs?" asked Talanov.

Tyrone simply chuckled and escorted Talanov inside.

Arnie's Ammo Emporium was a rectangular warehouse with metal beams spanning the store. Along one wall were racks of rifles and shotguns. They were displayed in vertical arrangements. Below the racks were shelves full of ammunition. On other walls were racks of assault rifles, sniper rifles and machine pistols. Display counters were filled with scopes, pistols, knives, brass knuckles and slingshots. Scattered around the warehouse were more than thirty security cameras. A metal door with mirrored strips on the window led to a back room.

Arnie stepped behind the main counter and waited.

"*Very* nice," said Calvin, looking around with admiration.

"How can I help you boys?" asked Arnie, his hands resting on the counter as the four men approached.

Talanov noted the security cameras and the layout of the store. He saw where the sniper rifles were located to his left.

"We're here about the Mark-12 you sold recently," said Calvin.

"I already told the *po*-lice everything I know."

"Were you the one who sold it?"

"Yep. All sales like that go through me."

"Did either of these men purchase that weapon?" asked Tyrone.

"Yep," said Arnie, pointing at Talanov. "He did."

CHAPTER 19

"MAKE him show you the security camera footage!" said Talanov as he was yanked away from the counter by Tyrone. "It wasn't me! I did *not* buy that rifle!"

"Sorry to have bothered you," said Calvin.

"No problem," Arnie replied.

With Ilya in hand, Calvin followed the others outside.

"Make him show you that camera footage," Talanov said again. "Get a court order. I *didn't* do it."

"Court order won't do you no good," said Tyrone, opening the car door and pushing Talanov inside. "You won't be around long enough to need one. And if you start with any more of that *bruh-thuh* stuff, you'll be suffering multiple injuries from resisting arrest. You get what I'm saying?"

After a short ride on the 405, they took Century Boulevard to the airport. Their destination – Tom Bradley International Terminal – was at the farthest end of the "horseshoe" arrangement of nine terminals that comprise Los Angeles International Airport, or LAX as it was known. In the center of the horseshoe were several multi-level parking facilities, along with the soaring crossed arches of the iconic "flying saucer" Theme Building. Traffic for departures was directed along an elevated upper deck, with plenty of sky overhead. Traffic for arrivals was directed along the lower deck, which was situated beneath the upper deck. The lower deck was a claustrophobic place. There was concrete everywhere. Traffic was a heavy mix of cars, shuttle busses, and taxis. The air was thick with exhaust. The noise of distant jet engines was amplified off the concrete before reverberating off the terminal in a suffocating roar. It was not the kind of place a person wanted to spend much time.

Calvin parked in a reserved space at one end of the Arrivals section. He and Tyrone removed their prisoners from the car and marched them into the crowded terminal. Lots of people paused to stare. In the lead was a giant of a man – Tyrone – escorting a man in handcuffs – Talanov. Tyrone was scowling and Talanov was being muscled along. It was an arresting sight and people parted to make way for them. More arresting, however, was the gorgeous blonde in tight jeans being escorted by Calvin. She, too, was in handcuffs, as was Ilya, whom Calvin was also escorting.

Talanov began assessing his surroundings the moment they stepped into the terminal. Crowds like this were good for making an escape. The handcuffs would be a challenge, as would the two armed Homeland Security agents he had already pushed to the brink. One wrong move and he would be deported in a coffin. And yet, even if he could somehow manage to break free, which was unlikely, it would mean leaving Larisa and Ilya, and that he would not do.

Tyrone paused to let Calvin take the lead against the river of pedestrians pushing baggage carts toward the exit they had just entered. Their destination now was a sterile facility deep within the bowels of the terminal. Calvin led the party along a tunnel to a guard who was checking the documents of arriving passengers. Calvin showed the guard his ID and explained where they were going. The guard nodded and allowed them past. Calvin led the group through the baggage area, with its slowly turning carousels laden with suitcases. On the other side of the baggage area, they entered a hallway. At the end of the hallway was a locked door. Calvin touched his ID to a digital reader on the wall and the door clicked open.

"In here," Calvin said, ushering the group into a windowless waiting room. Chairs lined the perimeter of the room. The walls were painted pastel green, no doubt for its calming effect. A few magazines were stacked on a small table in one corner. Above the table was a security camera.

"Face the wall," Calvin instructed. When Talanov obeyed, Calvin removed his handcuffs and nodded for Tyrone to do the same for Larisa and Ilya.

"I demand the use of a phone," said Ilya, rubbing his wrists once the handcuffs were removed.

Without answering, Calvin walked to a second door and touched his ID to the digital reader mounted on the wall. The door clicked open and he and Tyrone left the room.

"They ignored me! Did you see that?" said Ilya, who was now pacing the floor.

Larisa sank into a chair and Talanov sat beside her. Larisa leaned her head against Talanov's shoulder.

"What now?" asked Larisa.

"We wait," Talanov replied.

"This is unacceptable!" protested Ilya, still pacing the room. "I refuse to be treated this way. I am here on official business!"

After nearly fifteen minutes, the door opened and Calvin stepped into the room. "You, come with me," he said, pointing at Talanov.

Talanov squeezed Larisa's hand reassuringly and went with Calvin. Before the door clicked shut, he looked back and smiled. A teary-eyed Larisa did not smile back. Talanov followed Calvin along a corridor past several uniformed guards, who stopped talking when they approached. "Where are you taking me?" he asked.

Without answering, Calvin led the way to a door. This time there was no digital reader. This door had a handle, which Calvin used. "In here," he said, opening the door.

The room was like all the interrogation rooms Talanov had seen on TV. It had gray walls and a large one-way mirror in the middle of the far wall. In the center of the room was a table and several chairs, except in this case, there was a man seated in one of the chairs. Behind the man were two men in suits. On the table was a pitcher of water, some glasses, a selection of sandwiches, and a bottle of wine.

Talanov stared incredulously at the man.

"Hello, Alex," said Wilcox, standing. "Me? A wine snob? Seriously? I should have you deported for that."

CHAPTER 20

TALANOV could not believe eyes. Wilcox was *here?* He stared at him, wanting to say something but not knowing exactly what to say. His mind was a blizzard of questions and emotion, not all of which was pleasant.

"Aleksandr Talanov at a loss for words," Wilcox said, unscrewing the cap on the wine. "Hard to believe after the colorful scoldings you've been giving my colleagues. Come in, come in, have a seat. I remember your fondness for the rather peppery Shiraz, seeing as how you lived in Australia for many years. McLaren Vale, as you know, produces some of the best, as does the Coonawarra region of the Limestone Coast, although they're better known for their excellent Cabernet Sauvignon, which of course is my preference. So I compromised and found this wonderful blend. May I pour you a glass?" With the bottle in hand, he lifted a wine glass inquiringly.

"Was this your idea?" demanded Talanov, approaching the table.

Wilcox started to reply but Talanov cut him off.

"Your men dragged me through the airport in handcuffs! And who the hell is Connor Jax? I know he's one of yours, but why is he after me?"

When Talanov planted his hands confrontationally on the edge of the table, the men behind Wilcox stepped forward. They were big guys and they were armed, as evidenced by the slight bulges in their suit jackets, near their armpits. Which meant they were some of Wilcox's boys from the Agency.

"Sir, I need you to sit down," one of the agents said.

"I'll sit down when I'm ready," replied Talanov, who could tell the agents weren't military, judging by their posture and their lack of "presence," which was a euphemism for a whole host of indefinable military qualities related to alertness, edge, attitude, and precision. That meant they were university boys, fresh from the Farm and probably former football players or weight lifters, which accounted for their sloppy confidence and cocky attitude. Which didn't mean they weren't capable. They no doubt were. Otherwise, they wouldn't be here.

"And I'm telling you to sit down *now*," advised the agent.

Talanov looked back at Wilcox. "I believe I asked you a question."

"You asked me several, to be precise," said Wilcox, "which we shall get to in due course. Now, please, Alex, won't you sit down?" He sat, hoping Talanov would do the same.

"Why have I been marked?" demanded Talanov, still glaring at Wilcox from the front edge of the table.

"Sir, I need you to sit down," emphasized the agent.

Talanov ignored him. "Why have I been *marked?*" he demanded of Wilcox again. "Because Connor Jax *missed* me and killed my *wife!*"

"Sir, for the last time, I need you to sit down," the agent said, rounding one end of the table while his partner rounded the other.

Talanov leveled his eyes at the agent. "Was your wife the one who was killed?"

The agent said nothing.

"I didn't think so," said Talanov.

"Alex, will you *please* calm down?" said Wilcox calmly. "We didn't kill your wife."

"Yes, you *did!*" shouted Talanov, jabbing a finger at Wilcox. "Connor Jax tried killing me and shot her by mistake."

"Will you *please* listen to me?" said Wilcox, sitting forward for emphasis. "We did *not* kill your wife, and we are not trying to kill you."

"I saw the report!" yelled Talanov, slamming his palm on the table. "Connor Jax works for *you!*"

"Sit down!" commanded the agent, grabbing Talanov by the arm.

Most people would have tried pulling away. It was a natural reaction to resist that way and the agent was trained and ready for such a reaction. But Talanov did not respond that way. He tucked his shoulder, spun into the agent and flipped him over his shoulder. When the agent was high overhead, Talanov plunged a hand inside the agent's suit jacket and grabbed his SIG P226. The agent catapulted away from Talanov into the other agent, leaving the pistol in Talanov's hand. Both men crashed to the floor and scrambled to untangle themselves, kicking and sliding and pushing until they finally found their footing. By the time they had clambered to their feet, Talanov had already unloaded the SIG and tossed it on the floor.

The other agent whipped out his gun but Wilcox held up a hand.

"Alex, *please!*" pleaded Wilcox. "Sit down and have a drink. It will make everyone feel much better knowing you are not going to vault the table and attack me."

"The thought did cross my mind."

Wilcox gestured to one of the chairs. Talanov glared at Wilcox for several seconds then pulled out the chair and sat, his eyes never leaving Wilcox, who looked much the same. He had always been bald, but his beard was now grayer, his face more lined, and his stomach much more pronounced.

"Thank you," said Wilcox with a sigh of relief. He again held up the wine bottle inquiringly.

"Coffee," said Talanov. "Black."

Wilcox looked hurt. "But I bought this for you."

Talanov folded his arms and said nothing. Wilcox shrugged agreeably and held up two fingers to one of his agents. The agent left just as a knock sounded on the door. Talanov swiveled in time to see Larisa being shown into the room by Calvin, who then closed the door.

Talanov whirled toward Wilcox. "What the hell are you *doing?*" he said in a low voice.

But Wilcox didn't hear him because he was staring at Larisa, who was standing near the door, unsure what to do. He had seen her on the CCTV, while she waited in the holding room, but in the flesh she was truly stunning. He had seen lots of beautiful women in his time and, on occasion, had seen exceptional women. Larisa was exceptional. In fact, she was more than exceptional. Tousled blonde hair, slender ankles, gorgeous legs, and hips you just wanted to grab with both hands and caress all the way up to those two voluptuous, perfect—

"*Wilcox!*" Talanov whispered harshly.

Wilcox blinked and refocused. "Of course, yes, come in, my dear, and have a seat," he said, glancing uneasily at Talanov before smiling warmly at Larisa. He gestured to the chair next to Talanov. Larisa nodded, hurried over and sat.

"Hey," said Talanov with a smile.

"Hey," Larisa replied.

"She should hear what we have to say," Wilcox explained while Talanov threw him a disapproving glance.

"What is going on?" Larisa asked, looking at Talanov, then at Wilcox, then at the large agent standing behind Wilcox.

"Larisa, meet Bill, an old friend," Talanov replied. "Bill's with the government. He's helping us out."

"You can keep us from being deported?" Larisa asked eagerly.

"I'll do my best," answered Wilcox, working hard to keep his eyes from drifting down to her breasts. "Would you care for a sandwich? Some wine?"

Larisa pointed to a sandwich, which Wilcox unwrapped while apologizing for the rough treatment they had endured. It was not entirely his fault, he hastened to add just as a carafe of coffee and several mugs were brought in. Matters were already spiraling out of control by the time he had learned Alex had been trying to reach him. And, yes, the company switchboard was being manned by young brainiacs who spoke six languages but possessed little common sense.

"That's an understatement," muttered Talanov.

"These aren't the old days," Wilcox replied.

Talanov poured two mugs of coffee and gave one to Larisa. "All right," he said, looking at Wilcox, "start talking. Who the hell is Connor Jax?"

Wilcox filled a glass with wine. "No pleasantries after all these years?"

"I'm not in the mood. Now, who is Connor Jax? I saw your leaked report saying Jax works for you, and that his fingerprint was found on the shell casing used to kill my wife, with an identical fingerprint found at the murder scene of an FSB captain in Moscow, which is why Russian State Security is involved."

Wilcox started to reply but Talanov cut him off with a demand to know how a trained CIA assassin could miss such an easy shot. "Me as a target, I can understand," continued Talanov. "Well, actually, no, I can't. I can't begin to understand why you'd want to kill me after all I did. But you didn't kill me. You killed my wife. You killed *an innocent woman.*"

Wilcox again assured Talanov the CIA was not trying to kill him.

"Then who is Connor Jax?" said Talanov.

"I'm not able to speak to that," answered Wilcox after a sip of wine. "But he didn't kill your wife. That I promise."

"Why the hell should I believe you? I've seen evidence to the contrary."

"It's false information."

"In what way?"

"I'm not able to speak to that."

"Not good enough, Bill. In fact, it's nowhere *near* good enough. I want his head on a platter. My wife is dead because of him. *She died in my arms.* And I've read what looks like credible evidence that Connor Jax – who is one of your guys – is responsible. And here you are, asking me to believe the CIA had nothing to do with it. But when I ask for elaboration, you say you can't speak to that. That tells me you've got something to hide. That tells me you're protecting an asset."

"I'm sorry, really, I am, and I wish I could explain, but I can't. You know how it is."

"I *don't* know how it is. Now, who the hell is Connor Jax? You *owe* me an explanation!"

"Look, we go back a lot of years. Enough for you to know that I would tell you if I could. But I can't. Do you hear me? I *can't.* But I can tell you this and I swear it's the truth: we are *not* trying to kill you. And we did *not* kill your wife. You have my word."

Talanov had been carefully scrutinizing every micro-expression while Wilcox talked: muscle movements, pupils, nostrils, overall body language and breathing. Wilcox was telling the truth.

Larisa raised her hand, as if she were in a classroom, and Talanov and Wilcox both looked at her. "What if Alex was not the target?" she asked.

"Who else would it be?" growled Talanov.

Larisa shrank back slightly and averted her eyes, not wanting to speak the obvious and irritate Talanov further.

Talanov swiveled and faced Larisa directly. "You think the killer was after *Andrea?*"

Larisa shrugged.

"That is absurd!" exclaimed Talanov.

"I think it is something you have not considered," Larisa replied quietly.

"It makes *no sense* that someone would want to kill my wife. She was a *caterer.* She had no enemies."

"What if it had nothing to do with her personally, but she was still the target," offered Wilcox after another sip.

"What the hell does *that* mean?"

"I don't know. But Larisa raises a valid point and I think we should consider it."

"You're stalling and evading," declared Talanov.

"No, I'm not."

"Yes, you are. You're trying to get out of telling me the truth."

"The truth is, Alex, if we were trying to kill you, especially from that range, you'd be dead. For another, we would never have been so careless as to leave a fingerprint on a shell casing."

"The casing was forty-five caliber."

"Which of course is the right caliber, but our people don't make those kinds of mistakes."

"You did this time."

"Did you hear a shot?"

"Yes! I was there, remember?"

"More evidence that it wasn't us. We would have used a long-barreled automatic rifle with an infrared laser and scope. The ammunition would have been subsonic, and the gunman would have used a silencer packed with Nomex strands. Due to special honing of the weapon, there would have been no mechanical sounds associated with the firing, so this, coupled with the silencer and subsonic velocity of the round, would have made the rifle entirely silent. So to repeat, if you heard a shot, then it wasn't us."

Talanov scowled and looked away.

"A shell casing was all that was found, is that correct?" asked Wilcox.

"No weapon was recovered, if that's what you mean," replied Talanov.

"Nor will they ever find one. But let's say one of ours had been used. It still could not be traced back to us because our specialty rifles have no manufacturer's markings. They have nothing – no markings, no bore, no anything or any sort – that identifies it as one of ours. Nor will anyone outside this room admit to us using such sanitized weaponry. So if word reaches me about this conversation, I'll know where it came from." Wilcox stared hard at Talanov and Larisa to let them know he wasn't kidding. "Plus," he continued, looking back at Talanov, "our rifles can be disassembled in seconds and packed away in a special case protected by a thermite self-destruct system. The complete unit weighs twenty-six pounds, and that's with everything. Scopes, tripod, weapon, ammunition, suppressor. If ever compromised, the whole case would be found in a burned and melted heap, which would further render it untraceable. Furthermore, our marksman would have had at least ten thousand rounds of practice before assignment to the field. So, to repeat, we would *not* have missed. It's as if somebody is wanting you to believe it's us, which, again, it's not."

"That's quite an explanation," said Talanov.

"Because it wasn't us," said Wilcox, finishing his wine. "Which is why I went to the trouble of bringing you here. To reassure you of that fact."

"So this whole deportation thing was nothing but an act?"

Wilcox nodded and smiled.

"Why didn't you just drive out to my house and tell me what's going on?" asked Talanov.

"Because you'd already gotten yourself into a right royal

mess with the LAPD, and by the time I became involved, thanks to your scathing phone call, I knew I had to act quickly. If you don't mind me saying, I think the deportation idea was rather clever."

Talanov raised an eyebrow skeptically.

"Are you sure you don't want some wine?" Wilcox asked, looking first at Talanov, then Larisa.

"An explanation is what I want," Talanov replied, leaning back in his chair.

"And you shall have one," Wilcox said. "Are you sure I can't pour you a glass?"

Talanov's impatient glare made Wilcox raise his hands in surrender and set the bottle aside. He then started at the beginning, when American Express reported the unauthorized purchase of a sniper rifle. When the police asked for the cardholder's name, Talanov's name was supplied, whereupon his driver's license details were located, whereupon his photo was recognized by the same officers from the nightclub – Diego and Carlos – who promptly organized a raid on his property.

"So that's how they found me?" said Talanov.

Wilcox nodded. "And by the time I got your message, operations to apprehend you were well underway, which meant I had to do something fast to keep you from being thrown into jail, where things would have gone from bad to worse. Really, Alex, threatening to call the media?"

"I needed to get your attention."

"Well, it worked. My old buddy, Calvin, was in on my plan, but because you kept mouthing off to his partner, he ended up having to take you by Arnie's Ammo Emporium."

"He was *lying.*"

"I know."

"What do you mean, you know?"

"Arnie works for the mob and the mob's been expanding their activities here in Los Angeles. We've had him under surveillance for quite some time, and when I say 'we,' I mean the JRIC – the Joint Regional Intelligence Center – which is comprised of us, the FBI, Homeland Security, and a whole range of state, regional, and local law enforcement agencies, including the LAPD. It's a cooperative between Federal, State, and local law enforcement on matters relating to terrorism and intelligence analysis. The question is why you're being set up."

"Any ideas?" asked Talanov.

"No. But I think I know someone who does."

"Who's that?"

"She happens to be sitting right next to you."

CHAPTER 21

TALK about dropping a bombshell, and Larisa looked as stunned as Talanov. She sat staring at Wilcox for five of the longest seconds on record, mouth open in shock, while Talanov sat staring at her for the same five seconds, mouth open in shock. Wilcox looked back and forth between them, watching their reactions.

The genuineness of a person's reaction can be determined by a composite of non-verbal clues called micro-gestures, which are beyond voluntary control. Taken together, these minute signals can indicate with a high degree of accuracy whether or not a person is lying, or what they are feeling.

Talanov's five-second reaction was easy to read. His first response had been shock and disbelief, which gave way to perplexity with the surfacing of several memories and recollections, which in turn gave way to disbelief of a different quality than the disbelief he felt at first. It was disbelief mixed with a suspicion that he had been betrayed.

Larisa's five-second reaction had likewise been easy to read. Her shock and disbelief were of a different nature than Talanov's – that of being discovered – which in turn gave way to fear.

Talanov read Larisa's face as accurately as Wilcox had. He shot forward in his chair, then slumped back and stared at her as the implication of her betrayal sank in. "You're working with them, aren't you?" he asked. "You're working with the mob!"

Larisa reached for Talanov's hand but he pulled away. "I tried telling you," she said, tears welling up. "Twice. But something always got in the way."

Talanov looked away bitterly.

"I did not know what they were going to do with your credit card and ID," she pleaded. "They told me what to do and I did it."

"I guess everything Ilya said about you was true. You're nothing but a cheap, thieving whore."

Larisa began to sob.

Impervious to the crying, Talanov looked at Wilcox. "How'd you find out?" he asked.

Wilcox watched Larisa sobbing for a moment and then said, "Once I became involved, I read everything the police had on file. Believing you were being set up but not knowing how or why, I ran traces on your bank transactions, internet usage, and phone calls."

"And?"

"During the time when you said you were asleep at home, after your rather exciting rescue from the hospital, two calls were made from your landline to a local number owned by the Russian mafia. Unfortunately, the recording was corrupted by what is no doubt a signal jammer at their end. They're a sophisticated lot, and careful. Nevertheless, the phone calls were made, and not once, but twice."

"You called them *twice?*" said Talanov, staring at Larisa.

"I wanted to tell you," she sobbed. "I tried, but something always happened. Please, I beg you to believe me."

"Believe you?" shouted Talanov, jumping to his feet. "How the hell can I believe you after what you just did?" He kicked his chair across the floor and it crashed into the wall.

Larisa's sobs had now turned to wails. She heaved uncontrollably, her head buried in her lap, her hair hanging loose and tangled.

Wilcox nodded for his men to leave and they looked at him, unsure. He nodded again and they left.

"You phoned them from my *home,*" Talanov railed, standing over her. "Everything you did was for *them!*"

"Not everything," Larisa cried, unable to look up at him.

"You picked me up in a nightclub. You drugged me and stole my wallet so that one of them could buy a sniper rifle and pin it on me. You then pretended to give a damn by bringing my wedding photo back. The good-hearted nurse. And then, while I slept, you *called* them. You called the Russian *mafia!*"

"I guess he's one KGB operative that didn't go over to the dark side," said congresswoman Diane Gustaves in the darkened observation room behind the one-way mirror. At fifty-six years old, Gustaves had streaked blonde hair that was swept back in a Washington power bob. Her designer slack suit reflected her prestige as Chair of the House Intelligence Committee. "Maybe we can use him after all."

"I don't trust him," said Jackson Teague, a bald-headed African-American who was the Acting Director of Operations for the CIA. Teague was fit for a man of forty-seven, with big arms courtesy of the Company gym. "He wasn't just a KGB operative. He was a colonel. A man trained to be our enemy and view us as *his* enemy. Yes, Wilcox recruited him as a spy back in the day. So that's good. But that was then. This is now. What's Talanov been doing since the Wall came down? How bitter is he that we didn't catch his wife's killer? How eager is he to blame us? There are too many unanswered questions for me to be comfortable offering him a position within our ranks."

"My thoughts, too," said Martin Posner, Assistant Director in Charge of the FBI's Los Angeles Field Office. He had thick hair that stood straight up, like a Shetland pony. Together with Gustaves and Teague, they formed the core of the oversight committee for the JRIC.

"Marcy, what do you think?" asked Teague.

Twenty-nine year-old Marcy Foley was Teague's assistant on the JRIC. She had short bleached-blonde hair that was almost white except for a crown of dark roots.

"I don't trust Talanov, either," she said. "He's a Russian and the Russians tried hacking our election. Who's to say he's not part of that network? Like a Trojan horse in our midst?"

"The Russians did not hack our election," said Teague. "That whole blame-the-Russians smokescreen was actually an inside job leaked through a hacker in France using a server in San Francisco."

"How come I haven't heard that?" asked Marcy.

"Because the evidentiary chain and names of the smoking guns have been classified, and I bring it up here only to dispel that ridiculous myth. My mistrust of Talanov resides on a whole different level."

"Copy that," said Marcy. "Even so, I question whether Wilcox should be in there with Talanov. In fact, should Wilcox be in Los Angeles at all?"

"Why shouldn't he be?" asked Posner.

"He's been deep cover for more than a year," answered Teague. "Off the grid completely, tracking the mob. Word is, they'd like him gone."

"Why didn't he say something?" asked Gustaves. "He didn't have to come to LA and blow his cover like this."

"He came because you're one of his favorites and he knows how important this organized crime convention of yours is," answered Teague. "Don't worry. Nobody knows he's here."

"Except now. Does our meeting here today compromise his cover?"

"It could," answered Teague, "which is why I tried talking him out of it. But Wilcox has always wanted to bring Talanov aboard in some capacity, so when Talanov phoned trying to get hold of him, he jumped at the chance to meet."

"So Wilcox trusts Talanov?" asked Gustaves.

"Completely," said Teague.

"Wilcox was Talanov's handler during the Cold War," said Posner. "He's biased."

"A bias formed because he knows Talanov better than any of us," Gustaves replied.

"There's the matter of that sniper rifle," said Marcy.

"I don't think there's any doubt that Talanov did *not* buy that rifle," Gustaves said. "Assuming the reports that I've read are correct."

"Agreed," conceded Teague, "but your efforts to take on the mafia have made you as much of a target as Wilcox already is. The purchase of that rifle using Talanov's ID suggests a hit's being planned, the timing of which is no coincidence given the fact that you're tonight's keynote speaker. We can't risk that somebody being you."

"Wilcox is the one who's been crippling their activities," said Gustaves, "along with you, I might add. Any one of us could be a target."

"You're the one who's been receiving death threats."

"Everybody on the Hill gets those."

"Don't play glib, Diane. You're the one who's been pushing to expand law enforcement's extraterritorial jurisdiction to investigate and prosecute organized crime activities around the world. Make no mistake, you're on their hit list, and I'm guessing they were hoping to assassinate you and pin it on Talanov, which would deflect blame back on the Russians. Relations with them are already strained to hysterical levels, so this would help ice that cake."

"All the more reason he'd want to help. To set things straight."

"We don't know that he'd even want to," said Posner, "or if he should. Many of his old buddies work for the mob. Who's to say he wouldn't turn against us and begin helping them? There's a growing nexus between organized crime and terrorism, especially with the Russians. We'd be jeopardizing national security by using Talanov."

"Come on, Martin," said Gustaves. "Talanov provided us with some of the most strategic intelligence of the Cold War. Not only that, during that time he supplied us with the names of countless KGB agents operating here and abroad, and he knows their terrorist operations like none of us do, especially with all the fresh faces we've been hiring out of university. They know theory, but Talanov was actually there. He knows *who* they trained, *how* they were trained, and where they are now. The very fact that there *is* a growing nexus between organized crime and terrorism means that he'd be a valuable asset."

"I just don't trust him," said Teague, his eyes on Talanov, who was standing over Larisa. "I don't trust him one bit."

"*Why?*" shouted Talanov on the other side of the one-way mirror. "What is it you people *want?*"

Larisa looked up at him with red, puffy eyes. When she spoke, her words were punctuated by sniffs and sobs. "They told me to steal your wallet. I do not know why. I did only what I was instructed to do. Then you returned to the nightclub for your wedding photo, and I see in your eyes how much she mean to you. So I bring wallet to you at hospital. See you running up hill. Take you to house. Stay there while you sleep."

"And while I slept you *called* them!"

Larisa again buried her faced in her hands.

"How could you *do* that?" he shouted. "I *trusted* you!"

"They have my family!" cried Larisa. "They say they will *kill* them if I do not do what they say. They post photos on wall, showing Gorsky with my mother or sister, smiling, like he is their friend. But he will *kill* them if I try to escape, or if I call police, or if I do not do what they say. So they tell me to steal your wallet and I do it. And I call them from your house because I have been gone for very long time and I am afraid what they will do. So I tell them where I am, and they say for me to stay and take care of you. To call them back and tell them how you are."

"Why do they care how I am? What do they want?"

"I do not know!"

Larisa buried her face in her hands again and continued weeping. They were deep, anguished sobs, from the very core of her being.

Behind the mirror, Marcy smiled. "I think I see an opportunity."

CHAPTER 22

MARCY conferred with the others in a discussion that took roughly three minutes. The consensus, however, was not unanimous because Gustaves had serious objections. But Martin Posner, who was in charge of the oversight committee, had the final say and he felt Marcy's plan was their best opportunity to penetrate the mob's operation in Los Angeles. That meant Wilcox needed to implement the plan since he was in the room with Talanov and Larisa. And since Wilcox worked for Teague, it was Teague who was asked to issue the order.

Teague contacted Wilcox over the intercom and Wilcox listened to the new directive by means of his wireless earpiece. The instruction took fifteen seconds, and during the next fifteen seconds, the others watched Wilcox's reaction through the one-way mirror.

"Pursed lips," said Marcy, pointing. "He's imposing a non-reaction on himself. That means he doesn't like it."

"I don't like it, either," Gustaves said. "Tell him to stand by. We need to discuss the ethics of this further."

The order was relayed to Wilcox, who nodded imperceptibly.

"With respect, Madam Congresswoman," said Posner, "I think the question we should be asking is whether this plan will give us what we need given the urgency of the situation. I think it will."

"As do I," agreed Teague.

"My hesitation," said Posner, "is whether or not Wilcox can make it happen. Perhaps someone else needs to take over."

"He'll do what I tell him to do," answered Teague.

Posner looked over at Gustaves and said, "Madam Congresswoman, the JRIC is my committee, but you chair the House Intelligence Committee, so if push comes to shove, you can shut this down."

"It's your call, Martin. I won't interfere."

"Then let's do this," said Posner.

"Permission to proceed, then?" asked Marcy.

Teague gave her the nod before putting the intercom to his mouth. On the other side of the one-way mirror, Wilcox listened to the confirmation. The plan was a go.

Talanov had been pacing the room while Larisa continued to cry. Wilcox invited Talanov to sit. Talanov did not want to sit. He wanted to destroy something. Wilcox pointed out the obvious, that destroying something would accomplish nothing, and again asked him to sit. With a huff, Talanov pulled back the chair and sat just as the door opened and Marcy entered the room. Talanov and Larisa both looked to see who had arrived.

"My dear, this is Agent Foley," Wilcox said to Larisa. "She'll take you to the ladies' room so that you can freshen up."

With a stone-faced expression, Marcy came over and took Larisa by the arm. Larisa stood and looked tearfully at Talanov, who refused to make eye contact. And with a dejected sigh, Larisa turned and left with Marcy.

On the other side of the one-way mirror, Martin Posner smiled. Everything was going as Marcy had said it would. Larisa had been removed from the room without the slightest objection from Talanov, which meant they had managed to separate the two without alerting Talanov to what they were doing. Larisa could now be turned against him.

When the door to the interrogation room clicked shut, Wilcox again offered Talanov some wine. Talanov again declined. So Wilcox refilled his own glass. He knew Talanov was too angry to have noticed what he had noticed, which made saying what he had to say all the more difficult.

And yet it also made it easier, because Talanov would never know how much Larisa really cared. Wilcox had seen it in her eyes. As expected, she was shocked at being discovered. She then showed fear – again, a normal response – after which she showed something completely unexpected – shame – especially when Talanov was staring at her with open disbelief. In other words, she cared about Talanov and what he thought. And she cared that she had hurt him.

Yes, Larisa was genuinely ashamed, even though she had had no choice because of the threats against her family. If she had been willingly complicit, she would have shown contempt. He'd seen that reaction on many occasions. But not shame. Nor would she have been sitting here crying her eyes out all this time. He'd seen enough fake tears to know the real thing when he saw it. This girl was crushed, as if an earthquake had rattled the foundations of her world and she was powerless to keep it from crushing her.

Wilcox had also seen how hurt Talanov was. The intensity of his reaction had been an indication of just how much he cared for her, too. It also showed that he did not want to admit that fact to anyone, especially himself.

Which made turning him against her all the more difficult. Finding someone to care for you in this world was hard enough, let alone in their particular line of work. He should know. He had ruined every relationship in his own miserable life. But this was not about him. It was about Talanov. And they needed him without any baggage.

Baggage. Wilcox was disgusted with himself for using the word in reference to Larisa. But that's what the committee thought of her, which was a sad testimony as to how far they would stoop to get what they wanted. But priorities were priorities, which meant he had a job to do.

"In truth, it's just as well," Wilcox said, taking a sip of his wine. "I can't believe what she did."

Talanov did not reply.

"She played you, Alex, and I'm sorry. But you should have known better. I mean, honestly, a hooker? A pretty one, yes, but a *hooker?*"

Talanov looked away bitterly.

"The mob traffics them into the US," Wilcox continued. "Some come here by choice, most through some sort of a scam. The mob then turns them into money-making machines, and those girls will do anything they're told to do, including what happened to you. Bottom line: I did you a favor."

Talanov folded his arms and looked hard at Wilcox, who

hoped Talanov was not reading his micro-expressions. He had to play it carefully here.

"I can tell you liked her," Wilcox said. "So did I. She has a certain something that catches you off guard. A certain innocent quality, at least on the surface. But deep down, her loyalty's with the mob, and, like it or not, she belongs to them, and she will continue to do anything and everything they tell her to do. My advice is to forget her. In spite of what the movies lead us to believe, fairytales like this never have happy endings."

Wilcox then laughed to avoid the heat of Talanov's stare.

"Not that I'm much of an expert when it comes to relationships," Wilcox continued affably, leaning back. "The CIA is murder on your health, brutal on marriage, and a lot of us drink too much. Look at me. Three wives. And three houses that I'm paying for and don't own." He shook his head. "Hell, number three bought a Ducati and used it to run off with my lawyer on a cross-country romp. No wonder there are so many lawyer jokes. Never mind that one of my exes happens to actually *be* a lawyer. I learned real fast about assets and liabilities. So, as much as I enjoy the fair sex for a weekend fling ..."

"Enough with the sales pitch, all right?"

"I'm merely reminding you of the facts."

"I don't need to be reminded. I get it."

"Do you?"

"Yes, I do."

"I'm not so sure. That's why you're sitting there glaring at me. You're pissed off that I burst your bubble. She *betrayed* you, Alex. She works for the mob. She called them from your house while you were asleep, and she's been doing what they tell her to do. Look, if the stakes weren't so high, I'd say go for it. Have your little fling. You deserve to mourn and get wasted after what happened to your wife. But this hooker you picked up – who picked *you* up – did it to steal your credit card and ID, which she then handed to the mafia, who used them to buy a sniper rifle. You're being set up! This may not bother you but it bothers me. I don't know who they're planning to kill, but I've got to find out and stop them. And right now, your hooker friend is the only lead that we've got."

"Isn't this a domestic issue? How come the FBI isn't taking the lead?"

"They are. I'm here because you and I go back a lot of years, and right now you need a friend."

"Maybe Larisa needs a friend, too."

"Oh, *please*. Why do you care about her, anyway? She's a *prostitute*. Who works for the mob."

"And you know as well as I do why that is. She was trying to save her family. I never had any family to save other than a wife I never learned to love. And she took a bullet in the neck. And her blood kept pumping through my fingers until there wasn't any of it left. So I'm not about to crucify Larisa for trying to save her family. You got anyone who would do that for you? Who would do whatever it took to save your ass?"

Wilcox did not reply. He wished he could reply, but he couldn't. That's because Talanov was right. There was no one. His wives had all left him. His son wanted nothing to do with him. He didn't even have a best friend apart from the man sitting across from him right now. A man he was cheating and deceiving while looking him in the eye. A man who trusted him. The loneliness and depravity of it all was one reason he *did* drink so much. And now, here he was, trying to destroy another person's chance at happiness with someone who genuinely cared. Teague, of course, had given the order. He could have raised an objection, but he hadn't. Moments ago, he had told Talanov how he needed a friend. Was this what a friend would do?

Unfortunately, the CIA was not in the business of making friends. They were in the business of achieving objectives. And the objective here was to recruit Talanov for the JRIC. Still, what Alex had said was true. He had no one.

"Me neither," said Talanov, reading the truth in Wilcox's eyes. "I've got nobody. Do you hear me? Nobody. But I have the feeling there's a lot more going on here than what you're letting on. What are you hiding? What are you not telling me?"

Wilcox decided the best defense was a strong offense. He remembered this from his football days. "I could say the same about you," he replied firmly. "A lot of people are wondering what *you're* hiding."

Talanov glanced quickly at the one-say mirror, then back at Wilcox. When he did, he saw Wilcox's pupils dilate briefly. Saw him inhale and hold it for an instant. With a cold smile, Talanov stood and walked to the mirror. He cupped his hand on the glass and peered into it.

"Can he see us?" Gustaves whispered, instinctively stepping back.

Posner responded with a finger to his lips.

"Who's back there?" demanded Talanov. "CIA? FBI? DHS?" He turned away from the mirror and came back over to Wilcox, where he leaned down and stared directly into his eyes. "You're hiding something, Bill, and one way or another, you're going to tell me what it is."

CHAPTER 23

LARISA finished washing her face and Marcy handed her a paper towel. "I know you're in a hard spot," Marcy said. "The Russian mafia's got you by the neck and you don't see any way out." Larisa nodded despondently and Marcy touched her gently on the arm. "Don't worry, I can help. But I need to set you straight."

"Set me straight? I do not know what you mean."

"Talanov's Russian. Former KGB, in case you didn't know. We've got a file on him a foot thick. Men like that have hearts of stone. It's who they are. It's why they're so good at their jobs. It's also what got Talanov's wife killed, in case you didn't know that, either. She loved him. He didn't love her. And after she gets killed by someone trying to kill him, he hooks up with you. Is that the kind of man you want to fall in love with?"

"I do not think that is correct," answered Larisa. "It has been a year since the death of his wife. He has been sick with grief."

"Point is, what if the same thing happens again? He's still got enemies, you know, and they're liable to come after you."

Larisa did not reply.

"Look, if the romantic side of you thinks Talanov is different, *he isn't*. Do you get that? He isn't. If something happens to you – you get old, lose your looks, lose your *life* – he'll move on. It'll be like you never existed."

Larisa looked away thoughtfully just as a woman came into the bathroom.

"Beat it, we're closed," said Marcy. The woman spun on her heel and left. Marcy turned back to Larisa and placed a consoling hand on her shoulder. "Men like Talanov don't care what happens to people like you and me."

"I do not believe you."

"Don't get me wrong. Men like Talanov have their uses. Like I said, it's why he's so good at his job. Do you know how many people he's killed?"

"He has *killed* people?" Larisa asked, bringing a hand to her mouth.

"Again, don't get me wrong. He was attacked – in East Germany, smuggling a family of Soviet Jews into the West – six kids and their parents – and a team of KGB agents was after them. By then, Talanov was helping us, but the KGB didn't know that. So when they were caught and two of the children were shot, one of whom would later die, Talanov doubled-back and took the agents out bare-handed, one man against three highly trained men. He was wounded, but not before killing all three. Why am I telling you this? I'm telling you because killing people hardens you. And that's only one of a dozen instances. I know because I've read his file. Who knows how many other unrecorded instances there are?"

"But he was helping people, and like you say, he was attacked."

"He's a hardened killer, Larisa! Not the kind of guy that works nine-to-five and coaches Little League. The best thing you can do is forget him. Forget him and let me help you."

"Help me how?"

"I'm part of an interagency task force that wants to put a stop to the mob's organized crime activities in the United States, in particular, here in Los Angeles. In other words, we want to break their necks before they break yours."

"There is nothing you can do. My family is in Ukraine and I am here."

"Yes, there is. Once we take down the mob here in LA, the whole chain of command falls apart. You and your family will no longer be in danger."

Larisa looked warily at Marcy. "What would I have to do?"

"Are you willing to forget Talanov and not see him again?"

"Why is that necessary?"

With a reprimanding glare, Marcy pointed in the general direction of the interrogation room. "Did you see the way he treated you? Kicking chairs and yelling like that? Do you seriously want a man around who treats you that way?"

"He thinks I betrayed him."

"Just because he didn't get his way doesn't mean he has a

right to treat you like that. You of all people should understand what I'm talking about. Look at the way men use you. It's unforgiveable. Not only that, Talanov's a Russian. He's no different than the Russians threatening your family and the Russians who forced you into prostitution. Ukrainians have been bullied by Russians for centuries."

"Alex is not like that."

"Yes, he is."

"No, he is not."

"Will you shut up and listen to me?" shouted Marcy, causing Larisa to shrink back. "He's using you and he'll use you again. Men like that are animals. They use women for their own selfish purposes and their own gluttonous appetites."

Larisa stood leaning against the counter with her head lowered, looking at the floor while Marcy stood facing her, seething, hands on her hips, lips pinched so tightly they were drained of color.

"He is not like that," Larisa said softly.

"Yes, he *is*, you stupid—"

Marcy stopped mid-sentence, and with a growl of frustration, raked a hand through her hair and began pacing the floor. Larisa watched her take several deep breaths to calm herself before rolling her shoulders and coming back to her with imposed control.

"I said I was willing to help you and I will," Marcy said, placing a hand on each of Larisa's shoulders. "But it has to be on my terms. And my terms do not include a former KGB agent who has friends in the Russian mafia. Fact is, we don't trust Talanov. But we trust you. What you need to decide right here and now is whether a man who uses and mistreats you is worth the lives of your family."

Larisa stepped past Marcy and threw her paper towel in the trash. "Alex was furious because he thought I betrayed him. And I did. I had no choice, but I did betray him to try and save my family. But you yell and call me stupid, and I have done nothing to you. You say men want to use me – that Alex wants to use me – but you are no different. You dangle the safety of my family in front of me because you want me to help you. Your assistance has strings attached. Alex is a good man. The best man I have ever known. He has principles that you and I do not have. So if you want me to help you, then it will be on *my* terms. And the first thing you will do is apologize."

"*Apologize?* Listen, you worthless whore!"

Tensions can escalate to actual combat in various stages. Accusations escalates to finger pointing, and then pushing, back and forth. That is not what happened here. This time Larisa threw a punch. No warning, no name calling, no baring of claws. Just an unannounced right hook that caught Marcy beneath the eye and knocked her into a toilet stall, where she lay sprawled and dazed. Larisa stepped over to the sink and pulled several paper towels from the dispenser. She soaked them in water and handed them to Marcy, who was struggling to her feet.

"Where the hell did you learn to throw a punch like that?" asked Marcy, accepting the wet towels. She held them to her eye then stepped over to the mirror to inspect the damage.

"Do not ever talk about Alex that way again," Larisa replied. "And you will apologize to me for what you said."

Marcy scowled angrily at Larisa. Folding her arms, Larisa raised an eyebrow expectantly.

"All right, I'm sorry," growled Marcy.

"Good. I will help you now. What do you want me to do?"

CHAPTER 24

SQUIRMING in the heat of Talanov's glare, Wilcox felt like fresh meat to a predator. To make matters worse, he knew the committee was watching him from behind the one-way mirror. And what they were seeing did not look good. Talanov had taken control.

"I think I need a drink," Wilcox said.

"You've been drinking for the better part of an hour."

"Something with a little more kick."

Talanov scrutinized Wilcox for a moment. The old fox had a look in his eye that said he needed to talk. And not here. "I take it you're buying?"

"I just saved you from being deported. I'd think you'd be a little more appreciative."

"Appreciative of what, exactly? Being dragged out of my house? Being dragged through the airport in handcuffs? You're buying. End of story."

"Ungrateful."

"Cheap."

"Bully."

"What about my friend from the FSB? He's been waiting over an hour and is probably climbing the walls since it's a no-smoking zone."

"You've got friends in the FSB?"

Talanov laughed. "Acquaintances, yes. Friends, probably not. They guy you're still holding out there – Ilya Filishkin – I remember from the old days, when he was coming up through the ranks. Back then, the KGB was training snipers to take out people like you. Then the Wall came down and everything changed. I left. He stuck around."

"Why didn't you stick around?"

"I think you know the answer to that. KGB, FSK, FSB. Different acronyms but still the same. I wanted nothing to do with them. Period."

"Do you trust him?"

"Why do you ask?"

"Because if Ilya's trustworthy, a man in his position could be very useful."

"Useful how? What exactly are you doing these days?"

"A little of this, a little of that."

Talanov stared hard at Wilcox. It was a reprimanding stare and Wilcox raised his hands in surrender. "All right, all right. Don't yell at me with that look. I've been living in Cyprus the last few years."

"And you flew in just to see me?"

"Don't flatter yourself. I'm in town because my boss and I are briefing our congressional delegate to the Regional Congress on Organized Crime Prevention."

"Briefing them on what?"

"The Russian mafia, who, as you know, operate out of Cyprus."

"And you were in Cyprus because?"

"I was doing undercover surveillance."

"On?"

"Their shipments of nuclear materials and weapons, as well money laundering and drugs as they relate to the financing and supplying of terrorist activities. The mob's become a major player, not only in these departments but also in human trafficking, which generates billions in revenue. They make more money trafficking humans than they do weapons, if you can believe that. So we're starting to pay attention. Which means a man in Ilya's position could be invaluable. The mob has infiltrated the Russian government, particularly the FSB. Ilya could tell us who they are and help us penetrate their activities from the inside."

"Why would he want to do that?"

"Because I'd make it worth his while. Obviously, we'd check him out. Every now and then, we come across a decent Russian."

Talanov chuckled and said, "Speaking of which, there's something else I'd like checked out."

"What's that?"

"Ilya says Connor Jax killed his boss, Ivan Moroshkin, who

was an old colleague of mine. I read Ilya's reports but would still like your people to find out what actually happened. Ivan was a good guy. One of the honest ones."

"Already on it," said Wilcox. "I scanned everything Ilya had with him after we confiscated his files back at your house. They've been copied and sent to Charlie."

"Who's Charlie?"

"Charunetra Suri – Charlie – my technical analyst at Langley."

"Indian?"

Wilcox nodded. "Moved here with her parents when she was two. Computer geek. Speaks more languages than I can count. If she finds anything relevant, I'll let you know."

"Who determines what's relevant?" asked Talanov.

"You'll have to trust me on that."

"If Connor Jax is behind the killing of my wife, I won't let it go. You know that, don't you?"

"What exactly are you hoping to accomplish?"

"Justice would be nice, but I know it doesn't work that way. He's one of your assets and you're not about to admit he screwed up. I also know you're not going to just hand him over. So I'll probably have to do things my way."

"We didn't kill your wife."

"So you say."

"Look, I can understand your wanting to kill the man who did. But it wasn't us. You may think that's easy for me to say. After all, it wasn't my wife."

"You've got that right."

"And I know that. Believe me, I do. I've never been lucky enough to have what you had. I can't imagine losing the love of my life."

"That's just it. She wasn't. She should have been, and she deserved to be, but she wasn't. Simply put, I didn't know how. And I thought I had come to grips with that. But then her father showed up ready to blow my head off. Understandably, he blames me for what happened. His only daughter is dead."

"And?"

"I took the gun away from him and sent him back to Australia.

But it reminded me how I needed to put this right. To make Andrea's life count for something. So that's what I'm going to do."

"How do you plan to do that?"

"By killing the man who shot her."

"And you think that will, what, redeem you? Redeem her? Add meaning to her life? To yours?"

Talanov shrugged.

"Your wife's legacy is not dependent on you killing the guy who killed her. It's got nothing to do with that. Her legacy lives on in others. In the people whose lives were made better by the good things she did."

Wilcox kept talking but Talanov wasn't listening. He was thinking about Andrea's work at The Shelter and all of the kids she supported with her time and money. It had been her escape from the unfulfilled life she endured at home with him. He could still see her scrapbook full of photos. Andrea sitting in a group of smiling children. Andrea helping children learn to read and write beneath the palm trees of an outdoor classroom. Andrea comforting sick children in a medical clinic, some with sores, others with bandages or missing limbs. Andrea playing jump-rope on a dirt road with a group of girls.

"Have you been listening to me?" Wilcox asked after a long moment of silence.

Talanov refocused. "Have you been listening to *me?* Whoever killed her needs to pay."

"And he will," Wilcox replied. "All I'm saying is, don't do go after him thinking it's going to make everything right, or that it will make her life count for something. Her life already counts for something."

"She didn't deserve what she got."

"No, she didn't, which is why you and I do what we do."

"And Larisa. What about her?"

"She's being questioned."

"About what?"

"The mob. We need to figure out what they're planning to do with that rifle and why they wanted to pin it on you."

"I doubt she knows the answer to that. She was a pawn, nothing more."

"Which is why we're questioning her. We need to make sure. So, come on, let's go meet your buddy and see what he knows. Maybe he's interested in coming to work for the good guys."

"Are you serious? You want Ilya to come work for you?"

"The dynamic duo, Talanov and Ilya. You're the KGB veteran and he's in the FSB. Like I said, having someone in Moscow could be very useful. Naturally, Charlie's vetting him to see if he's on the level, but I'd like you to be there when we talk to him so that you can tell me what you think."

"I just met the guy."

"I thought you said you knew him."

"Once, maybe. Not now."

"What's your opinion so far?"

"That he's a jerk. He insulted Larisa but, to his credit, made it right. But that's after I threatened to break his legs."

"That's my boy," said Wilcox with a grin.

After motioning Talanov to follow, Wilcox led the way out of the room, down a corridor and through a locked door into the waiting room, where Ilya jumped to his feet. Wilcox introduced himself, apologized for the inconvenience, and reassured Ilya that he was not being deported. He then confessed how he had been forced to come up with a ruse in order to keep Talanov out of jail. When Ilya looked at Talanov for an explanation, Talanov said it was a long story and apologized again that Ilya had been swept up in the drama.

"So I am free to go?" asked Ilya.

"Unless you'd care to join us for a drink," Wilcox replied.

"You are serious? This is no trick?"

"No trick. You're free to go."

"Where is the girl?"

"She won't be joining us."

"She has been deported?"

"I really would like you to join us upstairs for a drink."

Ilya hesitated, unsure.

"He's on the level," Talanov said.

"To be fair," added Wilcox, "I'm hoping you can help fill in some blanks about the Russian mafia here in Los Angeles. But like I said, you're free to go."

"You are going with him?" Ilya asked Talanov.

"Absolutely. It's not often the old man opens up his wallet." Wilcox threw Talanov a scowl.

"I am not sure how much help I can be," said Ilya, "given you are no doubt more aware of their activities here than I."

Wilcox maintained a neutral expression and did not reply. A long moment of silence ensued.

"Naturally, I will help if I can," Ilya said with an agreeable nod.

"Wonderful," Wilcox replied. He signaled the security camera and a few seconds later, the door clicked open and Calvin appeared carrying Ilya's briefcase and two shallow gray plastic tubs, like the kind used in airport security. Calvin handed the briefcase back to Iyla, then allowed Talanov and Ilya to scoop their belongings out of the tubs. Ilya then asked if he could buy some cigarettes in one of the shops upstairs. Wilcox smiled and led the way to the elevator.

The concrete monolith that is Tom Bradley International Terminal has a soaring entrance of huge columns bracing massive girders and a flat roof that covered the loading and unloading zones. Cars nosed out of the steady crawl of traffic and into parking spaces under the watchful eyes of police. Departing passengers jumped from cars, yanked open trunks, and pulled luggage out onto the sidewalk.

While Ilya stood near the luggage carts smoking his second cigarette, a silver Chrysler inched out of the flow of traffic and parked next to the curb. The door of the Chrysler opened and Slam-D climbed out in a vibrating cloud of heavy *Gangsta Rap* music. He was dressed in a pair of baggy denim jeans, an oversized Lakers jersey, a sideways New York Yankees baseball cap, and enough gold bling to ballast a freighter.

After the trunk clicked open, a shapely black girl named Kono got out. She had a tiny waist, generous bust, and was dressed in red stilettos, a Killer Panda Hoodie, and skinny jeans that hugged her hips.

Slam-D strutted to the rear of the car and lifted the trunk. "Yo. Take care o' ma wheels," he said, lifting out two large suitcases.

"How long are you gonna be gone?" asked Kono.

Slam-D shrugged.

"The band's not happy. They want to know when you're gonna be back. *I* wanna know when you're gonna be back."

"Nunnaya concern, bitch," Slam-D replied, slamming the trunk. "Jus' make sure dat ya—"

"Going somewhere, Dennis?" asked a voice.

Slam-D whirled around to see Talanov standing directly behind him.

"Holy *shit!*" cried Slam-D, recoiling and almost falling over. "Who *are* you, man?"

"Your worst nightmare if you don't make that donation."

Talanov glanced at Kono, then at Slam-D, who was scrambling to get away. "You think there's a place on earth that I can't find you?" said Talanov in an icy voice. With eyes like lasers, he strode after Slam-D, who scrambled around the front of the car. "Try leaving town again and I *will* come after you." Talanov made a slicing gesture in front of his groin.

"Da trunk! *Open da trunk!*" shouted Slam-D. Kono reached inside the car and pressed a button. The trunk sprang open. Slam-D raced to the rear of the car, threw in his suitcases and slammed the lid. He then ran to the passenger door and jumped inside. "Get us outa here!" he yelled.

Talanov rounded the rear of the car just as Kono jumped in, cranked the wheel to the left and hit the gas.

"You're crazy, man!" shouted Slam-D as they peeled away. *"Crazy!"*

Talanov watched the Chrysler weave around several cars, squeal around the bend and disappear out of sight.

"What the hell was that about?" asked Wilcox as Ilya approached.

"Redirecting one of LA's troubled youths," Talanov replied.

"He looked terrified. Does he know you from somewhere?"

"Not really," answered Talanov. "Let's go."

Wilcox led the way through the automatic doors into the cavernous interior of the terminal. In front of the various airline counters, long lines of people stood waiting with their luggage in roped-off lanes. High above, a large information board ticked over new departure times. At the far end of the terminal was an escalator leading up to a mezzanine food court.

"Where are we headed?" asked Talanov over the echoes of announcements about departing flights.

"Someplace quiet where we can talk."

"And eat, and drink," Talanov told Ilya. "Order whatever you want. Like I said, Wilcox is buying."

Ilya grinned. *"Znaet li on, skol'ko my p'em?"*

"Yes, I know how much Russians can drink," answered Wilcox. "And I can still deport you both."

"Oh, yeah, Wilcox speaks Russian," explained Talanov.

"Now you tell me," said Ilya.

CHAPTER 25

WITH Vic standing over him yelling insults in Russian, Nick bench pressed four-hundred-and-seventy-five pounds just as Borzakov strode into the club. Dressed in a slick gray suit, open shirt and the usual excessive jewelry, he looked out of place among the sweaty gym junkies working away on the chrome-plated equipment. Beyond the weight room was another room full of treadmills, stair steppers, elliptical trainers, and stationary bikes. On the wall were three flat screen television monitors featuring the latest news and celebrity gossip.

Wearing a tight Lycra tank top to highlight his sculpted physique, Nick jumped up from the bench and punched the air with a victorious shout. People throughout the gym barely glanced his way, not wanting to attract the volatile attention of the steroidal giants.

"Kiski, vse vy!" shouted Nick.

"Who are you calling a pussy, *Midget?"* retorted Vic, inflating his chest and stepping up to Nick. Vic was half an inch taller than the six-foot-four Nick and called him "Midget" because of that slight difference in height. The two men laughed and bumped chests, then slapped double high-fives.

"Get dressed, we have problems to take care of," said Borzakov, straightening his cuffs.

"We just started our workout," said Nick.

"I'm not paying you to work out," said Borzakov. "I'll meet you in the car." He turned and walked out of the club.

Taking care of problems was what Nick and Vic did. "Better than sex," was how both men described the exhilaration of inflicting pain on those who did not abide by their rules. They loved busting heads, breaking kneecaps, and blowing huge holes in chests with their forty-four caliber magnum Colt Anaconda revolvers, not that either of them got much sex. The larger the arms, the tinier the testicles. It was an unfortunate consequence of long-term steroid use.

The shower stall in the locker room was ten feet square and stylishly tiled, with a dozen shower heads located on three of the walls. The room was filled with hissing torrents of water and a group of men comparing views on the Lakers' chances. When Nick and Vic entered, the shower stall cleared in just under twenty seconds. Fifteen minutes later, Nick and Vic stepped out into the bright sunshine dressed in shiny bronze suits.

Borzakov was parked on the street in front of the club, which occupied three floors of a large contemporary warehouse. The entrance was like a funnel, with walls angling back to a glass door flanked by two mosaic mirrored columns and some palm trees. Traffic whooshed by as Nick and Vic approached the car.

Borzakov glanced at his two henchmen. They were stupid but useful because of their size and limited intelligence. Why they dressed the same was beyond him. "Have you got everything?" he asked.

Nick and Vic knew what he meant and Vic patted the bulge in his jacket where the Anaconda was holstered. "Ready to rock 'n' roll, baby."

Their first stop was to a sports-themed nightclub that had been robbed recently. Twice, actually, and within a matter of weeks, and not for money, either, but for the club's rather large cache of colorful methylenedioxymethamphetamine tablets, otherwise known as MDMA, or "ecstasy", which had been supplied to the owner by Borzakov.

The owner's name was Chad Harris, a former professional quarterback who had purchased the club after a series of shoulder injuries ended his career. A notorious party-boy throughout his college and professional days, Chad was more than happy to augment the club's income with some of Borzakov's colorful tablets. However, after the robberies, he found himself in the rather delicate position of owing Borzakov more than a quarter of a million dollars. And Borzakov was stopping by to discuss payment options.

The interior of club was dark and elegant. Chad loved the refined quality of brass and oak and the club was full of it in the form of tabletops, barstools, trimmings, and wall panels.

The bar itself was polished oak, with brass beer taps and piles of NFL throwaway coasters. Behind the bar were mirrored shelves full of gleaming bottles of liquor. Autographed photos of famous athletes adorned the walls, along with other sports memorabilia, including a bat once used by Babe Ruth and one of Jim Thorpe's medals.

Borzakov paused at the end of the bar to show his appreciation to the waitress who had phoned earlier to say Chad was in. He slipped five hundred dollars down her bra and gave her a kiss on the cheek. *"Krasivyĭ zhopa,"* he said, patting her on the bottom while Nick and Vic watched a touchdown being scored on one of a dozen television monitors mounted overhead. "When are you going to come work for me?"

"When are you gonna come work for *me?"* she countered while sticking wedges of lime into the necks of some Corona beer bottles.

Borzakov laughed. "That is what I like about you, *moya malen'kaya lisitsa."*

"What did you just call me?" she asked.

"Come by one night and I will show you."

"You are *so* bad," the waitress said, slapping him playfully on the chest before leaving with her tray of drinks.

Borzakov led the way upstairs but was stopped at the top by two bouncers. One was a former lineman for UCLA and the other was a local bodybuilder. They were big guys with short hair and enormous arms. Together, they formed a wall of muscle. "I am here to see Chad," said Borzakov.

"Chad's busy. Make an appointment."

"He does not return my calls," said Borzakov, adjusting his cuffs to reveal gold nugget cufflinks with embedded one-carat diamonds.

"Then I guess he don't want to see you."

"He probably does not. But I want to see him."

"Beat it, pal."

Borzakov shrugged and sighed. An instant later, Nick and Vic stepped around him with their Anacondas. The eight-inch gun barrels grabbed the immediate attention of the two bouncers.

"Whoa, there, pal, take it easy," the lineman said as he and the bodybuilder stepped back, their hands held up in surrender.

"Whoa there, *pal,*" mimicked Vic an instant before he smashed the butt of his Anaconda into the lineman's forehead. It dropped the big man where he stood. Vic watched him crumple backward to the floor with a thump, where he lay sprawled and bent.

"Break his legs," Borzakov said, again straightening his cuffs to make sure they were even.

With Nick's Anaconda pointed at his forehead, the bodybuilder watched Vic stomp the lineman's kneecaps. Snapping and popping noises could be heard as bones broke and joints were smashed.

"*Okay,* you made your point," the bodybuilder said, pointing to a door.

Borzakov smiled and headed for the door.

Nick motioned the bodybuilder over to a wall, where he punched him in the stomach, kneed him in the face, then pistol whipped him to the floor. "Whoa there, *pal,*" he said. He giggled and kicked the bodybuilder in the face, then followed Vic into Chad's office, where Borzakov was seating himself in front of Chad's desk.

"I'll pay, I swear I will," Chad said just as Nick and Vic strode to Borzakov's side holding the largest pistols he had ever seen. "A week, that's all I need. Some friends, they owe me money."

"You really should hire yourself decent protection," Borzakov replied. In fact, for signing over just forty-five percent of the club – and Borzakov happened to have a document in his pocket drawn up for that very purpose – Chad's debt would be forgiven. Completely. Not only that, Chad would also enjoy the protection of Borzakov and his organization, which of course meant no more thefts. How could Chad say no?

Chad knew he was in deep with these guys and it was about to get deeper. The mob would own him, but what could he do? "I could go maybe thirty percent," he said, attempting to sound in control like he was against the New York Jets the day he threw for six touchdowns. His perspiring forehead, however, reminded Chad that today was not one of those days.

Nick and Vic rounded the desk and stood on each side of Chad. Nick was on Chad's left and Vic was on his right. The Anacondas were still dangling from their hands.

"Chad, Chad, this is no time to be quibbling about points," said Borzakov with a smile so cold it could freeze an open-air flame.

Nick clasped Chad on the shoulder. It was the kind of gesture a good friend would give another good friend, except Nick let Chad know they weren't friends when he dug his fingers into the tiny hollow between the clavicle and trapezius muscle. Chad got the message, and less than a minute later, Borzakov was tucking the signed document inside his pocket.

"Where to next?" asked Vic as they climbed into their car.

"The apartment. We're sending home one of our girls."

Nick and Vic knew what that meant. When a girl had outlived her usefulness, she was "sent home." The process was usually quick and painless, except when they needed to teach the other girls a lesson or issue them a reminder. In cases like this, the girls would all be called in for a meeting, whereupon the intended victim would be pulled from the group, bound, and then hanged in front of the others so they could watch her writhe and twist inches from the floor until she was dead. It was an effective tactic to keep the others in line. And that's what would be happening today.

Vic opened the car door and Borzakov slid into the back seat. Vic shut the door and climbed into the front seat beside Nick, who was already behind the wheel. "Which one?" he asked as Nick pulled away from the curb and entered the flow of traffic.

"Larisa," answered Borzakov.

"The one who stole Talanov's ID?"

"Da. She has become a liability."

"What do you want us to do?"

"Make it a party the girls won't forget."

Nick grinned. "I like parties."

CHAPTER 26

WILCOX led the way upstairs to the Qantas club, which offered an atmosphere of tranquility away from the clamor of pedestrian traffic that filled the cavernous terminal. After showing his membership card to the smiling young woman at the counter, Wilcox signed Talanov and Ilya in as his guests.

"I come here to get away," Wilcox explained as they stepped around the partition and entered the club. "It's private, it's quiet, and it's in a sterile section of the airport. A great place to talk. Plus, the chef's an old friend who cooks me up a special platter each time I come in."

The club was a long L-shaped room with some curtained windows on one side. The windows overlooked the main concourse below. The floor space of the club was filled with stuffed chairs, couches, and small tables. A food and beverage buffet ran the length of one wall. A counter of internet computers ran along the other. At the far end was a fully stocked bar. On the wall above the bar were several flat screen televisions. Showers and bathrooms were off to the right.

Wilcox stuck his head in the kitchen for a quick word with the chef before leading the way to a quiet corner table, where the light was dim. Talanov sat on the couch, with his back to the wall. Wilcox and Ilya sat across from him.

"Help yourself to whatever you want to drink," said Wilcox.

Ilya went for Scotch, Talanov for coffee, and Wilcox for a bottle of wine. By the time they returned to the table, a platter of breakfast burritos had arrived. Accompanying it was a small platter of fresh fruit.

Ilya savored a long swallow of Scotch.

"I thought you'd have gone for the vodka," said Wilcox, sipping his wine.

"I get enough of that as it is," Ilya replied.

Wilcox laughed. "I guess you do. So tell me, how did you meet Alex?"

"By the time I was promoted to the First Chief Directorate under Gorbachev, *ledyanoĭ chelovek* – the ice man – was already a legend. I did not know him well, but I knew who he was and how he worked ... like a machine, seeing everything. The man was amazing. A genius."

"And ... with that I'll go visit the men's room," said Talanov, excusing himself from the table.

Once Talanov was gone, Ilya leaned forward and said, "No one could understand why Talanov did not come to work for the new Ministry of Security. A man of such skills and experience." He shook his head. "Yeltsin himself tried to recruit him and still he refused."

"Really?"

Ilya nodded. "Not that I blame him for choosing Australia. Plenty of sunshine, beautiful women, the beach. Besides, he had money, so why not? Not all of us had the luxury of such a choice."

Wilcox did not reply.

"May I ask you a question?" said Ilya.

"Of course."

"I had with me a number of police reports, which were confiscated by your men when we were taken into custody."

"The ones we returned to you downstairs?"

"Yes. They are with me now, in my briefcase."

"Is there a problem? Is something missing?"

"No, no, of course not," said Ilya. "But among those documents is what appears to be a leaked report from your CIA. At least that is what my superiors in Moscow told me, and they are the ones from whom I received this report."

Wilcox kept his expression neutral and said nothing.

Ilya squirmed slightly in the ensuing moment of silence. "I mention this," he said, "because the report specifies an assassin named Connor Jax. The report goes on to say how he works for the CIA. According to fingerprint records, it appears Connor Jax not only killed Talanov's wife, but also my boss and friend, Ivan Moroshkin."

Wilcox took a sip of his wine.

Ilya shuffled nervously and said, "Do you have a comment about this?"

"Not really."

"I am here to investigate whether or not this is true. That is why I flew all the way from Moscow. I need to figure out why Connor Jax killed my boss and tried to kill Alex, which, as we both know, resulted in the death of his wife. Surely there is some piece of vital information common to them both. Something they know. Some*one* they know."

"What do you think it is?"

"I am hoping you can tell me."

"I'm afraid I can't."

"Forgive me, for I know this is awkward, and believe me, I would not be asking if—"

"I can't help you, Ilya," Wilcox said firmly. "But I do need you to help me." He placed his wineglass on the table and leaned forward for emphasis. "Like I said downstairs, I need you to tell me about Russian mafia activities here in Los Angeles. Help me fill in the blanks."

Ilya started to reach for his cigarettes then settled back in his chair and rubbed his forehead, clearly uncomfortable.

"I can make this worth your while," said Wilcox, "and in the long run you may well get the answers you seek. But I first need something from you."

"What do you mean?"

"Who their leaders are. What their focus is. Which of your old colleagues went to work for them?"

Ilya deliberated for a moment than said, "Well, similar to the United States, where domestic and foreign intelligence activities are assigned to separate agencies, the Russian government has—"

"I know your history," Wilcox cut in, "and how the various directorates of the old KGB were morphed by Yeltsin into your domestic security agency, the FSK – now the FSB – and the SVR, your espionage agency. And let's not forget your buddies in the GRU, your foreign military intelligence directorate. I also know how organized crime began spreading like wildfire once Yeltsin's power began to erode. Which gets us to where we are today: in a huge stinking mess. What I need from you are names and details, such as where they are, who's linked to whom, and who's working both sides of the fence."

Ilya took a drink of his Scotch. "Is this an official request?"

"Unofficial. Off the books."

"You can appreciate that such information will be – how should I say – of a sensitive nature," he said, jiggling the ice in his glass, "and very difficult to obtain without attracting attention. If I were discovered to be helping the CIA, well, I think we both know what would happen."

"We're talking about a common enemy here, Ilya, as in organized crime groups that both our countries want to stop. Competing mafia groups fighting for control of the various black markets in drugs, weapons, nuclear materials, human trafficking, extortion, money laundering, assassination, and credit card fraud. The list goes on."

"I agree that our official interests are the same. Still, if I am caught passing sensitive information to the CIA, my career would be over. I could go to prison."

"We're not talking betrayal. We're talking inter-agency assistance."

Ilya didn't quite buy that description and his expression said so.

"Okay, so it's way off the books," admitted Wilcox, "but don't forget, someone did a favor for you."

"For me? What do you mean?"

Wilcox lowered his voice. "You came here with a leaked report from the CIA about an assassin named Connor Jax. That report came from within my agency. In other words, someone did you a favor by slipping you a copy. I'm asking for a favor in return."

Ilya stared at Wilcox for a long moment. "You place me in a difficult position. I cannot afford to lose this job."

"You won't."

"Compiling such a list would take time."

Wilcox handed Ilya one of his cards. "We need to move quickly on this. Call me as soon as you get something."

"But if something goes wrong. I am not a wealthy man."

"You could be," Wilcox replied as his cell phone rang. He looked at the caller ID just as Talanov returned to the table. "Sorry, I have to take this," he said, standing. "Where are you?" he asked, walking away.

"Almost there," Marcy replied from her government sedan. Larisa was in the front seat beside her and they were heading north on La Cienega Boulevard. There were dry hills on both sides and oil rigs dotting the landscape. "Incidentally, the bitch gave me a black eye."

"What?"

Marcy glanced over at Larisa, who was smiling while looking out the window at a cluster of rocker arms going up and down. "Yeah. She threw a punch that landed me face-up in a toilet stall. Don't worry, she's agreed to help."

"What happened?"

"I tried talking sense into her about Talanov. It didn't quite go as planned."

After listening to the rest of Marcy's recap, Wilcox told Marcy to call him when she arrived at their destination. He then ended the call and stood there for a moment, scratching his head with disbelief. *Larisa had punched Marcy.* Some people never ceased to surprise him.

Wilcox dialed another number that routed his call through the CIA's encrypted bandwidth in a constellation of satellites known as the Advanced Extremely High Frequency network, which was operated by the United States Air Force. It was answered on the second ring by Charlie. With her mane of thick raven hair tied back in a loose knot, the mocha-skinned beauty was sitting at a cluttered desk in her cubicle at Langley surrounded by several flat screen monitors. Beside her was a tall glass that held a liter of green vegetable juice. It had a bent straw sticking out of it. In a collapsed heap on the floor beside her lay an oversized handbag. A parachute could fit in the bag. It was shiny and black with chain straps and lots of zippers.

"Charlie, it's me," said Wilcox.

"How's LA?" Charlie asked.

"Those rumors about me and those actresses are not true."

"Everyone will be so disappointed."

"What have you found on Filishkin?"

"Heaps," said Charlie, her fingers flying over a keyboard. Within seconds, reports and verifications were layering onto her screen. Reading from highlighted sections, Charlie said, "Ilya appears to work in the Investigations Directorate, which combats corruption and organized crime, plus illegal trafficking in weapons and drugs."

"Appears to work, did you say?"

"He may also work for Directorate T, which is a special unit responsible for counterterrorism activities, including operations carried out against organized crime groups supplying arms to Russian separatists. He's also helps combat the illegal export of nuclear materials and technologies, including sporadic interrogation work for the Antiterrorism and Anti-Extremism Directorate. In short, he looks like a troubleshooter."

"What's his background?"

Charlie told him how Ilya came up through Department Thirteen, the most feared unit of the KGB, which to this day is not even officially recognized as having ever existed. This was followed by a number of stints in other directorates. Then, once the Soviet empire dissolved, he transitioned to the FSK and then the FSB, as it was restructured and renamed.

"So he's on the level?"

"Yes, sir."

"Good, because I've asked him to supply me with the names of Russian mafia leaders he knows and any people in the FSB who may be working both sides."

"Isn't that why you're recruiting Talanov?"

"Talanov doesn't know the inner workings of today's FSB. Ilya's there, in Moscow, in the middle of the action. He could become a valuable asset. Besides, he has what looks to be a leaked report from our Sensitive Compartmented Information Facility. I want to know where he got it. Anything yet on Ilya's boss?"

"Ivan Moroshkin was Ilya's captain in the Investigations

Directorate of the FSB. He was investigating the assassination of some British foreign agents in Moscow when he was murdered. I also found a link between Moroshkin and Talanov."

"What's that?"

"Moroshkin and Talanov were both in Directorate Nine back in the eighties, where they were assigned to protect the ailing Leonid Brezhnev after the poisoning of Fyodor Kulakov, Brezhnev's likely successor. This cleared the way for Andropov to step into the position once Brezhnev died. Andropov kept them on to protect him because he was impressed by their efficiency and honesty, even though many people thought Andropov was actually the one who poisoned Kulakov. When Talanov prevented a retaliatory attack on Andropov's life, Andropov promoted him to the First Chief Directorate, which is where he met Ilya. What I haven't found is a common denominator that would make Talanov and Moroshkin both targets. Like I said, Moroshkin was murdered while investigating those British agents, so the FSB thinks the British had the CIA kill Moroshkin as a favor to protect their agents. Ilya was said to be making all kinds of vows to track down and kill an assassin of ours named Connor Jax."

"Which explains why Ilya's here," said Wilcox just as a family of travelers entered the club. The parents pulled small suitcases on wheels and the kids carried brightly-colored backpacks of cartoon character material. "He believes Connor Jax works for us and that he's responsible for the murders of Moroshkin and Talanov's wife."

"And he's there to try and prove that?" asked Charlie.

"I think he's here to see if Talanov can give him any leads on Connor Jax. Who he is. Where he is. That sort of thing."

"Maybe he wants to swing Talanov over to his way of thinking – that we're the bad guys who murdered his wife – with the hopes of recruiting him into the FSB."

"I don't think Alex would go for that."

"Does he believe Ilya's story about Connor Jax?"

"I told him we weren't involved."

"Does he believe you?"

"He and I go back a lot of years and those years are friendly years, so – yes – I think he believes me. For the most part, anyway."

"What if he really does believe we killed his wife?"

"He may have some lingering doubts," answered Wilcox, "but that's all they would be, just doubts."

"How did he respond when you told him we weren't responsible?"

"He wasn't pleased. After all, I told him I couldn't elaborate on the evidence, meaning the leaked report on Connor Jax, which means he pretty much had to take my word for it."

"Would you know if Talanov was plotting some kind of revenge?"

"He was hell-bent on it for a while, but I think I changed his mind."

"With respect, sir, if you were able to talk him out of it, then someone else could talk him back in. Ilya aside, it could be anything that flips his switch. A mood swing, a reaction to something, a frustration that nothing's happening. What if he decides he needs to take matters into his own hands and – ding – he gets angry and you become his punching bag?"

"He wouldn't do something like that."

"He might if he thinks we killed his wife."

"A woman he says he didn't love. Besides, Talanov is not the emotional type. He's not the kind to suddenly explode."

"Something's driving him," said Charlie. "Look, you may have talked him into letting this slide for now, but the kind of atrocity he witnessed can eat at a person, hour after hour, in the dark of the night, when he's loneliest and alone. There's no way we can prove we didn't kill her."

"He has my word."

"Is that good enough? Is the strength of your word good enough against a leaked report that says otherwise?"

"There's not a lot else I can do."

"Yes, there is. You can tell him the truth."

CHAPTER 27

"YOU and Wilcox, how did you meet?" Ilya asked Talanov as the arriving family settled at a nearby table. The kids immediately dropped their backpacks and raced for the soft drinks. The mother scooted the backpacks under the table and hurried after them.

"What did Wilcox tell you?" asked Talanov, taking a bite of his burrito. It contained scrambled eggs, refried beans, fresh salsa, avocado, and cheese.

"Nothing," said Ilya, leaning closer and lowering his voice. "As you know, he wants me to supply him with information about Russian mob activities here in Los Angeles."

"Yeah?"

"Is he trying to – how do you say – recruit me?"

Talanov knew the danger in this line of questioning. Whatever noncommittal answer he gave, Ilya might respond by asking if Wilcox had recruited *him*. It was not out of the question that he already knew about a Cold War spy for America called November Echo. If someone within the CIA had leaked information about Connor Jax, then that same someone could have leaked information about November Echo. Or worse, could have leaked the truth that *he* was November Echo.

The fact that he had been able to move to Australia after the Cold War was evidence that he possessed the means to do so. Former colleagues had occasionally asked how he could afford such an affluent lifestyle, so it was natural for Ilya to wonder, too. An outright lie to Ilya's question would be visible on his face, even if Ilya did not possess the ability to fully interpret it. He needed to be careful about not giving anything away. How would Ilya respond if he discovered the truth? How would others in Moscow respond? Could this be the reason someone had tried to kill him but instead killed his wife?

Downstairs, Diane Gustaves was talking about the same thing with Jackson Teague and Martin Posner. The three were sitting around the same table in the interrogation room where Wilcox and Talanov had been. The wine bottle and glasses were gone. In their place was a carafe of freshly brewed coffee. Cups and small plates with half-eaten sandwiches were in random placement around the table. Notepads and copies of reports were scattered in disarray.

"Assuming it wasn't us, who's got a motive for wanting Talanov dead?" asked Gustaves. "We *can* make that assumption, can't we? That it wasn't us?" She looked over at Teague with one of those penetrating stares for which she was famous as Chairman of the House Intelligence Committee, known officially as the House Permanent Select Committee on Intelligence.

"It wasn't us," Teague replied. "To fill you in on what we know, the LAPD did find a forty-five caliber shell casing bearing an unknown fingerprint. IAFIS was not able to identify that fingerprint because it was buried in our Sensitive Compartmented Information Facility at Langley."

"But you're saying without question the CIA was not responsible for the death of Talanov's wife? You're telling me that?"

"Yes, ma'am."

"And the report. Is it genuine?" asked Gustaves.

"It has the appearance of being genuine," answered Teague, "meaning it has all the right markings and blackouts. But since I know without a doubt that we're not responsible for Mrs. Talanov's death, it's definitely a fake."

Gustaves raised a skeptical eyebrow.

"Where it came from and how someone put it together, I wish I could tell you," said Teague. "But at this point, I can't."

"You can't because you don't know, or you can't because the information is classified and you don't want to elaborate?"

"I can't because I don't know. And that's the truth."

Maintaining a neutral expression, Posner had busied himself with a sandwich during the exchange between Gustaves and Teague. That's because Gustaves would not hesitate to turn her congressional wrath on him if she smelled any signs of the competitive bickering and gloating that had divided the two agencies in the past.

Gustaves glanced at her watch. "I've got another hour."

"Then let's use that hour to pick this apart," said Teague. "Talanov's goal is to find who killed his wife. My goal is to find out *why* someone would want to kill her."

"How sure are you that she was the target and not him?"

"Pretty sure," answered Teague, "although we still can't figure out why. Once we know the answer to that, we can figure out who."

"Why on earth would she be the target?" asked Gustaves. "Talanov himself thought the idea was ludicrous, and I tend to agree. She was a caterer. She had no enemies."

"By all appearances, that's a logical assumption," said Posner. "But if someone wanted to get even with Talanov and simply missed, they would have had plenty of other chances to finish the job. But they haven't. And Talanov hasn't exactly been in hiding. To me, that suggests he wasn't the target."

"Then why would someone go to all the trouble of faking a report to make it look like we – meaning the CIA – were the culprits?" asked Gustaves. "Why go to all that trouble, with the fingerprints and all?"

"If someone knows Talanov was November Echo," answered Posner, "then they'd know about the long-standing relationship between him and CIA. By planting those fingerprints, they hope to sour that relationship, which sets up Talanov to be recruited back to Moscow to work for the FSB. Even if the FSB wasn't aware of his role as November Echo, they still gain by turning him against us, which explains the fabricated report."

"Is that why Ilya's here? To try and recruit him?"

"We heard for ourselves what Talanov thinks about the FSB," answered Teague. "He wants nothing to do with them. Plus, to our knowledge no one has tried to recruit him since the death of his wife, so I seriously doubt that's why Ilya is here."

"Unless he's that at hiding it," suggested Gustaves, sitting forward and placing her elbows on the table. "Maybe he's doing it in baby steps. Maybe he's trying to change Talanov's mind little by little. Let's say the FSB learns Talanov's wife has been killed and that he's now alone, and probably bitter. Remember, at first he was the prime suspect. Didn't the LAPD cause him all sorts of grief with accusations?"

Teague rifled through his documents and found a copy of the police report. "Yes, they did," he said, scanning the report. "It's all right here. Opinions, accusations, conclusions."

"Then the FSB would know all of that because the LAPD supplied them with a copy of their investigation report. In the name of cooperation and good will, of course, and the LAPD went along with it."

Teague tapped his pencil on his notepad. It was an annoying reality, but true.

"What do we know for sure?" asked Gustaves. "One: someone wanted to frame us to look like the bad guys, and to do that they fabricated a report that said the CIA killed Ilya's boss. Who was he again?"

"Ivan Moroshkin," said Teague, glancing at his notes.

"Two," Gustaves continued: "judging by the ballistics reports, the same person who killed Talanov's wife also killed Ivan Moroshkin, which means the two murders are somehow related."

"Actually, we don't know that," said Teague.

"What do you mean?" asked Gustaves. "We have the same fingerprint on two identical shell casings."

"Says a leaked report I know to be false," Teague replied. "We have two *murders* – that's undeniable – but they could in fact be totally unrelated, and to tell you the truth, I think they are. Obviously, somebody *wants* us to think they're related because of that fabricated report."

"And the only people who could have fabricated that report is the FSB," replied Gustaves.

"Don't you see, Jackson? The FSB *wants* us to look guilty so Talanov can be recruited back to Moscow to work with them."

"Either that or they want him to stay in LA to work for them," said Posner, "which explains why he moved here and why he wants citizenship. Ilya may well be his go-between with Moscow."

"We don't know that," said Teague.

"No, we don't, not yet," conceded Posner. "But it's certainly not out of the question."

"Given Talanov's service to this nation, I think it *is* out of the question. Plus, Wilcox trusts him like a brother and he knows Talanov better than all of us put together."

"Then why is Ilya here?"

"Personally, I think he's here to take down Connor Jax, or at least find out enough about him to launch some kind of vendetta. Or at least expose him. That's why he's sharing everything he knows with Talanov. He's hoping Talanov has information to share with him, or that Talanov knows someone who does."

"Like Wilcox?" asked Gustaves.

"It's not out of the question," answered Teague, "especially if knows Wilcox recruited Talanov. If so, he's hoping Talanov will milk Bill for some answers. What I still don't get is why this is all happening now."

"What do you mean?"

"The report about Connor Jax is fake. Why go to all this trouble for something you know is fake?"

"Maybe he's come here to kill Talanov. To finish the job."

"Then why hasn't he killed him, to put it bluntly? From what I understand, Ilya approached Talanov at his home late at night in order to show him reports pertaining to the murder of his wife. If Ilya were here to kill Talanov, he could have easily waited in the shadows and put a few bullets in his head. I think Ilya's being used."

"To what end and by whom?" asked Gustaves.

"That we don't yet know, because we don't know who fabricated that report."

"Could it have been us? As a ruse to bait the FSB?"

"Absolutely not," answered Teague. "Someone in Moscow fabricated that report, and leaked – or gave – it to Ilya, for what reason we don't yet know."

"Then if that report is definitely a fake," asked Gustaves, "who is Connor Jax?"

Teague swallowed hard but did not reply.

CHAPTER 28

THAT has to be it, thought Talanov upstairs. *The FSB knows Wilcox recruited me.*

"My friend," said Ilya. "You've obviously known Wilcox for some time. How you met him, I do not care. It is not my business. But you know him, so what should I do? He has asked me to provide him with information on the Russian mob. To tell you the truth, I would like to help. My government has been unable to stop them, in part because the mob's influence has penetrated the FSB, in part because we do not have the budget or manpower to pursue them effectively."

Talanov was genuinely surprised. Instead of snooping into the origins of his relationship with Wilcox, Ilya was actually considering Wilcox's offer.

"I think Wilcox can stop them," said Ilya with conviction.

Talanov saw Ilya make a fist, which affirmed that conviction. But Ilya's eyes were squinting slightly, which was a sign of evaluation and uncertainty, although sometimes squinting can indicate deception if the person is trying to masquerade that deception. His brow was furrowed thoughtfully, which was a sign of concentration. His eyes were moving back and forth, then up and down and to the right, which were signs of emotional wrestling, and possibly shiftiness. Overall, mostly good signs.

"I am not naive," Ilya continued. "I know the mob has friends in Washington, and that certain politicians are being blackmailed, or have been bought. But America still has a moral compass few other nations possess. There are many good people in here, people who want to do what is right, who take stands based on conscience and conviction. Wilcox, I think, is such a man. Do you agree?"

Talanov nodded and Ilya nodded in agreement, obviously relieved. A long moment of silence passed.

"This matter with Connor Jax," Ilya finally said. "Wilcox would not speak of it, which of course does not help my investigation. He is not easy to read. In fact, I could not read him at all."

"Join the club," said Talanov. "He swore the CIA had nothing to do with the murder of my wife, but when I tried pressing him on the matter, he wouldn't say anything more."

"Do you believe him about your wife?"

Talanov thought about what to say. All along, the big problem for him regarding CIA involvement had always been one of motive. There was simply no reason for them to kill him, much less his wife. This had been confirmed not so much by what Wilcox had said, but by his facial language. People can lie. Expressions don't. Even so, the issue of Connor Jax still nagged him. Had Jax gone rogue? If so, who had hired him? The Deep State? Was this why Wilcox was being so evasive? Wilcox was shrewd, and with him exact wording mattered, which may well explain the vague explanation he had given. If Connor Jax had indeed gone rogue, then by responding the way he had, Wilcox could truthfully deny CIA involvement.

"So you do not believe him?" asked Ilya in the absence of a reply.

"Actually, I do," Talanov replied, refocusing. "He's a good man. One of the best."

"Should I do it, then? Researching the kind of information he wants will take time."

"That's up to you."

"What would you do?" asked Ilya.

"If it were me, I'd help him any way that I could. I like what he stands for. Who he is."

Talanov suddenly realized he had said too much. It wouldn't take a mathematician to add two and two and figure out the obvious, that he had once done the same thing himself. *Divert him. Don't let him have time to think about what you just said.*

"Be warned, though," added Talanov quickly. "He's a horrible snob about wine. Much like you and chess."

"Me? You were the – how do you say – fanatic one. You had this unbelievable memory for strategy and why games were won and others were lost. No one had an analytical mind like yours."

"Except you," countered Talanov. "You would play an entire game in your mind. I remember those darting eyes moving around the board like you had had too much caffeine. Then, suddenly, you would say, 'Checkmate,' and not a single piece had been moved. What a showoff, and we all knew it."

"Look who is talking!" said Ilya with a laugh. "You were always the one to beat because you played so fast and made everyone nervous with that drilling ice-man stare."

Back and forth the two men bantered, so that when Wilcox returned five minutes later, he found them locked in friendly debate.

"What's going on?" asked Wilcox, sitting. "I could hear you two arguing all the way out in the foyer."

Ilya said, "Alex, the traitor, leans toward Bobby Fischer as the greatest player of all time. I, on the other hand, cannot decide whether it should be Kasparov, Karpov, Botvinnik, or Alekhine."

"Fischer won eleven out of eleven at the US Championships in 1963/64, which is the only perfect score in the history of the tournament. He also holds the modern record of twenty consecutive wins, having burst onto the world stage at the age of thirteen with his stunning Game of the Century, which is one of greatest contests of all time."

"I will allow you that one," said Ilya. "However—"

"Allow? What about Fischer's game in Reykjavik against Spassky, in seventy-two?"

"Granted, that Cold War game attracted lots of attention."

"It attracted more worldwide attention than any game before or after!"

"True," said Ilya, "but that game does not rank with the truly great ones."

"As you can tell," Talanov explained to a bewildered Wilcox, "my colleague here loves the classics. Petrov's Immortal, Greco's Game, the Opera Game, the Peruvian Immortal."

"You're kidding me, right?" said Wilcox. "You actually sit around and analyze this kind of stuff?"

"Chess is the ultimate game of strategy," Talanov explained.

"It requires one to outwit an enemy mentally before engaging that enemy physically."

"Yeah, well, your girl 'engaged' one of my agents. Seems Marcy made a remark about you that Larisa didn't like. So Larisa punched her in the chops."

"She did *what?*"

"Punched her in the face," said Wilcox with a chuckle. "Sent Marcy sprawling into a toilet stall."

"What did your agent say?"

"No idea. Whatever it was, Larisa didn't like it. Which means, I guess you were wrong."

"About what?"

"About having no one to stick up for you," said Wilcox. He chuckled again and shook his head with disbelief. "Who'd have guessed it would be someone like Larisa?"

Someone like Larisa. The remark made Talanov stiffen, especially when Wilcox imitated a right hook and said, "Pow! Hookers, one, Agency, zero." When Ilya laughed, Wilcox noticed Talanov glaring at him.

"Is your agent all right?" asked Ilya.

Talanov did not hear Wilcox's answer. His mind was replaying what Wilcox had told him earlier about Larisa and how he should forget her because she had played him. If that were the case, why had Larisa defended him by punching Marcy?

Slumping back in his seat, Talanov could see now what Wilcox had been doing. He had been exploiting Larisa's betrayal to turn him against her. Without a doubt, he *had* felt betrayed, mostly because he had felt a genuine connection with Larisa. Exactly what that connection was, he was not entirely sure, but it had been a lot more than a one-night stand. He looked over at Wilcox, who was making a point by tapping the palm of one hand with his index finger. Wilcox had always been one of the good guys. And yet Wilcox was also a Company guy who did what was best for the CIA, which was what he was doing right now. He was recruiting another asset. He was selling the benefits of Ilya's information to their mutual best interests. He was letting Ilya know about the good things that would happen as a result of his bravery and commitment to a higher good. It was marketing at its best. Yes, Wilcox was a salesman, and he had done his best to sell him on Larisa's betrayal. The question is: why? What was Wilcox not telling him?

"Speaking of which," Wilcox was saying when Talanov rejoined the conversation, "do you know anyone from the old days who might be living here in LA? Any of your old colleagues who may be working for the mob?"

Ilya thought for a moment. "I cannot think of anyone off the top of my scalp."

"Top of my head," said Wilcox. "And please don't ask me how someone came up with that saying."

Ilya laughed, swirled the last of the ice in his glass and drank the melt. He then paused with his glass in hand. "There is one man that I recall," he said. "He had a colleague named Gorsky, and after the Soviet empire crumbled, they began scamming rich Westerners – mostly Americans – into coming to Ukraine to find young brides. One thing led to another and they soon discovered there was a lot of money to be made trafficking young women into countries where beautiful young women were prized. Thailand, Japan, India, Western Europe, the United States, Turkey, Kuwait, Oman, Qatar, Saudi Arabia, and dozens of others. And I mean big money. Human trafficking has always been around, of course. They just took it to new heights. Or depths, I guess I should say. Several years ago, he was able to get a cultural exchange visa into the United States, and to my knowledge, has been here ever since. I knew him because we came through training together. He always bested me in marksmanship, although I did beat him once and he flew into a rage and stormed away."

"Anyone I know?" asked Talanov.

"Roman Borzakov," Ilya replied.

Talanov's mouth fell open. "Borzakov is *here?*"

"Do you know him?" asked Ilya.

"Yes! A sadistic killer. Cruel and ruthless. What's he doing in LA?"

"His partner, Gorsky, is running a trafficking operation out of Ukraine – Kherson, I think – so I would guess that is what Borzakov is also doing, but from here, at the other end."

"Did you say Kherson?" asked Talanov.

"Yes, why?"

"Larisa's from Kherson," he replied, shifting his focus onto Wilcox. "Did you know about this?" he asked.

"Know about what?" asked Wilcox.

"About Borzakov, dammit."

Wilcox averted his eyes.

"You *knew,* didn't you?" said Talanov, standing and glaring at Wilcox. "You *knew* Borzakov was here."

Wilcox did not reply.

"Didn't you?" repeated Talanov. It was a demand, not a question. "That's why Larisa's with Marcy, isn't it? Marcy's interrogating Larisa about Borzakov. About his operation, how often he's there, do any cops ever stop by, how many people work for him, how many weapons do they have. You're using her to gather intel, aren't you? That's why you wanted to turn us against each other, and why Larisa punched Marcy, because Marcy was saying things about me and it backfired."

"Will you please sit down?" said Wilcox quietly but emphatically.

"It all makes sense now," said Talanov, shaking his head with disbelief. He turned away then turned back around to look at Wilcox again. "You didn't want me caring what happened to her, did you? She's just a hooker, right? Someone who doesn't count. Never mind that Borzakov *brutalizes* her and the other girls he's holding prisoner. They're throwaways, anyway, right?"

"Keep your voice down," said Wilcox, noticing people glancing their way.

"Where is she, Bill? Where is she *right this moment?"*

"Will you *please* keep your voice down?" said Wilcox.

Talanov planted his hands on the table. "Don't make me ask you again."

"She's on her way home," said Wilcox, motioning Talanov down into his chair.

"On her way *home?* Do you have any idea what Borzakov will do when he finds out she's been helping you?"

"She already works for him," said Wilcox.

"No, she doesn't!" Talanov replied. "Larisa did what she did because she had no choice. If she refused, her family would die. If she involved the police, her family would die. If she did anything to displease Borzakov, her family would die. Which means she's now in a boatload of trouble because Borzakov will question her to find out where she's been and what she's been doing. Trouble is, Borzakov doesn't ask questions like you and I do. He's one of the most sadistic killers I've ever known. He'll do unspeakable, inhuman things just for the fun of it. And you sent her right back to him. There's no way she can hold out without telling him the truth."

"She had to go back sooner or later."

"No, she didn't, not that way!"

"One of my agents is with her."

"To do what? Drop her off at the door? Have a nice day? When Borzakov finds out she's been helping you – and he *will* – Larisa is *dead*. And you sure as hell better not have asked her to plant a bug in the office."

Wilcox did his best not to react. He knew Talanov could read the tiniest of reactions and he kept his expression noncommittal. But Wilcox could not control the dilation of his pupils. Or that split second of holding his breath. Or the brief instant when his lips and other facial muscles tensed.

"You son of a bitch!" exclaimed Talanov, pounding a fist on the table. "What did your agent tell her? That if she helped you, you'd get her family out? Or that by helping you bring down Borzakov, the domino effect from that arrest would destroy their operation? Is that it?"

Wilcox did not reply.

"Call her *right now,*" said Talanov. "Get your agent on the phone *right now!*"

"Stay out of this, Alex. I mean it."

"Get her on the phone, Bill, or I'm handling this on my own."

CHAPTER 29

MARCY prepared to park her sedan on a side street near the apartments where Larisa lived. She could see them up the block. Six stories of tiny balconies on walls of faded pink stucco. All of the windows had security bars, just like many other windows in this area.

A silver Land Cruiser was parked behind her. She hated parallel parking in the first place, but parking next to one of these monstrosities made her especially nervous. They filled the entire rearview mirror, which made parking difficult because they stuck out into the street when parked poorly like this one was. They also took up more space than a normal car. Thankfully, the vehicle in front was a normal car. It was a black Lexus and it had been parked like cars were supposed to be parked.

After several tries, Marcy eased her sedan into the space and switched off the engine. She then swiveled in her seat to look at Larisa, who had said very little the entire trip. Marcy had tried making small talk, hoping to create some kind of rapport, but Larisa had not been the least bit interested. It didn't take a psychologist to read the obvious, that Larisa didn't like her. Not that she cared. As far as she was concerned, any bimbo foolish enough to fall in with the mob deserved what she got. Still, she needed Larisa to do a job and that meant acting like she cared. It meant saying whatever was necessary in order to secure Larisa's cooperation. She just hoped the stupid bitch believed her about the safety of her family.

"Any questions?" asked Marcy with a pleasant smile.

"Do you enjoy your work?" asked Larisa.

The question caught Marcy off guard. "Do I enjoy my work?" she repeated, her eyebrows arched with surprise. "I think we should keep our attention focused on—"

"You know what I mean," Larisa cut in. "The kind of work where you use people, and lie, and manipulate them, but secretly despise them while smiling and pretending to be their friend."

Marcy stared dumbfounded at Larisa.

"So, no, I do not have any questions," Larisa continued. "I think I understand perfectly. You want me to go into the office and hide a tiny listening device in a location where they are not likely to discover it. That is correct, yes? You know Borzakov will take me into office to interrogate me, and if I am caught with device, I will be tortured for punishment and then killed in a slow and very painful way. But these are bad people who are doing terrible things, and since to you I am only a stupid person of no importance, you are not concerned about any consequences I may suffer. This is also correct, yes?"

Marcy stammered but could not answer.

"Good," said Larisa. "I think now we understand each other. So, if you will show me this device and what I am to do."

Back in the Qantas club, Wilcox was trying his best to calm Talanov down. "Will you *please* sit down? You're making a scene."

"You've got no idea the scene I'll make if you don't call Marcy right here and now," declared Talanov, refusing to sit. "Do you have *any idea* what you've done?"

"Larisa volunteered to help us out with this."

"Bullshit! She's doing it because she thinks you're going to rescue her family. *That's* why she's doing it. She trusts you. She doesn't know the safety of her family is something you can't guarantee."

"There are no guarantees in life."

"Don't play word games with me, Bill! You know damned well what I'm talking about. Bringing down Borzakov will *not* protect her parents. Gorsky is in Kherson and he'll have standing orders to kill them if anything happens. So call your agent *now!*"

"And I'm telling you to stay out of this."

"Then I'm afraid you leave me no choice."

A group of backpackers had just entered the club and paused to look for seats. One of the backpackers saw Talanov pulling

Wilcox to his feet and hurried over. "Hey, man, are you leaving?" he asked. He was slender with dreadlocks and a friendly smile.

"No," said Wilcox brusquely.

"As a matter of fact, we are," said Talanov. To Ilya: "Grab your stuff."

The backpackers swooped in while Talanov marched Wilcox toward the entrance. A few steps away, Wilcox dug in his heels and stopped, like a mule refusing to go any farther.

"Will you please listen to me?" said Wilcox, shaking off Talanov's hand. "Okay, so we weren't completely honest with Larisa, but she's the only one who can get in there and do this. Once she's planted that bug, we can hear everything they're planning. Know what they're doing."

Talanov grabbed Wilcox by the arm again and marched him toward the entrance. Wilcox dug in his heels again and twisted out of Talanov's grasp. "Okay, you win, I'll call her," he said. "Just quit with the bully tactics, okay?"

"Speaker phone," said Talanov.

"You are a major pain in the ass," said Wilcox, fishing out his phone and motioning for Talanov and Ilya to follow him out into the foyer, where he swiped his finger over the screen, found Marcy's name in his directory and dialed her number. He held the phone between them, his expression one of aggravation and impatience. But as the phone continued ringing, Wilcox's expression morphed from aggravation and impatience to concern, and before long, it had turned to worry. "She's not answering," he said, disconnecting. He took out his Agency ID and showed it to the young woman behind the customer service desk. "I need a private room," he said. "It's an emergency."

"Right this way," the young woman said. She led the trio down a short hallway into a small conference room. The room contained a long table and some chairs. Wilcox smiled his thanks and the young woman closed the door.

Wilcox dialed another number and held the phone near his mouth. Three seconds later it was answered. "Charlie, it's me," he said. "Agent Foley isn't picking up and I need you to triangulate her signal and tell me where she is."

Charlie activated a program on her computer, entered Marcy's cell phone number, and triangulated her last call from La Cienega Boulevard, near the oil fields. No calls had been made since.

"Where is she now?" asked Wilcox.

"No idea. Her phone's gone dead. Someone's removed the battery."

Talanov and Wilcox exchanged glances. Batteries did not fall out of phones.

"So we're not able to locate her using GPS?" asked Wilcox.

"No, sir," answered Charlie.

"What about her car?"

Charlie was already ahead of Wilcox and had called up the details on Marcy's rental car, which was linked to the Agency credit card that Marcy had used. "It's a rental and the company does indeed have GPS tracking. I'm connecting with their server now."

A long moment passed while Charlie entered the car's details, plus her CIA authorization code, which were streamed over the internet to the rental agency's server. More seconds ticked by before Charlie's screen lit up with a reply.

"No signal," Charlie said.

"Meaning?"

"Meaning it's either been disabled or someone's using a jamming device."

"Maybe it's malfunctioning?" asked Wilcox.

"It was operational earlier."

Charlie allowed Wilcox to deduce the obvious, that the loss of one signal could be chalked up to an accident or malfunction. But not two. Someone had deliberately disabled Marcy's cell phone and the GPS in her car.

Talanov made a gesture to ask Wilcox if he could speak.

Wilcox nodded and said, "Charlie, Aleksandr Talanov is with me. He wants to ask you a question."

Talanov accepted the phone from Wilcox and said, "Charlie,

this is Alex. Are you able to locate a photo of Roman Borzakov?" He described Borzakov then spelled his name. "He's former KGB and now works for the mob here in LA. When you get something, would you please send it through to Bill?"

"Sir?" asked Charlie, her voice broadcasting from the phone's tiny speaker.

"Do it," Wilcox replied.

"Thank you, Charlie," said Talanov, returning the phone to Wilcox.

"I'll phone you back in a moment," said Wilcox, ending the call. "All right, let's have it. What's going on? Why do you need Borzakov's photo?"

"To ID the guy. If he's their ringleader, then I want a photo to show around, to see if any witnesses recognize his face. Plus, the night before your boys busted into my house—"

"They did *not* bust in," protested Wilcox. "They knocked and you let them in."

"—there was a girl with Larisa named Jade. One of her co-workers – Asian – with blue streaks in her hair. Short little thing, maybe five-one or two. She took my Lexus and drove Andrea's father to the airport."

"You let a stranger, who's also a prostitute, take your Lexus? Are you out of your *mind?*"

"What else was I going to do? Andrea's father was there to kill me and I was in no condition to drive him to the airport myself. Besides, it's only a car."

"You could have called a taxi. And a Lexus is not just 'a car'."

"Point is, I told Jade to take Harry to the airport and then drive the Lexus to her apartment. I told her I'd pick it up later."

"So you *do* know where she and Larisa live. Why didn't you tell me this before?"

"Because I don't know where they live. But my Lexus has GPS. Find my car and we find them."

CHAPTER 30

TALANOV called Lexus and said he needed to locate his car. He gave them the car's license number, a password and his cell phone number. Seconds later, the coordinates were sent to his phone.

"Where is it?" asked Wilcox.

"Follow me," Talanov replied, leading the way downstairs.

"Where *is* it?" Wilcox asked again, hurrying to keep up.

Talanov was not about to give Wilcox the address. That's because he knew Wilcox would phone it in, which would result in a police response. And the last thing he wanted was a dozen squad cars surrounding the building with sirens blaring. It was probable that Borzakov was using a police scanner, which meant the minute he heard his name or address, he would kill the women and disappear. Assuming, of course, he hadn't killed them already. Plus, Wilcox was CIA, which meant the FBI, or the LAPD, or both, would be handling things, which meant multiple agencies with competing sets of egos worrying about who got the credit. Having that many variables was a recipe for disaster. And he was not about to take that kind of a chance with Larisa's life.

Right now, the element of surprise was on his side. Right now, there was no ridiculous chain of command comprised of people who worried and fretted about making the wrong decision rather than doing what needed to be done. In operations like this, split second timing was everything.

The first thing he needed to do was ditch Ilya, and possibly even Wilcox. Ilya may be an expert shot, but he, Talanov, had never worked with Ilya in a crisis situation. And while he knew and trusted Wilcox – mostly – plausible deniability was important for someone in Wilcox's position. Plus, if Wilcox got even the slightest hint that he would kill Borzakov on the spot, he would stop him.

He had to admit the situation did not look promising. They

were a good half hour away from his Lexus, so even if Larisa and Marcy were still alive at this moment, they might not be by the time he got there. Borzakov was a merciless killer who enjoyed the suffering of others, so there was no telling what he would do. And yet sadistic killers like Borzakov liked to first toy with their prey. They liked to make them sweat. They enjoyed seeing fear in their victim's eyes. Thus, calculation and probability told him they had an hour at most, depending on when Larisa and Marcy had been taken.

Talanov told Ilya that he could stay at his house and asked Wilcox if one of his agents would drive him there. It was a polite way of stating the obvious. Ilya preferred to come along and stated the obvious as he saw it, that he was a trained agent in the FSB who was an expert marksman, which meant he would be useful if things got sticky. He also knew Borzakov by sight. Talanov declined but Ilya insisted, with Wilcox finally weighing in on Talanov's side by saying he preferred Ilya to put together his list of names and call him tomorrow. Not able to hide his disappointment, Ilya nodded.

On the way down to the Arrivals area on the ground level, Wilcox called one of his agents and told her to drive Ilya back to Talanov's house. Talanov gave her the address while following Wilcox outside to a parking area. A jumbo jet was taking off and the thunder of its engines thickened the atmosphere with sound.

"Give me your keys," said Talanov. "It's best I handle this myself."

"And you're out of your freakin' mind if you think I'm letting you do this alone."

"Don't worry. I'll be all right."

"I'm not worried about you. I'm worried you'll kill Borzakov and screw things up."

"Don't go getting all gushy on me."

"Shut up, Alex. I'm coming with you, and that's that."

"This isn't your problem, Bill, although – come to think of it – you *are* the one who got her into this mess."

"Don't go getting all gushy on me," Wilcox replied with a

sour glare. He pulled a key ring from his pocket as they approached a silver sedan. It was as boring and basic as a car could get. Wilcox pushed a button on the fob and the taillights flashed with a chirp.

"You're kidding me, right?" remarked Talanov. "No one but a government hack would drive a car like that."

"It's called nondescript."

"Nondescript? The car's so tasteless and ugly it screams government. You actually stand out in a car like this."

"Get in and shut up."

"Man, it is a miracle you won the Cold War."

Wilcox scowled and opened his door. Talanov opened his but paused to look at Wilcox over the top of the car. "Seriously," he said. "I need to go this alone and you know what I'm talking about. Larisa's life is on the line and I can't risk doing things by the book. If I do – if *we* do – she'll get killed. Borzakov does not play by the rules."

"Maybe I didn't make myself clear. No *way* am I letting you off your leash. I know you, Alex. You're liable to shoot Borzakov on sight. I know why you want to and I don't blame you. If you do, however, they'll replace him with someone else before moving their operation underground, and we are back to square one. I *have* to know what they're planning to do with that sniper rifle. You remember the sniper rifle, don't you? The one purchased with *your* ID. I need to know who they're planning to kill, and I won't have you ruining the best chance we have of finding that out. Now, get in. We're wasting time."

Talanov glared at Wilcox. "This car really sucks."

"Quit bitching. Where are we going?"

"West Hollywood," said Talanov, getting in.

Wilcox backed out and peeled away and they were soon driving along West Century Boulevard. When they came to the 405, they turned left and sped up onto the giant six-lane interstate, heading north. The flow of cars was heavy but evenly spread out.

"All right, start talking," said Talanov. "I want the truth about Connor Jax."

"Are we back to that again?"

"We are until I get some answers."

Shaking his head, Wilcox merged into the freeway traffic. He knew this moment would come sooner or later and sooner or later was now. Under ordinary circumstances, he'd simply refuse to answer, and there wouldn't be much Talanov could do about it. But this case involved the murder of Talanov's wife, and Talanov would not let the matter be swept aside. Plus, he wanted Talanov to come and work for the JRIC, and that meant granting him certain concessions.

"Well?" said Talanov, who had rotated in his seat and was looking directly at Wilcox, who was passing cars left and right. "Who the hell is Connor Jax?"

"What I'm about to tell you stays between us. Agreed?"

"Agreed."

"Connor Jax doesn't exist."

CHAPTER 31

"HE never has," Wilcox explained, gunning the sedan over into the carpool lane. "He's a myth. A name we created as a diversion and a ruse, complete with fingerprints and profile."

"Ruse for what?" asked Talanov.

"Our dirty little secrets."

"In other words, people you've killed."

Wilcox nodded. "We leak his name whenever we need someone to blame. Someone to take heat and suspicion."

"So Connor Jax is pure fabrication?"

"We needed a scapegoat so we invented an assassin. Connor Jax is someone who supposedly worked for us but has now gone rogue. Someone we're supposedly chasing but can't quite seem to locate and apprehend."

"Ilya's report says he's yours. That he's not someone you're chasing, but yours, as in currently employed."

"Obviously, somebody altered the profile, which is easy to do when you're making copies of copies."

"Then why'd you hide his profile in your most secure facility?"

"Because that's where it would normally be found. Anywhere else – someplace a little too unguarded – and the traitors leaking our secrets would know it's a fake."

"Are you saying you have a leak?"

"Deep State appointments from a previous administration who are working to undermine the current administration. Diane and I are working quietly to expose them, but it's slow going and understandably delicate. As for the Connor Jax report, I don't know where that piece of paper came from."

"So Connor Jax is not real, although his name is, but *he* isn't, not as a person, anyway."

"That's correct."

"This is all sounds too convenient," said Talanov. "Don't get me wrong. I don't blame you for protecting your asset. For keeping his identity under wraps. But this involves the murder of my wife. Who killed her, Bill? I want the truth. You owe me that."

"That *is* the truth, Alex. It wasn't us, and that's a promise. You know how to read faces, so look at me when I tell you we did *not* kill your wife. And I don't know who did. And I don't know how else to prove that to you. In my mind, the question we need to be focusing on is, *why*. Why would someone shoot her and try to blame us? What do they stand to gain?"

Talanov could indeed see that Wilcox was telling the truth. He didn't like to admit that, but it was true. Wilcox was on the level. He had seen it on his face before and he was seeing it again now.

"And I do hope you'll believe me when I say, I really am sorry," Wilcox said gently.

Talanov nodded. "Then if Connor Jax didn't kill her because there is no Connor Jax – and I'm still having trouble getting my head around that – and, yes, I do believe you – then who did? Could it have been Borzakov? If he ordered Larisa to steal my wallet in order to buy a sniper rifle, then it's logical to believe he killed Andrea. Him or someone he works with."

"Why is that logical? I don't see any evidence of a connection."

"Inverse logic. In other words, if the opposite possibility is illogical, then the first option has to be the most logical, even if we haven't yet found any evidence. It's a big stretch to consider the murder of my wife and the theft of my credit card and ID as random incidents. My wife was killed by a sniper. My credit card and ID were used to buy a sniper rifle. That's too many coincidences for it to be coincidence. Conclusion: if the Russian mob was involved in the purchase of that sniper rifle, it makes Borzakov or someone he works with the likeliest candidate to have killed Andrea."

"Evidence, or the absence thereof – which, of course, is evidence in the negative – trumps logic every time. You know that."

"Yes, when there's genuinely no evidence. However, just because we haven't found any evidence doesn't mean it doesn't exist. So until that's been definitively decided, logic wins."

"I'm not so sure," said Wilcox, checking his rearview mirror as they sped along the freeway. "I think you're looking for an excuse to put a bullet in Borzakov's head. And I'm not about to let you do that."

"Then prove me wrong. Send your boys to Arnie's Ammo Emporium with Borzakov's photo and make that liar tell you the truth. Better yet, let me do it. I'll make him talk."

"And you know damn well that's not going to happen. Look, I don't blame you for wanting revenge."

"I never said that I did."

"You've been obsessing about it ever since Ilya arrived on the scene and told you who killed your wife. What else could it be? A scolding? Give me some credit, Alex. You want Borzakov in a coffin, and like I said, I don't blame you. He may have killed your wife – *may* have – and we are going to stop him, okay? We will."

Talanov did not reply. He just kept staring straight ahead. Jaw set. Arms folded. Breathing deliberate and measured.

"Quit yelling at me with that look," said Wilcox, steering the sedan out of the carpool lane and over into the right-hand lane. Up ahead was the Santa Monica Boulevard exit.

"What look would that be?" asked Talanov.

"That Ice Man death ray glare look of yours."

Talanov did not reply.

"Quit trying to laser burn a hole in the windshield. I get it, okay?"

"Get what?"

Wilcox growled with frustration. "You're going to make me say it, aren't you?"

Talanov did not reply.

"Okay!" said Wilcox. "It's my fault that Larisa's in this mess. I should never have consented to the plan."

"Who concocted that brainless scheme, anyway?"

"It doesn't matter. What matters is that I didn't put a stop to it. And I'm sorry. Really, I am."

"Sorry won't cut it if something happens to her," said Talanov. It was not an emotional statement, nor a threat. Just a factual declaration that hung in the air.

"I know," Wilcox replied.

Both men fell silent until Wilcox's phone chimed receipt of a text message. He picked up his phone and saw a picture of Roman Borzakov on the screen. "Is this him?" he asked, handing Talanov the phone.

"That's Borzakov, all right," Talanov replied.

The photo, a head shot, was nearly three years old and had been retrieved from Borzakov's visa application into the United States. He had dark wavy hair and cold eyes staring straight into the camera.

"Let's assume for the moment that Borzakov did kill my wife," Talanov continued, laying the cell phone on the console. "He may not have, but let's assume that he did. Why wait until now to pick up where he left off? He could have sent anyone this past year to steal my wallet and ID. I was at rock bottom most of that time. An easy target. Why now? Why not then?"

"What are you getting at?" asked Wilcox.

"What window of opportunity is occurring now that didn't occur this past year?"

"Obviously, the regional congress on organized crime and terrorism. It starts tonight and Gustaves is giving the keynote speech. That makes her a prime target along with other members of the JRIC oversight committee."

"I don't know what that is," said Talanov.

"The JRIC is the Joint Regional Intelligence Center, and the oversight committee, who steers the JRIC, is comprised of Congresswoman Diane Gustaves and representatives from the CIA, FBI, Homeland Security, and a bunch of others, including the LAPD. In fact, that's something I wanted to talk with you about. We want you to come aboard as a consultant."

"To do what?"

"Help bring down people like Borzakov," answered Wilcox, taking the exit ramp off the 405. "Which you're in a unique position to do because you know how he was trained, how he operates, and who his friends are. And not just Borzakov, but hundreds of other KGB agents who scattered to the wind once the Soviet Union dissolved."

"Is this why you want Ilya to come aboard as well. As another set of eyes?"

"Exactly."

"Then why do you need me?"

"Because I trust you and you've already proven yourself, which is not as important to me as it is to others on the committee. I know you. They don't."

"Who are they?"

"Gustaves, who chairs the House Intelligence Committee and leads the pack when it comes to fighting organized crime and terrorism. Like me, she favors bringing you aboard. Jackson Teague and Martin Posner have reservations. Teague's the Acting Director of Operations for the CIA. Posner's the Assistant Director in Charge of the FBI's Los Angeles Field Office."

"Is this something recent?" asked Talanov. "You wanting me to join your committee?"

"I see where you're going with this. Our wanting you to join the committee is something occurring now that didn't occur this past year. Meaning, if word leaked about us bringing you aboard and it reached Borzakov, he would not want you being empowered with any kind of authority to hunt him down, since you know him better than anyone and how he works. This would also explain why Borzakov waited until now. When you were at rock bottom, you weren't a threat. Now you are, or will be once you join."

"Then why go to the trouble of buying a sniper rifle with my stolen credit card and ID? Why not just shoot me if he wanted to keep me off the committee?"

"Maybe he wanted to accomplish two things at once," offered Wilcox. "Maybe he wanted to cripple the committee by shooting one of its members – i.e., Gustaves – then use her murder to get rid of you by making it look like you did it, which gets you the needle or sends you to prison."

"That's elaborate and clumsy and a lot of maybes, and I don't remember Borzakov being that much of a strategist. He was always more of a thug."

"It fits the facts."

"Maybe," Talanov replied.

At the stoplight, they turned right onto Santa Monica Boulevard, which bore little resemblance to its heritage as the western end of historic old Route 66. Gone were the eccentric, rounded art deco shapes of yesteryear, when quirks and originality flourished. Overlooking the boulevard now were fast food outlets, strip malls, and office towers of reflective glass and ribbed concrete.

The boulevard angled northeast until it reached the intersection of La Cienega, in West Hollywood, where it turned east. They followed the boulevard to Fairfax and turned north, and after a couple more turns, ended up on the street where Talanov's Lexus was located.

"There it is," he said pointing to the shiny black sedan with several parking tickets fixed to the wiper. "The apartments will be nearby."

"Yeah, but which one?" asked Wilcox. "The neighborhood is full of apartments."

Wilcox was right. The entire street was a canyon of apartments. All were roughly the same height and all were pink stucco or white. Some had sliding gates that led to underground parking. Most had fences, small balconies, and security bars on the windows. All looked pretty much the same, except for a two-story white adobe house tucked quietly away between two of the apartment blocks. It had palm trees out front, a red tile roof with several broken tiles, and a blue garage door facing the street. A curved walk led to an arched doorway. A bay window offered a clear view of the street.

"Park in that driveway," said Talanov.

"What's your plan?" asked Wilcox, parking in front of the blue garage door and switching off the ignition.

"We need to find somebody who's lived here a long time. Somebody who's seen the neighborhood change and knows what's going on."

"A busybody," said Wilcox.

"Exactly. Bring your phone and let's see who lives in this house."

With Wilcox accompanying him, Talanov led the way up the curving walk and knocked on the front door. The door was solid wood and contained a tiny panel behind two decorative wrought iron bars. "Got your ID?" Talanov asked Wilcox as the tiny panel opened.

"May I help you?" a woman's voice asked.

Talanov could tell it was an older woman. She was probably in her late sixties, judging by her voice, which was cautious and polite yet hesitant and inquisitive. He showed the woman Wilcox's ID. "Ma'am, this is Agent Wilcox and I'm Aleksandr Talanov," he said. "We're looking for a block of apartments owned by this man." He nodded for Wilcox's cell phone and Wilcox showed the woman the picture of Borzakov. "We think he's holding two women hostage and that the apartments are being run as a brothel."

"Sorry, can't help you. I don't want any trouble."

"Anything you tell us is confidential," said Talanov. "You'll remain completely anonymous."

"I really can't get involved."

"Lady, those women are about to be *killed,*" said Wilcox, edging Talanov out of the way, "and one of them works for me. She's a Federal agent, which makes this a Federal crime, with severe consequences for *anyone* withholding—"

"*Oy!*" said Talanov, easing Wilcox aside with a scolding glare. He looked again at the tiny window. "Ma'am, I'm sorry about my friend. He's uptight and kind of rude right now because of the strain he's under. But he's right. This guy will kill those women. So if you do know something, we really could use your help. By the way, did you know you've got a few broken tiles up top? It's brittle stuff, terra cotta. My house was so bad I had to replace the entire roof."

"I used to handle those kinds of repairs," the woman said. "In fact, I mortared all those cap tiles myself. But that was a few years back."

"Check out The Roofster. He's on the web."

"On the what?"

Talanov smiled. "The internet. I'll have him slip a brochure in your mailbox. He'll give you a good deal, and he's honest." To Wilcox: "Hand her a card."

"Alex, there's no time!"

"Give her your card. We need to keep knocking on doors."

"There are no other doors," the woman said. "Just security gates and intercoms."

Talanov smiled and waited for the grumbling Wilcox to dig a card out of his wallet.

"You say those women are in danger?" asked the woman.

"Yes, ma'am," answered Talanov. "She and hundreds of others were sold into prostitution against their will, which means they're being abused and beaten, and most will eventually be killed. Look, I'm not with the police, so that means there's no record of this conversation. Anything you tell me goes no further than your front porch."

"What about the guy with you? The one with shifty eyes?"

"Granted, the eyes are scary. That's because he works for one of those secret departments of the government that you read about in spy novels. Like me, he gets things done off the books. Now, *please*. Are you able to help?"

The woman was silent for a long moment. "I knew he was scum the minute I laid eyes on him," she finally said. "He's been coming here off and on for well over a year, usually with two big goons in slick suits. He drives a fancy car of some kind and often has young women with him. He handles them rough, like they're his prisoners."

"They are. Do you know where he lives?" asked Talanov handing the woman Wilcox's card.

"Across the street, on the corner. The place with pink stucco and bars on the windows. But you'll never get in, not without him seeing you. He's got cameras all over the place. And a high fence with a locked gate of heavy steel mesh."

"You're a sweetheart," said Talanov. "Thank you."

"Sweetheart? Young man, I think you need glasses."

Talanov chuckled. "I appreciate your help."

"You're welcome. Now, go get that bastard."

CHAPTER 32

"COME on, Shifty," said Talanov, leading the way to his Lexus.

"Oh, you are just hilarious," Wilcox replied.

"I told Jade to leave the keys on top of a tire," explaining Talanov, removing the tickets from the wiper and handing them to Wilcox.

"What are you giving them to me?"

"Take care of 'em."

"What is wrong with you? It's your car. Take care of them yourself. I'm not one of those bikinied meter maids you've got in Australia."

"That's for sure, but you *are* part of the JRIC, which means you've got friends in the LAPD. So don't tell me you can't get 'em fixed."

"Fix them yourself. I'm not your gopher."

"How badly do you want me to come and work for you?" asked Talanov, feeling along the top of a front tire.

"Sometimes I want to punch you," grumbled Wilcox just as Talanov located his keys and held them up with a big smile. Wilcox rolled his eyes.

Talanov pressed a button on the fob and the doors of the Lexus unlocked. "Throw me your keys," he said.

"What for?"

"In case we need to trade cars."

"Why would we need to do that?"

"Throw me your keys. I don't have time to explain."

With a growl of protest, Wilcox dug out his keys and tossed them to Talanov just as Talanov did the same. But Talanov's toss went wide and his keys slid across the sidewalk into some shrubs.

"Seriously?" complained Wilcox. With an exasperated huff, he walked across the sidewalk to the shrub.

When Wilcox turned his back, Talanov opened the front door of the Lexus, felt under the front seat and entered a four digit code into a touchpad. A metal door slid open and Talanov pulled out a Belgian-made Herstal semi-automatic pistol. It was matte black, with a threaded barrel and fully loaded magazine. He screwed a suppressor onto the barrel and slid a lever that cocked the weapon.

Wilcox heard the sound of the ratchet. "Where the *hell* did you get that? You said this was your wife's car!"

"I fitted it with some extras. Wait here."

"You are out of your *mind* if you think I'm going to let you go after Borzakov!"

"That's why I didn't ask permission," said Talanov, sprinting toward Wilcox's nondescript sedan.

"Like *hell!*" shouted Wilcox. He ran after Talanov but looked like a duck chasing a thoroughbred.

Talanov easily out-sprinted the overweight Wilcox to the sedan, where he jumped behind the wheel, locked the doors, and started the engine. Wilcox banged on the passenger window but Talanov backed out of the driveway, shifted into drive, and sped away down the street. Wilcox made a token effort to run after him but gave up after a few steps and a string of curse words.

The old woman's house was in the middle of one side of the block. Borzakov's apartment building was at the end of the block on the other side of the street. It was a distance of maybe two hundred feet. Talanov slowed the car at the corner and looked the place over. The old woman had been right. The building was wired with cameras. They were all over the place. The building was also protected by a security fence. The front gate was reinforced mesh. That meant the front door would no doubt be heavily fortified as well. Getting in that way would be virtually impossible.

Talanov took a second look at the security fence. It had vertical I-beam posts of heavy gauge steel and horizontal rails mounted to the posts by straight-line brackets and tamperproof bolts. All of the posts were set in concrete. But there was no retaining wall or other buffers between the curb and the fence. Just flat ground, a sidewalk, and a wheelchair ramp on the corner. After a quick look to make sure no one was coming, Talanov sped across the intersection, did a quick u-turn in the middle of the block and returned to the stop sign.

The corner of the fence was most accessible, but ramming it was a huge risk. For one thing, the corner post was thicker gauge steel than the others. It also had two diagonal posts bracing it, with the added strength of two sets of horizontal rails angling away at ninety-degrees. The corner of the fence would be strong, like the bow of a ship.

But the flanking sections along the side of the apartment building were braced only by vertical posts. The second or third section of fence, then, would be his point of entry.

Depressing the brake pedal, Talanov gunned the engine, released the brake, and jammed the accelerator to the floor. Squealing forward with a plume of smoke, the car shot across the intersection and up the wheelchair ramp. Both front tires could not fit on the narrow ramp, so one of them hit the curb and bounced into the air. Being a front-end drive, the tire hit the ground and hopped twice before catching traction again. Seconds later, the clang and screech of ripping metal filled the air as the sedan smashed through the fence. One of the vertical posts tore into the radiator and slowed the vehicle by roughly twenty percent. But it was no match for the car's velocity and mass. With steam flying from the hood, the car tore through some rosemary bushes and into the side of the building. Like most California construction of this vintage, the walls were made of insulation-packed timber studs covered with chicken wire and stucco. No match at all for a car. The wall splintered and caved. Chunks of stucco flew everywhere. Windows shattered, voices screamed, dust and debris filled the air.

Talanov was ready for the airbag deployment and let it absorb his forward momentum. He unsnapped his seatbelt, shifted into reverse, and backed out of the gaping hole. After jamming the gearstick into park, he jumped out and looked in through the jagged opening.

He had figured right. The office was situated toward the front of the building, where control over who came and went was easy to maintain. If there was trouble, the guys with guns were right there to control the situation.

The crash had filled the office with dust. It was everywhere, and it made visibility difficult. An alarm was going off and a blue light was pulsating. Two men were lying dazed on the floor. They had been seated at the security console and had taken the brunt of the crash. Their handguns were laying on the floor.

Pushing aside a splintered stud, Talanov started to enter but paused when he saw movement in the dusty haze. A figure was dashing toward what looked like a red door in the far wall. The figure twisted and lifted his hand. Talanov ducked out just as two shots sent wood chips flying.

Talanov returned fire with the Herstal, then squeezed in through the opening just as the figure raced out the door. Had it been Borzakov? Talanov couldn't be sure because of the dust. In the distance he heard screaming and pounding.

One of the men on the floor reached for his pistol but Talanov knocked him unconscious with a kick to the head. He then did the same to the other man.

Seconds later, Wilcox arrived. "Do you have *any idea* the trouble I'm in because of what you just did? *Look* at this place!"

Talanov raced across the office to the red door, which was standing open. He peeked out into the hall then ducked back quickly as a shot punched a hole in the jamb.

"Show yourself or I kill her!" shouted Borzakov.

Leading with the Herstal, Talanov knelt and looked around the corner. The weapon was an extension of his eye. He sighted in on Borzakov standing midway along the corridor. Dressed in one of his designer suits, now covered with dust, he was holding Jade in front of him, like a shield.

"Help us!" shouted a girl from the open the doorway into Jade's bedroom.

Borzakov fired two quick rounds and the girl flew back as blood and brains splattered over the other girls standing behind her. They screamed and dove to the floor before scrambling to the back of the room. "Shut the door!" Borzakov shouted. One of the girls pushed it closed.

"Let her go!" commanded Talanov. He had the Herstal trained directly at Borzakov's head. But Borzakov kept ducking and weaving behind Jade, not giving Talanov a clear shot. Under normal conditions, he would have no trouble putting a bullet between Borzakov's eyes. But these were not normal conditions. His hatred of Borzakov was so intense it was causing his aim to waver. He had allowed emotion to cloud his ability.

Talanov had never hated a man so much. He hated who he was, what he had done, what he was doing right now. And he had never been in this position before. He was trained not to allow emotions to interfere. He was trained not to care about any collateral damage that got in the way. But he did care. And he was furious at the prospect that his wife's killer might get away.

Dust floating down the hallway made things worse. It was hanging in the air and sticking to the perspiration on his forehead, which was trickling into his eyes. He wiped his eyes with his left hand and then used that hand to steady his right hand, which was holding the Herstal in a grip that was way too tight. He needed to relax.

Talanov did not allow himself to look at Jade, who was quivering in Borzakov's grasp, eyes pleading, desperate and frightened. Instead, he kept his focus on Borzakov. Looking into Jade's eyes, even for an instant, would give Borzakov the split second he needed to shoot. But by keeping his eyes fixed on his, he stood a good chance of reading Borzakov's intentions before he had time to act. No doubt, this was why Borzakov had chosen Jade. He knew they had met and was hoping to distract him.

"Did you do it? Did you kill my wife?" demanded Talanov.

But Borzakov kept moving from side to side, keeping Jade in front of him.

"Answer me!" shouted Talanov. "Did you kill her?"

Borzakov grinned while backing slowly toward the open stairwell at the end of the hall. All along the corridor, girls pounded on doors, crying for help. Dust continued drifting down the hall.

"Did you kill her?" yelled Talanov.

"Ice Man is angry, yes? He wants to know who killed his wife?"

"Yes, damn you!"

Talanov kept his eyes locked with Borzakov's while advancing slowly forward. Borzakov jabbed the gun into Jade's neck and she cried out. Talanov stopped and Borzakov laughed.

"You have grown soft, I think," Borzakov said, pulling Jade's head in front of his and licking her on the ear. Jade shuddered and tried leaning away. Borzakov pulled her tightly against him and stroked her face with the gun. Jade's eyes were tightly closed but tears streamed down her cheeks.

"Let her go!" said Talanov, imposing calm on himself.

"And if I do you will – what – let me go? You will let me just walk out the door? Is that what you will do?"

They both knew that would never happen. Borzakov was not about to let Jade go and Talanov was not about to let Borzakov walk out the door. Both men were set on one thing: *killing each other.*

And Jade was standing between them.

Borzakov laughed again. "I think you like this one, yes?" He yanked Jade's head back and jammed the gun barrel into her neck. Jade's eyes flew open with a gasp. When Talanov instinctively glanced into Jade's terrified eyes, Borzakov whipped his gun down and fired. The explosion reverberated through the hallway.

Borzakov shoved Jade toward Talanov. She weighed maybe ninety-five pounds. Thin frame, no fat, light as a feather. She flew toward Talanov, arms flailing, eyes wide with panic when she hit the floor at the same instant pain sensors in her brain received shock waves from the bullet that had just ripped through her flesh.

Talanov watched Jade hit the floor. Saw her grab her leg and scream. Saw blood start gushing everywhere. Three seconds, that's all it took. When he looked up, Borzakov was gone.

CHAPTER 33

THE gunshot brought Wilcox into the hallway. He had purposely remained out of sight because he knew he would be a distraction that may well get Talanov killed. He saw Talanov drop to Jade's side, and over the sound of screaming and pounding on doors, saw Talanov pull off his shirt, rip out the sleeves and tie one of them around Jade's thigh, above the wound. But the blood continued to pump onto the floor with each of Jade's heartbeats.

For Talanov, the sight of the blood brought back memories of Andrea lying on stage, and it was the same now with Jade, who lay writhing on the floor, crying and screaming while girls up and down the hallway continued pounding on their doors. Talanov recognized many of the languages – Russian, German, Ukrainian – and many he did not. But he understood their desperation well enough to know they were crying for someone to help them.

Talanov tied a knot in the tourniquet, stuck his gun barrel through the loop and twisted. It slowed the flow of blood but did not stop it. The wound was deep and at an awkward angle on Jade's thigh, and Talanov had not been able to tie the tourniquet high enough to stop the hemorrhage completely. He saw Jade looking up at him. She was shivering with pain and terror. Her eyes met his and held them.

"They t-took her," Jade said between sobs. "B-Borzakov's men. To k-kill her." Shock was setting in. She was shaking violently.

Wilcox came to Talanov's side. "Police and medics are on their way. I put out an APB. Borzakov won't get far."

Jade started jerking uncontrollably. Her eyelids started fluttering.

"Stay with me! Help's on the way!" shouted Talanov. He twisted the tourniquet tighter and slapped Jade lightly in the face, recalling how he had said the same words to Andrea when she lay dying in his arms. *And here it was, happening again.* To Wilcox: "In the office. Get me some coffee."

Wilcox ran into the office.

"Don't want to die alone," whispered Jade, whose face was losing color.

"You're not going to die," said Talanov. He squeezed Jade's hand reassuringly and brushed a streak of matted blue hair out of her face. "But you've got to stay with me. You can't let yourself fall asleep." He looked toward the end of the hallway, toward the open doorway of what was obviously a descending flight of stairs. The fact that Borzakov had run down those steps meant there was an escape tunnel at the bottom. Borzakov the butcher was getting away.

"Larisa ... got to s-save her," Jade whispered as her eyelids sagged closed.

Talanov slapped her lightly in the face again and Jade's eyelids snapped open. He looked down at her thigh and saw blood still pumping out onto the floor. His tourniquet was failing. Grabbing his other sleeve, Talanov wrapped it above the other tourniquet and twisted.

Jade flinched and coughed. "Larisa," she said in a voice that was barely a whisper.

Talanov leaned close to Jade's ear. "Larisa," he said. "Where did they take her?"

Jade did not answer.

Wilcox appeared from the doorway and hurried to Talanov's side. "It's cold but it's coffee," he said, handing Talanov a mug.

Talanov lifted Jade's head and held the mug to her lips. "Drink," he said. "It will help."

Jade took a sip and coughed. "Hate ... c-coffee," she said. "Green tea."

Talanov held the mug to Jade's lips again. But she was too weak to open her mouth and Talanov set it aside.

What to do? If he left now, he could probably catch Borzakov. He didn't need to run him down. He just needed to get him in his sights. Borzakov might be fast, but a bullet from his Herstal would be faster. In the distance, he heard a siren and looked down at Jade. Her eyelids were closed. He again slapped her lightly in the face. "Don't give up! Help's on the way!"

She didn't move.

Talanov felt Jade's neck for a pulse. He looked at Wilcox then at the petite body of Jade lying in a pool of her own blood. He looked again at the doorway where Borzakov had disappeared.

Pursuing Borzakov was the logical thing to do. It was something the Ice Man would do. Avenge Andrea. Stop the killer. Prevent him from killing again.

Avenge Andrea. Everything he did and thought about had brought him to this very moment. Borzakov was within reach. Andrea would finally get the justice she deserved. The redemption he craved was within reach. What should he do? *Protecting the living is more important than avenging the dead.* The words seemed to hover in his mind.

He looked down at Jade again. "Come on, Jade, *fight!*" he said, knowing he had to stay. He twisted the tourniquet tighter just as a siren stopped outside. "Hurry!" he said to Wilcox. "Get them. There may be time."

Wilcox ran to the front door just as Jade exhaled a slow, final breath.

"Not now, Jade!" shouted Talanov. "They're here! The ambulance is here!" He kept slapping her lightly in the face, not wanting to commence heart massage for fear of pumping out the last drops of her blood.

Paramedics rushed in the door. Talanov discreetly removed his Herstal from the tourniquet and stood to let them take over. One look was all it took for him to know that Jade was gone. He had seen dead people before, and after her final sigh, he had felt her spirit linger for a moment before vanishing. It was as if she had stayed around long enough to say thanks. Thanks for trying, for not giving up, for not letting her die alone.

Borzakov will pay. I promise, Talanov mouthed wordlessly to himself. He took Wilcox aside while paramedics commenced emergency procedures. "We need to get out of here," he said quietly.

"This is a crime scene, Alex. We can't."

"And if we wait around to answer questions and fill out police reports, Larisa and your agent will be killed."

"I can't leave without telling the police what happened. You crashed my car into a building. There's been gunfire. People are dead and we have *no idea* where Borzakov's men have taken Larisa and Marcy. We need to follow procedure."

"What's it going to be, Bill? People or paperwork? Or have you forgotten what this fight is about?"

"It's not anywhere near that simple and you know it!" Wilcox shot back.

Talanov stared at Wilcox for a long moment and seemed to sigh with surrender. He then plunged his hand into Wilcox's pocket. Wilcox tried twisting away but Talanov found the Lexus keys and yanked them out.

"Give me those!" demanded Wilcox. He grabbed for the keys but Talanov pulled away.

"They're mine. Are you coming or staying?" asked Talanov, holding the keys out of reach.

One of the paramedics came over and explained how they had tried in vain to save the girl. He asked who she was, what their names were, and what had happened.

"Last chance," said Talanov. "People or paperwork?"

Muttering angrily, Wilcox pulled out his ID and showed the paramedic. "My name's Wilcox, CIA," he said, "and I'm part of the Joint Regional Intelligence Center. The LAPD will be here shortly but we can't wait around. Tell them we're part of Operation Red Star and we're in pursuit of a suspect. Did you get that?

"Yes, sir," said the paramedic. "Operation Red Star."

"Have you got an extra shirt?" asked Talanov.

The medic took a blue hospital shirt out of his kit and handed it to Talanov.

"There's another casualty in that room," said Talanov, slipping on the shirt and pointing at a locked apartment door. "You'll also need to restrain the two guys in the office. Duct tape works really well."

"That's not our job."

"It is now."

Before the paramedic could reply, Talanov ran into the office and out through the hole in the wall. With a growl of frustration, Wilcox ran after him.

"Why the hell didn't we go out the front door?" yelled Wilcox, who had trouble squeezing through the opening.

"Because I wanted these," answered Talanov, waving several envelopes he had scooped off the floor.

They ran through the ring of spectators and over to the Lexus, and within seconds were speeding away from the scene just as the flashing lights of three police cars appeared in their rearview mirror.

CHAPTER 34

"OPERATION Red Star?" asked Talanov with a look of incredulity while racing south toward Hollywood Boulevard. "Are you serious? Your initiative to infiltrate the Russian mob is actually called Operation Red Star?"

"What's wrong with that?" asked Wilcox, who was in the passenger seat while Talanov was behind the wheel.

"It's as corny as that car of yours."

"You mean the car I *used* to have, which you destroyed?"

"It was ugly. You can thank me later."

With a shake of his head, Wilcox began sorting through the small stack of envelopes Talanov had picked up off the floor. "What do we do with these?"

"They're utility bills. Call Charlie and have her find out who owns the apartment and what their phone number is. Then have her run a trace on that number and tell us what numbers were called during the last four hours. If we're lucky, we'll get a cell phone number that we can track using GPS."

"What's the plan?" asked Wilcox, dialing Charlie's number.

"Since Larisa and Marcy weren't at the apartments, I'm thinking Borzakov's men are going to kill them someplace else. Someplace remote."

"Why didn't they kill them in front of the others? The mob does that, you know, to teach the other girls a lesson and keep them in line."

"Killing a Federal agent in front of witnesses is a different ball game than killing an illegal alien in front of other illegal aliens," answered Talanov, turning left onto Hollywood Boulevard. "Doing something like that would put the girls in a position of power with law enforcement. Borzakov would never allow that. His men will do it in a place where they can easily dispose of the bodies without being seen."

"That means ocean or desert," Wilcox replied.

"That's what I'm thinking," agreed Talanov.

"The mob is heavy into shipping. That's how they smuggle drugs and human cargo and all kinds of black market goods. Unfortunately, there are ships and boats all up and down the coast. Where the hell do we start?"

"That's what we need Charlie to tell us," said Talanov as they sped past the old Pacific theater, which occupied half a block with its grand rundown façade and twin radio towers on top. Running the yellow light at North Cahuenga Boulevard, they crossed the double yellow lines in order to get past a bottleneck of slow-moving traffic.

Charlie answered Wilcox's call on the second.

Wilcox filled Charlie in on what had happened, gave her the utility bill information and told her what they needed. He then switched the call to speakerphone while Charlie went to work on her keyboard. The wait was not long.

"The apartment's owned by a shell corporation called California Living Enterprises," said Charlie, reading from her monitor, "which is owned by a shipping company called Spice Lines East."

"Out of Hong Kong?" asked Talanov, looking at the phone with surprise.

"That's right," said Charlie. "How did you know?"

"They smuggled a team of Department Thirteen killers into Australia back when I was married and living there. They destroyed almost everything we had, which is why we ended up moving to Los Angeles, to try and start a new life, not that it did much good."

"Well, get this," said Charlie, snapping and popping a wad of chewing gum. "Spice Lines East is owned by NOVO Maritime, which is a shipping company out of the Russian port of Novorossiysk, on the eastern shore of the Black Sea, just south of the Sea of Azov."

"Spit the gum out, Charlie," said Wilcox. "I can hardly understand you."

Charlie spit the gum into an empty coffee mug. It normally held four cups of liquid and was a souvenir from Disneyland, complete with a giant smiling face of Mickey Mouse. "California

Living Enterprises has an unlisted number," she continued, "which of course I accessed and traced all outgoing and incoming phone calls made during the last four hours. Every one of them was made to and from prepaid cells, one of which has been accessed three times. Twice outgoing and once incoming. I ran a GPS on that particular cell, which is currently heading south on the 110, toward the Port of Los Angeles. Right now they're crossing the Pacific Coast Highway."

"Patch that signal through to my phone so that we can follow the flashing dot."

"Patching through to you now," said Charlie.

"Charlie, can you jam that number?" asked Talanov. "I don't want Borzakov phoning his goons to let 'em know what happened back at the apartments. If he does, our chances of finding those women alive go from slim to none."

"If I do, you lose tracking capability. I'll effectively be removing that number from service."

"Can you block it now and then unblock it when we get closer so that we can tell where they are, then block and unblock it at intervals until we find them?"

"In theory, yes," answered Charlie, "although the process is slow and we may temporarily lose their signal until our algorithms lock on again."

"In other words, attempting both may compromise both to the point that neither is effective."

"That's right."

"So, which do you want more?" Wilcox asked Talanov. "Keeping track of their location or preventing Borzakov from communicating?"

A long moment of silence ticked by.

"Location," said Talanov. "I'd rather know where they are. Being on the run, Borzakov may not have immediate access to a phone, since he left the apartments in such a hurry and the police are after him."

"You heard him," said Wilcox. "Do it."

"You should be able to track them ... now," answered Charlie just as a small stack of pink slips were laid in front of her. All of them were from Teague. All of them demanded to know where Wilcox was. All of them concerned reports of Wilcox's rental car being driven into the side of an apartment building, with Wilcox then leaving a crime scene involving gunfire and two murders.

"Uh, sir, I just got a stack of messages from Teague," said Charlie. "It looks like all hell is breaking loose."

"Fill him in and tell him I'll phone when I can," said Wilcox just as Talanov sped through a yellow light.

The tarnished luster of vintage Hollywood soon gave way to trashy strip malls, parking lots, and fast food outlets. Talanov ran another yellow light at Bronson, flew past the 76 station and squealed right onto the 101 entry ramp. He gunned the Lexus, which downshifted with a throaty whine and sent them flying past apartments with panoramic views of traffic. Before long, they were on the freeway.

This section of the 101, known as the Hollywood Freeway, was like a shallow canyon, with concrete retaining walls and sloping sides blanketed with shrubs and ground cover. The lanes were narrow, with a waist-high concrete divider separating southbound traffic from northbound. There was no shoulder, either, so that if a driver broke down, there was no place to go.

Talanov had the accelerator to the floor and Wilcox had his hands on the dashboard hoping they didn't crash while Talanov weaved back and forth from lane to lane, roaring past cars and in front of others. To their right, the skyline of downtown Los Angeles jutting into the clear blue sky.

The distance from their entry onto the freeway to the port of Los Angeles is roughly twenty-five miles, and during non-peak times, traffic often moves at speeds of up to eighty-five miles per hour, even though the posted limit is sixty-five. The "flow of traffic" was the unofficial speed limit, and so long as one traveled at the relative speed of other cars and did not zigzag all over the place, the police tended not to notice. Which is precisely why they *did* take notice of Talanov, who was violating those principles.

Talanov was not sure when they noticed him because it took the first squad car a while to catch up, even with its lights and siren. But Talanov soon saw the patrol car closing in, with another one farther behind. "Bill, we've got trouble," he said.

Wilcox turned and saw flashing lights.

"We can't let them pull us over," said Talanov.

"This may actually be a good thing," Wilcox replied. "We'll lead the police right to Borzakov's men."

"Are you crazy?"

"It's not like the police are going to shoot us for speeding. We can explain everything when we get there."

"If Borzakov's men hear sirens, they'll kill the women."

"Then I'm open to suggestions about what to do."

"You're part of the JRIC, which includes the LAPD. Phone your boss and have him call off the cops."

"I'm not exactly real popular right now, thanks to the mess you've created."

"This is no time for being sensitive."

"Sensitive? Really? You crashed my rental car into a building. Shots were fired. People were *killed*. And we left the scene of the crime!"

"Quit complaining and get on the phone," said Talanov, his eyes on the rearview mirror. "Those squad cars are closing in."

Behind them, Talanov could see traffic moving aside to let the powerful patrol cars roar past. To make matters worse, a third patrol car was speeding down an entry ramp.

Talanov continued weaving in and out of traffic, trying to stay out of reach. Swaying side to side while muttering curses, Wilcox touched the screen of his phone, found his directory and dialed Teague's number. It was answered immediately after the first ring.

"You'd better have a damn good explanation for what you're doing, is all I can say," barked Teague.

Wilcox filled him in on where they were, what they were doing, and what he needed done.

Teague said, "So you're adding speeding, endangering human life, and evading the police to this growing list of infractions?"

Wilcox did not reply.

"Is this your doing or Talanov's?" asked Teague.

Wilcox did not reply.

"And you want me to *hire* this guy?"

Before Wilcox could respond, the line went dead.

Wilcox slumped back in his seat and stared out down at the floorboard for a long moment. Talanov glanced over and saw the abject look on Wilcox's face.

"What is it? What happened?"

"That didn't quite go as expected," Wilcox replied.

CHAPTER 35

TALANOV watched the third black-and-white join the other two as more traffic on the 110 kept pulling over. The situation was getting critical.

"Where are Borzakov's men?" he asked.

Wilcox looked at the flashing red dot on the tiny map on his phone. "Crossing the Vincent Thomas Bridge onto Terminal Island," he replied.

The police were right behind them now. There were two squad cars, side by side, with a third one following, all with lights flashing and sirens screaming. "Pull over to the shoulder!" a voice called out over a loudspeaker. Ahead, cars were moving over for the phalanx of police cars behind the speeding black Lexus.

A slow-moving white panel van with Griff's Electrical written on the side was in the lane directly ahead. The cars in the right lanes had moved over to the shoulder, out of the way. Talanov veered into the left lane and shot around the van just as a squad car passed it on the right. When Talanov sped ahead of the van, the squad car pulled over into the lane beside him. Talanov was now trapped between the center divider and the patrol car, with another patrol car directly behind him. The third patrol car had dropped back and was weaving back and forth across all the lanes, its lights flashing as a warning not to pass. They were clearing the freeway and preparing to squeeze him against the center divider.

Talanov looked over at the Latino officer in the patrol car beside them. It was Diego, from the nightclub. Talanov's heart sank and it must have shown on his face because Diego replied with a sneering grin. Diego then patted the shotgun mounted vertically in a bracket on the dashboard.

"This does not look good," said Wilcox as they roared beneath an overpass. High on their left was an elevated section of concrete where Interstate 105 intersected the 110. It was an impressive confluence of concrete ribbons on massive columns over crisscrossing bridges and thoroughfares. Talanov was still in the center lane as they sped beneath the elaborate tangle. Ahead, a fresh flow of cars was feeding onto the 110. Diego's squad car was still right beside him. The second patrol car was still directly behind, with the third police car still weaving back and forth to hold back traffic.

Talanov knew the Lexus had plenty of room to spare on the speedometer. But he was reluctant to open it up all the way. There was a lot of traffic ahead. Many cars had seen the flashing lights and were moving over. Many were not. Many were ignoring the flashing lights, or hadn't seen them, so if he pushed the Lexus up over 140, he would be an accident waiting to happen. They had to pull over. They were out of options.

He thought of Larisa in the trunk of a car, frightened but alive. He had to keep thinking of her that way rather than seeing her chained to some piece of scrap iron at the bottom of the harbor. Such thoughts gave him hope. Wilcox, no doubt, was more worried about his agent, and probably would not be giving him so much latitude if she weren't in danger, too. Nevertheless, he was glad to have the old fox along. At least it would help calm things down with the police.

Talanov was about to signal Diego that he was pulling over when he saw Diego look toward the dashboard and cock his head. An incoming call over the radio had caught Diego's attention. An instant later, Diego shouted angrily and pounded a fist on the dashboard.

Wilcox had been watching Diego as well. "What's that all about?" he asked. He watched the furious policeman spit words at his partner. The partner said something back, which resulted in another string of angry words before Diego yanked the microphone from its clip and said something into it. He then slammed the microphone back in place, fumed for a long moment, then looked over at Talanov and made a circular motion with his finger for them to follow. And with the other patrol car pulling up beside it, they sped ahead.

Wilcox's cell phone sounded and Wilcox answered it. It was Teague, telling him the LAPD would clear the two center lanes all the way to the port.

"I spoke with Chief Cruz and he gave the order," said Teague. "He told them to cut their sirens, figuring you didn't want to announce your arrival. He also told them to back off once the freeway ended. Before you cross the bridge, though, you'll be met by two unmarked police cars. They'll give you back-up and run interference."

"Thank you, sir."

"Get Marcy back alive, Bill. Make this worth the heat I'm going to take for being involved where we don't belong. I don't need to tell you, Talanov really *is* on the verge of being deported, a situation that is much more likely to be forgiven if you manage to come through with the goods. Bring back a dead agent and heads are going to roll."

"I understand, sir," said Wilcox, ending the call and sinking back in his seat.

"What was that about?" asked Talanov.

"Oh, just teetering on the brink of destruction for the mess you've gotten us into."

"You're acting like this was all my idea. Like I randomly decided to go on a rampage or something."

"You crashed my car—"

"—into an apartment building, yes, I know, as you're constantly reminding me."

"A young woman was *killed,* Alex. She wouldn't have been shot if you hadn't crashed into the building and gone after them the way you did."

Talanov's knuckles were white from gripping the steering wheel so tightly. "I know," he said, "and I'll have to wear that for the rest of my life. But I also know that Borzakov would have killed her, anyway, because she and Larisa were loose ends in whatever it is they're planning to do with that sniper rifle."

"Oh, yeah, that."

"Oh, yeah, *that.* So don't give me any heat about what I'm

doing to try to save Larisa and Marcy. If I hadn't done what I did, they'd be dead by now for sure. So instead of complaining, why not figure out where Borzakov is and what he's planning to do with that rifle. He *is* planning on using it, in case you'd forgotten, and you'd better figure out who he's planning to shoot before he puts a bullet in someone's brain."

Within ten minutes, the patrol cars switched off their lights and pulled over, allowing Talanov to speed by. Talanov waved his thanks but Diego did not wave back.

They soon took the exit ramp to the right, which swung left under the freeway and merged with the Seaside Freeway, which was a pleasant strip of highway with a grassy median and palm trees in the middle. Parked on the median were two unmarked cars, which fell in behind them. Up ahead was the Vincent Thomas suspension bridge over the ship channel. It had two giant towers that looked like sections of upright ladders. Through the lower rungs was threaded the arching deck that was the freeway. It was suspended from massive cables, with a high chain link fence on each side and a concrete divider topped with reflective green posts. To their right was the dogleg channel that led out to sea. To their left were the port's deep-water fingers, where several freighters were docked. On both sides were towering cranes, industrial yards, and waterfront warehouses.

The panorama on the downward span of the bridge was much the same. More cranes, some enormous fuel tanks, more industrial yards, a freight train inching along, and more docked ships. The cranes stood like giant insects against the horizon.

Following the blinking red dot on Wilcox's phone, they turned right on Ferry Street, which was bordered by warehouses and storage yards containing hundreds of ribbed steel containers piled five and six high, side by side, row after row. They made several more turns before entering a side street. The flashing green dot that was their car was now approaching the flashing red dot that was the other car.

"Slow down," said Wilcox. "We're getting close."

To their left were a row of more warehouses. Many had loading docks piled high with pallets and wooden crates. Big rigs were pulling in and out. On the other side of the street was another storage yard full of steel containers. Ahead, the street widened to form a parking lot behind a concrete barricade. The lot contained dozens of cars and pick-up trucks. Farther ahead was a small marina. In the distance across the harbor was another marina.

"In there," said Wilcox, directing Talanov into the parking lot.

Talanov parked in an angled space near the entrance and the two unmarked patrol cars pulled up beside him.

"Leave your pistol here," said Wilcox in a low voice.

"I may need it."

"Every one of those officers is armed. It's why they're here. Now, put it away and quit arguing."

After slipping the Herstal under his seat, Talanov and Wilcox joined a team of three men and one woman. All were in their twenties. All were fit and capable. Everyone introduced themselves before the officers drew their weapons and followed Wilcox across the asphalt.

While they walked, Wilcox rang Charlie and told her to get a satellite visual on the parking lot. "I want to see both dots and what the overall scene looks like."

"You got it," said Charlie, snapping and chewing her gum while her fingers flew across her keyboard. "Enhancing satellite imagery ... now," she said, entering a command.

The image on Wilcox's screen became a fuzzy satellite view of the parking lot, but after two seconds became clear again. It showed every vehicle, including shadows, and the progress of the group walking toward a car that had been juxtaposed with a blinking red dot.

"Over there," said Wilcox in a low voice, pointing to a maroon-colored Crown Victoria.

"Is that pounding I hear?" asked one of the officers to a series of repeated thumping sounds coming from the trunk of the car.

The four officers fanned out and surrounded the Ford. Approaching slowly, they held their guns low, in two handed-grips to one side, their eyes focused on the sedan.

"LAPD!" the female officer shouted. She had a blonde pony-tail and she was nearest the trunk. "Identify yourself."

Suddenly, they all heard vigorous pounding on the lid and muffled cries for help.

This all seems too easy, thought Talanov, turning a full circle to scan his surroundings. Across the street from his Lexus was the row of warehouses he had seen earlier. They were old buildings, sooty, and mostly brick, with low roofs and elevated freight platforms facing the street, where semi-trailers were being loaded and unloaded by workers driving forklifts. Two of the warehouses looked deserted and empty. No activity there at all. One had a sliding door standing partly open. To the left of the warehouses was a freight yard full of ribbed steel containers. There were hundreds of them, stacked four and five high, in neat rows, in a variety of colors, many rusty and scarred. Beyond the freight yard was the Vincent Thomas suspension bridge over the ship channel. Across the channel were more commercial buildings and warehouses, and a small factory of some kind. Following the channel to the left, Talanov saw a number of giant round fuel tanks. To the left of these were some freighters being loaded by towering gantry cranes. Then came the two marinas – one on each side of the channel – then several more freight yards, another parking lot with more cars and trucks, then the row of warehouses across the street from his Lexus. A full circle completed. A full assessment made in just under a minute.

This all seems too easy, he thought again.

CHAPTER 36

"HANG tight, we'll get you out!" the officer shouted back. To the officer in front of the vehicle: "How does it look?"

The officer had been looking through tinted glass of the windshield with a special scope from a variety of angles, not getting too close before they knew the car was unoccupied.

"Looks clear," he said.

The female officer approached the trunk cautiously at the right rear corner. She crouched and knocked on the lid and identified herself. Two female voices inside the trunk began yelling for help. The female officer calmed them down and asked who they were. Larisa and Marcy responded with their names. The female officer gave a thumbs-up to the others. She then asked if the car had been rigged with explosives.

Marcy identified herself as a Federal agent and demanded to be let out. The female officer said they first needed to ascertain the car's safety and repeated her question about explosives. Marcy said she didn't think so. The female officer then asked if either of them had heard anything suspicious, or if the drivers had mentioned setting any kind of a trap. Marcy said the two drivers had simply parked the car and left, and that nothing had been rigged, so would the officers hurry up and open the damned trunk. The female officer said they needed to check things out first. Marcy told her to hurry up, that she was tired of having her face in the ass of a whore. The other officers grinned at their colleague, who shook her head then peered under the car to see if any explosive devices had been planted on the undercarriage. Once the car had been thoroughly checked out, one of the officers opened the driver's side door. The car was empty. He looked up under the dashboard but saw nothing suspicious. He then popped open the trunk.

With a string of curses, Marcy clambered over Larisa and jumped out, where she began pacing back and forth, rolling her shoulders and stretching her muscles.

Talanov stepped past Marcy and offered his hand to Larisa.

While Larisa climbed out with Talanov's help, Wilcox took Marcy aside and asked what had happened. Marcy told him how they were sitting in the car when these two Russian goons – bodybuilder types – climbed in while she was explaining the transmitter to Larisa. She said the goons shoved huge pistols in their faces, then grabbed the transmitter from Larisa's hand. "One of them even ran his hands inside Larisa's bra cups for any hidden surprises, as he described them, which made them both laugh with high pitched giggles."

"Did they do the same to you?" asked Wilcox.

"I told them I'd scratch their eyes out if they tried," Marcy declared. "They said something in Russian and laughed, but I could tell they knew I was serious. So they left me alone."

Marcy went on to describe the slick, dark-haired man who drove up in the Crown Victoria. He had oily black hair, expensive clothes and was an arrogant show-pony type, with his shirt unbuttoned almost to his navel and lots of flashy jewelry. The goons showed him the bug and he grabbed Larisa by the face and told her she and her family would live to regret this. The goons then shoved them into the trunk of the Ford and shut the lid, but stood nearby talking. When Wilcox asked if Marcy had heard any specifics, Marcy said she could not understand what they were saying because they spoke Russian. Even more irritating, however, was Larisa's incessant crying about what Borzakov would do to her family.

"I tried getting the bitch to shut up, but she kept sobbing," said Marcy, glaring at Larisa in disgust.

Wilcox watched Talanov hug Larisa. For the longest time they just stood there embracing.

"Are you all right?" Talanov asked Larisa. He brushed some strands of hair from her face.

"Borzakov told them to kill me – kill both of us – for what I was going to do with that listening device," Larisa replied.

"And I was furious with Bill for asking you to do that."

"It was her – Agent Foley – who asked me to do it."

"I know. But Wilcox was in on it."

"But you came for me. No one has ever done anything like this before."

"We all need someone to fight for us."

"I would do the same for you."

Talanov smiled. "You already have."

"Nick, he touch my breasts. Say he is searching for additional surprises. Agent Foley, she say she will scratch their eyes out if they touch her. Nick and Vic, they look at one another and say in Russian not to worry, that they not touch back end of horse."

"They called her a horse's ass?"

Larisa stifled a laugh and nodded. "She think she scare them away."

Talanov's smile faded and he took Larisa by the hands. A long moment of silence passed while Talanov looked down at the pavement, not knowing how to say what he knew he had to say.

"What is it?" she asked, squeezing him by the hands.

Raising his eyes to meet hers, Talanov told Larisa about Jade and how Borzakov had shot her, and that he had tried everything to save her life, but couldn't. Larisa listened in stunned silence, her eyes searching his, not wanting to believe what she had just heard. But the solemn look in Talanov's eyes let her know it was true. Tears formed in Larisa's eyes. Her lips began to quiver. Talanov brought her to him and a moment later, Larisa began to cry.

A short distance away, Wilcox said to Marcy, "So, what's this about Larisa knocking you into a toilet stall?"

"I tripped. The punch wasn't much."

Wilcox smiled and nodded.

"Caught me off-guard, the bitch," growled Marcy, watching Larisa with disgust. "I'd have punched her back, but I knew we needed her help. Besides, have a look at her now. What a cry baby. Good thing I didn't punch her after all."

Fifteen feet away, Larisa wiped her eyes and looked up at Talanov. "Jade was my friend," she said. "We took care of one another. Help each other survive. Jade was from place that sounded like Song-choo, or something like that. I don't know exactly where. When she was born, her parents saw that she was a girl. They planned to kill her because they wanted a son, and can have only one child. But she was so pretty they could not do it. So her mother take her to Vietnam, to missionary group, where she was raised in an orphanage. Her new parents were Americans, who loved her as their own. Then her missionary parents were killed by rebels and she ended up in Hanoi, on streets. To survive, she lived as thief and prostitute from age of eleven. When she was fifteen, she was sold to mob and brought to LA. When I come, she take me under her wing. Protect me. Keep drugs away."

"Borzakov will pay, I swear," said Talanov, his expression hardening. "He just stood there in the corridor, sneering, using Jade as a shield. Then he shot her so that he could get away. And not a flesh wound, either. But through her femoral artery, knowing she would soon bleed out if I didn't do something to stop it. God knows I wanted to go after him. To kill him for what he'd done. But I knew I had to try and save Jade." Talanov's eyes grew moist with emotion. "I tried everything I knew to save her, to keep her alive, but she died, just like Andrea."

Larisa squeezed Talanov's hands.

"I should have stopped him," said Talanov. "I should have gone after him and chased him down and put a bullet in his brain."

"But you did something much more important. You chose to remain with Jade."

"Who *died*. I did everything I could, but she just ... died. Right there, in my arms. And I was helpless to do anything about it. If I'd have gone after Borzakov, at least something good would have come out of all of this, and that butcher would be dead right now."

"Protecting the living is more important than avenging the dead."

Talanov looked down at Larisa with surprise. "Where did you hear that?" he asked.

"Jade tell me."

"She actually said that to you?"

"She say she learn it from her missionary parents."

"It's as if she said those same words to me," said Talanov. "She didn't say them to me verbally, but those very words popped into my mind when I was kneeling beside her, trying to save her but knowing Borzakov was getting away."

"And you heard them, yes? Not in ears, but in your heart."

"Yeah, but what good did they do? Jade died and Borzakov got away."

"Don't you see, Alex? The good was for you, not her. Those words were her gift to you."

"But I failed her, Larisa. She *died.*"

"She died, yes, but you did not fail her. This is why Jade give you this special gift. Because you do this good thing for her. Because you stay. Because you not let her die alone."

CHAPTER 37

"TOUCHING," said Marcy sarcastically, "but the cops need Larisa's statement." Grabbing Larisa by the arm, Marcy began leading her toward several officers.

Talanov caught up with them and stopped her.

"Is there a problem?" asked Marcy.

"Yeah," said Talanov, removing Marcy's hand from Larisa's arm. "If the police want Larisa's statement, they can come over here and ask for it. Politely. But don't storm over here and grab her by the arm and treat her with that kind of disrespect."

"She's my package and she's coming with me."

"She's not a package and she's not yours or anyone else's."

"Are you interfering with a Federal officer?"

"Call it whatever you want."

"She comes with me *right now* or I'm arresting you for obstruction of justice."

"You can pop threats like that all day and it won't change a thing. Larisa goes nowhere with you."

Marcy jabbed a finger at Talanov's face. "Surrender her *now* or I'll—"

"Whoa, whoa, whoa, hold on," said Wilcox, who saw what was happening and hurried over.

"Your Russian pal here is interfering with a Federal officer," snarled Marcy.

"Let's dial it down a notch," said Wilcox, easing Marcy back.

"This whore – this *illegal* whore – needs to furnish a statement!"

"That's enough, Agent Foley! I'll take care of it."

"Fine. Take care of it any way you want. I'll be sure and let Teague know." With parting glares for Wilcox and Talanov, Marcy turned away. Wilcox watched her run to catch up with two of the male police officers who were walking back to their unmarked car. "Hey, guys, wait up!" she called out. When the two officers saw her coming, they groaned and kept walking.

" She wears brash and arrogant well," said Talanov.

"Yeah, well, keep this up and you'll get us *both* kicked off the committee," said Wilcox.

"They're not about to let me on that committee and you know it," Talanov replied.

"I'll give Teague a call and smooth things over, but you've got to quit antagonizing people, especially people like Marcy. She works for Teague and what she says carries a lot of weight."

"If joining your committee means working with her, then she's doing me a favor by killing my chances."

"Yeah, well, just watch it, okay?" said Wilcox, motioning for the female officer.

"Yes, sir?" the officer asked.

"Larisa here's been through a lot," Wilcox explained, "so with your permission, I'll take her statement myself and send you a copy. Is that okay?"

"No problem, sir. Here's my card. By the way, our boys back at the apartment were able to free more than sixty girls."

"What will happen to them?" asked Larisa.

"Some will be sent home. Happily, I might add, after all they've been through. Others will apply for a visa, which will allow them permanent residency. Some were already here legally, so they can stay for the duration of their visas. One already has an agent, if you can believe that, and wants to sell the film rights for her story."

"It's LA," said Talanov. "Nothing surprises me."

"You should see the squalor they – you – were forced to live in," the officer continued with a sympathetic smile for Larisa, who smiled back and nodded. "Herded each night into a communal bathroom to do your business and put on makeup while Borzakov and his thugs leered and watched. The ones who made the mistake of defecating or urinating in their rooms were made to clean up the mess and then punished. There was even an execution room at the end of the hall, with extra soundproofing and a noose mounted to a ceiling joist. One of the bedrooms attached to the office was a narcotics clinic.

Needles all over the place. No telling how many girls had been turned into junkies."

There were tears now in Larisa's eyes.

"I didn't mean to be insensitive," the officer said gently. "I can't imagine what you've been through."

"It is what happened. It is fine," Larisa replied, wiping her eyes.

"And Borzakov? What about him?" asked Talanov.

"Our boys found an escape tunnel in the basement," the officer replied. "It led to a neighbor's shed."

"So there's been no sign of him?" asked Wilcox.

The officer shook her head. "We're still searching but it doesn't look good. We'll run a trace on the phone left in the Crown Vic, of course, but it looks like a throwaway cell."

"They left their phone in the car?" asked Talanov.

The officer nodded.

"Doesn't that seem a bit odd?"

"It's a throwaway cell," answered Wilcox. "Which is what criminals do when they're finished with them. They throw them away, which allows them to vanish without a trace."

"That's certainly one explanation," said Talanov.

"Meaning what, exactly?" asked Wilcox.

"Meaning, they left that phone behind on purpose so that we'd trace it and find the car."

"Why on earth would they do that?"

"I'm not sure. But it's something we need to consider."

"It's a throw-a-way-cell," said Wilcox, enunciating each syllable. "Cell phones can be traced, which means they're liabilities for people not wanting others to know where they are. That's why Borzakov left it behind. Don't make this more than it is."

"What if he's baiting us? What is he wanted us to find that phone? We need to consider all the angles."

"You think too much," said Wilcox.

"Maybe you don't think enough."

Forcing a smile, Wilcox thanked the officer, took Talanov by the arm, and began leading him and Larisa toward the Lexus. "Come on. You can do your thinking from the car."

"Doesn't this bother you just a little?" asked Talanov. "Borzakov's men kidnapped Larisa and Marcy and drove them here with the intention of killing them and dumping their bodies. But all of a sudden, they unexpectedly abandon the car and leave the women alive in the trunk. But not only that, they leave their cell phone in the car, which we were able to trace and pinpoint its exact location."

"So they made a mistake. Or saw us coming and made a run for it. Don't over-think this, Alex."

Talanov looked at Larisa. "Didn't you say Borzakov was furious at you for what you were planning to do?"

Larisa nodded. "He grab me by the face and say my family and I would live to regret this. Then he tell Nick and Vic to put us in trunk of car and get rid of us."

"So why leave you alive in the trunk and a cell phone behind that he *knew* would lead us right to you?"

Talanov looked back and forth between Larisa and Wilcox but neither of them replied.

"What happened when you got here?" asked Talanov. "What did you hear?"

"What do you mean?" asked Larisa.

"Did you hear them talking to anyone? Did you hear a car door slam, or an engine start?"

"There were many noises. Trucks, cars, and a loud horn blast, from a ship, I think."

"But nothing specific? Nothing nearby?"

"I hear a car door slam, but like I said, there were all kinds of noises. And I was not listening to the noises. I was thinking of you and wondering and if I would ever see you again, and if I would ever see my family again, which I know I won't, for Borzakov will kill them."

"I won't let that happen."

"What can you do? Borzakov will phone Gorsky and Gorsky will kill them. He is a horrible man, very cruel, like Borzakov."

"Can't you call and warn them? Tell them to stay with a friend or a relative?"

"Borzakov say he has listening device on their phone, that he has them watched. He say if I ever try calling them, he will know and they will die. Maybe I should call them, anyway. What is there to lose if he is going to kill them, anyway? Perhaps they are already dead."

"Don't think that way, okay? We'll work something out."

Larisa smiled and shrugged and Talanov could tell she appreciated the sentiment but really didn't believe anything could be done.

Talanov turned to Wilcox. "We've got to help them, Bill."

"We can talk about that later."

"Let's talk about it now."

Wilcox started to reply but could only make a series of tongue clicks and sighs and awkward glances in various directions.

"Bill!"

"I can't," said Wilcox with genuine regret. "We have no assets in Ukraine and I can't very well send in a team on such short notice."

"Gorsky will *kill* them if you don't," replied Talanov.

"And I'm sorry, really, I am."

"Sorry doesn't cut it, Bill."

"It has to be when I have nothing else to give."

"I don't believe you," said Talanov. "That's because I know you *do* have assets in Ukraine, in Kiev, and if I had more time, I'd get you their names and addresses. But I don't. So let's say for the moment that you can't redirect them without compromising an ongoing operation. What about a neighboring country? Don't tell me the CIA has no available assets in all of Eastern Europe, or Western Russia, or Istanbul for that matter, because I know for a fact that you do, and if I had enough time, I'd get you *their* names and addresses as well. *Do* something, Bill. Fight for this! Fight for *them.*"

"I would if I could, Alex, but I can't, and I think by now I would have earned enough of your respect for you to believe me when I tell you I can't."

"You've got that backwards, Bill. Completely. Respect isn't earned. It's given. Right up front. Everybody deserves your respect until they earn your *dis*respect, and right now, you're earning mine."

Wilcox looked up with a frustrated sigh.

"How badly do you want me to come and work for you?"

"Not this again."

"I'll do anything you want. Give you any help I can give. But you've *got* to save that family."

"I just told you, there's nothing I can do."

"And I know there is, so promise me you'll look into it. Once Larisa's family is safe, I'm yours. But not until."

Wilcox looked away.

"Come on, Bill," said Talanov, repositioning himself to look Wilcox directly in the eyes. "Promise me you'll look into it."

Wilcox ran a hand across his forehead. He was clearly uncomfortable with being pressured into a corner.

Talanov stuck out his hand. "Do we have a deal?"

Larisa watched Wilcox closely. Her eyes were desperate with hope. Wilcox started to speak but didn't know what to say.

"I don't care how many favors you have to call in," said Talanov, "or how many strings you have to pull. If you want me to come and work for you, I'm willing to do that, but this is what it will cost."

Wilcox looked down at Talanov's hand then into his eyes. The two men stared at one another for a long moment. Finally, after an awkward glance at Larisa, who stood nearby wringing her hands, Wilcox shook Talanov's hand. Larisa responded by leaping into Wilcox's arms and hugging him.

"I haven't had this much affection in years," Wilcox said when Larisa finally let go. "But I really must caution you against—"

"I'm going to stop you right there," said Talanov, clasping Wilcox on the shoulder. "You said you'd try and that's good enough for me."

Wilcox sighed with resignation and nodded.

Talanov looked over at Larisa and said, "Now, back to what you can tell us about Borzakov and his men. I need you to focus on the drive over. Did you hear them say anything?"

"They were laughing and telling crude jokes in English," Larisa recalled, "until one of them got a phone call."

"A phone call?" asked Wilcox.

"Yes. I hear cell phone ring. Then they were quiet, but the one who take call, he speak Russian to whoever was on phone."

"They spoke in Russian? You're sure?"

"Yes. They speak to him like he was important man."

"So Borzakov got through," said Wilcox.

"Maybe," said Talanov. To Larisa: "Did you understand anything they said?"

"Agent Foley was complaining about being locked in trunk, so I could not hear very much. But I did hear them laugh and say, *'Shah i mat.'*"

"Checkmate?" said Talanov. "Are you sure?"

"Yes. That is what they say."

"Why would he say that?" asked Wilcox.

"Many of us in the KGB were chess fanatics," explained Talanov. "Ilya was, and I was, but I'm not that sure about Borzakov. I don't remember him in any of our classes."

"I still don't understand your obsession with chess," Wilcox replied, shaking his head.

"We studied its strategy," answered Talanov, "to develop our ability to think laterally and three-dimensionally, and were graded by the great Mikhail Botvinnik, who held the World Championship at various times from 1948 through 1963, when he turned to coaching others, including Karpov, Kasparov, and Kramnik. He made us study all the great contests. The Opera Game, The Immortal Game, Greco's Game, and others. We analyzed how they were won and what principles were involved."

"They mentioned Greco's Game," said Larisa. "I thought I was not hearing correctly."

"Why would they talk about that particular game?" asked Wilcox.

"In 1619, Gioachino Greco played the first recorded chess game in history," Talanov explained, "and that particular game, which bears his name, refers to his famous victory against an unidentified opponent. Botvinnik used it as the classic example of how gambits can be employed to lull your opponent into a false sense of security."

"I have no idea what you're talking about," said Wilcox.

"Picture a chess board," said Talanov. "Black is on top, with Greco, who was white, on the bottom. The opening moves see white with two pawns in the center of the board and black pretty much hanging back. Black finally decides to break up that two pawn defense and attacks with a pawn. White responds by taking the pawn. Black strikes with his bishop and white's rook is now trapped. So Greco strikes with his queen and threatens black's king. Black blocks the queen with a pawn. White takes the pawn with another pawn. Black then pulls a slick move with his knight and threatens two of white's most powerful pieces, the queen and rook. Greco then does the unimaginable. He takes one of black's pawns with a pawn. Black cannot believe his luck and he hurriedly takes Greco's queen with his knight. At that point, black must have felt the game was his. He had just taken Greco's queen. But Greco had been watching his opponent carefully and saw that he was hasty, and that he had tunnel vision. So he lured him into a trap by sacrificing his queen. When black fell for the gambit, Greco struck with his bishop. Checkmate, in only eight moves. It is the single finest example of how to trap a hasty opponent."

"Why would they be talking about that?" asked Wilcox. "I can't imagine two animals like – what were their names – Nick and Vic – is that a joke?"

"It is no joke," Larisa replied. "Nick and Vic are their names. They are very bad men."

"Well, I can't imagine *Nick and Vic* deciding to have an intellectual discussion about chess." He shook his head and continued walking toward Talanov's Lexus.

Talanov paused and looked back at the Crown Victoria being searched by the remaining officers. *Something still doesn't fit,* he thought, *especially with that cell phone left in the car.* He turned another full circle and scanned the cranes, storage yards, containers, and warehouses. Another blast from a freighter echoed across the parking lot.

"Are you two coming?" asked Wilcox, looking back.

"Is there any way for Charlie to gain access to our old KGB records?" asked Talanov.

"If a record or file exists, Charlie can usually get hold of it. Why?"

"I'd like her to check out the enrollment sheets for our chess classes. To see the scores."

"You really are taking this chess thing a little too far."

"I want to find out what Borzakov's chess scores were. I want to see how good he was. Or if he was even there."

"Why?"

"Because Greco's Game, which is what Nick and Vic were talking about, was a brilliant use of gambits, which are traps based on the sacrifice of your own chess pieces."

"So?"

"In that game, Greco sacrificed his queen in order to check-mate his opponent."

"I hear them say checkmate," said Larisa.

"But *why?*" asked Wilcox. "What does checkmate and Greco's Game have to do with Larisa and Marcy?"

With Wilcox and Larisa walking ahead, Talanov again looked back at the Crown Victoria, then at his surroundings, then at the row of warehouses across the street, where he noticed someone step quickly out of sight from the partially-open doorway of the deserted warehouse on the end. Had someone been watching them? He was certain he had seen movement. He paused and stared at the doorway. Why would someone be watching them? Why would someone not want to be seen? A dock worker would simply exchange glances and go about his work. This person, however, had deliberately jumped out of sight. Someone agile and quick but large enough to catch his attention. There he was again. Deep in the shadows but definitely stepping back into view and definitely watching them.

Talanov saw Wilcox and Larisa approach the Lexus. Saw Wilcox turn and motion for him to hurry up.

Greco's Game. A hasty opponent. Tunnel vision. Checkmate.

Talanov lunged forward and grabbed Wilcox and Larisa by the shirts. "Get down!" he yelled, yanking them back just as his Lexus exploded in a massive fireball.

CHAPTER 38

TALANOV watched the Lexus burn. The bomb had turned the interior into an inferno that raged until a fire truck arrived and doused the flames with a dry chemical spray. It had been the perfect trap, leaving the two women alive in the trunk to draw everyone's attention. Tunnel vision. Haste. Checkmate. *Except their gambit had been discovered and their checkmate foiled.*

This time. Barely.

"Borzakov obviously wants revenge for what you did back at his apartment," said Wilcox as paramedics treated them for minor abrasions from the back door of an ambulance.

"We don't know that for sure," Talanov replied. "He could have been after you."

"He didn't know I was even there."

"Maybe he saw you leave the apartment."

"Which of us drove a car into the side of his building? Which of us ruined his operation?" asked Talanov, wincing when a paramedic cleaned his burns and scrapes with iodine.

"Sorry," the paramedic said.

"So Borzakov and his men get away and we've got nothing," said Wilcox, watching police search the warehouses and question dock workers.

"We're alive. That counts for something," Talanov replied.

"Why explosives? Why not a rifle? *Your* sniper rifle, for example. Wouldn't that have been ironic? You getting shot with your own rifle."

"Aren't you the gushy one? It's not my rifle and they used explosives because they wanted to get rid of us all. I'm guessing Nick and Vic were planned to kill the girls here at the port and then dump their bodies offshore when Borzakov calls with a new strategy and someone meets them here with a brick of C4. Checkmate."

"Remind me to take up chess," muttered Wilcox just as his cell phone rang and he took the call.

"Are you okay?" asked Teague.

"Minor scrapes. That's all. Talanov's quick thinking saved the day."

"You're sure you're okay? Nothing's broken?"

"I'm fine. Really, I am."

"Where do we stand with Talanov?" asked Teague.

With his phone to his ear, Wilcox turned away and lowered his voice. "He's willing to come aboard on one condition."

"He's really not in any position to be setting conditions."

"I know, but he wants us to rescue Larisa's family from Borzakov's men, from a thug in Kherson named Gorsky."

"We have no assets in Ukraine."

"That's what I told him."

"Then what's the problem?"

"He's insistent."

"We can't. End of story."

Wilcox did not reply.

"You didn't tell him we'd do this, did you?" asked Teague.

"I told him I'd see what I could do."

"Dammit, Bill!"

"He made me promise."

"Made you *promise?* Who's running this show, anyway? You or him? I'm beginning to think we're better off without Talanov. He does nothing but cause us trouble. Ilya identified Borzakov and he's a cop, who's perfectly placed in the FSB."

"Ilya hasn't been vetted yet."

"Isn't that what you're working on now?"

"Yes, sir, and so far, he checks out. In fact, he's compiling a list of KGB agents who stayed on to work for the FSB but who may also be working for the mob."

"As in double agents, working both sides?"

"Yes, sir. Plus, he's working on a list of KGB agents like Borzakov who ended up in the US. I should be hearing back from him any time."

"Well, there you go," said Teague. "Ilya's proving himself already. What has Talanov done?"

"I trust Talanov."

"And that's all well and good, but it sounds to me like he's becoming difficult to manage."

"He does tend to do things his own way."

"Leaving us to pick up the pieces. Do you have any idea the trouble he's caused?"

"Yes, sir, I do."

A huff of frustration was Teague's reply.

"What do you want me to do?" asked Wilcox. "He keeps asking me how badly we want him to come and work for us."

"The answer's, not at all, if he keeps talking like that. He's insubordinate and reckless and he's attempting to hold us hostage with excessive demands. I've a mind to deport his ass."

"Is deportation what you really want?"

"I want him to know his place!" fumed Teague, pacing the floor.

Wilcox did not reply.

"There is nothing we can do about the girl's family," Teague finally said.

"I told him I'd try."

"And you've kept your promise. You tried."

"He also wants me to have Charlie find out about some chess scores."

"We don't have time for stuff like that! I need you and Talanov to be at the Hollywood & Highland Center tonight for the Regional Congress on Organized Crime Prevention. Diane Gustaves is giving the opening speech."

"Does that mean you've cleared Talanov to work for the JRIC?"

"Just get him there."

"With respect, sir, I need to hear you say it. I need you to give me the green light to offer Talanov a position. Diane, I believe, is already in favor of bringing him aboard."

"And her convictions are based pretty much on yours since you know Talanov better than anyone."

"I appreciate the congresswoman's support, sir."

"Cut the crap, Bill. Talanov's a Russian and I don't trust him."

"Ilya's a Russian and you seem to trust him."

"You know what I'm talking about."

"With respect, sir, no, I don't. That's like people mistrusting you because you're black. Or me because I'm white. Or a white man. Or an old white man. Who mansplanes or whitelashes or whatever it is we're supposed to do. Haven't we had enough of that kind of ignorant nonsense and bigotry? If you've got something against Talanov personally, I'd like to know what it is."

"How about Ilya already coming through with some impressive results? You said so yourself. What has Talanov produced other than trouble?"

"Oh, how about some of the most valuable intel this country has ever received? How about the dozens if not hundreds of people he helped escape Soviet oppression? If you'd like, I can bring in some of those survivors and their families, who will be more than happy to—"

"All right, you've made your point!"

"Sir, Talanov may be arrogant, difficult, and frustrating, but he has been a trusted ally since the Cold War. In fact, he helped us win the Cold War. That's, what, thirty years of service and loyalty? And we've known Ilya for, what, a day?"

"Posner's against bringing Talanov on board."

"Posner's an idiot."

"Maybe so, but the LAPD agrees with him. Immigration is still not sure they want to let Talanov into the country, and Homeland Security is watching him like a hawk. Diane Gustaves has managed to give us some wiggle room, but bringing a Russian like Talanov aboard is still very tentative. Don't forget, we nearly lost Agent Foley to the Russians."

"With respect, sir, that's a pretty broad and inaccurate statement. Talanov is hardly in league with the Russian mob. He had nothing to do with what happened to Marcy."

"Maybe not, but a lot of his old buddies work for the mob. Who's to say he won't side with them if push comes to shove? Who's to say he's not still on friendly terms with some of them? Who's to say he won't double-cross us instead of turning them in? Who's to say those old buddies won't recruit him as a mole?"

"I've already said it but I'll say it again: Talanov put his life on the line many times for us during the Cold War. I think he's more than demonstrated his loyalty."

"For your sake, I hope you're right," said Teague. "Because if you aren't, you'll crash and burn. Are you willing to risk everything on Talanov's recruitment?"

"If I didn't think we needed his help, I'd say no. But we do. And I trust him. So the answer is yes. What you need to decide, sir – again, with respect – is whether *you* think we need his help. If you don't – if you think we're making adequate headway on our own – just say the word and I'll drop it."

"No one's been able to stop the proliferation of organized crime and you know it."

"Then I think you've answered the question. I just need to hear you say it."

"I really am tempted to deport you along with Talanov, you know that?"

"My being an American aside, if France is among your list of destinations, be my guest, especially the Burgundy region, although the Barossa Valley of South Australia is definitely a contender."

"Shut up, Bill. You've got your clearance."

"Thank you, sir. We can't assume he'll accept, though, given his demand."

"Just get him there, whatever it takes."

"I'll try."

"You better do more than try. Diane's life is on the line and we can't take any chances. Obviously, the LAPD and Secret Service are working overtime, but Talanov knows Borzakov better than any of us."

"I'll see what I can do. But if Talanov agrees and later finds out we let something happen to Larisa's family ..."

"Just get him there, okay?"

"Yes, sir," said Wilcox as the line went dead.

CHAPTER 39

WILCOX could feel his heart pounding when he got off the phone. No telling what his blood pressure was. What he wouldn't give for a glass – make that a bottle – of wine right now. At the moment, retirement to some far flung vineyard sounded pretty good.

He turned and looked at Talanov and Larisa sitting together in the open rear door of the ambulance. The medics – two young men in their twenties – were still cleaning and dressing Larisa's scrapes. Talanov was amused by the extra attention they were giving Larisa, who was shy and appreciative until she noticed his grin and punched him.

Wilcox smiled. If only he had someone to punch him like that. Perhaps his last wife had been right when she'd said he wasn't worth the price of a fifty-cent bullet or she would have shot him. She didn't mean it, of course – the part about shooting him – but the part about being worthless had wounded him more deeply than any bullet ever could have. He watched Talanov and Larisa for a moment. *Why had he tried to divide them? What a stupid decision that had been.*

By now, the fire trucks had extinguished the flames of Talanov's Lexus, which was nothing but a smoking shell with a distended roof from the force of the explosion. The seats were little more than charred springs. The dashboard was melted and burned. All four doors had been blown off their hinges. Police had taped off the parking lot with yellow crime tape, and a crowd of spectators, mostly dock workers and a few truck drivers, were watching from various positions around the perimeter.

Wilcox checked his phone. He had missed a call from a number he did not recognize. Whoever it was had left a message, so he dialed his voicemail and listened to the recording.

The message was from Ilya, who said he had good news. After making a few calls to some trusted colleagues in

Moscow, he had been able to put together a list of old KGB agents involved with the mob. Some were even in Los Angeles, and Borzakov was on the list, as were a number of covert operatives from the FSB. Of special interest was Ilya's comment that Borzakov maintained a safe house in Los Angeles. His source of that information was an FSB agent in Moscow, who knew a friend of a friend who knew Borzakov. The Moscow agent said he was working on an exact address, which Ilya said he would pass on to Wilcox once he received it.

Wilcox phoned Ilya to thank him and asked how quickly he could email him that list of agents living in Los Angeles. Ilya begged Wilcox to understand that he could not email anything which might in any way be traced back to him. He was happy to hand over the list personally, but to communicate it electronically was out of the question.

"I understand," Wilcox said just as another horn blast from a freighter echoed across the port.

"What was that?" asked Ilya.

Wilcox told Ilya where he was and briefed him on what had happened with Larisa and Marcy. "As for your list, how about we meet tonight, in my hotel room?"

"Of course. What time and where?"

Wilcox told Ilya where he was staying in and what room, adding that if he needed a hotel room of his own for the duration of his stay, he was happy to arrange a suite. "There's a bit of airport noise," he added, "but the hotel has gorgeous views all around. City lights on one side, ocean and sunsets on the other. Take your pick."

Ilya graciously declined, adding that if he were discovered to be staying in the same hotel with a senior official from the CIA, suspicions would be aroused. Staying with Talanov would arouse no suspicions.

"There's no way anyone could link the two of us together," said Wilcox. "I use a different name and my reservation, as always, was made through an ordinary travel agency."

Ilya expressed his appreciation but again declined. "Surely you understand," he said, "and I mean no disrespect to your generosity, but I simply cannot be too careful in light of what I am doing. You may call me paranoid, if you wish."

Wilcox assured Ilya that he understood. He then asked if Ilya remembered Borzakov being a chess player.

"Such an odd question. Why do you ask?"

Wilcox told him what Talanov had said about chess being studied as part of his training. He then recounted how Larisa had overheard the men who kidnapped her, Nick and Vic, mention 'checkmate' and 'Greco's Game.'

Ilya thought for a moment. "I do seem to remember Borzakov being in class. He always sat toward the rear of the room. We were in an old lecture hall, with rows of wooden seats that were very uncomfortable. Botvinnik would walk the stage, reciting strategies and moves from memory. I've never seen anyone like him."

"But Borzakov was there? You remember him?"

"Yes, although he didn't socialize with the rest of us like Talanov did."

"Look, I've got a prior commitment for tonight that I can't miss. Are you able to meet me at, say, eleven? Or is that too late?"

"Actually, late at night is my preference. Not that anyone is watching, of course, but I'd rather not be seen talking to you during daylight hours. I mean no offense."

Wilcox laughed. "None taken. I'll phone you later with an exact time. Where will you be?"

"With Talanov."

"He won't be home tonight."

"Oh?"

Wilcox wondered if he should fill Ilya in on what was happening. Ilya knew Borzakov, too, but he had not been cleared for tonight's convention. Still, if there was a chance he could obtain additional information on Borzakov's attempt to assassinate Gustaves – assuming that was his objective – then it would be gross negligence not to see if Ilya could be of help.

"Obviously, you are not able to discuss what you and Alex will be doing," Ilya said in the absence of an explanation.

"Actually, I would like your opinion on something."

"Of course."

"We're worried Borzakov may try to assassinate someone tonight," Wilcox said.

"Are you able to say who and why?"

"Congresswoman Diane Gustaves. She's received dozens of death threats because of her tough stance against organized crime. She's giving a speech tonight in Hollywood and we think Borzakov may use the occasion to try to kill her."

"She would definitely be a logical choice."

"How do you think he'd pull it off?"

Ilya thought for a moment. "In my estimation, he would send one or two men on a suicide mission. They would not know this, of course, thinking they would be on a legitimate assignment to kill the congresswoman. But they would be apprehended and probably killed. This would be his diversion. Then, when everyone relaxes after what they assume will be a failed attempt, he will assassinate her when people least expect it."

"Like in Greco's Game?"

"Yes. Do you know chess?"

"Not really. But something like that happened today and Talanov mentioned it."

"It is the reason we studied the game. For situations like this."

"So you think Gustaves is the target?"

"From what you have told me about her, yes. I don't think there is any doubt."

"And Borzakov, is he our man?"

"Unless you think the kidnappers, Nick and Vic, are more of a danger."

"They're henchmen. Not the brains. Will Borzakov use the sniper rifle he bought with Talanov's ID?"

"I think so, but not because he thinks Talanov will be blamed for the attempt. That opportunity has passed. Nevertheless, it will be one of the components of his plan, simply because it is an effective weapon."

"How, when, and where will he make his attempt?"

"Will tonight be when the congresswoman is most vulnerable?"

"Yes."

"Then tonight he will make an attempt."

"How can you be so sure?"

"It is simple and clean, and the weight of evidence points to this moment, which makes perfect sense when seen through the eyes of someone like Borzakov, who views Americans as typically having tunnel vision, which is why he will use a diversion. When I see you later tonight, I will tell you about some case studies of planned assassinations and how diversions played an important part."

"Planned assassinations? Of whom?"

"Certain political and industrial leaders in the West," Ilya replied. "The case studies were from our KGB days, and reflect how we studied the arrival and departure patterns of your leaders, as well as their personal habits, in order to deduce those occasions of greatest vulnerability and least expectancy of an attack."

"You studied our movements in that much detail?"

"As I am sure you studied ours."

Wilcox laughed and said, "Thanks, Ilya. We'll talk more tonight." Ending the call, he turned to see Talanov standing directly behind him.

CHAPTER 40

WILCOX jumped back a step. "Quit sneaking around like that! Are you trying to give me a *heart attack?*"

"You're that trusting of a man you've known for a day?"

Wilcox let out a deflated sigh. There was no use trying to duck out of this one. "You've got to understand," he said. "Prior to that call, my boss put me through the worst grilling of my career."

"About?"

"Bringing you aboard."

Talanov raised an eyebrow but did not reply.

"They don't trust you," said Wilcox. "They think you're a loose cannon who may have loyalties to the mob, which is populated with many of your old buddies from the KGB."

"You've got to be kidding."

"I told Teague how I trusted you and convinced him to bring you aboard. He wants you with me tonight."

"What for?"

"As you know, Congresswoman Gustaves is one of the biggest thorns in the side of the mob. She's giving a speech tonight at the Regional Congress on Organized Crime Prevention."

"And your boss thinks the mob is going to try and assassinate her?"

Wilcox nodded. "Which is why they want you along tonight as a consultant. To try and prevent that from happening."

"So you ran this by Ilya to get his take on what Borzakov might try?"

"Ilya thinks Borzakov will make a diversionary attempt on the congresswoman's life to distract us. Then, when we foil that attempt, he'll strike when we least expect it. He says it's a classic chess strategy that's right up Borzakov's alley."

Talanov did not reply.

"You don't agree?" asked Wilcox, noticing Talanov's hesitation.

"Those who study chess can see when an opponent is too

eager, too greedy, and too inexperienced. You're obviously not inexperienced. But your boss has got you rattled and you're scrambling to try and get back on his good side by using sources that aren't properly vetted. You're too eager, Bill, and maybe too greedy. I'm not saying Ilya's a bad guy. I wouldn't have offered to let him stay with me if I thought he was. We simply don't know him well enough – or long enough – to bring him in on something like this."

"Charlie ran a background check. He's a cop. He's on the level."

"I'd want him passing a lot more than an internet background check before I trusted him with that kind of information."

"Ilya knows Borzakov, knows his chess strategies, knows how he thinks."

"Does he now?"

"He says that he does and I've seen nothing that would lead me to suspect otherwise. Have you?"

Talanov did not reply.

"He's trying to help, Alex. Ilya's not exactly my style, but he *is* trying to help. He told us about Borzakov. He's compiling a list of old KGB agents who hired on with the mob. Including a list from the FSB."

Talanov did not reply.

"For heaven's sake! He came here trying to help you track down your wife's killer!"

Talanov did not reply.

"Why don't you cut to the chase and tell me what all this is about?"

Talanov looked away.

"Out with it!" said Wilcox, keeping his voice low so as not to alert Larisa, who was still being fussed over by the medics. "What's going on between you and Ilya?"

"I don't like the guy. I'll admit that. And if he hadn't been here trying to help me find my wife's killer, I would have kicked him from here to tomorrow for what he said about Larisa. And if he does it again, I will."

"Oh, that will do a whole lot of good."

"As opposed to you throwing Larisa under the bus to get what you want?"

Wilcox looked away.

"The truth is, I'm just not sure I want to work with you and your committee. Because I'm not willing to throw people under the bus, Bill, and I'm not willing to involve people in the decision-making process that I've known for only a day. Diane, or whoever it is they're after, deserves better than that."

"Okay, so maybe I deserved that. But the fact is, we need you. Teague needs you. He said so himself."

"Obviously, not that badly."

"Look, I'll admit you and Larisa nearly got killed because of what we did. I screwed up, Alex, and I'm sorry. And, yes, my career is on the line and the pressure of everything's got me rattled. We've got a sniper on the loose and it's up to us to try and stop him. That's why I went to Ilya."

Talanov did not reply.

"Do you think he's wrong about Borzakov?" Wilcox asked.

"On the surface, what he said sounds logical, but I really can't make that call because I don't have enough information."

"What kind of information would you need?"

"You're missing the point. I'm not telling you not to work with him. I'm saying you need to keep him at arm's length until he's proven himself."

"He *is* proving himself. Why can't you see that? I know you don't like him. The question is whether or not you can put those feelings aside."

"I'm not sure that I want to."

"What would it take?"

"You rescuing Larisa's family."

"Come on, Alex, my boss already thinks you're holding me hostage. That you're pushing me around with these demands of yours."

Talanov laughed. "The most secretive and powerful branch of the mighty US government is whining about getting pushed around? Do you have any idea how ridiculous that sounds? The only reason your boss gives a damn about me is because he wants something. Otherwise, he'd have me deported. I am nothing but a commodity and I know that. It's not because he likes me. It's because I'm a valuable commodity, and so he makes certain allowances. He makes them under protest and probably while yelling at you, but he makes them nonetheless. That shows me I have negotiating power. Am I asking for the unreasonable? No. Am I trying to be difficult? No. Believe me when I say I am *not* trying to make your life difficult. But I do have a few requests that I think are justified and moral."

"Requests?"

"Okay, demands, which, if your boss is unwilling to grant, tells me he's not the kind of guy I want to work with."

"And you know as well as I do that we don't have enough resources and manpower to save every family on earth. It can't be done. It's not because we don't care."

"I'm not in a position to help every family on earth, either. I *am* in a position to help this one."

"I already told you I'd see what I could do."

"I need you to fight for this, Bill. Don't say that just to get me off your back."

"I said I'd see what I can do, and I will. You have my word."

Talanov nodded. "Okay."

"In the meantime," said Wilcox, "I need you to do something for me."

"What's that?"

"I'm meeting Ilya tonight, after the convention. I'd like you to be there as well."

"What for? You've already brought Ilya on board."

"He's bringing me a list of double agents and moles. I'd like you to look over that list."

"On one condition."

"We're not back to *that* again, are we?"

Talanov laughed and patted Wilcox on the shoulder. "No, not that. Something else. I still need Charlie to grab a copy of our old KGB chess scores."

"Is finding out whether or not you beat Borzakov really that important?"

"It is, but not for the reasons you think."

"Mind telling me why?"

"For now, call it curiosity. Secondly, I'd like you to put Larisa up in your hotel for a few days. She can't go back to the apartment, and the mob is sure to be looking for her at my place. Register her under a different name."

"That request makes sense, unlike your obsession with those old chess scores of yours."

"Just do it as a favor, okay?"

"Anything else?" asked Wilcox with a sigh of exasperation.

"That's it for now. I'm yours."

CHAPTER 41

THE glamorous Hollywood & Highland Center is an example of architectural confusion and marketing genius. Built along the famous "Hollywood Walk of Fame," where the brass stars of entertainment personalities are embedded in the terrazzo sidewalk, the multi-level complex, with its soaring electronic billboards, sits on the corner of Hollywood Boulevard and North Highland Avenue. It covers a massive portion of the block and includes the elegant Kodak Theater, home to the Academy Awards, and Grauman's Chinese Theater, where the signatures, handprints and footprints of Hollywood legends are preserved in the concrete of the forecourt.

The five-story complex resembles a Babylonian palace, with escalators and staircases leading to higher levels, which are set back like terraces. Gigantic elephants overlook the open courtyard from atop huge pedestals. The courtyard itself is lavishly adorned with palm trees, shrubs, and fountains. Tenants include boutique shops, trendy nightclubs, name brand stores, and a variety of restaurants. The towering Renaissance Hollywood Hotel is nestled up against it, and the Red Line subway terminal sits beneath it. The complex epitomizes the evolving, uncertain identity of the new Hollywood, with nostalgic splashes of art deco amalgamated with massive sections of concrete and glass.

Linked with the Kodak Theater on an upper level is the Grand Ballroom, which was accessed by a number of walkways and open areas offering views of the Hollywood Hills and the Los Angeles skyline. It was an area of beautiful vistas. It was likewise an area of danger, being situated within several lines of sight from a number of rooftops and hilltops.

The Grand Ballroom was where Diane Gustaves would be addressing nearly six hundred delegates attending the Regional Congress on Organized Crime Prevention. It would be an eclectic mix of Pacific Rim nations, with an emphasis on human trafficking, cybercrime, money-laundering, and black market trade in arms and nuclear materials. Attending would be government representatives, parliamentarians, policymakers, academics, and law enforcement experts. And of course the international media.

Thwarting any attempt by Borzakov or his men to assassinate Gustaves was uppermost in the minds of everyone at the JRIC. To have the Russian mafia slay *anyone* at the convention, much less the leader of the US delegation, would be an unmitigated coup for the mafia and an unmitigated disaster for the United States.

Access to the opening session would be via the fifth floor escalators, where delegates would be required to present their identification badges and then pass through metal detectors. They would then proceed up a flight of steps to the landing, where identification badges would be checked again before admission into the Grand Ballroom. Security cameras utilizing facial recognition software would compare the faces of attendees with numerous databases containing images of terrorists, mafia leaders, and organized crime members. Agents would be stationed everywhere to monitor crowd activity.

Martin Posner was in charge of tonight's security, although he wanted Teague and his advisors – Wilcox and Talanov – in the command center with him, which was a large security tent set up especially for this convention. "We've got the place covered," Posner told Teague inside the tent, which was lined with monitors and communications equipment. "But you know Borzakov better than any of us, which is why I want you manning these monitors."

"I don't, but he does," Teague said, nodding toward Talanov.

The Shetland pony glanced dismissively at Talanov before looking back at Teague. "Then I'd like your man to remain here, where the cameras will pan the crowd and analyze faces."

"Waste of time," said Talanov.

Posner ignored the remark and continued addressing Teague. "Have him assist my people. The software will do most of the work, but it's nice to have human backup in case Borzakov alters his appearance. The software has compensation capability, but only so much."

"Do you seriously expect Borzakov to try something in a place crawling with Federal agents?" asked Talanov. "For one thing, are you absolutely sure Gustaves is the target? Have you considered anyone else?"

"Our simulators say Gustaves is the target," Posner replied.

"Your simulators?"

"Computers that factor every known contingency and come up with a prioritized list of likely candidates and scenarios. With over ninety-percent certainty, they say Gustaves is his target and tonight is the occasion."

"You are what you eat and computers are no different. Feed them crap and you'll get crap."

Posner glared briefly at Talanov, then looked at Wilcox. "What does Ilya think?" he asked.

Wilcox glanced nervously at Talanov before replying. "He thinks Borzakov is after the congresswoman and will attempt something here tonight. It may not be his only attempt, and it may only be a diversion, but something will go down tonight."

"Which is exactly what our simulators think," said Posner, glancing at Teague. "Maybe we should have brought Ilya on board. He seems to have his finger on the pulse of what's actually happening."

"This is exactly what I am talking about," said Talanov, shaking his head in the dim hush of the command center. "You've got tunnel vision. You're playing right into his hands."

"Are you saying you disagree with Ilya's assessment?" asked Teague.

"I'm saying we need to be looking in other directions as well, and not just in front of our noses. Diane may well be the target. She may not. Someone may try to kill her tonight. But they may also be setting us up, just as they did down at the harbor when they left Larisa and Marcy alive in the trunk of their car and a cell phone in the front seat. It was a trap. And we nearly fell for it. Let's not make a mistake like that again."

"That was you and this is me," said Posner, eyeing the various monitors lining the walls of the command center, "and I have a whole team of experts on hand and not just a disgruntled wannabe cowboy who drives cars into buildings and gets people killed."

"Are you really that stupid and arrogant?" asked Talanov.

Posner lunged at Talanov but Teague stopped him. "Ease off, Martin," he said after a reprimanding glare at Talanov.

"I want him out of here. Now!" shouted Posner, pointing toward the door.

"Gladly," said Talanov, who turned and walked out of the tent.

"Good riddance," muttered Posner, yanking away from the muscular Teague.

Teague scowled at Posner and hurried after Talanov.

"Hold on a minute," said Teague, catching up with him in the courtyard. Clusters of Federal Agents in suits were patrolling the area while delegates from all across the Pacific Rim were starting to trickle in, many in colorful native costume. Teague ushered Talanov aside to a quiet place where they could talk. "Posner can be difficult, but you've got to quit antagonizing him like that."

"I don't have time for buffoons," said Talanov. "The man should not be in charge."

"He's a decent guy when he's not being a jerk."

"The man doesn't trust me. I get that. And that's okay. I wouldn't expect any of you to take my word on anything. What bothers me is that you're basing your entire strategy on certain assumptions."

"Such as?"

"Such as Borzakov plans on shooting someone."

"He bought a rifle, Alex. With your credit card and ID. What can we conclude from that? That he plans on shooting somebody. Who's his greatest nemesis? Diane Gustaves."

"Again, those are conclusions based on assumptions. You're *assuming* he plans on shooting somebody."

"Why else would be buy a rifle?"

"I'm simply saying it's an assumption based on conjecture. We have no evidence that he plans on shooting anyone.

Prepare for it, yes, but don't rule out the possibility that it was a diversion. It's also an assumption that he plans on assassinating Gustaves. Prepare for it, yes, but don't rule out the possibility that he's planning to kill someone else. Or nobody at all. Maybe all of this is to get us looking one way when someone else is the real enemy. Maybe Borzakov's only a middle man. Someone to divert us."

"Ilya thinks there will be an assassination attempt tonight, using your rifle as part of some clever chess move. He knows Borzakov, same as you."

"It's not my rifle, and Ilya's an unvetted source."

"Are you saying he's lying?"

"Why should I be the one having to tell you to look in all directions? To be the lateral thinker? Ilya throws you a scrap of credible information and suddenly he's your golden boy. But you keep putting through me through the wringer because I'm telling you to be careful about making assumptions."

"Sounds to me like you're jealous," said Teague while men and women from various nations strolled by.

"Sounds to me like you haven't been listening to a thing I've been saying," Talanov replied. "Have you even considered the possibility that Ilya's being used? That maybe he's being fed a stream of disinformation from someone in Moscow, maybe by the same people who fabricated that report about Connor Jax? That's what I'm talking about when I say he needs to be vetted. You don't just need to check Ilya. You need to check his sources. You need to find out everything there is to know about him, and everybody he's worked, and that's before bringing him into an operation like this. For instance, are you absolutely sure Ivan Moroshkin is dead? Has a credible source verified his death? Also, Ilya says he doesn't know where the Connor Jax report came from. Thing is, someone had to give it to him. Either that or he fabricated it himself."

"Why would he do that?"

"I don't know. All I'm saying is that *you* should be the one asking those questions instead of me. And until I know the answers to those and a whole lot more, I won't work with him on something like this. It's not enough for him to say he has sources, like he's a journalist who doesn't have to explain any further. If you're going to build a security plan to protect one of your congressional leaders, then you'd better know where your intelligence is coming from."

The echo of footsteps suddenly reached their ears and they turned to see a winded Wilcox running toward them through the growing crowd of delegates. He half waddled when he ran and his belly bounced up and down. When he reached them, he bent over to catch his breath.

"What have I been telling you, Bill?" said Teague, his posture erect, like a coach.

"To lose twenty pounds, sir," panted Wilcox. "And I will, soon, I promise."

"And you and I both know that will probably never happen."

"You're right, sir, probably not."

"What is it, then? What's going on?"

Wilcox straightened and wiped his forehead. "Ilya just phoned. He found out where Borzakov is."

CHAPTER 42

THE news brought Talanov, Teague, and Wilcox running back to the tent, where Posner was communicating with two teams of FBI agents. The agents, sixteen in all, were in two shiny black vans that were speeding toward Borzakov's safe house, which was approximately two miles from the Grand Ballroom.

"Can you believe it?" said Posner, glancing at Teague. "He was holed up in our own backyard. Our own backyard! Thank God we've got Ilya on our side."

"Sir," said a female technician. "Two men with concealed firearms were apprehended in the lobby of the congresswoman's hotel. Both men were carrying photographs of Gustaves, and neither man appears to speak English. In fact, neither man is speaking at all except to ask for a lawyer. The congresswoman has been alerted and will be using an alternate route. She'll be coming through the upper breezeway in approximately six minutes."

"Get our people over there," said Posner. "I want a wall of protection around her."

"Yes, sir."

"Sir, over here," said another technician seated at a monitor showing a satellite image of a flat rooftop. "We have a lone figure on top of an office tower northeast of here."

"Is it a repairman, graffiti artist, or someone just walking around?"

"We're analyzing that now," the technician replied. "The building has a clear line of sight to the intersection zone of the upper breezeway and escalators."

"So this could be a credible threat?" asked Posner, looking over the technician's shoulder at the monitor, which showed an enhanced greenish image of the office tower. The building was in the shape of an L, which meant its rooftop was in the shape of an L.

"Yes, sir," the technician replied while Talanov, Teague, and Wilcox gathered around.

"Range?" asked Posner.

"About a thousand feet."

They watched the lone figure walk across the rooftop carrying a large case. Near the edge of the roof, the figure knelt, opened the case, and lifted out the chassis of a sniper rifle.

"Stop Gustaves!" shouted Posner. "And get a take-down team over there *now!*" He whirled and looked accusingly at Talanov. "Still think Gustaves isn't the target? Still think Borzakov would never try something in a place crawling with Federal agents?"

With his arms folded across his chest and one hand rubbing his chin thoughtfully, Talanov kept watching the monitor. Posner was a jerk, but what could he say? If Borzakov were indeed trying to kill Gustaves, it meant Posner was right and he was wrong. And yet, somehow, the sniper seemed a little too convenient, as did the two Russians carrying concealed weapons in the hotel lobby. Could this be a double diversion?

"What's the matter?" said Posner. "Cat got your tongue?"

"This is merely his opening gambit," said Talanov. "So if I were you, I'd spend less time gloating and more time figuring out what Borzakov is doing where you're not looking."

"You really are useless, with your idiotic theories about chess. Ilya, on the other hand, keeps bringing us solid intel. He confirmed Gustaves to be the target. He said Borzakov or one of his men would try something tonight, and may even try a preliminary diversion to distract us from the actual attempt. And what do you know? That's exactly what's happening. You, on the other hand, have brought us *nothing.*"

"All I've been trying to do is get you to vet your sources, look laterally, and proceed cautiously. Otherwise, you may find yourself in a trap."

"What is it with you? Afraid Ilya will prove himself more valuable than you? That you'll suddenly be out of a job?"

"I was simply trying to—"

"Enough! You've done nothing but hinder us from doing our job. And if I find out you've been hindering us on purpose, then you can kiss any hope of citizenship goodbye."

"I own a house here! LA's my home!"

"Ain't them the breaks?"

Talanov looked at Wilcox with an expression that said, *Is this guy for real?*

"Don't look to him for help," said Posner. "I don't know what things were like when you Commies were in power, but over here, when we get credible intel, we *act* on it rather than sit around talking about chess and drinking vodka."

"Thanks for clearing that up. Did you learn that in a seventies comic book?"

Posner looked over at Teague. "How long do we have to put up with this guy?"

The tent had already gone silent. Normally it was filled with quiet conversation and the pattering of keyboards and people scurrying about doing their jobs. Now it was chillingly quiet.

Teague thought for a moment, then looked at Wilcox and nodded toward the door. "Get him out of here," he said.

"But, sir," tried Wilcox just as Teague turned his back and continued watching the real-time satellite coverage of the unfolding action on the office tower.

Wilcox started to protest but Talanov stopped him. "It's okay, Bill," he said. And with a smile, he clasped Wilcox briefly on the shoulder and left the tent.

Posner watched Talanov leave. "If there was any lingering doubt about who belongs on this committee and who doesn't, I think we just settled that." To Wilcox: "Get Ilya on the phone."

After assembling his rifle, the figure on the rooftop clicked a Leupold infrared scope onto the mounting bracket above the bolt, slipped a fifty-caliber cartridge into the chamber, and racked the bolt. He was in the process of sighting in on the kill zone when his cell phone buzzed. He took the call, which was from Borzakov, who asked how things were going.

"Not now!" the sniper named Igor growled irritably. "I will text you when I am finished." After ending the call, Igor stuffed the phone back in his pocket. *He's becoming a liability,* Igor thought, looking again through the scope. In the crosshairs, he saw a steady flow of delegates in the fifth-floor patio kill zone. Some had come directly from the hotel by means of the breezeway. Others were coming up the escalators. *Fish in a barrel,* he thought with a smile.

Just over a mile away, the unmarked black panel vans screeched to a halt on a darkened side street. One van blocked the east end of the street and the other van blocked the west. No one would be getting in or out of that street without permission from the FBI.

Eight Federal agents in black fatigues jumped out of the rear of each van. Both teams wore helmets, body armor, and were heavily armed. All carried stun grenades and a variety of other specialty weapons. Both teams knew exactly where they were going and kept to the shadows beneath the sycamore trees lining each side of the street. The rubber soles of their boots made little noise on the sidewalk.

Their destination was a two-bedroom adobe cottage on the left. It sat on a narrow lot, had no front porch, and was a triple-fronted house, meaning the living room protruded farther toward the street than the dining room, which was set back. The single garage, which was so narrow only a small car could fit into it, was set back even farther. The front door was a rounded wooden panel in an arched opening beneath a lip of barrel tiles. It had two windows on each side. Holland blinds had been drawn down over the windows although strips of light could be seen along the edges. No front porch light was on. In the driveway sat an old car.

Teams A and B took up positions in front of the house, which is where the main breach would occur. To prevent escape, the commander motioned Team C, which was comprised of four agents, to the rear of the house. Using infrared night vision goggles, Team C proceeded cautiously along a narrow sidewalk between the house and a wooden fence.

"Advise when you're in position," the commander said into a tiny microphone positioned near his mouth.

"Copy that," the leader of Team C replied.

Inside the living room, Roman Borzakov's cell phone rang.

CHAPTER 43

WILCOX caught Talanov before he reached the top of the escalators. The colorfully-dressed delegates were passing by them on both sides in groups, chatting happily, heading toward the ballroom. Wilcox grabbed Talanov by the elbow and pulled him aside.

"Alex, I don't know what to say," Wilcox said, looking frustrated and defeated.

"I'm sorry if I caused you embarrassment," Talanov replied. "But I cannot, in good conscience, keep quiet. What's happening is classic Greco, who took out his opponent in eight moves – *eight moves,* Bill – and this time, the game is no game."

"Do you honestly believe this is a chess match?" asked Wilcox. "Do you think it's as simple as that?"

"Just as you often reduce strategies and metaphors to football, we do the same with chess. It's as national to us as football is to you, and I use it to illustrate the way many of us think. If you want to outwit your enemy, you've got to think like him. To imagine what *he* would do and not just what you would do if you were in his place."

"Meaning what, exactly?"

"Posner has tunnel vision. And he's hasty, like a charging bull who doesn't see there's a matador with a sword waiting for him behind the red flag."

"If you mean Borzakov, we have him surrounded. Ilya discovered the location of his safe house and we're within minutes of taking him down. Same with that sniper on the rooftop."

"I hope you're right," said Talanov, "because this is a lot bigger than Borzakov."

"What do you mean?"

"For one thing, we don't know what chess piece Borzakov is. Is he the king, the queen, a knight, a pawn? Is he a gambit? Same with that sniper. What piece is he? A diversion? The main event? That's what you need to figure out before it's too late."

"Too late for what?"

"Bill, I don't know. That's my point."

"Posner thinks you're a sore loser. That you're throwing cold water on a successful operation because you're pissed off that Ilya called it and you didn't."

Talanov smiled and did not reply.

"For the record, I don't agree," Wilcox hastened to add. "I am totally on your side and I have never doubted you for a moment."

"You sound like a politician," said Talanov with a laugh.

Wilcox laughed, too, and both men enjoyed a moment of levity before Wilcox turned serious and said, "I tried, Alex, really I did. But Posner wants Ilya on board."

"It's okay," Talanov replied, clasping his friend on the shoulder against the backdrop of delegates streaming past. "Larisa. Where is she?" he asked.

"My hotel. Two doors down, across the hall," answered Wilcox, telling him the room number. "By the way, I'd still like you in that meeting."

"What meeting?" asked Talanov.

"The one with Ilya, in my room."

"Why, if the decision's been made?"

"Because I trust you. I trust your ability to see what others don't see. What *I* don't see. Please, I'd like you there. But no more mixing chess metaphors with bullfighting, okay?"

Talanov smiled. "Okay."

"I'll let you know later what time."

"Let me know when you hear from Charlie," said Talanov. "I'd still like to know what Borzakov's chess scores were."

Wilcox chuckled and shook his head. "You really are a chess snob, aren't you?"

"Not as much as you with your wine."

The two men laughed again.

"By the way," said Wilcox, "I want you to know I was wrong."

"About what?"

"You and Larisa. I know I said it before, but I'm sorry I did what I did, trying to divide you like that."

"Don't worry about it," Talanov replied with a wave of his hand. "You were right. It was just a fling. Nothing more."

"Fling? Are you kidding me? This was anything *but* a fling. I mean, yeah, it probably began that way, after the drugging-and-robbing-you part, but this girl *defied* the mob for you. She risked everything. And if you don't see that for what it is, then you *do* need glasses."

"Maybe."

Wilcox threw up his hands in a gesture of disbelief. "What is wrong with you?"

"Easy, Bill. I'm just trying to maintain some perspective here. Larisa is everything a guy could want. There are just a lot of ... obstacles."

"Screw the obstacles," countered Wilcox. "It's not often guys like us find love. Someone who loves us for who we are, warts and all, and someone we can love back. I know you haven't been looking for any kind of a relationship, and I know you've got unfinished business, and that maybe you think you can't move on until that unfinished business is finished. But take it from someone who's an expert on failure. When you find someone like Larisa who sees you at your worst and still keeps throwing herself all over you – for what reason, I cannot *begin* to fathom – then you need to take it as a gift from heaven, my friend, because gifts like that – like *her* – do not come along very often. I know, because I've blown it so many times I've lost count. Don't let your life become as pointless and lonely as mine."

"It can't be as bad as that."

"I know I've done some good, but if you don't have anyone to share it with, what's the point? I'll die a lonely old man in some tiny village – near an excellent vineyard, mind you – but still alone and full of regrets. Your life doesn't have to end that way."

"What about your son?"

"He wants nothing to do with me and I don't blame him. He's done just fine on his own. Better than if I'd been around."

"I doubt that. Kids need their dads, even if they think they don't. You really should give him a call."

"It's way too late for that."

"Where does he live?"

"On the Marine Corps base at Camp Pendleton. I hear he made Gunnery Sergeant."

"Why don't you give him a call?"

"I've put him through enough as it is. I can't just show up now, after all this time."

"Why not?"

"Like I said, he wants nothing to do with me."

"How do you know?"

"Because we haven't talked in years."

"All the more reason to give him a call. Time has a way of working things out."

"I've tried."

"Then try again."

Wilcox's cell phone suddenly chimed with a text message and he looked at the screen. "Well, what do you know? Charlie *was* able to locate your old KGB chess scores. There are a number of pages, she said, and all of them are in Russian."

"No problem. Send 'em over."

"I can't. Teague said no."

"Come on, Bill. I need to look at those records."

"Not without Teague's approval," Wilcox replied.

"Then why tell me about them at all if you were going to pull something like this?"

"I probably shouldn't have, but I got the text and read it out loud and then saw Teague had nixed the whole thing. Sorry. But Charlie did find something else and it's something I *can* tell you. It concerns your father."

"My father was killed when I was an infant."

"Maybe not. I had Charlie do some checking and she found a Mikhail Talanov – which was your father's name – living near an old gulag in a remote village in Siberia. It may just be a fluke, but his arrival there coincides roughly with the reported date of your father's death in 1963. How old was he when he died?"

"Not quite thirty."

"And his middle name?"

"Ivanevich."

"Which happens to correspond with a birth certificate Charlie found for a Mikhail Ivanevich Talanov, born in New York on March 11, 1934. Do you know your father's birthday?"

"March 11, 1934," Talanov replied, his mouth hanging open in shock.

"Close your mouth," said Wilcox. "It gets better. Mikhail then migrated to Russia on July 19, 1956. Charlie found his name on the manifest of a passenger ship. Which means, my friend, if this man *is* your father, which we would need to prove, then you may already be an American since your father was an American."

"And he's alive and he's my father? You're sure about that?"

"There's no way to know for certain without further research or a DNA test, but if Charlie's right, then, yes, in Siberia."

"But my mother swore he was killed."

Your mother was strung out on drugs, Wilcox wanted to say. Instead, he said, "Is it possible she may not have known what was going on?"

Before Talanov could reply, Wilcox's phone chimed again. Wilcox read the message, then said, "We'll talk more later. Gotta run."

Talanov watched Wilcox hurry toward the command center. He still waddled while he ran but was amazingly quick at weaving his way through the steady flow of delegates strolling toward the ballroom. Up on the landing, where the actual doors into the ballroom were located, were more security guards and a steel drum band playing a calypso beat. Colorful banners welcomed delegates in a variety of languages.

Bypassing the escalators, Talanov crossed the small open plaza and walked to the balustrade, where he rested his elbows on the concrete railing and looked absently down at the crowds of shoppers below. They were wandering in and out of restaurants, boutique shops, and along the terraced walkways.

My father an American, thought Talanov with a chuckle.

That part of the equation actually made sense. "An idealistic fool," was about the only thing he remembered his mother, Nina, saying about his father, and she had been strung out on heroin at the time. Which is why, in a moment of bitter honesty, she had probably described him accurately, if, as he now suspected, his father had emigrated from America after Nikita Khrushchev's famous "Secret Speech" to the Communist Party Congress on February 25, 1956, where he denounced Stalin's purges and said he was ushering in a new era aimed at bettering the lives of ordinary citizens, which would have appealed to his dad, if indeed he was the idealistic fool his mother had accused him of being. Plus, if he happened to have been disillusioned with the inequities and excesses of American society after the Second World War, the prospect of returning to a simple life in his ancestral homeland would have been appealing.

But alive after so many decades? That part of the equation actually scared him, because it produced more questions than answers, and the questions it was producing were opening emotional wounds he didn't know he had. Had his father abandoned him and his mother? Was this why his mother became hooked on drugs? Had the KGB paid his father to leave? Was that why he moved to Siberia? Had the KGB set his father up with a new life and a new wife? Or had he committed some crime and had to disappear? Did he have a separate family? Or was all of this an illusion – a cruel coincidence – that would soon evaporate? So many questions. So few answers.

And an honest admission that, when it came right down to it, he just wasn't sure he wanted to find out the truth.

CHAPTER 44

THE Dallas Cowboys were playing on ESPN when Borzakov's cell phone rang. He watched the Cowboys score another touchdown, checked the caller ID and took the call. *"Chto eto takoe?"* he asked, keeping his attention on the game. He loved American football. Like chess, it was a game of strategy, with the players like pieces.

"Get out of there!" a voice shouted in Russian. "The FBI found you. They know where you are."

Borzakov switched the TV on mute and jumped out of his chair. Nick and Vic had to be the ones who tipped off the Feds. No one else knew where he was.

Outside, the FBI commander heard the TV sound go off and signaled everyone to hold steady, not wanting the noise of their movements to tip off Borzakov before his men were in position at the rear of the house.

Inside, Borzakov grabbed his pistol and ran into the dining room. A Holland blind was drawn down over the window and the room was dark. He peeked around the edge of the blind and saw teams of agents standing motionless in the shadows. *"Chert,"* he swore to himself. They're preparing to storm the house.

Outside the command center, Wilcox had paused to catch his breath when he saw Gustaves coming up the escalator. She had a minimum security detail – two agents – one in front and one behind – and her tailored sapphire-blue power suit stood out among the dark suits of her agents and the flowing costumes of the delegates surrounding her.

Dammit, she's doing it again.

Gustaves was supposed to be arriving by the upper breezeway. That was the latest word and security agents were waiting for her there. But Gustaves was famous for arriving early and unannounced by whatever route she chose, believing that heavy security and elaborate planning was not only unnecessary but created a larger target by attracting attention. To her, the fewer who knew her movements, the better.

"Cherokee is coming up the escalator," Wilcox said into his lapel mike, referring to the codename for the congresswoman.

"Stop her!" Posner radioed back.

With the TV remote in one hand and his pistol in the other, Borzakov ran quietly to the kitchen. There was a window above the sink and he carefully looked out. Nothing. He then moved to the door and lifted back the edge of the blind. Nothing. Everything looked quiet.

However, the FBI was not stupid. They would send agents to the rear of the house. The question was whether or not they were already in place. Maybe they had stopped when they heard the TV go quiet. Logic told him they were not in position. Otherwise, they would have stormed the house. That meant he had time. A minute at most.

He could of course give himself up. If he did, the Feds would take him into custody, where he would be convicted and sent to prison. Once in prison, he would be killed by one of the mob's hit men in order to keep him from talking. He wouldn't talk, of course, but the mob would not take that chance. So that option was out.

A second option was to make a break out the back door. Going out the front door was suicide and going out the back door was risky at best. A gunfight would ensue and he would be killed. So that option, too, was out.

A third option was the skylight in the bathroom. The roof was flat, with a scalloped facade on front that was topped with terracotta tiles. From the street, it looked authentically Mexican, which it probably was with so many Mexicans doing the physical labor Americans felt was beneath them. Once he was on the roof, he would wait until the FBI broke into the house. Then, in the resulting pandemonium, he would hop to a neighboring rooftop, pick up speed and leap from rooftop to rooftop. The Americans were so accommodating to build their houses this closely together. With so many fenced yards and tightly packed houses, this option offered his best chance of survival.

Borzakov hurried into the bathroom, paused in the door, aimed the remote toward the TV and switched back on the sound. *Go Cowboys,* he thought as the sound of cheering crowds and excited announcers again filled the house. He tossed the remote into a basket of magazines, switched off the light, stood on the sink and pushed up against the skylight. The clear acrylic dome hinged back. He grabbed the frame and pulled himself up through the opening and out onto the composite roof, where he quietly closed the dome.

"Go, go!" he heard a voice shout. An instant later, there was a loud crash. A battering ram had smashed open the front door. A stun grenade then went off inside, after which agents flooded the house.

With the sound of the game blaring over the shouts of agents, Borzakov looked toward the neighboring house and prepared to make his dash.

Suddenly, a figure rose from a crouching position on the rooftop across the street. Borzakov would not have seen the figure except for the red laser dot that flashed across his face and came to a rest on his chest. He knew immediately what it was and froze. That's when he saw the gunman's silhouette against the faint wash of light from a streetlamp. The figure clicked off his laser and rested the butt of his weapon on his hip. It was a stubby assault rifle with a long suppressor on the end of the barrel. Borzakov stared at the figure staring back at him. An instant later, the acrylic dome flew back and an FBI agent stuck his head up through the opening.

"He's up here!" the agent shouted.

The sniper across the street fired. The weapon made barely a sound. The agent's head exploded in a burst of red and he dropped back through the opening. The sniper then shot two of the four agents in the front yard, again in virtual silence.

"Men down, men down!" a third agent in the front yard yelled.

Borzakov saw agents pour out the front door.

"He's on the roof!" several of them yelled just as Borzakov looked across the street. The figure had disappeared.

"Take him down!" an agent shouted.

Borzakov threw up his hands. "Hold your fire! I didn't shoot those men!" he screamed as automatic gunfire cut him down where he stood.

CHAPTER 45

ON top of the office tower, Igor was lying in a prone position at a forty-five degree angle to his rifle. One leg was almost straight. The other was angled slightly. The rifle was resting on an adjustable bipod, and through his scope he was watching delegates stream through the kill zone. "Where are you? Where are you?" he kept muttering to himself, knowing satellite surveillance would no doubt have spotted him by now.

He had been timing how long delegates appeared in the zone, which at the casual pace most of them were walking was several seconds. One of his fifty-caliber bullets would travel at roughly 2800 feet per second, which meant he had more than enough time to accomplish his task. Unfortunately, his target had not appeared as expected. And time was running out.

Inside the security tent, Posner was in real-time communication with the take-down team. Teague was beside him and they were watching the satellite image of the sniper lying in position on top of the office tower.

"How long?" asked Posner into his microphone.

"Heading up the final flight of stairs," the team leader replied.

"Go in hot," said Posner. "Take him out."

"Copy that. Going in hot."

A thousand feet to the southwest, Diane Gustaves glided toward the top of the escalator just as Posner's security detail came running from the upper breezeway. Agent Rachel Dawkins, the lead agent, was cursing Gustaves for another of her unannounced entries. She shouted repeatedly for Gustaves to stop, that a sniper had been sighted, but was drowned out by the sound of the steel drum band.

In front of Gustaves were three enormous women from a Pacific island nation. They were dressed in flowing colorful attire, with head scarves wrapped into turbans. Gustaves was silent and her agents were guarded and vigilant, while the island women were chatting happily.

Wilcox was waddle-running along the waist-high wall next to the escalator when Talanov met him in a head-on collision, like two players in a football game. Wilcox flew backward to the concrete, arms flailing, just as Talanov turned and leaped over the waist-high wall into the escalator shaft. Gustaves and her agents saw Talanov descending upon them like a paratrooper without a parachute. The agents started to react just as Talanov landed on the moving metal steps.

"Get down!" he shouted. Startled, the island woman in front of the lead agent toppled backward, hitting the agent, who toppled backward into Gustaves, who created a domino effect of people falling down the escalator. Talanov sprang forward up the steps and tackled the two women ahead of him.

Through his scope, Igor saw Talanov tackle Wilcox, then vault down onto the escalator. Shouting a curse, he pulled the trigger. The bullet exploded into the wall where Talanov and the two island women had been standing. Talanov kicked the large red button located on the end panel of the escalator. The escalator jerked to a stop.

Knowing there was no time for a second shot, Igor jumped to his feet just as the door onto the rooftop exploded. He knew the FBI would show up sooner or later, which is why he had taken the precaution of wiring the door with explosives. The booby-trap injured the two lead agents and knocked the others back down the stairs. Running to the rear edge of the roof, Igor picked up the coil of thick rope he had placed there earlier. One end had already been secured to a vent pipe. Igor threw the rope over the edge, and, looping the rope around his back, jerked it to make sure it was secure, leaned back, and rappelled down the face of the building.

Inside the security tent, Posner pounded his fist on the counter while watching the real-time satellite feed. "East side of the building. He's getting away!" Posner yelled into his microphone.

By now, Dawkins and her security detail had reached the top of the escalator. Dawkins and two of her agents dragged Talanov off the women, slammed him to the concrete, and pinned his arms behind him. Other agents herded everyone else back down the escalator, while other agents surrounded Gustaves and rushed her to safety, her knees bleeding from her fall.

"What the hell are you *doing?*" yelled Wilcox, limping over to where Dawkins had her knee on Talanov's back while clicking handcuffs on his wrists.

"He assaulted three delegates and injured Congresswoman Gustaves," Dawkins replied.

"I wasn't talking to you," said Wilcox. "I was talking to him." He got down in Talanov's face. "I could have you *arrested* for what you did, tackling me like that."

"I heard someone shouting for Gustaves to stop, that a sniper had been spotted. So I reacted."

"By tackling *me?*"

"We don't know for certain who the target was, and I was not about to let someone put a bullet in your head. If you want to arrest me, go ahead."

Wilcox glared at Talanov, then stood. "It's okay. Let him up."

"Not without authorization," Dawkins replied.

"I'll vouch for him. He's a friend."

"He stays where he is until I get authorization."

Wilcox pulled out his ID. "Is this authorization enough?"

Dawkins looked at Wilcox's identification and handed it back, unimpressed. "Not your jurisdiction."

"Reckless as he was, he was trying to save lives," Wilcox replied. "Let him up."

"He stays where he is until I have proper authorization to release him. Which isn't you."

"I'm with the JRIC. So let him up."

"Back off, Wilcox! You're CIA and the CIA has no jurisdiction here. The assailant stays where he is."

"Let him up or I take this over your head."

With a reluctant sigh, Dawkins stood and brought her lapel mike to her mouth. "Sir, this is Dawkins," she said. "I have a William Erasmus Wilcox, with the CIA. He's claiming the assailant's a friend."

"Erasmus?" said Talanov, craning his neck to look up at Wilcox. "Who names their kid Erasmus?"

"It's a family name," growled Wilcox, bringing his own lapel mike to his mouth. "Sir, this is Wilcox. Talanov saved Diane's life and security has him handcuffed face-down on the pavement. I vouched for Talanov but Agent Dawkins refuses to release him."

Teague looked over at Posner while Wilcox and Dawkins waited for answers.

"Haul Talanov in for questioning," Posner replied.

"Wait," Teague called out, putting his hand across the microphone and looking straight at Posner. "He's innocent and you know it. Let him go."

"He's a pain in the ass. I want him locked up."

"You're making this personal, Martin. You're in charge here tonight and I respect that. But this is flat out wrong, and I'll take it higher if you don't let him go."

"He made me look like an idiot!"

"So Ilya was right and Talanov was wrong and you want to rub it in his face. This is not the way to do that."

Posner fumed for a long moment, then raised his microphone to his mouth. "Release him," he said.

"Copy that," Dawkins replied. To her partner: "Release that asshole," she said just as Gustaves emerged from the hotel breezeway. When Dawkins saw her, she rushed over and said, "Madam Congresswoman, you shouldn't be here!"

"I'll deal with you in a moment," Gustaves said, bypassing Dawkins and approaching Talanov. "Colonel Talanov, are you all right?"

"Yes, ma'am," he replied, standing. "My apologies for you getting hurt on the stairs."

"I'll take scrapes over a bullet any day," she said. "And, please, call me Diane. I hope you'll accept my apologies for the unforgiveable way you were treated."

"Your agents were merely doing their jobs."

"You're very polite. But Agent Dawkins was not only disrespectful of a senior colleague, but continued to violate protocol and good manners when Mr. Wilcox assured her you were a friend. She will be issuing you and Mr. Wilcox written apologies for her conduct and language, unless of course she wishes to be reassigned to the underground archives in Hutchinson, Kansas."

Dawkins swallowed hard.

"With respect, Madam Congresswoman," said Talanov, "Agent Dawkins was right. You shouldn't be here, even though you may not have been the target."

"What makes you say that?" asked Gustaves.

"Diane, thank *God* you're all right!" Posner called out, running toward her.

"I'm fine, Martin, but Colonel Talanov here seems to think I may not have been the target."

"I'd expect him to say something like that."

"Who else would it be?" asked Gustaves.

"The sniper couldn't have seen you from where he was," answered Talanov, "so there was no way he could know you were on the escalator. Simply put: that shot was a diversion."

"For what?"

"To fool the FBI into thinking this was their primary assault."

"What a load of crap," said Posner.

"It's true," said Talanov, "but you're too blind to see it. Nevertheless, you still need to get the congresswoman to safety. This area isn't safe."

"And I'm growing weary of you interfering in our business."

"Someone needs to. Before another sniper succeeds."

"Get him out of here!" barked Posner.

"All right, you two," said Gustaves. "You really do need to get along if you're going to be working together."

"He's not. Not anymore," said Posner.

"I thought we were bringing him aboard."

"Change of plans and Teague agrees. We're bringing Ilya on board. He's well placed in the FSB and he brought us credible intel that led us to Borzakov."

"You've got Borzakov in custody?" asked Talanov.

"Borzakov is dead," declared Posner.

Talanov was literally stunned speechless.

"That's right," said Posner with a cold smile of satisfaction. "While were complaining about Ilya not being vetted, he found out where Borzakov was and called us with directions. Borzakov tried making a run for it, and in the process killed three of my men. We took him down. The man is dead. And you know what the ironic part is? Ilya came here trying to help you track down your wife's killer. And where were you all this time? Running around with prostitutes."

Talanov stared hard at Posner before finally looking away. Sure, he was shocked at the news, but maybe Posner was right. Maybe he did resent Ilya for accomplishing what he had failed to do. Maybe he did feel guilty for spiraling out of control after Andrea's death. Maybe he needed to admit the truth about his failures and quit blaming Ilya for being the kind of person he wished he had been. After all, the sadistic butcher who had killed Jade – and presumably his wife – was finally dead. There was no way of telling how many lives Borzakov had destroyed. And while Nick and Vic were still out there, Borzakov's death at least raised the hope that Larisa's family would now be safe. Justice had been served.

And yet, on the other hand, something still troubled him. But since he didn't know specifically what it was ...

"I don't like to admit this," said Posner, "but I do think you were right about one thing. I think this was some kind of a chess game. Borzakov engineered an elaborate plan to kill Diane and we thought you could help us figure it out. But while you were wringing your hands about Ilya's credibility, Ilya helped us win the game. Checkmate, I think it's called."

"And you think the game is over. Is that it?" Talanov replied.

"You really are a sore loser, who just can't stand the fact that he didn't win. Well, you're finished here, Talanov. Done."

"You still don't get it, do you? This was never about me. I'm not the enemy. But you think I am, and that keeps you focused on me rather than looking where you ought to be looking."

"Which is where?" asked Gustaves.

"I don't know, Diane. And that's the problem. Posner thinks he's won a game that may not even have begun."

CHAPTER 46

THE ride east on Hollywood Boulevard was quiet. Wilcox was driving while Talanov stared out the window. Behind them, the western sky was a huge orange banner stretching the width of the horizon.

"So your middle name's really Erasmus?" asked Talanov.

"It was my dad's middle name and his dad's before him. Goes back generations, to the Civil War."

"Sounds like something out of those times. Erasmus Wilcox, the wounded soldier, head bandaged, returning home from battle using his rifle as a crutch."

"My dad's side fought for the North. Grand Army of the Republic. All the boys had the same middle name."

"And your son. What about him?"

Wilcox did not reply.

"You didn't."

"Why not?" asked Wilcox. "What's wrong with the name?"

Talanov grinned and shook his head.

"What?" pressed Wilcox irritably.

Talanov smiled and shrugged. It was an exaggerated shrug that said, "No comment."

"It's a family name!" said Wilcox defensively. "I named him Daniel Erasmus Wilcox, after my grandfather."

"O-kay."

"It's a name with history! A *legacy!*"

Talanov held up his hands in surrender.

"Hey, don't give me a hard time about my middle name, Aleksandr *Mikhailevich* Talanov. What kind of a middle name is Mikhailevich, anyway? Sounds like a girl's name. Who names their boy Mikhailevich?"

Talanov laughed.

Wilcox growled irritably, then said, "By the way, the sniper on that office tower got away. Seems he planted an explosive charge on the door to the roof, so when the FBI opened it—"

"Boom."

"The explosion injured two and knocked the others back down the stairs, and the sniper got away by rappelling down the east face of the building. The FBI ran a check on Borzakov's cell phone – which they confiscated from his safe house – and there were several calls to a throwaway cell leading up to the assassination attempt. Question is, was the sniper working for Borzakov, or was Borzakov working for him?"

"Any conclusions?" asked Talanov.

"Not enough intel to know. Shortly before Borzakov was gunned down, a couple of the Fibbies reported him screaming that it wasn't him, whatever that means."

They continued riding in silence while Talanov thought that over. Cars rushed past them in both directions. Los Angeles was a city in a hurry with more than enough stop lights to keep that from ever happening.

"So, you want to grab something to eat?" asked Wilcox. "I could use a glass of wine."

"You've got a meeting with Ilya, remember? Best you be sharp for that."

"We've got a meeting with Ilya."

"Come on, Bill, the decision's already been made about bringing him on board. You don't need me hanging around."

"Actually, that decision hasn't been made. Yes, Posner and Teague want Ilya on board. And Diane will probably go along with them if I give my stamp of approval. Meaning, I've still got a say in the matter, and I want you to be part of this interview process. I trust you. I want to know what you think."

"You already know what I think."

"Come on. Don't bail on me now."

Talanov told Wilcox to take the next left.

"Well?" asked Wilcox as they sped north. Ahead, the rugged tops of the Hollywood Hills appeared as dark jagged shapes against the luminescence of the sky.

"I'll pass. Larisa's been cooped up all day. She'll want to go out."

"How do you know she's been cooped up all day? She may have been out hitting the streets."

Talanov looked sharply at Wilcox.

"Sorry, that came out wrong. I was trying to be funny by suggesting she might have been out shopping. Please, Alex, I need you to be there with me. This is the last thing I'll ask you to do."

"What do I tell Larisa?"

"That this is all my fault. That you're doing this as a special favor to me, your oldest and dearest friend, who's always been there for you, like a brother, asking nothing in return, *ever*, until now."

"Seriously?"

"Come on! Don't bail on me now."

"Quit saying that."

"Then help me out this one time. I'll even buy you guys dinner. My treat. To make up for all the trouble."

"Who's buying? You, or your expense account?"

"Does it make a difference?"

"You better believe it does. "If it's you, then you'll get off for less than a thousand. If it's the CIA, then they can pay for whatever we feel like ordering, including a bottle or two of La Tâche."

"Come on, Alex! No way can I justify that."

"How badly do you want me to help you out?"

"Not *that* again," said Wilcox with a sigh of exasperation.

Talanov grinned and shrugged just as Wilcox's phone chimed. A text message had arrived. Wilcox glanced at the screen and saw it was from Ilya, asking what time they should meet.

"What time should I tell him?" asked Wilcox.

"It's your meeting. Whenever you want."

"I'm asking because I want you there."

Talanov shrugged.

"Dammit, Alex!"

Talanov shrugged again.

"All right, my expense account! Now, what time should I tell him?"

"Nine o'clock? Gives me time to shower and change."

Wilcox agreed and had Talanov text Ilya saying to come by his room at nine. "Tell him you'll be there, too," added Wilcox, and by the time Talanov finished sending the text, they had reached the base of the hills.

Talanov directed Wilcox up the dark, winding streets to his house. When Wilcox expressed concern that he might not be able to make it out again, Talanov said he would give him directions. "However, since I haven't lived here that long myself, I hope I don't send you the wrong way. Some of these old roads end up in desolate canyons. Some people never come out."

Wilcox could tell Talanov was joking but he didn't find it very funny. He was genuinely worried that he couldn't find his way out. So Talanov invited him to stick around while he showered and changed. He could then follow him to the hotel.

While Wilcox stood on the deck admiring the nighttime view of the city, Talanov stood under a steaming hot torrent of water thinking about recent events. Was Borzakov the "king" in this three-dimensional game? If he was, then Posner was right about the game being over. But what if Borzakov were the "queen" or some other piece on this chessboard called Los Angeles? If that were the case, and if Borzakov had been sacrificed as part of an elegant trap, by, say, whoever that sniper was on the officer tower, then the real game had not yet begun, and everything thus far had been only a diversion.

He thought again about the great Russian chess master, Mikhail Botvinnik, and the games he made them study back in their KGB days. All of them had one feature in common. The queen sacrifice. In all of them, the winner lured his opponent into a false sense of security through the loss of the queen. It was the ultimate gambit, the ultimate risk, the ultimate power play of feigning weakness and loss. It was the ultimate, strategic win. Was that what was happening here?

Talanov recalled what Wilcox had said, that a couple of the FBI agents had heard Borzakov scream that it wasn't him. Three men had reportedly been killed by Borzakov, and from snippets of conversations he'd overheard, one had been shot in the skylight after spotting Borzakov on the roof. Two more had then been gunned down in front of the house. Had Borzakov killed those men? Or had Borzakov been set up? Had Borzakov's pistol even been fired? Had microscopic comparisons of the bullets definitively pinned the murders on him and his gun? And who was this mysterious sniper who had escaped from the rooftop of the office tower?

After twenty minutes, Talanov switched off the water. He knew it was wasteful to stand under a shower that long, but sometimes he needed the prolonged pelting of hot water to help him think. After drying his hair, he slipped into a pair of khaki Armani jeans and a collarless, white Moroccan shirt. He then went to the closet and entered a security code on the touchpad of a heavy metal door located behind his hanging shirts. Inside was a selection of pistols and ammunition. He chose the Glock 19, which was a compact handgun that fit comfortably in the back of his jeans. After loading the weapon, he slid an extra magazine into his pocket. With Nick and Vic and an unidentified sniper still out there, he would not be caught unprepared.

CHAPTER 47

WILCOX was outside on the deck talking on his cell phone when Talanov entered the living room. He watched Wilcox pacing back and forth, gesturing with his hand, focused on the call. The call finally ended and Wilcox stood hunched over at the railing, staring down into the darkness of the canyon below.

"Everything all right?" asked Talanov, joining Wilcox at the railing.

"Borzakov didn't kill those agents," Wilcox replied. "They were killed by someone else. Ballistics confirmed it. His pistol had not even been fired."

"Who do they believe it was?"

"The slugs were 5.56 millimeter. The FBI thinks a Mark 12 was used."

"Like the one I supposedly bought?"

Wilcox nodded. "Diane's had her security tripled and Posner is livid. He thinks you purposely withheld information to make him look foolish. He wants to question you further. I told him that wasn't going to happen. Teague's backing me on this and says what happened proves we need your help on the JRIC. However, convincing Posner may still be a problem."

"I don't know that I want him convinced," Talanov replied. "First Marcy and now Posner. They're hardly great advertisements for what you're selling."

Wilcox chuckled. "Can't argue with you there."

"Ever think about retirement?"

"All the time."

"It definitely has its perks," said Talanov with a smile. "Come on, let's go."

With Wilcox following in his nondescript sedan, Talanov led the way out of the Hollywood Hills in his Boxster. Several times he had to wait at corners for Wilcox to catch up with him, but within an hour, they had arrived at Wilcox's hotel in plenty of time for their nine o'clock meeting with Ilya.

The hotel was one of several high-rise hotels set among a cluster of office towers near LAX. They had been constructed at odd angles on the wide strip of real estate between West Century Boulevard and 98th, no doubt to create panoramic views of something other than the faces of neighboring buildings. Wilcox's fourteenth-floor room faced northeast, toward the vast blanket of lights that was greater Los Angeles. Across a small side street were several more high-rise buildings that were mostly dark except for a few rectangles of light from the windows of offices being used, either by ambitious workers or cleaning crews.

Talanov handed his car keys to the valet and Wilcox did the same, and together they entered the hotel.

The lobby was spacious and decorated with artistic red, white, and blue furniture that looked horribly uncomfortable. Maybe that's why so few people were seated there. Large blue octagonal pillars supported a high ceiling. A polished counter was staffed by handsome young attendants who flashed gleaming smiles when Talanov and Wilcox passed by. The two men stepped into the elevator and punched a button for the fourteenth floor.

"Teague phoned me on the way over," said Wilcox while soft music played.

"About?"

"This conflict with Posner. Teague said he and Gustaves supported me in wanting to bring you on board, but Posner's opposition has intensified to the point that no one wants to go head-to-head with him over it. You making him look like an ass didn't help much, either."

"He *is* an ass."

"He's the Assistant Director in Charge of the FBI's Los Angeles Field Office, Alex. You can't go around embarrassing people like that. Teague and Gustaves probably agreed with everything you were saying, but they weren't about to go out on a limb without compelling evidence. Ilya *did* locate Borzakov, you know."

"It's a moot point now, anyway, and, frankly, I don't care.

Like I said before, I don't need the job, don't need the money, and I certainly don't need the headaches."

"What *do* you need, Alex? Are you going to end up a lonely old man telling stories in a bar to whomever will listen? Are you going to waste the remainder of your days playing golf or bridge or some other pointless game? What's your purpose?"

Talanov did not reply.

"Why did you come to us in the first place?" asked Wilcox. "Why risk a firing squad to help us win the Cold War? Was it the money?"

"The money was incidental."

"Then what was it?"

"Why are you asking me these things?" asked Talanov as the elevator pinged and the doors opened on the fourteenth floor.

"I think you came to us because you believed in the ideal that was America," replied Wilcox as they walked down the corridor. "What you were doing gave you a sense of purpose. That you were doing something that mattered."

Talanov shrugged.

"Look, I know you well enough to know you'd go crazy sitting around all day doing nothing."

"I'd rather do that than put up with Posner and his kind."

"Our government's full of his kind. That's just the way it is. But I'm not one of them and neither is Teague, nor Gustaves, nor any of the other people I work with."

"Look, I appreciate where you're going with this, and for your vote of confidence, but I'm just not interested in working for the JRIC. We're not cut out for each other."

"I couldn't agree more," Wilcox replied.

"You do?" asked Talanov with surprise.

"Absolutely. Which is why I'd like to offer you a chance to come and work with me at the CIA, with the very people you sought out in the first place. Do something with your life besides sitting around."

"Says the man who wants to retire to a vineyard in France and drink himself into oblivion."

"When I'm put out to pasture, it won't be by choice. It'll be because my expiration date has arrived. Which means I will retire to that vineyard and become that lonely old man telling stories to whomever will listen."

"You just tried telling me how pointless that is."

"I didn't say it was pointless for *me*. I just know that it's not for you."

"Oh, that makes a whole lot of sense."

"Really? Can you honestly stand there and tell me you could retire and sit around drinking yourself into oblivion? You and I both know the answer to that. Me? I could handle something like that quite nicely, thank you very much. In many ways, I already have. But you? No way could you do something like that. You're just too pigheaded to admit it."

Talanov chuckled and shook his head.

"Am I right?" asked Wilcox with a grin.

Talanov did not reply.

"Well?" pressed Wilcox. "Am I right?"

"You can wipe that stupid grin off your face, is what you can do."

The grin broadened. "Does that mean you'll come and work with me at the CIA? I've already run it by Teague and he loves the idea. It would be just like the old days, you and me, saving the world. Plus, you get the satisfaction of knowing you're helping out your oldest and dearest friend in his time of greatest need."

"You really are a scammer, you know that?"

"Guilty as charged. I'll phone Teague. He'll be ecstatic."

"Yeah, he looks like the ecstatic kind. Tell him I'll think about it. That's all."

"Come on, Alex, what else are you going to do?"

"How about me enjoying *my* retirement without you annoying me all the time?"

Wilcox laughed and patted Talanov on the cheek. "You're not meant for retirement. You know it and I know it. Besides, there isn't room for two of us sitting around feeling sorry for ourselves. That would be way too pathetic."

Talanov rolled his eyes.

"Together again, the Two Musketeers," exclaimed Wilcox happily. "Now, go see that girl of yours."

"Where is she?"

Wilcox told him the room number. "Two doors down, other side of the corridor. Say your hellos, then meet me back here again in ten minutes. Ilya should be here by then."

While Talanov continued down the hall, Wilcox stuck his card-key in the slot and opened his door. The room was dark but the drapes were open to allow enough ambient light to highlight the silhouettes of the furniture.

On the credenza was a bottle of Chopin vodka. It was standing by itself, as if on display, and the slender frosted bottle seemed to catch the reflected light and glow, even though everything else in the room was dull and shadowed. Wilcox had ordered the vodka for their meeting with Ilya. He knew Ilya preferred Scotch, but Chopin was Talanov's favorite, and this time he was giving preference to his longtime friend.

After the door clicked shut, Wilcox strode across the carpet to the window and looked out. The dark monoliths of the neighboring office towers reminded him of giant speaker cabinets. In the sky above them were the blinking lights of several aircraft taking off and landing. The vast expanse of lights that was Los Angeles at night was a spectacular sight.

He had seen many spectacular sights in his travels with the CIA. Antarctica, the jungles, the Sahara, Yellowstone, the Alps, and every ocean on earth, both from the decks of carriers and coning towers of nuclear submarines. The world was a beautiful place. Yet nothing compared to the great cities of the world at night. Los Angeles, Hong Kong, Sydney, Honolulu, San Francisco, Rio de Janeiro, Shanghai, Moscow, and dozens of others. Seeing them from an airplane or a mountaintop – or a hotel room on the fourteenth floor – took your breath away, just as being down there on the street, in the pulsating rhythm of the night, among the people, gave it back.

He would miss this part of the job when his time came to retire – or be retired – and he knew that time was not far off. He had asked Talanov about the meaning of life, had pushed him on it, in fact, but in truth, he didn't have much of an answer himself. Whatever purpose he may have once had was pretty much gone by now. Yes, he could feel it. Retirement, forced or voluntary, was near.

Talanov, however, still had a lot of miles left in him, and Washington needed him, whether pinheads like Posner realized it or not. Being an outsider, Talanov had the advantage of being unaffected by American politics, which meant he could call things as he saw them, and without bias. Plus, not only did he have a wealth of field experience, but he had also studied enough theory to choke a horse. That's because he'd started when he was a teenager, albeit for the other side, which would forever arouse suspicion in people like Posner. If Talanov could manage to quit deliberately antagonizing all the Posners in DC, he would be one of the most valuable assets this government would ever acquire.

A knock sounded that jolted Wilcox out of his reverie. He walked to the door and opened it. Talanov entered, looking disheveled and dazed.

"What's wrong?" Wilcox asked.

"Everything. I mean, nothing. Why are the lights off?" asked Talanov, entering the suite and falling into a stuffed chair. Across from him was another stuffed chair. It was part of a cozy arrangement positioned at right angles to a small desk set up by the window.

After closing the door, Wilcox took up a position directly in front of Talanov, standing over him, hands on his hips. "You just got laid, didn't you?" he asked.

"I tried telling her," said Talanov.

"Tried telling her what?"

"That I was too old. That one day some young stud would come along and sweep her off her feet."

"What'd you go and say something stupid like that?"

"Because it's true. How can I compete with guys half my age?"

"Because there *is no* competition, you idiot," cried Wilcox, throwing up his hands. "Don't you ever *listen?*"

"I listen to logic, and logic says—"

"Screw logic!" Wilcox cut in. "Since when has love been about logic? Larisa broke every rule in the book doing what she did for you. Did she ask herself whether it was logical to defy the mob in order to give you back your wedding photo and save your ass? Hell, no. She just did it. And *that* is what makes her the incredible woman she is."

"Yeah, but—"

"No buts, Alex. I'm not going to let you screw this up. *I* nearly screwed it up for you, so I'm not about to let you do what I almost did."

"And I'm telling you this cannot work. Read my lips. *This. Can't. Work.* Except you can't read my lips, can you, because the lights are still off. Why is that?"

"So that I don't have to read *your* stupid lips, that's why. Listening to you whine about logic is bad enough."

"Come on, Bill. She's got her whole life ahead of her, including a family with someone she can grow old with. And I just tried telling her that."

"What did she say?"

"She just threw me down on the bed and ripped off my—"

"*Stop!* That is *way* too much information for an old man with a heart condition."

"You don't have a heart condition."

"I will if I hear any more of that story."

Talanov took out his cell phone. "Maybe I should call her. Or send a text. Say what I couldn't say back in the room."

Wilcox grabbed the phone away. "You annoy the crap out of me sometimes."

"Why? What did I do?"

"Put that thing away," Wilcox said, tossing the phone back in Talanov's lap. "Most guys would *kill* to have a girl like Larisa ripping off their clothes."

"She's half my age."

"Do you hear her complaining?"

"She hasn't thought this through."

"How do you know? Have you asked her?"

Talanov did not reply.

"Look," said Wilcox, sitting across from Talanov. "Most guys look good in their twenties, although that number is shrinking because we're getting lazier and fatter. Still, most guys in their twenties look good, even dimwits who live on coffee and cigarettes. Or fast food junkies whose only exercise is tearing open a wrapper. Sooner or later it catches up with them. It always does. So if a hot tamale like Larisa wants to know the kind of man's she's getting, she looks for a guy who's older. A stud, to be sure, but not some kid whose only brain is between his legs. She wants a man with staying power. Take it from me. When a younger woman looks at an older man the way Larisa looks at you, it means she's serious about what she wants. Question is: are you going to grab hold of her the way she grabs hold of you?"

"You really annoy me sometimes."

"Good. You need to be annoyed, and kicked, and smacked around for even thinking something so mindlessly idiotic, not that I know anyone who is capable of smacking you around, not that it wouldn't do you some good. Now, snap out of it. We have a meeting with Ilya."

Wilcox walked over to the desk and switched on the lamp.

An instant later, the window exploded in a burst of automatic gunfire.

CHAPTER 48

SHARDS of glass flew everywhere while bullets shattered lamps, chewed up furniture, and punched out Wilcox's back with bright sprays of blood. Diving to the floor, Talanov screamed for Wilcox to get down. But Wilcox was already toppling to the floor before the words had left his mouth.

The killer had used a bracketing technique, which meant firing a heavy fusillade from right to left, thus compensating for wind drift, distance, and errors in judgment. It wasted ammunition, but it created a wider kill zone that boxed in – or "bracketed" – the target.

Those few violent seconds revealed something important to Talanov. The spray of gunfire had begun opposite Wilcox and swept toward him, confirming Wilcox to have been the primary target, not him. If he had been the target, the sniper would have bracketed from the other direction, hitting him first, not Wilcox. Which meant Wilcox, not Gustaves, had been the target all along, in spite of all the well-orchestrated diversions to the contrary. When he thought about it now, the rooftop sniper was probably waiting for Wilcox to run into the kill zone back at the Hollywood & Highland Center. But that plan had been foiled by a football tackle, no less.

So who was shooting at them now? The rooftop sniper? Nick or Vic? It wasn't Borzakov because Borzakov was dead. Who was it, then? No one knew which hotel Wilcox was staying in, much less where his room was, or what time he would return.

No one except Ilya, that is.

Ilya! Wilcox had told him which room he was in and when he would return. That's also why Ilya didn't risk coming in person. He knew Wilcox would not be alone, and that he, Talanov, would be there with him. Firing from a distance was the perfect solution.

If only he had listened to his hunches about Ilya. But Ilya had played him just like he had played everyone else, complete with supposedly leaked reports and a professional background that he knew would hold up under scrutiny. Ilya then worked his way into the confidence of everyone on the committee by providing credible intelligence on mob activities here in Los Angeles. All of it was a ruse. If only Teague had allowed Charlie to send through his old KGB chess scores. If he had, then Ilya's lie about Borzakov being in class with them would have been discovered, and Wilcox would probably not be sprawled out on the floor right now bleeding. Ilya's sole purpose in coming to Los Angeles was to not to help him find his wife's killer, but to assassinate Wilcox, the person most responsible for crippling the mob's operations. And, like in Greco's game, Ilya had been willing to sacrifice his most powerful piece, Borzakov, in order to achieve his goal.

Well, this isn't checkmate yet.

With bullets splintering wood and smashing glass, Talanov crawled over to his bleeding friend, who lay groaning on the floor with four bullet holes in his body. Pulling out his pistol, Talanov shot out the light, which again plunged the room into darkness.

The gunfire stopped, meaning Ilya would reload and hurry over to finish the job. Which meant they had two or three minutes at most. "Come on, we're getting you out of here," Talanov said, sticking the pistol in the back of his pants He grabbed Wilcox under the arms and dragged him across the floor to the bathroom.

"Tell son ... I love him," wheezed Wilcox, struggling for breath.

"Tell him yourself," said Talanov, dialing Larisa. When she answered, he told her what had happened.

"You must stop bleeding," she said. "Apply pressure to wounds with towels. Then get tea bags from tray, near mini bar. Wet them. Apply to wounds. I be there soon."

Talanov had barely ended the call when Larisa was pounding on the door. Talanov opened it and she slipped inside just as the elevator doors opened at the end of the corridor and Nick and Vic emerged.

"Oh, that's just great," said Talanov, quietly closing the door and raking a hand through his hair. *Nick and Vic. Just what we need.*

Larisa grabbed the bottle of Chopin still standing on the bullet-riddled credenza. There were window fragments strewn all around, but the bottle remained standing triumphantly. She ran into the bathroom, where Wilcox was lying on the floor. The bath towel around his chest was soaked with wet tea bags and blood. Larisa uncorked the bottle and doused the towel with vodka. "We need ambulance," she said.

"No time," answered Talanov. "Nick and Vic are coming down the hall. Let's get him up and get ready to run."

Talanov propped Wilcox up into a sitting position against the wall. "Stiffen your legs," he said. With a moan, Wilcox locked his legs straight. Larisa slipped her shoulder under one of Wilcox's arms while Talanov slipped his shoulder under the other. Together they hoisted him up into a standing position.

"He is heavy. He needs to lose weight," Larisa said.

"Too much French wine and Brie."

"He must go on diet. This much fat is not healthy."

"I'm right here," whispered Wilcox hoarsely.

"Take sip," Larisa said, tipping the bottle to Wilcox's lips. "Help with pain." After Wilcox had taken a couple of swallows, Larisa poured the remainder over the blood-soaked towels.

"You just wasted that entire bottle," Wilcox said.

"I buy you another. Be quiet. Save strength."

Pulling out his Glock, Talanov looked through the peephole and saw Nick and Vic standing outside the door. They were dressed in their shiny bronze suits. They looked up and down the hall, then reached for their Anacondas, When they did, Talanov yanked open the door and jammed his pistol up into their faces. "Drop them right now!" he commanded just as a woman came out of her room, saw what was happening and ran back inside, slamming the door.

Nick and Vic glared down at Talanov but did as they were told. The giant revolvers thudded onto the carpet. Talanov wanted to dismantle the pistols, or certainly unload them, but knew there was no time. Wilcox needed a hospital and needed one fast.

"Back down the hall. Let's go," said Talanov, kicking the pistols away and motioning the two musclemen back toward the elevator.

The big Russians did not move.

"We can certainly do this the hard way," said Talanov, aiming at Nick's kneecap.

"All right!" growled Nick, backpedaling with Vic toward the elevator.

"Hall's clear. Let's go," said Talanov.

Larisa struggled out of the room supporting Wilcox under one arm. Talanov slipped his shoulder under the other arm, and with his gun trained on Nick and Vic, motioned the two men back along the corridor. They arrived at the elevator and Talanov pushed the button.

"We will find you," vowed Nick.

The doors opened and Talanov and Larisa helped Wilcox inside. When the doors closed, Nick and Vic raced for their guns. Talanov punched the ground floor button.

"Where is nearest hospital?" asked Larisa.

"No idea," Talanov replied, sticking his pistol in the back of his jeans and covering it with his shirt.

"Bill must have medical help."

"Our biggest problem is getting out of here alive," said Talanov. "And I'm not just talking about Bill. I'm talking all of us. Nick and Vic will be hot on our heels, and Ilya may be waiting downstairs."

"Get off on second floor," said Larisa.

"Why there?"

"Take stairs down to kitchen."

"The kitchen? Why not the first aid clinic? The hotel should have one somewhere."

"No time. We must get Bill to kitchen. Stop bleeding."

They got off on the mezzanine floor and carried Wilcox along the corridor to the stairs. Hotel guests stopped and stared. Wilcox's legs were limp and dragging behind while

Talanov and Larisa carried him. They hurried down the stairs, into the restaurant, past the stunned hostess and into the kitchen, which was crammed with industrial stoves, stainless steel shelves and work counters. Flames leaped around sizzling skillets. Voices shouted orders. Kitchen staff bustled around.

Talanov swept everything off a stainless steel counter. Pans and casserole dishes crashed to the floor. By now, everyone in the kitchen had stopped to look while Talanov and Larisa laid Wilcox on the counter, where he moaned and coughed. It was a raspy cough from blood filling his lungs.

"I need chili pepper and curry powder," Larisa called out.

No one moved.

"Now!" Talanov shouted.

Several of the kitchen staff sprang into action and in less than thirty seconds Larisa was handed two industrial-size canisters of curry powder and cayenne pepper. Wilcox opened his eyes when she began untying the blood-soaked towel. He saw the canisters.

"You're not," he said weakly.

"It will stop bleeding," Larisa replied, opening the canisters.

Wilcox gazed up into Larisa's blue eyes. Her hair fell in loose tangles about her face. He reached up and touched her on the cheek. "How beautiful you are, my darling."

Squeezing Wilcox's hand, Larisa laughed and cried at the same time.

"It's okay," he whispered, "I'm ready to go. I've lived a good life."

"Shut up, Bill," snarled Talanov, glaring down at Wilcox with a reprimanding scowl.

Wilcox flinched and recoiled. "You know how to ruin a dying man's dream."

"You're not dying, so forget that vineyard-in-the-sky talk. The only place you're going is to a hospital." To Larisa: "We need to hurry."

Larisa tamped small mounds of spices into each of the four bullet holes in Wilcox's chest. She then rolled Wilcox onto his side and did the same for the exit wounds in his back. Wilcox began coughing up blood and Larisa glanced worriedly at Talanov.

"Not looking so good, is it?" Wilcox whispered. His breathing was shallow and rapid.

"Lie still, don't talk," Larisa replied. "Bleeding stopped. We take you to hospital."

While Larisa wrapped Wilcox's torso with a clean apron given to her by one of the kitchen staff, Talanov retrieved Wilcox's valet parking slip. He would prefer the speed of his Boxster to get Wilcox to the hospital, but needed a back seat for Wilcox to lie down, so that meant using Wilcox's sedan. He handed the slip to one of the dishwashers. He was a young man of maybe nineteen, with pimples on his face. He was dressed in kitchen whites that were soiled with food stains.

Talanov pressed a twenty dollar bill into the kid's hand. "Take this and the parking slip to the valet and get my friend's car. Bring it to the back door." He then handed him a fifty. "This is for you. Now, hurry." The boy nodded and ran out of the kitchen.

Out front, Ilya was approaching the hotel entrance when Nick and Vic ran out. "What happened? Where are they?" asked Ilya.

"Talanov burst out of the room with a gun and got the drop on us," said Vic. "They got away."

"Larisa is with him," added Nick. "Wilcox is wounded but alive."

Ilya punched the air angrily just as the young dishwasher ran past them and over to the valet. He gave the parking slip and cash to the valet, asked where the car was, and said there was a medical emergency in the kitchen.

"Over there," the valet said, pointing to the nondescript gray sedan parked in front of the black Boxster. The kid ran over, jumped in, started the engine, and roared past the three Russians.

Ilya watched the car squeal around the corner. "Get Gorsky on the phone," he said, walking over to the valet. "Whose car was that?" he asked.

"We don't give out information about guests," the valet replied.

Ilya jammed his pistol into the stomach of the valet. "I'll ask you one more time. Who was the kid and whose car was that?"

"He's a kitchen worker. He said there was a medical emergency."

Ilya ran over to Nick and Vic and Nick handed him the phone. Ilya put the phone to his ear. "Larisa's family," he said. "It's time we teach her a lesson."

CHAPTER 49

"NEAREST hospital?" shouted Talanov.

"Centinela," the head chef answered. "Down Century Boulevard past the 405 for maybe a mile. Left on Myrtle and it's six or seven blocks."

"Thanks," said Talanov. He pointed at two assistant cooks. "You and you, give me a hand." To Larisa: "Get the car door."

Talanov picked up Wilcox by the legs while the two assistant cooks grabbed him under the arms.

"Do those spices really stop bleeding?" one of the cooks asked.

"It is home remedy, but, yes, it works," answered Larisa.

"Is he going to make it?" the other one asked.

"Yes, he's going to make it," said Talanov. "Now, stop talking and let's get him to the car." They carried Wilcox out the back door. Everybody trailed after them to watch.

"We should sit him up," Larisa said, opening the car door. Talanov stepped backward through the open door and helped the two workers place Wilcox in the back seat. One of the workers handed Talanov the seat belt and Talanov pulled it across Wilcox's shoulder and buckled it. Talanov then backed his way out the other door and jumped behind the wheel just as Ilya ran into the kitchen and saw everyone gathered at the back door.

"Out of the way!" shouted Ilya. He began shoving his way through the crowd, tossing people aside, pushing toward the back door.

Larisa jumped into the front seat beside Talanov, who shifted into gear and hit the gas. The gray sedan squealed away just as Ilya shouldered his way outside and took aim. But Talanov was too far away. Seconds later, Nick and Vic arrived in their new silver Audi. Nick was driving and Vic was in the passenger seat with his Anaconda resting on his lap. Ilya jumped in the back seat and the Audi roared away.

Talanov sped down Avion Drive and turned east on Century

Boulevard. It was late and traffic was light and he was making good time. But so were Ilya and his men, who were in a much faster car. Talanov had the accelerator to the floor, but the sedan had an economical four-cylinder engine, which was great on mileage but lousy on getaway. Talanov looked in his rearview mirror and saw a pair of headlights closing in.

Wilcox coughed and Talanov glanced back at him. "Hang in there," he said.

Larisa reached over the seat and took Wilcox by his hand. "I am here."

A loud boom sounded and the rear windshield burst into thousands of tiny chunks. Larisa screamed and ducked. Another thunderous boom from Vic's Anaconda sent a second forty-five caliber bullet singing through the interior.

Talanov began weaving from side to side. It was about all he could do because traffic was so sparse and there were no other cars to use as obstacles and shields. *Where was LA traffic when you needed it?* They sped through the green light at International Road. An overpass was ahead.

Another boom from the Anaconda thundered and the front windshield shattered. With another scream, Larisa curled herself up in the front seat, head down, arms around her shins. Air blasted Talanov in the face as they raced beneath the overpass and through the light. On their left now was a Shell station. On the right was a Circle K. Vic fired again at Talanov, who was veering from side to side. The bullet missed.

Beyond the overpass and light, the median disappeared and Century Boulevard became a wide ribbon of concrete. It was as wide as a landing strip, counting the center turn lanes, which were designated by yellow lines. No curbs, no center divider, no palm trees and shrubs. Just open concrete and plenty of it.

An idea came to mind, but before Talanov could act, the median strip reappeared. He had missed his chance.

With the accelerator pressed to the floorboard, Talanov kept weaving from side to side. Thankfully, there were other cars on the boulevard now, so Talanov was able to race around and between them, like a game of cat and mouse. Unfortunately, the Audi was able to stay right with him, so the prospect of the mouse getting away from the cat did not look good. Plus, everyone in the Audi was armed. Talanov had his Glock wedged beneath his leg, but it was useless at the moment because he was driving eighty miles an hour and every bit of his focus was on driving and not colliding with anyone else.

The 405 overpass was up ahead. Before the overpass was the intersection at La Cienega Boulevard. Beyond the intersection, the median strip ended and Century Boulevard became a landing strip again. No center divider, no curbs, no palm trees and shrubs. Just more open concrete all the way to the 405.

When they raced through the intersection, the Audi was right behind him. Talanov took a steadying breath and swerved to his right. As predicted, the Audi did the same. "Hang on," he said. He hit the brakes and cranked the steering wheel hard to the left. With continuing forward momentum, the sedan spun left with a rotating turn, its tires skidding and squealing. As it did, Talanov used his right hand to slip the Glock from beneath his leg, and in one smooth motion, brought it down across his left arm, which was controlling the steering wheel while the sedan continued to spin.

The sedan was facing backward now in its rotating skid, which meant Talanov's window was facing the Audi as it passed by, its brakes screeching as Nick reacted to Talanov's unexpected maneuver. Nick looked over and saw Talanov staring right at him. He then saw the Glock staring at him as well.

Talanov fired six shots. In the light from an overhead streetlamp, he saw Nick's head explode and Vic's face get sprayed with blood. He saw Ilya duck down in the back seat as the out-of-control Audi sideswiped a car and skidded into a fire hydrant. The crash knocked over the cast iron barrel and shot a geyser of water into the air before bouncing to a complete stop. Completing the spinning circle, Talanov released the brakes, hit the accelerator and straightened the steering wheel. The sedan careered back and forth several times before the tires bit the pavement and the sedan sped east beneath the 405 overpass. Behind him, a car veered widely around the Audi and collided with another car before smashing headlong into a sign marking the Inglewood city limits.

"How does he look?" asked Talanov.

Larisa crawled over the top of the seat and settled in beside Wilcox, who was now slumped to one side. She felt his wrist for a pulse, then his neck. "Hurry! He's slipping away."

CHAPTER 50

"DON'T let him die!" shouted Talanov, who was gripping the steering wheel tightly as they raced through the next stoplight. He leaned on his horn before swerving wildly through an impossibly slim opening in the four lanes of cross traffic. Drivers honked and cars smashed into one another when Talanov shot through the intersection. He glanced in his rearview mirror at the pileup, then caught sight of Larisa in the backseat trying to revive Wilcox.

"I think he is giving up," she said.

"He can't! Not now!" Talanov replied.

Larisa slapped Wilcox lightly in the face.

"He's got a son and a grandson that need him," said Talanov. "We can't let him die this way."

"I am so sorry to do this," Larisa said, slapping him again, trying to rouse him. "I know it must hurt, that your whole body must hurt. But you must hang on, Bill. *Please!*"

Talanov's hatred of the mob was growing with each passing minute. Andrea had died in his arms. Jade had died in his arms. Now Wilcox was dying. It would be easy to play the blame game. If he went there, he would be tempted to deck Posner on the spot if ever he saw him again. Posner was not entirely at fault, and Talanov knew that. Posner had not pulled the trigger. Ilya had. But Posner and Teague had been foolish enough to fall for Ilya's charm, which of course laid some of the blame at his own feet because he had not seen through Ilya's game, either. He had jumped at the chance to uncover his wife's killer, which had been a calculated move on Ilya's part that had fooled him as much as it had everyone else. In fact, the whole Connor Jax fabrication was as brilliant as it was evil, for by making it look like the CIA had killed Andrea in an effort to kill him, Ilya had created an apparent motive for him to kill Wilcox, which might well have worked if Larisa hadn't decided to return his wallet. Still, Ilya's plan succeeded in drawing Wilcox into the open, mainly because Ilya knew he, Talanov, would phone Wilcox demanding answers. Which meant Ilya must have known that he was November Echo and that Wilcox had been his contact. Ilya had dropped hints in that direction and made suggestive comments, but he hadn't recognized them, and thus, by introducing Ilya to Wilcox, he had played right into Ilya's hands. Ilya then allowed events to play themselves out, and when all was said and done, he kept his scheduled appointment with Wilcox. But not in a way that anyone had anticipated.

The frustrating thing was that all of this could have been prevented if Posner and Teague had trusted him. Or if they had accepted Wilcox's trust in him. If only they had listened. But they hadn't.

"How close are we?" asked Larisa.

"A few more blocks," answered Talanov, noticing a pair of headlights closing in on him from behind.

They came to Myrtle Avenue and turned. The headlights behind him turned, too.

"How's he doing?" asked Talanov, keeping an eye on the car that was following.

Larisa was holding Wilcox's hand. The apron and towels covering Wilcox's chest were saturated with blood. "I don't know how long he can hold on," she said.

A car passed them from the other direction. Its headlights briefly illuminated Talanov's face, then the car behind them. In the rearview mirror, Talanov recognized the car. It was the silver Audi, which was damaged but very much functional.

Larisa saw Talanov stiffen. "What is it?" she asked.

"Trouble," he replied, placing his pistol in the seat beside him as they roared toward the hospital, which was visible ahead.

The Centinela Hospital was in a complex of buildings that included specialty clinics, medical offices, and a twenty-four-hour emergency room. Following the signs, Talanov skidded around a corner. The Audi stayed right behind him. But as he sped toward the emergency room entrance, he suddenly veered left, across the open parking lot. The Audi, however, did not follow. Whoever was driving would not be fooled again.

While Talanov steered the sedan in a wide circle, the Audi stopped in a darkened patch of asphalt between him and the hospital. The driver's door opened and Ilya climbed out. The passenger door then opened and Vic stepped out. Vic's face was still smeared with Nick's blood. In his hand was the Anaconda.

Talanov sped right toward a line of cars. Beyond them was a clear lane that led to the emergency room entrance. Vic trotted in the same direction, cutting him off. Talanov circled back to the right in another wide circle, his tires squealing as he looked for a way to get close to the entrance. But Ilya was already tracking him that way on foot.

And in the backseat, Wilcox was dying.

Talanov stopped in the center of the parking lot and shifted into Park. It was empty and dark where he was, with no light to give Ilya or Vic a clear shot. It was a standoff. But if he waited much longer, Wilcox would die.

Checkmate.

Talanov shifted into Drive and made a squealing wide turn toward the exit. Ilya and Vic ran back to the Audi and raced after him. But as he reached the street, Talanov hit the brakes. The car screeched as it stopped. Ramming the gearstick into reverse, Talanov hit the gas and roared backward at the Audi speeding toward him. Ilya swerved but Talanov swerved with him and the back of the sedan rammed the side of the Audi just as Vic fired two rounds from the Anaconda. The bullets missed because Vic was not wearing a seatbelt and the impact of the crash smashed his head against the windshield frame. When that happened, he lost his grip on the Anaconda and it bounced out the window and fell into a crease of crumpled metal on the trunk of the whining little sedan that was pushing the Audi sideways across the parking lot. The sedan's tires were smoking and its transmission straining against the resistance of two tons of Audi. The sedan soon ran out of momentum, however, and stopped, its engine tapping loudly as Talanov fell out the open door, jarred from the crash, panting for breath.

Looking up, Talanov saw Vic's head hanging out the window. Vic was dazed and moaning. Scrambling to his feet, Talanov slammed Vic's head against the side of the car. He then whirled around, looking for Vic's pistol. His own pistol was gone and he was not sure where it was.

In the corner of his eye, Talanov saw movement. Looking left, he saw Ilya holding Vic's Anaconda. Rivulets of blood were trickling down Ilya's face.

"I tell Nick he was driving too close," remarked Ilya, "that he should shoot out your tires. But Nick, he would not listen."

"Too bad for Nick," said Talanov.

Ilya motioned with the pistol and Talanov slowly raised his hands.

"Nice move, sacrificing Borzakov the way you did," said Talanov. "Knight to h5, taking queen."

"Bishop to g6. Checkmate."

"Borzakov never studied chess with us, did he?" asked Talanov.

Ilya smiled and shook his head.

"I thought not," said Talanov, lowering his hands. "I asked Wilcox to grab our old KGB chess records but his boss nixed the idea. He thought it a waste of time. You said Borzakov was in class with us. Those records would have told me you were lying."

"Ain't them the breaks? Is that not how the Americans say it? They love dispensing such abrasive advice. So now I rub this advice in your face, *November Echo,* since you love Americans so much."

Talanov said, "The longer we stand here talking, which is fine with me, the sooner the cops will arrive. You can't go around firing a cannon like that and not expect people to notice."

Ilya glanced toward the emergency room entrance, where a small crowd of onlookers had gathered. But the parking lot was dark and they both knew the crowd would soon disperse back inside.

"Americans have no attention span," said Ilya. "They will soon lose interest."

"One of them will call the police."

"I think not," Ilya replied as the crowd began trailing back inside.

"He's dead, you know," said Talanov. "Wilcox died on the way."

"Then he will not feel a thing," said Ilya, cocking the Anaconda. "The same, I am afraid, cannot be said for you."

"Or you," announced Larisa.

Ilya looked left and saw Larisa standing on the other side of the two crashed cars holding Talanov's gun. She was holding it with both hands and was aiming it directly at Ilya's chest. Her blouse was torn and she was covered in Wilcox's blood.

"But, I thought—" Ilya stammered.

"Ain't them the breaks?" Larisa replied, cocking the pistol.

CHAPTER 51

ILYA looked back and forth between Talanov and Larisa.

"Hand over the gun," said Talanov. He took a step forward but Ilya jerked the Anaconda in his direction and Talanov stopped.

"Give him gun," Larisa said. "Or I shoot."

"I think you should hear something first," Ilya replied.

Talanov took another small step forward but Ilya pointed the Anaconda straight at his face. "Try that again and I *will* kill you," he said. "Yes, your girlfriend will shoot me. Perhaps she will even kill me. But you will be dead and she will go through the rest of her life without you." He looked over at Larisa. "Is that what you want?"

Larisa did not reply.

"All I ask is that you listen to something," Ilya said. "Then do what you must do." He reached for his pocket and Larisa stepped forward with the gun. "I am only reaching for my phone," he said. "You *do* want to talk with your family, don't you? Before Gorsky kills them?"

Larisa stepped forward again but this time she was shaking with anger ... and fear. Her hands were starting to wobble as she fought back tears.

Ilya glanced at his watch. "If I do not call Gorsky in two minutes, he will start with your sister, Marina – what a beautiful girl – and then your brother. While your parents are made to watch."

"You are *lying!*" shouted Larisa, quivering with emotion. She looked at Talanov, hoping desperately for some kind of assurance that Ilya was lying and her family was safe.

"Do not look at Ice Man," said Ilya. "He has no part in this. But you do. And you can stop this tragedy from happening. All I ask is that you shoot Wilcox. He is already dead, I am told, so he will not feel a thing."

A weak cough sounded from the sedan and Ilya smiled.

Larisa glanced quickly at Wilcox. He was slumped in the back seat and was looking at her. He had not moved, but his eyes were open and Larisa could see a sliver of reflection.

"No!" Larisa shouted, looking back at Ilya.

"Three times in head, that is all."

"No!" she shouted again, but she was shaking with indecision.

"Are the lives of your family worth a man who will die, anyway?"

"It's ... okay," gasped Wilcox. "Life over. No reason to live."

Larisa knew what Wilcox was talking about. He was estranged from his son. He had no other family besides her and Alex. Which is why she had refused to give up on him. Everyone deserved love. Everyone deserved to live.

Just as her family deserved to live.

Could she do it? Could she kill the man she so desperately wanted to save? She knew how much Wilcox meant to Alex. But her family meant just as much to her. Either way, someone must die.

Everything hinged on whether Ilya was telling the truth. Even if he was, and even if she agreed to do what he was demanding, would he allow her family to live? There was really no way to tell.

"I assume you are wondering if I will allow your family to live," said Ilya. "Let me assure you, my sole purpose in coming here was to kill Wilcox. Talanov will tell you that. Once I have accomplished my mission, I have no further interest in killing anyone. You two can live happily ever after. Your family will be spared."

"How can I know you are telling me the truth?" asked Larisa. "How can I be sure you will not kill them, anyway?"

"You can't. But you *can* be assured that I will have them killed if you do *not* do what I say. Each and every one of them will die." He glanced again at his watch. "You now have less than a minute, he when Gorsky calls, I will put phone on speaker so you can hear him kill your sister. Then, while you listen to the wails of your parents, he will kill your brother, too, and he will kill him slowly and more painfully than you can imagine.

Gorsky is good at such things. Talanov should know. Gorsky was KGB. And you will listen to each and every moment."

Ilya took out his cell phone and placed it carefully on the crumpled trunk of the sedan. "Shoot Wilcox *now,*" he said.

Larisa ran a hand through her tangled hair. What should she do? The choice was between Wilcox and her family. Her *entire* family.

"I'll do it. Give me the gun," said Talanov. He reached his hand toward Larisa.

"Careful!" said Ilya, circling right.

"Stop where you are!" shouted Larisa, and Ilya stopped.

Talanov turned to Ilya. "I'm not going to shoot you because that would be the same as killing her family. Look at her. She can't do it. But I can, and you know it. Let her give me the gun."

Ilya looked toward the back seat of the car. He would do it himself but Larisa was probably unstable enough to shoot him. The Ice Man, however, was capable of doing it. He motioned for Larisa to give Talanov the gun.

"Lower your gun first," said Talanov.

Ilya laughed. "Do you take me for a fool?"

"We're wasting time!" declared Talanov. "You know I'm not going to shoot you because you've got her family. Even if Gorsky isn't there and you're bluffing, I won't take that chance. But you can shoot us while we're making the transfer, and no doubt would if Larisa didn't have you covered right now. And she may well shoot you, anyway, if that phone rings and startles her. So lower your gun so we can make the transfer without anyone getting hurt."

Talanov could see Ilya deliberating. See him biting his lip and cursing silently. Finally, Ilya lowered the Anaconda.

For Talanov, this was not a good sign. It meant that Ilya was telling the truth about Gorsky having Larisa's family. If he'd been unwilling to lower his gun, it would have meant he was bluffing, and he could have told Larisa to shoot. But Ilya had complied. And that was not good.

"I should kill you for doing this to us!" cried Larisa, advancing toward Ilya, her hands shaking.

"Larisa, give me the gun," said Talanov calmly. "He's got your family and *will* have them killed if we don't obey."

Larisa remained rigid with anger and hatred.

"Don't shoot him," Talanov said gently. "Don't give him the pleasure of killing your family. Hand me the gun."

Talanov moved over to the cars and reached out his hand. Keeping Ilya covered, Larisa handed Talanov the Glock. But instead of turning toward Wilcox, Talanov strode over and placed the pistol against Ilya's forehead.

"Did you do it? Did you kill my wife?" Talanov demanded.

Ilya did not flinch.

"Did you kill her?" shouted Talanov.

"Closure. Is this what you seek?" asked Ilya, smirking briefly before hardening his expression. "Remove your gun from my head."

Talanov did not respond.

"Now!"

Talanov's lips were pinched with rage, but after a long moment, he withdrew the pistol yet kept it aimed at Ilya's chest when he stepped back.

Ilya laughed. "You are such a little girl."

"Considering most of the women I know are twice the man you are, I'll take that as a compliment."

Ilya's eyes flashed briefly before settling into a cold smile. "Yes, I kill your wife, and, yes, I make it look like CIA was responsible. And now I am forcing you to kill your friend. And you will do it. That is because you are November Echo, the Ice Man, who makes decisions based on logic, and logic tells you that a dying man, even a friend, is not worth an entire family. Nor is shooting me."

Talanov glanced briefly at Larisa, whose eyes were pleading with him.

"Shoot Wilcox now!" commanded Ilya.

"I'll make you convince Gorsky to let them go," said Talanov. "Your life for theirs."

"Do you think Gorsky will fall for that? If he knows you have me, he will kill them, believing you will kill me, anyway."

"Convince him otherwise."

"You know we do not operate that way. Gorsky will simply hang up phone and shoot them, leaving you and your girlfriend to live with consequences. We are *mafia*, Talanov. It is why we are feared."

Ilya's cell phone suddenly came to life. It vibrated with an annoying ring tone that Ilya had downloaded from a heavy metal site. Shouts and growls and amplified bass music filled the air. Everybody looked at the cell phone as it rattled on the trunk of the car.

"Do it. Shoot Wilcox," said Ilya, stepping over and picking up the phone.

Keeping Ilya covered, Talanov moved to the rear passenger door and looked in at Wilcox.

"It's okay," he whispered. "I'm ready."

"Don't worry. We'll figure this out," Talanov replied.

"Shoot him!" commanded Ilya. He touched an icon and the phone went to speaker. "Are you there, Gorsky?" he asked.

"*Da.* I am here," Gorsky replied in a gravelly voice. "Who do I kill first?"

"Tell me about girl," said Ilya. "Maybe we sell her to rich Arab."

"Boy, maybe, not girl," Gorsky replied. "Too skinny. Teeth need fix."

"Shoot girl in ten seconds," said Ilya.

An instant later, three gunshots sounded over the instrument's tiny speaker. They sounded like party poppers. Ilya shrugged at the sound of screaming. "Oops," he said. "Too late. Shoot Wilcox now. Save others."

"*No!*" Larisa cried. It was a prolonged wail that faded into a deep sobbing agony. Larisa then fell to her knees, mouth open, tears streaming down her face.

"Do it," whispered Wilcox in the back seat of the sedan.

Talanov looked into the eyes of his old friend staring up at him.

"It's okay ... do it," said Wilcox again. He closed his eyes.

"Is this Ilya Filishkin?" a voice asked in cultured American English over the phone. It was a strong, almost friendly voice.

A stunned Ilya looked at the phone. "Who is this?" he said.

"Is Talanov there?" asked the voice.

A brief silence.

"Who *is* this?" Ilya demanded, tightening his grip on the Anaconda.

"Connor Jax," the voice replied, "and I'll take that as a yes. Talanov, Larisa's family is safe. No one's been hurt and no one's been killed, except Gorsky, of course. Made a horrible mess."

The connection was terminated and a faint hiss of static filled the vacuum of silence.

Ilya's reactive instincts immediately took over and he knew exactly what Talanov would do. Feinting left, Ilya dove right while raising the Anaconda. Talanov would be thrown off for a split second, which would be enough time to drop him where he stood.

Ilya was wrong, and it was the last thought would ever have.

Talanov followed Ilya's movements with the Glock and fired five shots in rapid succession. Five direct hits. Five hollow-tip bullets ripping through Ilya's skull as if it were a watermelon. Ilya was dead before he hit the pavement in a mist of blood and tissue. Talanov ran over, helped Larisa to her feet, then lifted Wilcox out of the back seat and began running toward the lighted entrance of the hospital.

CHAPTER 52

IT was almost 4:30 in the morning when the surgeon in scrubs came out of the operating room. Uniformed police officers constituted the majority of people filling the waiting room and most of them had gathered around Talanov and Larisa. Teague was also present and was talking quietly with detectives.

Both Talanov and Larisa were weary and showed it. Talanov's eyes were bloodshot, and his clothes were stained with blood. He'd received a gash on his forehead from ramming the Audi and it had not yet been treated. Nor had more than a dozen small cuts from the flying shards of glass in Wilcox's hotel room. Larisa's face was streaked with tears, and her eyes were still puffy from crying. Like Talanov, her clothes were dirty and stained. When Talanov and Larisa saw the doctor, they rushed over and waited anxiously for the report.

"First the good news," the surgeon replied. "Whoever packed his wounds with teabags and spices kept him from bleeding to death, and that kept the blood flowing to his brain."

"And the bad news?" Talanov asked.

"Internal damage," the doctor replied. "Those bullets tore right through him and did some serious damage, which we were able to repair. Again, penetration of the tea and spices helped seal the holes, but for some reason his body's shutting down. And we cannot for the life of us figure out why."

"Can't you give him a transfusion or something?"

"We replaced the blood. That was no problem. The real problem is his will to live. It's as if he's giving up."

"Can I talk to him? Find out what's going on?"

"I'm afraid not. He's in a coma."

"But he can still hear us, right?"

The doctor shook his head sadly.

"May we try?" asked Larisa. "Please. We will not stay long."

The doctor smiled and nodded.

"Who's in charge here?" Martin Posner called out, pushing

his way through the crowd of police officers. Two officers pointed to a lieutenant. The Shetland pony marched over to the lieutenant. "Martin Posner, FBI," he said, flashing his ID. "This is my case now and I'm taking over."

"On whose authority?" asked the lieutenant.

"Mine," said Posner, striding into the center of the room. "Everybody, listen up!" he shouted. "I want the waiting room cleared of uniforms and I want that man over there taken downtown and held for questioning." He motioned for several of the officers to take Talanov into custody.

The officers looked at their lieutenant but nobody moved.

Posner marched back over to the lieutenant, who stood several inches taller and was built like a lumberjack. Posner got right up in his face, like a terrier picking a fight with a bear. "Are your men hard of hearing? Clear the room *now* and take that man with you." He pointed again at Talanov.

"Take him yourself," said the lieutenant. "It's no longer our case, remember?" To his fellow officers: "Okay, let's go."

Posner grabbed one of the young police officers and demanded his handcuffs. When the officer hesitated, Posner threatened him with obstruction of justice.

"Ease off, Martin," said Teague, intervening. "Talanov is not a danger."

"He *killed* a man in the parking lot!" hissed Posner. "We have the victim's companion in custody and that's what he's claiming."

"It was self defense," cried Larisa. "Ilya was a Russian hit man. He was going to shoot us!"

Posner jabbed a finger in Larisa's face. "When I want to hear from a prostitute, I'll let you know. Until then, stay out of my way."

"Hey!" said Talanov, stepping between Posner and Larisa and easing Posner back.

"You're assaulting a Federal officer," declared Posner, glaring up at Talanov.

"She was trying to tell you what happened."

"I don't care what she claims. The testimony of an illegal

Russian *whore* does not carry weight in this town. In fact, I can't wait to deport her."

Posner did not see the blow coming. All he remembered was waking up to the pungent smell of ammonia salts being waved under his nose.

Talanov had tried to restrain himself, he really had. He understood that hard questions needed to be asked. He *had* killed a man and that needed to be explained. He had also been carrying a firearm, and that, too, would no doubt cause problems. If he hadn't been carrying it, they would all be dead right now, including Wilcox, who might well die anyway. But he had broken the law and he would willingly pay the penalty, including jail time, if it came to that.

Even so, Posner had crossed the line. Whatever Posner said to him personally meant nothing. Posner was a moron and what he said was equally moronic. Insulting Larisa, however, would not be tolerated.

Talanov had been careful to pull his punch so as not to leave Posner with any permanent damage. His Combat Sambo training had taught him how to control force and penetration. Hence, he had delivered a good solid blow to the maxillary section of Posner's jaw. It was enough to give him a black eye as a reminder to watch his mouth, but not enough to leave him with a concussion or missing teeth.

Two nurses helped Posner to his feet. He pushed them away and grabbed the nearest policeman and demanded that Talanov be arrested.

"What for?" asked the policeman.

"For assaulting a Federal officer!"

"I didn't see a thing," the policeman replied. "Any of you guys see what happened?" he asked, looking at his fellow officers.

"Nope," the others replied.

Posner, whose eye was already turning black and blue, ran over to Teague and grabbed him by the arm. "You saw what happened! Arrest him!"

"I didn't see a thing, Martin. What I *did* see is how your

extreme prejudice against Talanov caused a critical blind spot that nearly got Agent Wilcox killed. I, too, bear a large burden of responsibility and I will make myself accountable. But your behavior has been duly noted and *will be* reported. And if you decide to go head to head with me over this, I'll call Diane Gustaves right here and now and see what she has to say. Do I make myself clear?"

For almost an entire minute, Posner glared up at the ebony features of the Acting Director of Operations for the Central Intelligence Agency. He knew better than to tangle with Teague. He knew even better than to tangle with Gustaves. And with a bitter scowl, he stormed out of the hospital.

Inside Wilcox's room, Talanov and Larisa sat next to Wilcox's bed. The blinds were open and a beeping monitor was keeping time with his dangerously slow heartbeat. He was connected to all kinds of wires and tubes. His skin tone was pale.

"I wish I could have known you better," Larisa said, taking Wilcox's hand. "So you must come out of this so that we can change that. Alex told me you love to eat, so I will cook for you. I know many Ukrainian specialties that you will love."

"Do you remember that first day in France?" added Talanov. "I showed up looking like some noir character out of a black-and-white spy thriller. Black Fedora, sunglasses, three-quarter-length jacket. And there you were, decked out in that awful Hawaiian shirt, walking shorts, brown socks and sneakers. And the waitress caught you peeking down her blouse. Do you remember?"

Talanov searched Wilcox's eyelids for any kind of movement that signaled he had heard them. But there was nothing but the incessant beeping of the heart monitor and gentle hiss of oxygen.

"He *can* hear us, can't he?" Larisa asked.

"I hope so," Talanov replied.

CHAPTER 53

LARISA walked over to a small bedside table and opened the drawer. Inside was a Bible. She brought is back and opened it to the twenty-third Psalm. "The Lord is my shepherd, I shall not want," she began. "He makes me lie down in green pastures. He leads me beside the still waters."

"Here, let me have that," said Talanov, taking the Bible. He flipped some pages and found another verse. "A good woman, who can find?" he said, reading a passage. "She considers a field and buys it. From her earnings she plants a vineyard." He leaned closer to Wilcox and said, "Did you hear that, Bill? A *vineyard*. As in acres and acres of grapes. In France, no doubt. Perfect for an old wine snob like you." Closing the Bible, he said, "How beautiful you are, my darling. Your love is better than wine. Curvaceous hips, incredible breasts. Come and drink wine and eat cake."

"It doesn't say that!" said Larisa, snatching back the Bible.

"Yes, it does. Well, sort of, I think."

"A vineyard in France?"

Talanov grinned and shrugged.

"Curvaceous hips and generous breasts? Come and drink wine and eat cake?"

"That one I know. Song of Solomon."

"What is wrong with Psalms?"

"Nothing. But in case you hadn't noticed – and you *had* to have noticed, since he kept drooling all over himself at the sight of you – Bill likes gorgeous women. So maybe this will stir him up. Get the juices flowing."

Larisa gave Talanov a smack on the arm just as a young woman with flawless light brown skin and thick sable hair burst into the room. Adorned with colorful tassel earrings, she was wearing a short, tight black skirt and a shiny plaid blouse. She had an enormous magenta handbag over one shoulder, which she dropped on the floor as she came reverently to

Wilcox's side. She lifted one of his hands to her lips and kissed it. Talanov and Larisa watched the woman place her cheek affectionately against Wilcox's hand for a long moment before leaning back and wiping tears from her eyes.

"He's going to pull through this, isn't he?" she asked, looking at Talanov. "Promise me he's going to be fine."

"Have we met?" asked Talanov.

"Sorry, I'm Charlie," she said, shaking Talanov's hand and nodding at Larisa.

"Alex and Larisa. We talked on the phone," Talanov replied.

"You're one of the few people he trusts," she said, looking back at Wilcox again. With a quivering lip, she watched his chest move up and down with each breath. "Look at all of those tubes."

"They're keeping him alive until he comes to."

"So he will ... come to?" she asked.

"The doctors are hopeful," said Talanov.

The door opened again and a uniformed police officer stepped in. "Colonel Talanov, there's someone to see you."

Talanov stepped out of the room and into the corridor, where he was met by a uniformed Marine, who stood six-feet-two, had thinning hair and broad shoulders. Beside him was a pregnant brunette, who was holding the hand of a little boy, who was carrying a crayon drawing on a piece of construction paper.

"Gunnery Sergeant Danny Wilcox," the Marine said, shaking Talanov's hand. "This is my wife, Julie, and my son, Jake."

"I'm four," Jake said, holding up some fingers.

"I'm Alex. Thank you for coming."

"How's he doing?" asked Danny.

"Not good," Talanov replied. "He took four bullets and has lost a lot of blood."

Fighting back emotion, Danny looked up at the ceiling while Jake kept watching Talanov.

"I hope I wasn't out of place phoning you," said Talanov. "Over the years, your dad and I have been through a lot, especially recently. He told me all about you. How long it's been."

Danny kept looking up at the ceiling. His jaw was tight and his thumbs were rubbing his fingertips nervously.

"He may not make it through this," said Talanov, "so I'm going to tell you what he told me. What he was planning to tell you himself if he hadn't been shot."

"Who shot my dad?" asked Danny.

"A Russian hit man named Ilya Filishkin. Your dad was public enemy number one as far as the Russian mob was concerned. He was crippling their operations both here and abroad."

Danny smiled briefly with pride. "Where's Filishkin now?" he asked.

"Rotting in—" Talanov began, then glancing down at Jake looking up at him. "In a very hot place."

"Who sent him there?" asked Danny.

"I did," Talanov replied.

Danny exhaled with satisfaction and nodded.

Down the hall, an elevator dinged and the sound of footsteps and voices suddenly filled the corridor. Talanov looked to see Diane Gustaves and Jackson Teague leading a small contingent of aides and assistants. Gustaves was issuing orders left and right. Her aides were taking notes while virtually running to keep up with her.

Gustaves saw Talanov and hurried over to him. "Alex, how is he?" she asked.

"Congresswoman Gustaves, I'd like to present Marine Corps Gunnery Sergeant, Danny Wilcox, and his family."

"Wilcox? Is Bill your dad?"

"Yes, ma'am."

"Son, your father is a *hero!* A fu—" Gustaves stopped in the middle of the word and looked down at Jake looking up at her. "A bona fide hero," she said, finishing her sentence. "If there's anything you need, and I mean, *anything,* you let me know."

"Thank you, ma'am," said Danny, bowing politely.

Gustaves excused herself, then told her aides to wait in the corridor while she slipped in to pay her respects. Through the open door, Talanov could see her approach Wilcox and take his hand in hers. One longtime friend to another.

While Gustaves spoke quietly to Wilcox, Teague offered Danny his hand. "Jackson Teague, Central Intelligence Agency," he said. "Son, I've known your father for many years and he is without doubt one of the finest men I know."

"Thank you, sir," Danny replied.

Teague looked at Talanov and said, "Alex, we owe you and Larisa a debt of thanks for saving Bill's life."

"You saved my dad's life?" asked Danny.

"They took on the Russian mafia in order to save your dad," Teague replied, "including a high-speed chase across town to the hospital."

"About Connor Jax," said Talanov.

"No idea what you're talking about," said Teague, who turned to Danny and said, "General Stanfield's a good friend of mine. I'll speak to him on your behalf." He shook Danny's hand again and joined Gustaves at the side of Wilcox's bed.

"Thank you," said Danny, offering Talanov his hand. "For saving my dad."

Talanov smiled and nodded.

"They're calling him a hero," said Danny.

"He is."

"Why didn't I know this? Why didn't he call?"

"He felt he'd failed you. That too much time had passed and that you wouldn't want to see him."

Danny bit his lip and looked away just as Charlie came out of the hospital room and over to Talanov. "I just got a text," she said. "As you know, Langley never sleeps. But since Bill *is* asleep, I thought I should bring this to you."

"What is it?" asked Talanov.

"Our tech guys got hold of Ilya's cell phone from his car outside. Good job, by the way, ramming him like that. Anyway, Ilya made three calls to a throwaway cell while he was chasing you. The last was made just as he was entering the parking lot."

"Any idea what he said?"

Charlie shook her head. "Nope. All we know is that he called someone. We've got the number, obviously, but we don't know who purchased the phone. It was purchased with cash from a kiosk."

Talanov glanced into the hospital room and saw Gustaves and Teague reminiscing quietly with each other. They were including Wilcox in the conversation, as if he could hear them. The blinds were open and a few lights from neighboring buildings could be seen as tiny rectangles.

"Did we ever catch the sniper?" asked Talanov. "The one who took a shot at Diane?"

"I don't think so," Charlie replied. She worked her cell phone screen and gained access to the JRIC communications and records. "Still at large," she said, reading a police report.

"Can you do one of those things you do with cell towers to triangulate the location of whoever it was Ilya called?" asked Talanov. "Where he is now, or where he was when Ilya called him each of those three times?"

Charlie went to work with her cell phone again and within a minute showed Talanov a map of greater Los Angeles with several dots showing on it. "When Ilya first called, the throwaway was here, near downtown Los Angeles."

"In some cheap motel, no doubt. If I were a sniper, I'd want to stay where no one would notice me."

"For the second call," said Charlie, "the throwaway pinged off of a new set of towers, this time here, on the 110."

"Heading south out of downtown," said Talanov.

"Yep. And for the third call, the throwaway was triangulated here, on Century Boulevard, east of here."

"He's heading our way," said Talanov, glancing into the hospital room and noticing what he had failed to notice before.

The blinds were open.

"Danny, get your dad out of that room," said Talanov, running for the stairs. "Get everybody out of that room!"

CHAPTER 54

TALANOV ran down the stairs and out an exit. Ahead was the parking lot. Even at such an early hour before dawn, it was still fairly full. He looked up at the lighted façade of the hospital then at the darkened hulk of the neighboring medical tower roughly two hundred feet away. It was three stories tall, with vertical strips of inset windows. The building was entirely dark. No workers were working and no cleaning crews were cleaning. To the left and on the far corner of the block was another medical tower, this one slightly shorter and nearly identical in appearance. Both offered clear shots of Wilcox's window, although the first building was closer and offered a better line of sight. Still, for a skilled sniper, the differences in distance were inconsequential. Which building had the sniper chosen, then, assuming tonight was the night?

It had to be tonight. For one thing, Wilcox was most vulnerable right now, in the wake of his shooting. The sniper would no doubt have phoned the hospital to find out which room Wilcox was in. He would also know that guards would be posted in and around his room. No one but approved medical staff would get in. Posing as a doctor or an orderly was therefore not an option. Assassination with a rifle from a distance would therefore be his preferred method, just as it had been earlier with Gustaves.

Which building would he have chosen? There was no time now to deliberate. He had to make a choice based on instinct and experience. If he were the sniper, he would choose the nearest building. Why make this more difficult than it needed to be? The building was closer and the rooftop looked directly into Wilcox's room. Plus, no one would be expecting another attempt this soon. The nearest building was the most logical choice.

Talanov ran across the parking lot to the door of the first office tower. It faced Myrtle Avenue and a row of small trees separated it from the street. A few cars were parked at the curb. He peered in through the glass but saw no security guard in the darkened foyer. He tried the door but it was locked and none of the front windows had been broken. How, then, had the sniper gotten in? He wouldn't have had a key, and since Ilya had called him just a few hours ago, he wouldn't have been able to slip into the building unnoticed while it was still open. So either he broke in through a side window or scaled the outside of the building. Breaking in through a window would have triggered an alarm, so that meant using a grappling hook and rope to scale the outside of the building. Three stores was not that high, unless of course you didn't have a grappling hook and rope, which he, Talanov, did not. How, then, was *he* going to get up to the rooftop in order to stop a sniper from taking out Wilcox, Gustaves, Teague, and anyone else in the room?

On top of the roof, Igor had almost finished assembling his weapon. He would have preferred a grenade launcher for this kind of situation, but none had been available on such short notice. He was lucky to have had access to a Negev.

The Negev was an Israeli Defense Force gas-operated light machine gun, with a two-hundred-round belt of 5.56 mm NATO ammunition. It looked like most automatic rifles, with a standard barrel, suppressor, laser module, adjustable bipod, and folding lightweight butt. Even though the blinds had now been closed, two hundred rounds sprayed through the blinds into the room would be more than enough to finish Wilcox once and for all. Wilcox was on an elevated hospital bed in a second story room, which meant he had the advantage of a downward firing trajectory from where he was positioned.

The first call from Ilya had been frantic, saying that Wilcox had survived the attack and, thanks to Talanov's help, had eluded Nick and Vic. Ilya then called again, even more frantic, to say Nick had been killed by Talanov in a car chase. A final call had come from Ilya in the parking lot of the hospital, telling him to stand by, that he would phone again in five minutes. When Ilya failed to phone, and when he then failed to answer his phone, Igor knew something was wrong. So he destroyed his own cell phone to prevent his location from being traced. He then set out to finish what Ilya had failed to accomplish.

It had taken a bit of detective work to find out Wilcox's condition and which room he was in. But he had done it and was now minutes away from finishing the job. His colleagues in Cyprus will be pleased.

Suddenly, he heard the smashing of glass. The building's alarm then went off. Dressed in a black SDU – Strategic Deployment Uniform – Igor ran to the edge of the rooftop and looked below. It was dark on the ground but he could see the reflections of broken glass lying on the sidewalk. Someone had broken in through the front door.

The break-in was no coincidence. Someone – probably Talanov – had figured out what was going on. Had it been the police, they would have used a key and there would be officers swarming the grounds. That meant a single intruder.

At this point, he had two options. He could wait for the intruder to open the rooftop door and shoot him, or he could escape and live to finish the job another day. If he waited for the intruder to come through the door, that increased his risk of being captured by the police, who would also be arriving soon. That left only one option.

Leaving the Negev where it was, Igor ran to the far edge of the building, where the grappling hook and attached rope lay coiled. Making sure the hook was secured on a vent pipe, he tossed the coil of rope over the side. After looping the rope around his back, Igor rappelled down the side of the building, where he hit the grass with barely a sound. Fishing out his keys, he ran to his car, which was parked on a dark stretch of curb, away from the nearest streetlight. As such, he did not see Talanov lying on the top of his car when he ran up to the door.

"Warm engine hoods are such a giveaway," Talanov remarked. He was no more than two feet away from Igor, who was concentrating on getting his key into the lock and did not see him.

Igor grabbed for his pistol, but Talanov swung his foot like a hammer and caught Igor on the side of the head. Igor went down and his gun bounced free. Igor shook off the blow and lunged for the pistol. But Talanov had already sprung from the top of the car and stepped on Igor's wrist. When Igor cried out, Talanov grabbed Igor by the belt and lifted him off the pavement.

Talanov was about to smash Igor's head against the side of the car when a figure stepped out of the shadows.

"Hold it!" the figure commanded.

Talanov froze.

"Drop him and move away," the figure said.

Talanov dropped Igor on his face and stepped back. Glaring up at Talanov, Igor climbed to his feet just as the figure stepped forward.

"My turn," Danny said.

Danny's fist caught Igor in the jaw like a Louisville Slugger. "That was for my dad," he said, catching Igor before he fell and propping him up against the door of the car. "And this one is for me," he said, punching Igor again and again in the stomach, not letting him fall until Igor's knees finally buckled and he crumpled to the pavement in a heap.

Talanov and Danny looked down at the unconscious body of Igor.

"God, that felt good," Danny said, panting heavily, massaging his knuckles.

"Tell me something," Talanov said, slapping Danny on the shoulder. "Did he really name you Erasmus?"

Danny laughed. "Yeah, he did. And I cannot tell you how much I hated him for it when I was a teenager."

In the distance came the wail of sirens.

CHAPTER 55

ENTERING the hospital, Talanov and Danny were directed to a different floor, where they were met by a doctor. He was a slight man in scrubs, with neatly combed hair and fine features that were almost feminine. A stethoscope was slung casually around his neck.

"How's my dad?" asked Danny.

"Follow me," said the doctor evasively.

Danny grabbed the doctor by the arm. "How is my *dad?*" he asked again, this time more forcefully.

"Deteriorating fast. Having to move him was quite a strain."

While they hurried along the corridor, the doctor kept glancing around.

"Is something wrong?" asked Talanov.

"I'm just not used to this."

"Used to what?"

The doctor shook his head in frustration as they rounded a corner and he gestured toward four Marines guarding a closed-off section of the corridor. The Marines were in khaki fatigues and helmets. Each held an M4 Carbine.

"Ten *hut!*" the duty sergeant barked, and the Marines all snapped to attention. With their rifles held upward at precise 22.5 degree angles, the Marines parted, two on each side, to let Gunnery Sergeant Danny Wilcox and Talanov past. Two of the Marines opened the doors.

"What's going on here, Sergeant?" asked Danny, pausing.

"Standing guard, Gunny," answered the sergeant.

"On whose orders?" asked Danny.

"The very top, sir. General Stanfield."

Danny's eyes widened. "*Stanfield* issued the order?"

"Yes, sir. Said there was important cargo on board. That no one's to get by us who doesn't belong."

Seeing a faint, brief smile on the face of the stoic sergeant, Danny nodded appreciatively.

Down the corridor were another two Marines. They were stationed in front of the third door on the left. The Marines snapped to attention when Danny approached. One of them opened the door.

With an appreciative nod, Danny led the way into the hospital room. It was just like the other room and Wilcox was still connected to several drip lines and a monitor, which beeped with each of his heartbeats. In his nostrils was a clear plastic oxygen cannula, with a tube that ran to a panel on the wall. Jake's crayon drawing was now taped to the headboard of his bed.

"We'll talk later," Talanov said to Danny, motioning for Larisa to join him in the hall.

Danny nodded appreciatively, walked over and kissed Julie, then sat in a chair beside the bed. Jake hopped up in his lap.

"Mom says Grandpa's asleep," Jake whispered, placing a finger over his mouth. "When is he going to wake up?"

"I don't know, buddy," Danny replied. He scooted the chair closer to the bed and took Wilcox by the hand. "Dad, this is Danny," he began while Julie looked on. "I don't know if you can hear me, but I'm here. We're all here, all three of us, soon to be four. That's me and Julie, and little Jake – Jacob Erasmus Wilcox – who just turned four."

Julie walked over and stood beside Danny.

"I know we haven't seen each other in a while," Danny continued, "and I want you to know, I'm really sorry. I blamed you for a lot of things. Not being there, never calling, always putting other people ahead of us. Then it started happening to me. Missing Jake's birthdays, going away for months at a time, even though Jake kept asking where I was and why I wasn't coming home to take him to the beach. I know you didn't call, but I could have called you, too. I was stupid, hardheaded, and proud."

"Daddy said stupid," Jake whispered to his mom.

With a half-laugh and a half-cry, Julie wiped a tear from her eyes and took Jake in her arms.

"So I want you to know," said Danny, "that I'm real proud of you. And I'd like to start seeing you again. Because I miss you, Dad, really, I do."

Danny looked at Wilcox for some kind of a response. There was none. Just the gentle hiss of oxygen and the beeping of the heart monitor.

"I hope you can hear what I'm saying," said Danny. "You've just got to come out of this, okay?"

Danny kept looking for a response. Movement under his eyelids. The twitch of a finger. A nod. Anything. But there was none. Just the gentle hiss of oxygen and the beeping of the heart monitor.

"Give me *some* kind of a sign, Dad. Some kind of a sign that I'm not sitting here making a fool of myself."

Danny looked carefully for some kind of response. But there was none. Just the gentle hiss of oxygen and the beeping of the heart monitor.

Down the corridor, past the Marine guards, was a small waiting room. It was a typical waiting room. There were several chairs, an upholstered couch, a couple of small corner tables with lamps and magazines. On the wall was a framed print. A pastoral scene. On another wall was a flat screen television. Talanov and Larisa sat together opposite the television, which was switched to an early morning news program. But Talanov's attention was not on the television. He was staring absently at the floor, his lips pursed, his brow furrowed in thought.

"What are you thinking?" asked Larisa.

"Nothing much," Talanov replied.

"Tell me," Larisa said.

Talanov did not reply.

"Perhaps you are thinking how your friend Bill is lying near death," Larisa said, reading his downcast eyes. "Perhaps you are thinking how mob also killed Jade, and nearly killed me, and how they killed your wife in front of your eyes."

Talanov nodded without looking up.

"So now you are thinking of way to send me home," Larisa continued. "You will tell me that I will find happy life with another man, that it is better to experience pain in my heart now than death in a horrible way. You say I will get over you, but I think you say this more for you than for me. Perhaps you think I am foolish girl, who knows nothing about love, doing what I did. But you do not know what it was like, the horrible things they do to us and what I must do to survive. You think I do not know the kind of man you are, or what can happen if I am with you. But I know more than you think, and I am stronger than you think. Just because I am quiet and shy does not mean I am weak, or that I do not know how to fight for people I love. Two ropes are stronger than one."

"That is what I love about you," Talanov said, taking Larisa by the hand. "In spite of everything that's happened and everything you've been through, you have this wonderful, resilient, optimistic belief that love will conquer all."

"You are making fun of me," Larisa said, pulling away.

"I'm not. I promise," he said, taking her by the hand again. "I honestly love that about you. Don't ever change, okay?"

"You are saying goodbye, aren't you?" she asked.

"Not in the way that you think."

Larisa replied with a skeptical frown.

"People around me get killed, Larisa. My wife, Jade, Bill. Look at what happened to you and your family. You're safe for now, thanks to a miracle named Connor Jax. What about next time? If something like that happens again, they won't come after me, they'll come after you. That's the way those people operate. So until I figure out where things stand, we've got to let everyone think we've gone our separate ways. Until now, we've simply been victims swept up in something bigger than the both of us. But if you move in with me, or if we become an item, it makes you an immediate target. Go home for a while to Ukraine. Reconnect with your family. Figure out what you want to do with the rest of your life. You're a tough, intelligent, gutsy nurse. Correction: make that a tough, intelligent, gutsy nurse with a wonderful, resilient, optimistic belief that love will conquer all."

Larisa punched him on the arm just as a petite Chinese nurse with a clipboard walked by. The nurse was in her thirties, although her porcelain skin made her age difficult to guess.

"I'm serious," he said, recoiling with a laugh. "And I'm not poking fun at you, either. You've got incredible strength and experience, so if changing the world is something you want to do, then I've got a way to kill two birds with one stone."

"What do you mean, kill birds with stone? I do not know what this means."

Talanov started to answer, then paused to look at the Chinese nurse, who was watching them. When Talanov made eye contact with her, she smiled and continued down the corridor.

After a thoughtful moment, Talanov looked back at Larisa and said, "It means, I can accomplish two things at once by getting you a job with some people who are doing just that. They're changing the world by helping others. When I said love conquers all, I wasn't joking." With a sigh, he looked down the corridor to where the Marines were stationed on each side of the door into Wilcox's hospital room. "If only love could bring *him* back," he said, nodding toward Wilcox's door. "Bill and I bicker and fuss all the time, but the truth is, I love that old wine snob like a brother."

"It is possible he will make it, you know," Larisa said. "We cannot give up."

"Like I said, don't ever change," replied Talanov with a smile.

"You do not believe he will live?"

"I hope so," said Talanov, leaning back.

"See?" Larisa said. "You have hope. Hope means there is time for miracle to occur. Look at what happened to my family. We cannot give up."

Talanov started to reply when his attention was drawn to the television, where a female reporter in a business suit was standing before the camera with a man he had seen before. The man was wearing lots of gold jewelry and a baseball cap turned sideways. He and the reporter were standing in front of an office building in downtown Santa Monica. Painted on the window of the office was the circular logo of The Shelter. Inside the perimeter of the circle was an artistic rendition of a pair of interlocked hands. "Well, I'll be," he said, picking up the remote and turning up the volume.

"With me now is local LA rapper, Slam-D," the reporter said, "who has just made a one-hundred-thousand-dollar contribution to The Shelter." The reporter turned to Slam-D and said, "What motivated you to make such a generous contribution?"

"Dem kids got nobody, got nuthin," he replied. "So me and Dog, we decides to do sumpin about dat."

The camera pulls back to include Dog, who is standing to one side of Slam-D.

"One hundred thousand dollars will feed and clothe a lot of orphans," the reporter continued. "How does that make you feel?"

"I feels gud, ya know? Really gud," Slam-D replied, jivin' and swayin' from side to side. He pumped a fist in a rolling downward direction. A gesture of "cool."

"What made you choose The Shelter for your donation?"

Slam-D's face grew tense. "Someone tol' me about it. Said dey needed help."

"You must be very proud."

Slam-D nodded and he and Dog bump fists.

"Well, there you have it folks," said the reporter, turning back to the camera. "Local rapper, Slam-D and his band have just made a *one-hundred-thousand-dollar contribution* to a chain of orphanages called, The Shelter."

Suddenly, a group of nurses and doctors sprinted past the waiting room. Seconds later, one of the Marine guards stuck his head around the corner and said, "Sir, you'd better come now."

Talanov and Larisa ran down the corridor into Wilcox's room to see Gunnery Sergeant Danny Wilcox bent over the bed, wiping his eyes with a hand. Hugging him were Julie and Jake. Several doctors had gathered around the head of Wilcox's bed and were quietly conferring.

Marines don't cry easily. In fact they rarely shed tears at all. So when Talanov saw Danny's emotion, he knew immediately what had happened. *His old friend, Wilcox, was dead.*

Everything had been in vain. Packing his wounds with spices.

The race across town. The battle in the parking lot. Doctors working feverishly. The waiting and praying. He had even brought Wilcox's son, Danny, into the hospital to try and rouse the old fox. He had hoped Wilcox would hear Danny's voice – hear little Jake's voice – and start fighting again. But he had failed. Once again, someone close to him had died. And not just anyone, but someone closer than family. *So much for love conquering all.*

"Danny, I'm so sorry," said Talanov.

But Talanov did not need to be sorry. That's because Danny's tears were not tears of grief. They were tears of joy.

Wilcox opened his eyes and slowly moved his head to look at Talanov standing in the doorway.

"You're alive!" Talanov exclaimed, rushing to his side with Larisa, who had tears rolling down her cheeks.

"Here I was," said Wilcox hoarsely, "heading toward a better place, when all of a sudden I hear this voice talking about generous breasts and curvaceous hips. So I made a u-turn right then and there and back I came. No way was I going to pass up an offer like that."

Holding hands, Talanov and Larisa laughed while more doctors and nurses came and went.

"But if you ever call me a wine snob again," growled Wilcox, "citizen or not, I'm deporting your sorry ass."

At that very moment, two people passed by the open doorway. One was the Chinese nurse. Her name was Straw Sandal and she still had her clipboard in hand. On it was a photograph of Talanov. With her was an orderly in green medical scrubs. His name was Po Yong Shu. Lanky and tall, Po had shaggy black hair and wore glasses. They paused briefly for Straw Sandal to discreetly click several photos with her cell phone camera before continuing along the corridor.

Once they were beyond the cordon of Marines, Straw Sandal led Po into a stairwell. "Call Dragon Head," she said. "Tell him we have found Talanov."

"As you wish," answered Po with a slight bow. "And if Talanov refuses to cooperate?"

"Do Not worry. Talanov will cooperate."

Po bowed his head submissively but did not reply.

"You do not believe me?" she asked.

Po kept his head bowed. It was a polite gesture that acknowledged her superior rank as Dragon Head's sister, which meant she was arguably the number two most powerful person in Hong Kong's criminal underworld, second only to Dragon Head himself.

"Did you see the young woman beside him?" Straw Sandal asked.

"The pretty one, holding his hand?"

Straw Sandal nodded and smiled. "She is our means of getting Talanov to cooperate. Make the call."

END NOTE

The International Labour Organization, in Geneva, Switzerland, estimates the worldwide number of human trafficking victims to be more than fourteen million, with generated revenues for organized crime totaling more than 150 billion dollars annually. Responsible for the kidnapping and disappearance of countless men, women, and children, human trafficking is one of the most lucrative and heinous crimes on the face of the earth.

93187929R00187

Made in the USA
Columbia, SC
05 April 2018